Copyright©2014 Carole Anne Goodman
The right of Carole Anne Goodman to be identified as the Author of the Work has been asserted by her in accordance with the Copyright, Designs and Patents Act 1988.
Apart from any use permitted under UK copyright law this publication may only be reproduced stored or transmitted in any form or by any means without prior permission in writing by
Carole Anne Goodman.
First published as an eBook in the UK by Carole Anne Goodman in 2014

ISBN: **ISBN:** 9781980583394

THE SHENANIGANS OF CHAMPAGNE CHARLIE

by

Carole Anne Goodman

Contents:

Chapter 1 – page 4
Chapter 2 – page 14
Chapter 3 – page 17
Chapter 4 – page 29
Chapter 5 – page 38
Chapter 6 – page 40
Chapter 7 – page 42
Chapter 8 – page 48
Chapter 9 – page 55
Chapter 10 – page 60
Chapter 11 – page 74
Chapter 12 – page 78
Chapter 13 – page 84
Chapter 14 – page 97
Chapter 15 – page 108
Chapter 16 – page 116
Chapter 17 – page 120
Chapter 18 – page 138
Chapter 19 – page 143
Chapter 20 – page 150
Chapter 21 – page 161
Chapter 22 – page 169
Chapter 23 – page 174

Chapter 24 – page 183
Chapter 25 – page 192
Chapter 26 – page 199
Chapter 27 – page 203
Chapter 28 – page 208
Chapter 29 – page 217
Chapter 30 – page 223
Chapter 31 – page 233
Chapter 32 – page 244
Chapter 33 – page 253
Chapter 34 – page 263
Chapter 35 – page 267
Chapter 36 – page 274
Chapter 37 – page 279
Chapter 38 – page 289
Chapter 39 – page 301
Chapter 40 – page 305
Chapter 41 – page 311
Chapter 42 – page 318
Chapter 43 – page 323
Chapter 44 – page 331
Chapter 45 – page 340
Chapter 46 – page 347

he had. The only likely fly in the ointment was father who was determined his son should continue the set course into the Navy. When was the last time a ship's Captain became a millionaire? he wondered disdainfully.

Oh well, I've already made one decision about my future tonight, he thought contentedly, *how* I'm going to do it can wait till I leave school, and with a satisfied smile on his face he finally fell into a deep sleep just as the dawn was breaking.

With his school trunk unpacked and his bedroom all ship shape, Toby headed down to the kitchen, running his hands anxiously through his thick auburn hair, to have the difficult conversation with his father that he knew couldn't be avoided.

'Father, now that I'm out of school I've decided I'm not going into the Navy,' he told his perplexed parent. 'I've made up my mind, I'm going to make a million quid by the time I'm 30 and I can't do that poncing around in some fancy uniform full of gold braid and kissing Admirals' arses. I need to learn how money works. I know you'll be disappointed but this is something I have to do.' He was pacing up and down, trying to avoid his father's eyes and talking rapidly, needing to get out everything he wanted to say in one breath before he was stopped.

His father looked irritated. 'Of course I'm disappointed son, the reason for all those years at an expensive naval college was to give you a kick start in a steady job. What could be better than security in the Services? I've done well enough for the family in the RAF, and you could do a damn sight better learning to wear a Captain's uniform with pride than some fool's dream of making a fortune. Where did you get such a daft idea from anyway?'

How do you explain to your father that you are going to have more in your life than he had? How do you say "thanks but no thanks" for the sacrifices that he knew his parents had made to give him a better future? How do you tell them that determination to make a million is not a daft idea, but a total single-minded commitment to a brilliant and successful future? One day he would show the world his worth. He would sit on the board of banks, he would control an empire of his own, he would have all the Champagne he wanted and he would drive the most expensive cars. Best of all, he would have his pick of the girls who enjoyed the jet set life style he was planning for himself. Following orders and saluting senior officers could achieve none of this. He was becoming aware of the world and what adventures were available to the right man, and they were going to be his for the taking.

'I'm sorry, I have to do this, but first of all I need to find out how money works, so I've decided to get a job with a firm of accountants in Bournemouth for a bit, see what happens. One thing I've always been good at is figures.'

His father put his forehead in his hands as he considered this change of direction from the one he had envisaged for his eldest son. 'I must confess I don't understand, but if you're not going to go into the Navy with total dedication then there's not a lot of point, is there?'

'Honestly father, I'm going to do well in life, I promise. I will make you really proud of me, just not in the Navy though.'

Working as an articled clerk quickly taught him he didn't want to get into accountancy. His first Monday morning, wearing the obligatory collar and tie, had been passably interesting and challenging, but from Tuesday onwards it went rapidly downhill. His was a free spirit that was going places, and free spirits don't sit tied to a desk for eight hours a day grappling with the problems of extended trial balances, corporation tax and other such uplifting tasks. His efforts were helping to make profits for his bosses whilst he was not getting on with conquering the world. Six months as a drone was enough, but at least he had learned the basics of a balance sheet.

'Father,' he started. 'I'm fed up with accountancy, I've given it my best shot but it's not teaching me what I need to know. I'm bored with checking other people's affairs, but it has taught me one thing – I think I've found out where there's big money to be made quickly – property. You remember my friend Jack Weston? Well he says his father is looking for someone to work in one of the London offices of his estate agency. I've had a word with him and . . .'

Father and son had a row – a serious row. 'I hope you're not telling me what I think you're telling me son,' growled his father. 'Your mother and I gave you an expensive education with secure prospects but you said you didn't want to join the Navy because accountancy called, so we supported your decision; now you don't want to do that either. We can't keep this up Toby, your mother and I have three others to look after besides you. Anyway, at 19 years of age you're now old enough to leave the nest and make these crazy, stupid ideas work for yourself if you're so damn certain it's where you want to go. You've had all the support you're ever going to get from me.' And with that he reached into the kitchen drawer, where he kept his chequebook, and quickly wrote out a cheque for £100, made payable to his son. 'There you are, sink or swim you're on your own now. Good luck son.'

into the night for three days getting his facts and figures together. He could see that this young man had certainly done his homework, but how to get him checked out by Tuesday though?

'Who are you currently working for son?' he asked. Toby hadn't reckoned on Abe talking to Jack's father, but he should have, they were both in the same club after all. 'I've been with Harry Weston for the last year, but to be honest I haven't told him of my plans yet, and would prefer not to until things are sealed. Property marketing is a fiercely competitive industry, and I want to get into the niche before anyone else wakes up to the availability of those premises. I am going to make a huge success of this, it's just a question of who gets into bed with me to share it.'

He held his breath as Abe sat back thoughtfully. He hardly knew this boy, and at 20 he was still a youngster, and a very forceful youngster at that. What he did know, though, was that whenever he had seen him, mainly at the club, he had been confident and opinionated – just like me at that age, Abe reminded himself with a wry private grin. This was no shrinking violet before him. Buying a property in a prime location in Sevenoaks next to the station would be no bad thing, and he could always get his lawyers to tie the boy up in legal knots to protect his investment. His name above the door? Nice touch.

On the other hand, there'll be the office to furnish, the equipment to buy, the printing and advertising to be paid for, and probably months before commissions from any sales came in. And what about a secretary's salary and the business rates that will need to be paid, not to mention the interest repayments? Oi vey, what if the boy isn't as good as he thinks he is, and it fails?

As he sat deep in thought Toby was getting very close to biting his nails, but he dared not show any sign of nervousness and sent up a quick prayer to any God that might have been listening at the time to hurry things along a little, and preferably in his favour.

Abe continued his shrewd mental process, up and down the scale of possibilities, completely oblivious to the mental turmoil of the young man opposite him, finally sitting back and letting out a long breath of decision.

'Let's get back to the yacht club young man, I've left my wife alone for far too long on a Sunday, and you've got yourself a deal. Champagne's on me now.'

Toby didn't remember driving back to the yacht club; he had had far too much to drink and his adrenalin high had evaporated into mental exhaustion. Back at the yacht club he drank some more Champagne, courtesy of Abe and his wife, and finally made his departure just after 4 o'clock, waving to his boss, Harry Weston, on his way out.

Learning to bid at auction was a new experience for Toby, and he felt the adrenalin sting through his veins as each bid across the room increased the price of the property that was to kick-start his dreams of success. His whole body was rigid with trepidation, only his eyes moved, darting from one bidder to another, and adding to his tension was the fact that Abe was keeping strangely silent throughout the whole bidding process, watching the other buyers with deep concentration until the hammer was about to drop closing the sale of Toby's entire future to A.N. Other. He was silently panicking; what was wrong – why wasn't Abe bidding? But he didn't dare take his focus from the auctioneer's gavel. His heart was pounding, his mouth was dry and his hands were wet with perspiration, his eyes boring into the Auctioneer's hand holding the gavel, willing it not to drop by sheer concentrated force of his determination. Just as all hope seemed inexplicably lost, the index finger of Abe's right hand pointed skywards, the gavel's descent was arrested and Toby started breathing again.

Chapter 2

Toby Havers and Abe Silverman made a good team. Abe paid the bills for the first few months without question, and left his young partner alone to run the ground floor offices of his new empire exactly the way he wanted.

He made his customers feel welcome and comfortable on sofas rather than perched on hard chairs facing desks. Coffee was always on tap, as was his brightest smile. He made it his business to learn that Mr Jones's gallstones were something of a trial, never failing to sympathise with him when he called, and was always happy to spend a few minutes discussing Mrs Smith's endless problems with her children.

Soon properties were coming his way, sales were being achieved and commissions paid, slowly turning the large red figure at Abe's bank into black, and he congratulated himself on something of a find in Toby Havers; it was obvious that the boy had something, and that something was going to do well for both of them, of this he felt certain.

Toby worked the full seven days a week himself, allowing himself just a half-day off on Sundays. He wouldn't trust anybody else with his precious and hard won properties, he knew he could hold a sale together where others might lose it. Some of his early tactics were a little less than professional, but he became shrewd at playing a purchaser against a vendor in order to make them both feel he had achieved a well fought battle for the best possible price for them, and buyers and sellers alike loved him for it.

Life was exciting, life was a challenge and he was winning. At the end of his first year a new estate agency opened its doors next to him. He watched it being transformed from the old café into a smart new office with professional interest, and as soon as they were ready to open for business Toby made sure he was first through the doors with a bottle of bubbly in one hand, two glasses in the other and a huge grin lighting up his handsome face.

'Welcome to Sevenoaks!' he cried. His new competitor, Alex Burton, viewed his neighbour with a degree of suspicion.

'Got any properties yet?' Toby demanded.

'Mind your own bloody business.' came Alex's sharp response, and Toby roared with laughter. Alex found his laughter infectious and a firm friendship was born, a friendship that was to last a lifetime.

The powder blue E-type Jaguar that sat outside his office was his pride and joy. It had been a challenge getting Abe to agree to the purchase of such a car, a car he had always dreamed of owning. After the first few successful months of trading Toby had started to put pressure on him to agree to buy a car that would advertise his success.

'There's no point in getting a boring, old man's saloon car,' he had said. 'That doesn't make any sort of statement. I need something that shows we are a success.'

What he didn't say was that he was even more successful than he allowed Abe to know. The second of books that enabled him to siphon off a percentage of commissions received was his secret. His six months of accountancy training was being put to good use, and a nice little nest egg was accumulating.

After twelve months of hard work without a break Toby felt he deserved a holiday. He found that the initial euphoria of his success had dulled somewhat under the weight of mental and physical exhaustion, so he welcomed the call from Pat Bennett to tell him that some of his friends from Bournemouth were talking about taking a short trip to St Tropez. They were planning to drive their cars through France and spend three days in the glitzy coastal resort rubbing shoulders with the likes of Brigitte Bardot. Why not, he thought; I really could do with a bit of a break. The idea of driving his very own E-Type all the way through France was mouth-wateringly tempting. He pictured himself, hood down, sun glinting off the gleaming paintwork, wind in his hair, stopping en route to snack on French bread and good cheese, not to mention some interesting red wines.

With the agency doors carefully locked on the Friday evening, he drove down to Dover where he met up with the others, each driving their own sports car. The ferry docked at Calais on time, and as they drove onto French soil the race was on: *'Last one at the bar of the Victoria buys the round'*, went up the cry! No thoughts now about leisurely refreshment stops, it was foot hard to the floor; Toby was not about to come second. He never came second, whatever the cost.

After a hard drive through the night, determined to be first, he drove into St Tropez on the Saturday morning to find the town buzzing with activity. His tired red eyes sprang to life immediately at the sight of all the skimpily clad girls parading the beaches and streets in the warmth of the Riviera sun, and property matters under the grey murky skies of London were quickly pushed to the furthest recesses of his mind as he hungrily absorbed the scene from paradise before him.

As the temperature had cooled during the night he had reluctantly stopped for a few minutes to close the soft top of the sports car, but now he know – strong meat; I do feel rather overpowered by him. Think I'd best tell him to forget 22 Uphill Drive if he really is waiting at the station for me, that property is definitely not for us, and I'll get Adrian to ring his office to make appointments for us to see some of the other houses on his books together. Perhaps once he's met Adrian he will realise I really am going to get married; that would be far safer. And she felt a little more resolute with her decision made.

As the train pulled into the station she saw him waiting on the platform for her; she allowed herself a secretive smile and felt rather flattered. No, she thought pushing her resolve to the fore, I must stick to my decision and tell him to let me get on with house hunting with my prospective husband.

'Hello old thing,' he called as soon as she alighted onto the platform, and with a beaming smile guided her gently out of the station. 'I've been thinking, maybe Uphill Drive isn't quite what you're looking for, a bit too rambling, so I've got a another property for you to look at, just came in this afternoon, not even on the books yet. It's a steal; you have to see it tonight before someone else snaps it up. Come on, I've got the car waiting.'

How did he do that? How did he know she was going to pull out?

The property turned out to be far too small for Sally and rather run down, hence the reduced price. For a moment she wondered why he had bothered showing her round. But only for a moment.

'Well, you can never tell what clients really want,' he said, as she questioned his motives. 'I get people coming into the office who definitely won't settle for anything other than a three bed semi in Sevenoaks near to schools and bus routes, but finally end up buying a four-bed farmhouse in the countryside around Manchester. You just never can tell. But since we're here, I just happen to know a great little restaurant around the next corner that does the most amazing lobster – I took the liberty of booking us a table – won't get in without a reservation you know, it's terribly popular but the owner happens to be a friend of mine. How about a quick thermidor in the garden washed down with a nice bottle of something bubbly? Come on old girl, seems a shame to waste such a lovely evening.'

He's done it again, she thought. 'Now just a minute, Toby, this is not right. You know perfectly well I am getting married soon and it's wrong for me to be out having dinner with you like this. I would really rather you just drop me off at home, please.' The water was getting a little bit too hot for her and she could feel herself mentally back-pedalling.

'Oh come on old thing, nothing sinister in this, nothing sinister at all. I just calculated the time we would finish the viewing, knew I would be

20

hungry, thought you would be too. What could be more innocent than two friends sharing a meal together at the end of a busy day? You'll be telling me next you don't drink Champagne and can't stand lobster. If that is the case perhaps you won't mind watching me get through them as quickly as I can on my own – then I'll take you home. Well, what's it to be?'

Oh hell. 'All right then, I'll eat with you, and thank you,' she said with as much good grace as she could muster. This whole thing with Toby Havers was very strange, very strange indeed. She had the distinct impression she was being pursued, albeit in a softly-softly way, and found it completely unnerving; she could feel herself getting drawn into a situation that she wasn't sure how to handle. What *was* she going to tell Adrian? She still hadn't told him another man had taken her out for a pub lunch the day before, now here she was with him again, sharing the most beautiful Champagne meal with him. I must get my head round this before it goes any further, she promised herself.

Toby was really entertaining and he seemed to like poking fun at himself as much as others. He certainly enjoyed holding court and had an unending repertoire of jokes. The Champagne helped her to relax, the lobster was every bit as delicious as he had promised it would be, and all in all she was beginning to thoroughly enjoy herself, against her better judgement. She really should be at home with a good book and looking forward to chatting to Adrian about their wedding arrangements. But instead, here she was enjoying the company of another man.

The reminder of Adrian made her confusion get the better of her, and she asked Toby to take her home. He immediately called for the bill and happily guided her to the car. The sun had set and the evening was becoming a little chilly so he put the roof up for her comfort. On the way home he continued with the verbal entertainment and several times patted her knee to make a point. Oh God, she thought, how do I get out of this without seeming rude; the evening *had* been wonderful, the car *was* exotic and he *had* been great company, but now he really was going too far. She should have listened to her instincts on the train and never agreed to come out for the evening. Would he try anything when they said goodnight, she wondered?

He limited himself to just a chase kiss on the cheek, which left her feeling relieved that things had not developed into something more awkward, although she had no way of knowing that he had guessed at her unease, nor at the effort it had cost him to restrain himself.

'Was that property of any interest dear, and did you have a pleasant evening with that nice young man?' asked her mother, Hilda, as Sally sank into an armchair, kicking off her shoes.

'Do you know I'm not sure?' she replied, breathing deeply. 'It was a great evening but I'm sure he was trying it on with me. Anyway, I certainly shan't agree to see him alone again, it's not fair on Adrian. And no, the property was not for me – I'm sure he knew it all along.'

As she lay in bed that night thinking over the evening she had spent with Toby, she found her mind was in turmoil. Something about him had got under her skin forcing her to confront her future plans, causing her to toss and turn sleeplessly until the early hours.

Toby was struggling with sleep too. The last time he had been on such a high was when he had completed his very first property deal at his agency, the feeling was unbelievable. He wanted to scream from the rooftops that he had just dated the most incredible woman in the world, he didn't know why – she just was. His whole body was bubbling with excitement, so he gave up the unequal fight with sheets and pillows, threw on some clothes and jumped into his car. Quickly lowering the roof, he fired up the powerful engine and roared off through the dark, silent streets of Sevenoaks. As he left the town behind him he put his foot down and managed to hit a hundred miles an hour in record time, and for the next hour he concentrated on every twist and turn in the road, getting round faster than he dreamed he could in his adrenalin fired mood. Without realising in which direction he was heading he found himself on the well-known route to Bournemouth. By now, bursting with uncontained joy, he put his foot down even harder and raced into the town at 1 o'clock in the morning. He banged on the door of his friend Pat Bennett's parent's home, it never occurring to him for one moment that anyone would mind being so rudely woken up, his news was so good. 'Come on Bennett, open up!' he yelled at Pat's window. 'We've got some serious celebrating to do.'

Pat's crumpled features appeared at the door; he had enjoyed an evening with his friends at the tennis club and hadn't long been asleep. The last thing he needed was Havers thundering on the door waking the entire neighbourhood.

'What the hell are you doing here?' he mumbled crossly. 'What time is it for Christ's sake? Is something wrong?'

'Wrong? Wrong? Couldn't be more right you silly arse. I've just met the woman I'm going to marry and you're going to celebrate with me. Come on, get the scotch out.'

'What do you mean "met the woman you're going to marry", you never said you were getting married, you always said there are far too many girls you haven't laid yet. Anyway, who is she, and more importantly why on earth would she want to marry an idiot like you? Has the woman got no brains?' queried Pat, as he padded his way through to the dining room, leaving his friend to follow.

'Oh, she doesn't know it yet, she's engaged to some boring bloke from a bank but I'll soon change her mind. There's no way this one's getting away from me.'

He told Pat how she had walked into his agency only two days ago, the pub lunch they had shared on the Sunday and the meal they had enjoyed this very evening.

'You don't wait about, do you?' said Pat, knowing full well that when his friend set his mind to something he made it happen. Poor girl, whoever she was. He wondered if she knew yet what she was letting herself in for, and how difficult it was going to be to refuse Toby once he got his teeth into something. And he certainly seemed to have his teeth into her, by the looks of him tonight.

The fine, warm weather of the evening before had given way to overnight storms and a dark, wet Tuesday morning. Just matches my mood, thought Sally; she felt distinctly unbalanced and out of sorts. Putting aside for a moment the question of his intentions, the evening spent with Toby had made her sure of one thing: If another man could confuse her that easily, perhaps she should reconsider her commitment to Adrian, she man to whom she was planning to devote her life, forsaking all others, in sickness and in health, till death do them part.

At work that day nothing went right either; none of the garments fitted properly which put the pattern cutter into a foul temper, and zips and darts were unceremoniously ripped out to be realigned. Then the buyer expected at 11 o'clock cancelled at the last minute upsetting the showroom schedules. Eventually she got away from all the discontent going on around her and headed back to her desk to bury her head in some typing she had been asked to do, but the typewriter keys kept jamming as she hit them too sharply. Today was not turning out to be a good day. She couldn't stop thinking about the previous evening spent with Toby, and finally allowed herself to admit how much she had enjoyed most of it. Perhaps if she had not been seriously committed to another man she would have thoroughly enjoyed all the attention he lavished on her. But that was not the case – come on now, time for honesty. She cupped her hands around her neck and silently asked herself: Do I want him to call me again? Would I like to know a little more about him? She shocked herself as the questions entered her head. Even more so when the honest answer in each case was: Yes, I think I do, but only in small doses.

The next thing to sort out was whether her feelings for Adrian were really strong enough now that they had been so easily interfered with. He was such a kind and loving man who made her feel secure, but a successful marriage needed more than that. Even if Toby never called her again she knew she needed to question her commitment.

The bank didn't encourage personal calls, but she needed to talk to Adrian urgently, to hear his calm voice, to put her mind at rest, so she lifted her extension and called, but he was busy with customers. Damn. She left a message for him to please call her at work, and the next few hours were an absolute misery for her as they dragged by. She felt so confused at how could everything could have turned around so quickly.

Adrian called back at lunchtime just as she had popped out to get a sandwich. She tried to get him on her return only to find him back on the desk again and unavailable. The torment of not being able to speak to him, to reassure herself that he really was the one for her was driving her crazy. As she sank into her chair with her sandwich, trying to distract her thoughts with the crossword, her phone rang. At last, she thought, gazing intensely at her engagement ring, now I can clear my head and get Toby right out of my mind, then I can get a different estate agent to show us some houses together, perhaps even in a different area.

'Hello, old thing.' said Toby, 'fancy a drink this evening – how about I pick you up from the showroom?'

Oh no, it's him, and I haven't even spoken to Adrian yet. I really can't cope with this right now, and she felt her cheeks begin to flush with her confusion.

'No, no, Toby.' she stammered. 'I'm sorry; there is no way I can keep doing this. You know perfectly well I'm getting married soon; that was the only reason I came into your office on Saturday in the first place, if you remember. Thank you for the lovely evening last night, you were great company and I thoroughly enjoyed myself, but it's not right, you know that. Please don't call me again. If you get any interesting properties for me perhaps you could ask one of your staff to contact me. Goodbye.' Her forehead furrowed as she concentrated on getting her message across correctly. She quietly replaced the receiver with her heart racing but feeling very relieved that she had done the right thing, yet still hopelessly confused. Her phone rang again almost immediately and she looked at the instrument in some alarm. Surely not, he wouldn't would he? As she cautiously lifted the receiver she heard Adrian's measured tones asking why she had needed to call him at work, which was rather frowned upon, as she well knew. What was the emergency?

For a moment she was speechless, but only for a moment. Here she was in the middle of an emotional crisis, and all he could do was worry about the heinous crime of being called at work. Instead of being thrilled at hearing his voice as usual, she felt very let down and rather flat. For the first time she questioned what life would be like for her being discouraged from phoning her husband at work, so staid. But that was Adrian's world – very safe but very staid. Yesterday evening she had been shown another side to life, she had been wined and dined by a man who knew how to live and hang the consequences. And she had just told him not to contact her again.

'Sorry Adrian, it will keep,' she said flatly.

'Look dear, if it's really urgent I can spare you a couple of minutes but you'll have to be quick, otherwise you're coming over on Friday evening, as usual – we can talk then.'

'Yeah, sorry, it can wait.' She hung up, wondering why on earth she was apologising for needing him. As she moved away from her desk her phone rang again. Oh no, I can't do this any more, she thought, her eyes filling with tears, and fled to the toilet where she locked herself in until she felt sufficiently composed to face the showroom again.

Her breathing calmed, she left the cloakroom, and as she passed the telephonist she whispered: 'If anybody calls for me please tell them I've gone home with a headache.'

'Oh, you've just missed a call from some bloke; it didn't sound like your Adrian, sounded very dishy though, gorgeous deep voice. When I said you weren't at your desk he said he'd call again.' Gorgeous voice – that had to be Toby; he did have the most amazing deep, throaty voice that positively purred.

'Well, if he does, please remember my awful headache,' Sally reminded her as she disappeared into the showroom for the afternoon customers.

Walking home from the station meant passing his office. She was concerned that if he saw her it might start things up again, and she would rather not have any further contact with him if she could avoid it. She needed to stay right away from him, so took a slightly longer route hoping that he wasn't looking out of the agency window when he would be bound to spot her.

About a hundred yards from home a pale blue E-Type drove up next to her and kept apace with her steps.

'I was told you had gone home early with a headache and I've been looking out for you from every train since 3 o'clock,' said Toby. 'What happened? You've just come off your usual train. Look, I've bought you these in case you weren't feeling well.' And he produced an enormous bunch of white roses from the passenger seat, but instead of passing them to her through the open window he turned the engine off and got out of the car, and as he handed them to her he leaned in a little to give her a quick peck on the cheek before she had a chance to pull back.

'Whatever's wrong I hope these will put it right for you,' he grinned. 'Look, I know you said you didn't want me to contact you again, but I'm afraid I can't do that. I need to get to know you, and I know you feel the same.'

'Toby, please, back off,' she groaned. 'I've already explained to you that I can't see you any more; it's all getting too heavy too fast. Please, just leave me alone!' She put both hands up in front of her face, palms towards him refusing the flowers, then turned and ran the remaining hundred yards to her home slamming the door closed behind her and bursting into the kitchen where her startled mother asked: 'Whatever's the matter dear? You look quite upset.'

'It's complicated, mummy, I'm going upstairs for a moment, I need to be on my own for a while, I'll tell you about it later.' As she lay curled in a ball on her bed she was vaguely aware of the murmured sound of voices in the front hall, but she was too preoccupied with her spinning head to give the matter anything other than a passing thought.

An hour or so later she came down for the dinner that her mother had cooked and kept hot for her, to find the huge bunch of white roses arranged in two separate vases on the large refectory table in the kitchen that the whole family used for their meals together. Propped up in front of one of the vases was a hand written note on a page torn from a large notebook:

Sally, I am so sorry that I seem to be the cause of your distress, but for the first time in my life I have found something in you that has switched on a light in my soul. Please, don't run away from me. Please let us explore our hearts and minds together. I promise to stop frightening you and will hold my breath until we speak again. T x.

As she read the scrap of paper for the third time the phone rang and her mother went to answer it.

'It's for you, dear, it's that nice young man who brought the flowers round for you.' Hilda was burning with curiosity, but looking at her daughter's distraught burning face, realised that this was not the time for questions.

Sally picked up the receiver that her mother had left lying on the telephone table. 'Hello,' she said, quietly, waiting.

'I'm sorry – I couldn't hold my breath any longer.' She could hear the soft smile in his voice. 'If you didn't find the note too awful will you please have dinner with me tomorrow evening. I'll pick you up from the showroom and we'll have a meal in town, somewhere special. Please, don't tell me to leave you alone – you might have guessed by now I really can't do that, but I promise not to put any pressure on you. Just a meal. Just to talk.'

She could almost hear him holding his breath, hear the pleading in his silence, waiting for her answer. 'OK, but just to talk. I finish work at . . .'

'I know – 5.30,' he interrupted softly, his deep gentle voice caressing her down the telephone line. 'I'll be there, waiting for you.' And he hung up.

Now he needed a drink. All the other women he had ever taken out had been easy compared to her. They fell over themselves to get into his car, got turned on by his flattering ways, his humour, and were impressed by the way he spent money on them. What was it about this one that made it so difficult? This was more than just about winning, for some reason this one was serious. He didn't know why, but he wasn't about to mess it up.

He picked up the telephone again and dialled. 'Hello – put me through to the restaurant, please. I'd like a reservation for two tomorrow evening, say about 8 o'clock – the name's Havers. Good, thank you.'

Now at least she knew where she stood. She had just deliberately accepted an invitation for dinner from a man whilst she was preparing to commit herself to another. Oh dear, this was not a situation she was comfortable with but was something that needed to be handled. She was not due to see Adrian until Friday – that was their routine – their safe, staid routine. She also knew that she could not marry him now, no matter what happened with Toby; she had been too easily swayed to honestly believe that she was deeply committed to marriage. Their life together would be a sham, it wouldn't last five minutes, but she certainly wasn't going to tell him over the telephone, that would be cruel and cowardly, it would have to be face to face on Friday. His mother would be mortified, she had already welcomed Sally into their family and made it clear she considered her to be the daughter she had never had.

She returned to the kitchen and sat down to eat whilst her mother sat quietly opposite hoping her daughter would tell her what was going on, because clearly something was upsetting her.

Between mouthfuls Sally told her what had been happening since walking in through the estate agency doors on Saturday morning (my God, was it only three days ago?). As she talked her younger sister Jenny came in to make a coffee and sat in on the conversation.

When she had finished her tale there was silence around the table. 'Well, what are you going to do?' her sister asked.

'I don't know,' Sally replied. 'Toby Havers is really too forceful for my liking, he scares me a bit. But I will have dinner with him tomorrow night and just see what happens. All I do know for sure is I've got to tell Adrian on Friday that I can't marry him, that's got to be sorted out before anything else, and that's going to be the hardest thing.'

Now that she had made her decision she felt that some of the weight that had been accumulating on her shoulders over the last few days had been lifted. There was still the black cloud of the forthcoming meeting with Adrian on Friday evening, but that was a separate issue.

She allowed herself to look forward to the following evening with Toby and began to consider what she should wear. Somewhere special, he had said – I wonder what that means, she thought. Probably one of those new Italian restaurants, he's bound to be up on those. She decided to take a change of clothes for the evening, nothing too glamorous, just one up from what she would wear for work.

She slept soundly that night. So did Toby.

Chapter 4

He stopped the elegant open topped sports car outside the Grosvenor Street showrooms at exactly 5.15 and jumped out over the side. The double yellow lines painted on the road forbade parking but he couldn't have cared less, such rules were for lesser mortals. He positively bounced up the two steps to the front door, running a comb quickly through his hair and breezing through the showroom doors as though he owned the place.

'Hello sweetheart, you ready yet?' he called to her as she sat at the other end of the showroom sorting out sample books. His eyes were dancing with happiness and Sally found it hard to silence him – she wasn't ready to leave yet, there were still two more sample books to finish, and anyway she hadn't yet changed and freshened up her make-up. His sparkle was infectious though, so she sent him back out with a smile and instructions to wait for her in the car. Her boss had watched this exchange with amusement, and told Sally to get off early and enjoy her evening with her young man. *Her* young man? Well, perhaps he was for that evening, and she grinned to herself as she popped into the changing room.

It was difficult to ignore the admiring glances that were directed towards the car as they drove down Regent Street towards Piccadilly Circus. Toby was certainly glowing with pride and she felt extremely cosseted; she wondered where on earth they were going, but had twice been told it was a surprise and to stop asking. They drifted around the northern side of Trafalgar Square before turning left up the Strand, and as they turned right into the forecourt of the Savoy Hotel her jaw dropped open, this certainly was a surprise – she wasn't dressed for the Savoy. She had never been taken anywhere like this before and felt completely overawed by such opulence.

'Let's get some fizz before we eat,' said Toby, leading her into the American Bar. 'A bottle of The Widow please, barman,' he ordered, whilst she looked around her at the sumptuous but understated surroundings in which he seemed to be completely at home. She felt even more aware of the difference between this man and Adrian – good, solid, safe Adrian. But she and Adrian were not going to happen now, so she could sit back and enjoy this amazing experience.

They chatted amicably as the waiter discreetly topped up their glasses from the Champagne bottle nestling in the wine chiller by their side, gradually working their way through the bottle. He was full of questions about her and she found herself telling him all about her family and their life in Sevenoaks. She wasn't quite sure how she got into modelling. She had

29

left school at 15 with no qualifications of any description, someone had mentioned Lucie Clayton's, the modelling school, so she decided to have a go at that, and after a couple of job changes she had ended up in Grosvenor Street, having learned a bit of typing and bookkeeping somewhere along the way. Not a very complicated or stimulating story, his life had to be far more interesting. She tried to ask him about himself, but he only wanted to learn as much as he could about her and was reticent at talking about himself; he remembered the painful loneliness he had endured during his early years at boarding school, where hard-learned lessons had taught him much about the value of keeping his own counsel and not allowing any weakness to be seen. The boy in him was full of pranks, practical jokes and laughter, but the man in him had learned to use these faces as a cover when necessary.

'Me? There's nothing special to tell you about me. I'm the eldest of four, ex-RAF father, housewife mother – mind you, with the four of us to control she had no time for anything else. I've decided that I'm going to rule the world by the time I'm 40.'

He turned to her, his eyes twinkling with mischief:

'*She walks in beauty, like the night*
Of cloudless climes and starry skies;
And all that's best of dark and bright
Meet in her aspect and her eyes;
Thus mellowed to that tender light
Which heaven to gaudy day denies.'

'That's beautiful,' said Sally. 'Why did you learn that?'
'It's the first verse of a poem by Lord Byron, he replied. 'Why did I learn it? Well, I was bored with Shakespeare so Byron made a change.'

Three glasses of Champagne later and she was definitely ready to eat, especially since she had only had a sandwich for lunch and her head was spinning furiously.

Dinner was an equal joy and she loved every minute of it. Toby spent some time in conversation with the wine waiter going through the various red wines to accompany their perfectly grilled steaks, and seemed to know exactly what he wanted, but she had really had enough to drink with the Champagne and her head was feeling distinctly fuzzy. He does drink a lot, she thought; still, he seems to be able to hold it but I hope he'll be OK to drive home. She managed one glass of the Beaune and had to applaud his choice, it was the nicest red wine she had ever drunk, so rich and full of flavour. He explained about the different varieties of grape and the regions that produced such a wide variety of wines. 'Blindfold me and I can tell from a sip which grape has been used to create that wine,' he bragged. 'I'm happy to drink plonk at home, but when I'm out a good bottle can last me for hours, it should be savoured.' She wondered what was going to happen to the bottle he had just bought – she wasn't going to drink much of it so there would be a fair bit left – how long would he make that last? Three hours later they were still sitting at the table and he had managed to get through nine-tenths of the bottle by himself but still appeared to be sober.

Through their conversation they had touched on a whole range of subjects but she still felt she didn't know much about him. He had so much knowledge and enjoyed such a broad range of subjects, but was a closed book when it came to personal matters. When the waiter came to take their order for coffee Toby asked her if she wanted a brandy or a liqueur. 'No thank you,' she replied. 'I've had more than enough to drink, and do you think you should have any more, you still have to drive home, remember?'

'Don't worry about it, I'm fine, the evening's still young and anyway I haven't had that much,' he replied breezily.

But by now it was nearly midnight and she had had enough, she was feeling very tired, full of Champagne and wine and ready for home, but he wanted to go on to a nightclub. 'I'm sorry to be a party pooper' she said. 'But I've got work tomorrow and would really rather go home now, it you don't mind.'

'Oh come on sweetheart, just for a couple of hours please, then I promise I'll take you straight home.' The doorman had brought the car round, been generously thanked and Toby set the E-Type's engine purring.

'No, Toby,' she insisted. 'I'm dead on my feet now; the evening will be really spoilt for me if it goes on any longer.'

'Nonsense,' he snorted. 'I'll take you somewhere that will make your eyes pop; I'll bet you've never been to Annabelle's have you?'

'No, you're right, I haven't, and I don't want to go there tonight, please.'

He drove to Annabelle's, London's top aristocratic nightclub in Berkeley Square, of which he was a new member.

'Come on sweetheart, just one drink, just for me, be a great way to end the evening,' he pleaded. The last thing she wanted to do was cause a scene, but she equally did not want to get out of the car; she could see how difficult it was going to be to get him back behind the wheel. Besides, he had had a brandy with his coffee at the Savoy on top of the wine and Champagne and she really did not want him to drink any more before driving her home.

So she put her foot down. 'I am not getting out of this car Toby, so rather than end this lovely evening on a sour note, please let's go home right now, remember what we have enjoyed tonight and maybe we could plan to come here another night,' she argued.

He looked across at her, weighing up his options; this must mean she would agree to see him again. Surely she would. They had had a really good time tonight and she had seemed to be impressed with the Savoy, perhaps he had better not push his luck. If he upset her now it might not be so easy to see her again, he was learning that she could be a little difficult.

'Oh, all right then' he said, rather disappointed. He was desperate for the evening not to end, their first proper evening together, but he restarted the engine and headed for Sevenoaks. She breathed a quiet sigh of relief.

When they pulled up in front of her parent's house she was even more relieved that the journey home had been without incident. He had been driving far too fast through the darkened streets of London, showing off actually, and she had felt distinctly unnerved.

As the car came to a halt she didn't want to let him put her in a difficult situation and immediately opened the passenger door, leaned over to give him a quick peck on the cheek and prepared to jump out with a thank-you-for-a-wonderful-evening-but-it's-terribly-late sort of exit. His strong arms reached for her and held her in a firm embrace as his lips sought urgently for hers. 'No Toby, no, stop it. I'm sorry, please, that's all too much. Please don't do that!' She knew she was babbling but was desperate to get away from the car. She pushed at him with both hands and scrambled out of the low sports car with as much dignity as she could muster and fled into the house feeling upset and confused. She had thoroughly enjoyed the evening and his company, so why did she not want to let him get close to her? He was charming, erudite, entertaining, fun, protective, knowledgeable, successful and not afraid to thumb his nose at convention. He was also pushy, arrogant, over powering and dominant and these were the characteristics she found so unpalatable. On the other hand, these were possibly some of the traits that helped him towards success. Then perhaps a successful man was not for her. And there was still Adrian to talk to. She was too tired and confused to work it out right now and watched him pull aggressively away from the kerb, feeling relieved that he didn't try to follow her to the door.

He cursed under his breath, his emotions vacillating between happiness at the time he had spent with her and annoyance that he hadn't been able to even get a proper kiss. Tomorrow, he thought.

True to form he called her the next day at work, by which time she had come to view the previous evening with something akin to alarm. Yes, she had enjoyed it but it was all a bit excessive wasn't it? Too much Champagne, too much red wine, for him, then there was the argument over Annabelle's and the fight to get out of the car. No, that's really not my scene, she thought. So his phone call did not get the reception he had expected.

'Hello sweetness.' was his greeting. 'Did you sleep well?'

'Yes, thank you,' she replied, somewhat coldly.

'Where would you like to go this evening? I thought we could take in a show, or maybe just spend the evening at my pad – I could cook for us.'

Whoa! She wanted to shout – just you back off. Instead she said, very coldly: 'Look, I'm sorry but I really don't think you're my type Toby; I don't think I fit into your social life. Last night was memorable, it really was, but it was a one off. Please don't keep calling me, it really isn't going to work.'

'Bollocks,' he said confidently. 'I know this is all a bit new for you but we'll have some great times together, I've got some fantastic plans for us. I promise I won't put any pressure on you, I won't even phone you so much, but please don't tell me not to call you again, I don't deserve that. Didn't you enjoy the Savoy last night?'

'Yes. I already told you I did, very much,' she relented under the rich, velvety tones. 'But let me call you next time – that way I won't feel so pressurised.'

When she put the phone down she felt she had been weak, that was not the decision she had made for herself, but he was very persuasive and his gorgeous deep voice did make her melt just a little. She felt sure he knew that, it was certainly not quite the same voice as when they spoke face to face. And there was no need for her to ever make that phone call. Perhaps after a little while he will have cooled off.

Getting off the train that evening she knew she was going to have to take the circuitous route home to avoid passing his agency door, just to be on the safe side.

Friday morning for Toby meant preparations for the weekend. What would really turn her on, he wondered? He did his best thinking with a glass in one hand and a cigarette in the other, so trundled over to the pub at 11 o'clock; the agency was fairly quiet and the girls could cope without him.

His recently awarded Private Pilot's Licence hadn't had many outings, so he spent the first couple of hours of the day on the phone to

33

Biggin Hill Airfield trying to hire a small plane, planning to take her to Le Touquet for lunch on Saturday, then a flip around southern England on the Sunday – that ought to impress her. He smiled to himself as he anticipated enjoying the icing on the cake of the weekend, provided all went according to plan, of course. He had agreed not to phone her, but this was different. She would be pleased to hear from him when he told her of the plans he had made. Best not to call today though, he thought, she's seeing that bank bloke tonight to give him his marching orders so she won't be in the most receptive of moods, if I read her correctly. And if there was one thing Toby knew he was really good at it was reading women, he had certainly had enough practice, but she was proving a little trickier than others though.

Sally had found her evening with Adrian was breaking her heart as well as his. No, he did not understood what was wrong, and no, he was not going to take it without a fight.

    Was there someone else?

    No, not really.

    What did 'not really' mean?

    It meant that she had discovered another world that she had not experienced before and it had seriously unsettled her. They had talked until the pub closed; they hadn't eaten, neither of them feeling much like food. When they parted he tried to give her back the solitaire she had handed him earlier, but when she refused to take it he finally understood that she was lost to him. They both felt cold and hurting as they went their separate ways, not only to their respective homes but also into their respective lives.

    She thought she would feel a sense of relief that this roller coaster of a week was over and she could take a whole a new look at life tomorrow morning. But all she felt was empty and desperately guilty; Adrian didn't deserve the unhappiness she had just heaped on him, and all because she had gone house hunting last Saturday morning, just six days ago.

'Morning, sweetheart,' was Toby's bright start to his telephone call on Saturday morning. 'How about lunch in Le Touquet? Got a small plane booked for the day, and after that we could . . .'

    Sally was incensed. 'I told you to stop phoning me, you're driving me nuts. Please, get off my back, just leave me alone!' she yelled at the receiver before slamming it down on its rest. She had asked him to leave the next contact between them up to her, why the hell wouldn't he listen to her? He certainly unsettled her and she needed time to clear her head, especially after her evening with Adrian. All this talk of dinner at the Savoy, lunch in

Le Touquet. It was all moving far too fast, and that she hated.

How could the silly bitch not want to fly to France for lunch, he wondered in amazement? Every other girl he had ever dated would have jumped at the chance. Bloody woman, she wasn't normal. Sod her, I'll take someone else. No I won't, I'll cancel the whole fucking weekend and see what the boys in Bournemouth are up to. Perhaps there'll be more receptive female company down there, take my mind off her. Who needs her anyway, plenty more where she came from.

Over the next six months Toby went from strength to strength, plots of land for sale were in plentiful supply and he had no problem finding buyers. His ability to entertain people had brought him a large portfolio of contacts, one of whom was a city accountant who also sat on the board of a small private bank. Could be useful.

Toby was very favourably impressed with the suite of offices when he was called in to sign his first set of accounts.

'Morning, old boy,' said Toby, shaking hands with Hymie Goldstein and taking in the opulent surroundings. 'This all looks very plush – is this where all the fees are going? You're obviously charging too much – ha ha!'

Over coffee Hymie presented the balance sheet and accounts showing a tax liability of £1,000. Toby was tickled pink, he had calculated the liability would be nearly six times that figure. He had obviously landed on his feet with Hymie – must remember to give the friend who recommended him a bottle of fizz to say thanks.

Hymie then presented his fee account of £2,000. Toby exploded! 'How much? You thieving bastard. You know where you can stick that bill don't you!' He was furious, no wonder the guy can afford such an expensive desk, and he mentally cancelled the friend's fizz, the bloke was a con artist.

'Never mind, it was worth a try,' said Hymie. 'I thought you might think it was a bit on the steep side.' He tore up the fee account and the balance sheet, which made Toby sit up in surprise. 'Here's a new fee account.' And he passed over an invoice for £300.

'That's more like it, old son,' said Toby. 'But why have you torn up the balance sheet and accounts?'

'The work involved for a fee of £300 produced this set of figures,' said Hymie, and he produced a new set of accounts, which now showed a tax liability of £6,800.

Toby slumped back in the chair, absolutely aghast at the implications.

'Is there anyway I can get the first set of accounts back – and the

35

first fee account?' he enquired.

Hymie grinned at him, 'I just happen to have a duplicate set here. You're not the first client of mine to learn the hard way how I work; don't suppose you'll be the last either.'

Toby had certainly learned a lesson that day. Hymie was his sort of man, and he hoped he could be of some financial use to him in the future, especially with his banker's hat on rather than his accountant's.

His Christmas break was going to be a great one, he had already decided on that, but hadn't yet figured out the fine detail. Try skiing perhaps, can't be too difficult. Zermatt looked nice.

The ski resort of Zermatt was every bit as wonderful as he had been told. The scene that greeted him on his arrival was like something from a classical Christmas card that had been sprinkled with glittering stardust. Fairy tale carriages with jingling bells were being drawn through the thick white snow by high stepping horses, crisscrossing the town, taking their passengers from hotel to restaurant to hotel, and the couples inside were wrapped snugly together against the crisp, cold air. As he stood and looked around, drawing a deep breath of clean mountain air into lungs that had suffered from polluted city air and cigarettes, the ski slopes beckoned him to accept their challenge of learning to get down from the top in one piece. After which the anticipation of the promised après ski was a mouth-watering joy to be sampled. If the fruits of success were Zermatt and St Tropez then he was going to be even more successful; he was going to have it all, including that bloody woman. She had been a thorn in his side for the last six months and he had drawn on every ounce of his formidable will power not to ring her again after she had refused to fly to Le Touquet with him. Serve her right; let her go back to boring Adrian, that's where she belongs.

But once he had brought her to the forefront of his mind he was finding it hard to shake her out again. He had been so sure she would have been tempted by the private flight, all women were, and after a decent interval had passed she should have called him; he could understand that she wouldn't want to be seen to be too keen, that was how it always worked in his experience of difficult women. But six bloody months. Damn, it was starting to eat at him now; he was going to have to call her from Switzerland if he didn't want a completely ruined Christmas.

'Hello, sweetheart. Remember me, blue E-Type, Savoy and all that bullshit?'

He found to his horror he was nervous waiting for her response. Would she hang up on him again, would she be angry that he had called?

Had she got someone new? Please, oh please, let her be happy to hear from me, he prayed.

'Yes, of course I remember you, Merry Christmas Toby,' she replied.

Great, she sounds OK, confidence back on full power again. 'I'm in Switzerland at the moment, thought I'd take myself off skiing for a few days, fancy a quick trip out to Zermatt – join me for a few days after Christmas, old thing?'

Oh my God, here we go again, Sally thought.

'No thank you, Toby,' she replied wearily. 'I'm pretty busy right now and I have to tell you I am seeing someone, so enjoy the rest of your holiday and please don't call again.'

So that was his Christmas ruined in one phone call. Why couldn't he shake her out of his system, she was only a woman for God's sake. Right, that's it, no more. I'm never going to call her again; she can stew in her little suburban life. I need a bloody drink.

Chapter 5

The following year went by in something of a blur for him. Through his covert double set of books he was able to persuade Abe Silverman that the agency was ticking over reasonably well but not brilliantly, and with all the land deals he had done quietly in his own name he had managed to amass enough money to make an offer to buy Abe's shares in the business, which was accepted. Abe was busy with other larger fish now and was losing interest in a small agency that had not done as well as he had hoped. He was surprised though, Toby Havers had certainly looked as though he was going places in the beginning. Pity – he was obviously just all talk.

Early in the New Year the name of Havers Silverman was taken down and Toby had his own name painted above the door, his very own baby now. New stationery, new advertising, nothing could wipe the smile off his face, not even the niggling itch of Sally still at the back of his mind. No, damn it, she doesn't exist. No, I'm not going to call her.

She had become accustomed to taking the longer walk home from the station, but of course he had seen her. That evening he just happened to be coming out of the newsagents next to the station as she passed.

'Why, Sally,' he beamed, heart thumping. 'Fancy seeing you.' It had been extremely hard judging the exact moment to leave the shop to guarantee bumping into her without it seeming at all suspicious.

'How are you doing old thing? Got time for a quick drink? I've just bought out my partner and I'm in serious celebrating mood. For old time's sake, please. I'll give you a lift home later in my new . . . Sorry, there I go again. Just the one, come on.'

Did this man never give up? 'Just the one Toby, and only to celebrate your business deal.' She had noticed the name HAVERS ESTATES go up over the door a month back, all of Sevenoaks had noticed, the local rag had picked it up too, it would have been churlish to have refused him.

'Give us a bottle of your finest, please Jeff,' Toby shouted to the landlord as he held the door open for his girl. No, she wasn't his girl, he really must stop thinking like that – for now.

'I thought you said just one drink. How are you going to manage just one drink from a bottle?'

She was here with him, back where she belonged and he had to learn to stop frightening her away. 'Don't worry sweetheart, the buggers won't

38

sell Champagne just by the glass. I promised you just the one, and just the one it will be.'

And it was. He was a little calmer than she remembered, but she had no idea how his heart was racing as he tried desperately to keep a lid on his enthusiasm for her. After half an hour he guided her to his brand new car, this time a pale yellow E-Type, and quietly drove her the half mile home, wishing her a sedate goodnight and making no attempt to give her more than a chaste peck on the cheek. He then drove straight back to the pub and polished off the remains of the Champagne. No sense in letting good fizz go to waste.

'Do you know, mummy, I think Toby Havers is calming down,' Sally said to her mother as she closed the back door behind her. 'I've actually enjoyed a very civilised half hour with him, celebrating his business purchase, and for once he didn't try to impress me.' Without all the high-flying pressure she found he was actually quite a nice man. Still, no point in going down that route, she had decided to live on the Spanish island of Ibiza for the summer of '68 since she had enjoyed a beautiful, peaceful holiday on the island the previous year. Spanish lessons at night school in London had meant later trains home so she had rarely needed to pass his office door when he was there. Her flight was booked for the next day, but Toby had been so busy chatting about his ideas for his business – almost nervously she thought – that there had been no opportunity to tell him of her plans; no reason to anyway.

'Hello Jenny, it's Toby Havers. Is that sister of yours there please?'

'I'm sorry,' Jenny responded to the telephone question. 'Didn't she tell you when she saw you yesterday evening? She left for Spain this morning. We don't know when she'll be back, she's planning to be out there for the whole summer at least, maybe longer.'

He was mortified, after all his hopes for the coming months. Planning to bump into her was just the first phase of what was going to be a beautiful summer with her. He was proud of the way he had managed to control himself, and for what? She had buggered off to Spain. Shit!

Chapter 6

Out of season there was plenty of accommodation to choose from and Sally quickly found a small affordable pension in the pretty town of San Antonio. The owner, Miguel, told her he had work for her running a tiny beach bar and selling deckchair tickets in a nearby bay until she found a more suitable job.

Once she had unpacked her suitcase Sally spent a happy couple of hours wandering around the quiet, narrow, sunlit streets admiring all the brightly coloured hanging plants that were encouraged to trail over the many balconies of the little snow white houses. She walked around the bay and marvelled at the sparkling clarity and absolute stillness of the water, a stillness broken only by the few boats that were chugging across the bay, ferrying passengers to and from the hotels on the other side. There was a peaceful tranquillity about the town and she felt as if she had come home.

The resort was paradise, the pension was situated right on the beach, it was clean and the small staff were a very happy and friendly bunch who were all keen to help her develop her Spanish. At night an external staircase allowed her to climb to the upper terrace and sit gazing at a sky so close and crystal clear she felt that if her arms had been just a fraction longer she could surely have plucked one of the sparkling diamonds from its deep, dark velvety place. Never before had she experienced such total contentment, and felt herself drifting off to sleep in the balmy early spring night. This sort of feeling doesn't wash over you on the heavily overcrowded 5.57 from Charing Cross, that's for sure, she thought. After a while the night air cooled and she made her way to bed, feeling that she had done rather well for day one in San Antonio.

Over the first few weeks working in the beach bar she got to know some of the local fishermen who regularly used the little beach to launch their boats, and early one Sunday morning a group of her new Spanish friends went up into the hillside behind the beach to prepare a fire before taking a small boat out to catch enough for supper for ten people. As the sun began its dip towards the western horizon at the end of the day, the boat returned to the cove, and the contents of the net, seaweed, shells and all, were dropped into an enormous pot that required two strong men to carry up to the fire in the hills. They added some water, fresh tomatoes and rice then ran back down to the beach, whooping with the sheer joy of life, to start some serious liquid preparations for supper under the stars.

By early evening the impromptu paella was ready. Miguel's beach tables and chairs were prepared, bottles of rough red wine appeared from the back of someone's truck together with several loaves of freshly baked coarse Spanish bread, and the group of friends sat together in the golden glow of the setting sun with the waves lapping around their feet. Such a meal, so fresh, the flavours so powerful and the companionship so warm. Toby thinks he's got it sorted with his lobster, Champagne and the Savoy, thought Sally – he knows nothing. Give me this any day. There now – how on earth did he pop into my head, she wondered?

As Easter loomed Miguel told her he needed her room for tourists who would soon be paying him a proper rate, so she scoured San Antonio until she found a spacious room in a large airy house that had been converted into individual accommodation. Perhaps it was time to get a proper job now that the tourists were expected imminently and she had proper rent to pay. As she climbed up to the flat roof of the house and discovered glorious uninterrupted views right across San Antonio bay, she felt a happy flutter in her tummy at the sight of living so close to such paradise.

Miguel introduced her to Pepe who had opened a new car hire venture and was looking for two Spanish speaking English girls to run the business for him. By now Sally's Spanish was good enough to hold a simple conversation confidently, and she managed to muddle her way though a brief chat with Pepe who had already hired one English girl, Lesley, and wanted another to cover a working day from 7a.m until late.

Joy of joys, she got the job. Lesley turned out to be great fun; a tall, beautiful redhead who spoke impeccable Spanish and who had already been living on the island for a year. The two girls became good friends.

And so the lovely summer wore on. The Spanish sunshine and seawater bleached her blonde hair to palest cream and turned her skin a beautiful golden bronze. She wasn't earning much but her needs were small; instead of eating hot English meals every day she survived on tapas and salad, and found that the less she had to eat the less she needed. Without her own transport she walked a lot and loved swimming in the sea, so by the end of the summer she was slender, toned and healthy.

But she had promised her father she would return at the end of summer, so in October she made her way home. She was touched by the surprise leaving party that Pepe and Lesley had arranged for her – all of her friends came to say goodbye.

Chapter 7

England in October was grey, cold and wet but she could not have wished for a warmer welcome home from her family and friends. Hilda made sure that her daughter's first meal back at home was her favourite beef stew, but Sally found it couldn't compare with homemade paella on the beach under the setting sun, washed down by a rough red wine that someone had collected from the local bodega in old martini bottles. There would have been work for her during the winter months, enough to see her through to the beginning of the next tourist season, her Spanish was fluent, but she had promised her father that she would come home, so she had better make the most of it and look for a job in London. Next spring I'm going back, she promised herself. Definitely.

As the weeks went by she realised that it was very quiet on the Toby Havers front, he obviously didn't know she was back. Good, because she wasn't going to be around for long. She kept the hood firmly up on her warm coat as she took her circuitous route home, keeping as far away from the agency door as possible. She knew his personal office was at the back of the estate agency, so unless he was actually standing in the doorway he would be unlikely to pick her out at that distance. She didn't see his E-Type parked in its usual spot in the street outside the office either, and hoped that he was leaving early these days. Less hassle.

'Silly bitch,' Toby muttered to himself. 'Does she really think I can't see her?' He was highly amused to see Sally trying to hide beneath the hood of her coat. If she thinks I have any interest in her now she's mistaken, he thought. The day she left for Ibiza he had resolved to get on with his life doing the things he liked, when he liked and with whom he liked. That woman seemed to have a problem enjoying the finer things in life. Sex was another thing – just how long did she think she could keep him waiting?

He turned away from watching her moving quickly away from the station, trying to avoid passing his door, and his whole being ached for her.

The summer had been good to Toby as well. The profits he had made from two clever land deals had allowed him to take over the whole of the first floor as his personal office from which to control his burgeoning empire, and his huge leather-topped kidney shaped desk was placed to give him a commanding view overlooking the entire street below as he swivelled in his leather executive chair. He had a secretary with him now too, Sylvie; the paperwork generated by the property deals coming his way was too much for him to handle on his own, and his brand new Daimler sat away from the street in a private parking spot. He crossed his ankles on the desk as he leaned back in his comfortable chair, clasped his hands behind his head and considered how he felt.

On the one hand his plan for his first million was well on target, he owned his own flat and office block. Got a smart car and his name over the door of his own successful estate agency together with a thriving property developing business. There was also a string of beautiful women falling over themselves for the Champagne lifestyle he could give them. Not bad for a 25-year old from a modest family. It's been bloody hard work but the results speak for themselves old son, he told himself.

On the other hand he didn't have Sally. Fuck it!

He slammed his feet to the floor with an angry crash that brought Sylvie through from her typewriter in a rush.

'What's happened, Toby?' she asked in alarm 'Did you drop something?' She peered quickly round the room and didn't see any breakages, but she couldn't see the breakage in his mind. Why couldn't he get that wretched female out of his mind, for Christ's sake? It was driving him quietly insane.

'Sweetheart, get me booked on a flight somewhere hot for a week or so. Don't bother with hotels, I'll sort something out when I get there. I just need to get away for a bit.'

'OK, but where do you want to go?' she queried.

'I don't care where it is, just get me somewhere nice and now, there's a good girl.'

The next day Sylvie went early to the local travel agents before going into the office to decide which of the locations he would like, and as she settled back at her desk with arms full of brochures her eyes settled on a beautiful scene in Nassau in the Bahamas. Oh, if only I had the money, she drooled to herself. I bet Toby would like that – I'll do it – I'll book a week for him if there are any flights available. I know it will be expensive but I reckon he can afford it; anyway he didn't give me a budget, she thought. She popped back out again and surprised the travel agent with the speed of her decision, especially on someone else's behalf.

'Just book it please, I know he'll love it. I don't know what's happened but he's been in a funny mood recently and this will be just the ticket.'

Three days later Toby flew to Nassau for his first ever week-long sunshine break. Skiing for a few days was a great buzz, and St Tropez was amazing for a weekend, but what he needed now was a proper rest for a whole week, right away from everything familiar, not to mention the bleak November weather. As he alighted from the BOAC flight into the warm Bahamian sunshine and took a long sweeping look around he thought: Good old Sylvie, she's got this absolutely right – Nassau is something else. Sally might think she's done well by spending a summer in Spain – what does she know? She hasn't got a bloody clue.

'Which hotel you want sir?' enquired the cabbie espying Toby looking rather lost in the arrivals area.

'I've no idea sport – surprise me,' he replied, feeling more relaxed than he had felt for years.

'You want to spend some money my friend?' Although his fare was casually dressed the cabby's instinct told him this man could be a big tipper if he made the right choices for him.

'How about I take you to the Ocean Club? You look like a man with taste and like the nicer things.'

'Right-oh, old son, whatever you say.' And he settled back into the seat of the cab smiling contentedly as they drifted past the beautiful old colonial buildings of Downtown Nassau. As they headed out to Paradise Island he caught his breath at the exquisiteness of the islands, the clarity of the water as they passed over the bridge joining New Providence Island with Paradise, and the picture postcard beauty of the incredible beaches.

Yes, the Ocean Club was indeed for those who wanted to spend some money. Well, to hell with it – why not? He didn't treat himself to holidays that often, he'd earned this one and it was going to be enjoyed to the full. As he looked around the area after dinner that evening he was delighted to find the newly opened Paradise Island Casino and, joy of joys, a lot of female flesh on display.

This holiday was definitely going to be a good one.

After Christmas he could stand it no more. His iron will power was gradually being filed away by the sight of the love of his life walking along the far side of the street, trying to avoid him every time she left the station, and he found himself glued to his window every day as her train was due in. He was not a loser, he had never lost at anything in his life and he wasn't about to start now. He reached for a large whisky to steady his nerve.

Her phone rang. She recognised the deep, dark, silky tones instantly as he murmured the words: 'Hello old thing, I've missed you.' He felt her silence and steeled himself for the now familiar rejection; perhaps she had found herself a new boyfriend. 'I've been frightfully busy since you've been back from Spain,' he babbled on. 'But I've got a quiet evening tonight and

44

wonder if you feel like a quick drink – for old times sake, just to fill me in on your summer in the sun. I really do want to hear all about it.'

It was the voice that did it. Not the content of those few words, just the deep rumbling sound that silenced her and caused her to catch her breath. She was surprised that she had missed hearing those beautiful tones. Her breath was coming a little quicker, her pulse beating just a fraction faster and she felt an almost palpable need to see him and listen to his mesmeric voice first hand. But she wasn't about to tell him that. Besides, she was a little older now and a little wiser than the last time she had seen him, perhaps she would be able to handle him a little better.

As he called for her that evening he struggled to keep his hands from shaking. He didn't want to frighten her off again, and mentally ticked off each point that he knew he had to follow: No pressure, no showing off, go easy on the drinking, no touching – yet – and definitely no bullshit. God, it was going to be hard, but if he remembered the rules and learned how to walk on eggshells he might, just might, pull it off and make her relax enough to agree to see him again. All the complicated deals he had done where he'd put his future on the line, dealing with hard-nosed bankers and come out on top, difficult local authority planners and parish councillors that he had succeeded in winning round, all the beautiful women he'd had to work hard on to get into bed, and won – nothing had been as troublesome as this one woman. And now he had to obey some stupid self-imposed rules just to get her to spend a relaxed evening with him over a drink.

The evening went surprisingly well, she even agreed to have a quick meal with him in the new local Italian restaurant. She was impressed that he seemed to have both his feet in the vague direction of the ground now, if not exactly rooted in the soil. He couldn't resist showing off his new found knowledge of Italian pastas and Chianti; but it was just as well he did know his tagliatelle from his penne because Sally hadn't a clue. She had forgotten how he made her laugh, his jokes were endless and he seemed to enjoy entertaining, not only her but half the restaurant as well given the slightest encouragement. She thoroughly enjoyed herself that evening and his eyes danced with the joy of being close to her again. At last he felt he had got it about right. He pushed his luck a little further and asked her to attend the ballet with him on Saturday evening, and was rewarded with the warmest of smiles. 'I'd love to do that,' she said. 'I've never been to the ballet before.' Through their conversations he learned that a few years earlier she had developed a taste for classical music, and although he didn't really share her taste, felt the ballet might be something new that she would enjoy and perhaps identify with him.

She kissed him gently goodnight and thanked him for such a lovely evening. She had genuinely enjoyed herself and found herself looking forward to Saturday and the ballet.

Toby was floating. He'd cracked it. All he had to do now was remember the rules, they seemed to be right. Roll on Saturday – and afterwards? Easy tiger, he reminded himself, one thing at a time.

The ballet was a blur of joy for Sally. Toby certainly seemed to be drinking a lot less these days, she noticed with approval, when they shared just a half bottle of wine with their quick spaghetti after the show before driving home to Sevenoaks. She snuggled into the comfort of his new Daimler as he drove them home in a far more disciplined manner than she remembered. The winter air was sharp and cold, the sky clear and the stars crystal bright as the car purred gently through the streets of South London. They were both lost in their own separate world of happiness. His: Sally was in his care and she was happy. Hers: surprised at how much she had enjoyed every single aspect of the evening, from Toby's company, through the ballet, past the meal and now this beautiful ride home.

They were fast approaching the point in the journey where he was going to have to make a decision. Should he take her straight home and let her give him a quick peck by way of goodnight and guarantee himself another chaste date, or take it to the next level and suggest going back to his place for a quick nightcap?

'You haven't seen my pad yet have you sweetheart? Fancy a quick nightcap then I'll run you straight back?' he asked, heart in mouth. Had he pushed it too far?

Sally sat up from her relaxed reverie of the journey with a sharp prick of consternation and considered this twist. She wasn't stupid, she knew what he wanted and knew that she wasn't going to give it to him; going back to his place would have been like walking into the lion's den – far too dangerous. Was it then fair to go for the nightcap and get his hopes up? There was no way she was going to leap into bed with him, and if he was looking for rewards for evenings out then she would not see him again.

'I don't think so, Toby. I've had a fantastic evening, you have been wonderful company, but I would rather go straight home, please.' Was she being selfish? Was she leading him on? She had always been much more relaxed with other boyfriends, always able to draw the line easily enough. Why was she so confused about him?

The familiar feeling of emptiness washed over him. He had really hoped she would say yes, and had actually convinced himself that he would have been strong willed enough to give her a simple guided tour of his flat, including just a tantalising glimpse of the black satin sheets, then drive her home in the most chivalrous of fashion. Now it was just going to be a chaste peck and hopefully the promise of another chaste date.

Christ! He thought on his lonely way back to his flat, I'm really pissed off with this pussy footing around her. Who the hell does she think she is anyway? If she thinks I'm going to keep taking her out, giving her a good time and spending time and money on her for no return she's got another think coming. He fumed with frustration.

Chapter 8

Sally went back to work in the rag trade in London and continued with the nine to five routine that she had been so pleased to leave the previous spring. An elderly friend living a few miles away asked her to spend one evening a week helping him with the paperwork involved in buying and selling the small amount of paintings and antique furniture in which he was interested. All the items were sold from his home, and Sally spent a very pleasant three hours one evening a week logging the newly purchased items, pricing them for sale and recording the sales from the previous week.

'Bye, Mr Langdon,' she called, as she put on her coat and picked up the keys to her father's estate car she had borrowed for the evening. 'See you next week.'

'Goodbye my dear, and thank you for your help tonight. A splendid job, as always.' The most courteous of men, he never forgot to thank her. He held the door open for her to pass out into the frosty night air, then hurried back to his place in front of the fire where his wife had his cocoa ready for him.

Sally looked up at the stars in the clear winter sky and though how much further away they seemed than in the Spanish sky. Stupid thought, she told herself out loud. She turned the ignition on, took a quick look up and down the road, her way was clear so she reversed out, settled into first gear, whacked the heating up and began her fifteen minute journey home, humming to the radio. Almost immediately a car came up fast behind her and stayed with her for the next two miles, twisting and turning at exactly the same junctions she did, at times accelerating up tight against her rear bumper as though the driver wanted to force her off the road. She quickly locked her door and tried hard to see a number plate or at least an outline of the vehicle but the lights of the following car were too close and too bright. It was a terrifying journey; her heart began to race and she became undecided – should she run for home and reveal to this weirdo where she lived, or should she head for the nearest police station? But she had no idea if there was a police station anywhere in the vicinity. Nothing for it, she would have to go home, she couldn't drive around aimlessly looking for help. She would try to get a number plate when she got home, he would have to either pass her or stop with her – that would be her only opportunity. Please let her be fast enough to get out of her car, grab a sight of the following vehicle and get into the house without mishap; she found her hands were shaking and her heart pounding as she turned into her road, still

48

closely followed by her pursuer. She threw the big estate car into the driveway, jumped out and fled for the house in wide-eyed terror.

'Hey, sweetheart, aren't you at least going to say goodnight?' called Toby.

She skidded to a halt at the sound of his voice, her hands flying to her face.

'It's you! What the bloody hell do you think you were doing, Havers?' she blazed at him. 'You have just given me the fright of my life. Why the hell were you following me?' She began pacing in small circles, bending over at the waist, holding her stomach and trying to stem the feeling of nausea.

'Who did you think it was? You told me about these Thursday evening jaunts of yours and I just wanted to make sure you got home safely, old thing,' he beamed back, pleased with himself.

'You are never to creep up on me again, no matter what the excuse, do you hear me?' she yelled at him over her shoulder as she stalked into the house. 'And another thing, I'm perfectly capable of looking after myself, thank you. Don't ever do that again.' She was furious and still shaking when she closed the door firmly behind her and switched the lights off, then had to wait for the coast to clear before going out again to lock the car doors.

The following Thursday she told Mr Langdon what had happened and asked if he would mind if she began her labours a little earlier and finished by 9.30 instead of 10 o'clock. He was most concerned about her and readily agreed, and when she left the driveway she was pleased to see the road was absolutely clear of traffic as she reversed out. But after a hundred yards there he was in her rear view mirror, she recognised the headlights now. Her heart sank as he raced past her, threw the Daimler to a skidding stop at a 45-degree angle in front of her and climbed out of the car.

He slowly sauntered towards her, hands in pockets, but as he drew close to her door she put her foot down onto the accelerator as hard as she dared causing the big car to lurch forward leaving rubber on the road and narrowly avoiding colliding with him. She raced round the nearest corner into a small housing estate and turned her lights off, her erratic path now only lit by the occasional street lamp and the glow from the lighted windows that she passed. She suddenly found herself in a cul-de-sac, but thankfully at the end of the road she saw a screened darkened driveway and threw the car into it, turning the engine off immediately she came to a halt. Within seconds Toby's Daimler whispered past the entrance to the road as he slowly surveyed the area looking for her. She sat back, closed her eyes and prayed that no-one would come out of the house to challenge her – she didn't really feel up to explaining herself. After ten minutes she felt it was OK to creep out and took a circuitous route home, wondering if he would be waiting for her there. He wasn't.

I've really got to sort this out, she told herself. Not only can I not walk home from the train past his office door in case he leaps out at me, but now I can't even leave my evening job when I want to. Good fun he might be sometimes, but this is becoming ridiculous, and I don't like it.

The next morning she took a deep breath and rang him. 'Hello Toby, it's Sally. I wondered if you are free tonight for a drink – no meal, just a quick drink, I need to talk to you.'

Free tonight? For you? Stupid girl, I'll crawl over hot coals to be free for you tonight. This is the first time she's ever called me – I must have cracked her at last. Hang on a minute though, after last night's little fiasco she can bloody well wait now that she wants me.

'Sorry sweetie, got a bit of a bash to go to on a yacht in Poole, won't be back till Monday. Feel free to call me next week if you want.'

She could almost feel the smirk on his face and realised the game he was playing. He really thought she was doing the chasing now. Fine, if that's how he sees it he'll be in for a surprise next week.

He knew he couldn't hang around the locality that weekend, the temptation to call her would be too great; he needed to get away quickly before he changed his mind. Where better to go than the Yacht Club, at least he wouldn't be telling a lie when she called him next week. His toes curled in anticipation of the sweetness of that call.

The weekend crawled by; during the winter months the activity at the club was not as vibrant as during the summer. The boats were all protected against the winter weather, which was particularly foul that weekend, and only the screaming, wheeling gulls and the crashing of the rigging on the moored yachts gave any life to the harbour. Where the hell is everyone, he wondered to himself?

So he rang home and asked his mother if she still had his old room free for the weekend. She was delighted to see him again and lost no time in quizzing him about his London life. His siblings were still at home, and since they saw each other so rarely there was a great deal of catching up to do, much to mother's delight. His father was in ebullient mood and lost no time in telling his first born how proud he was of the success he was obviously making of his young life so far. Of course it had all been against his better judgement on day one, nothing wrong with a disciplined career in the Navy, but so far so good. The continual family chatter was tiring, so on Sunday morning he made his excuses and returned to his empty flat in

Farnborough.

The week went by and she didn't call. She did say she would call, didn't she? He had to wait this out, his male pride was at stake here. He kept himself busy with work during the day, with the pub and friends during the evenings but the nights were not good. He tossed and turned, he fretted and worried and found himself drinking a medicinal whisky at 3 o'clock in the morning to help get some shuteye, but it was desperately important that she should call him, not the other way round. By Friday he was really beginning to feel the effects of the strain and by Saturday he couldn't stand it a minute longer and rang her.

'Hello, sweetheart. I know you said you'd call me but my phones have been playing up all week and you would have had a problem getting through. I'm giving the phone people hell at the moment, but I thought I'd see if you still wanted that drink you mentioned last week?'

'Yes, I do, I need to sort things out with you, Toby, but I'm afraid it will have to be one evening next week now, if that's OK? Maybe Tuesday? I could meet you in the pub near your office; my train gets in around 7 o'clock – as you know – how would that suit you?' She could almost hear him grinding his teeth at more delay, but since she and some of her friends had planned a long weekend away at a wedding in the Midlands, including the Monday, their little fireside chat together would have to wait. At least whilst she was away from home he would not be able to chase her – either by car or by phone – and she would have some peace.

He had to keep busy and Alex Burton had just the answer for him. He and a couple of friends were going to play squash, a game that he hadn't played before but had heard about. Apparently it was hard and fast – just what he needed right now. He quickly picked up the rules and thoroughly enjoyed thrashing the little black ball at the front wall, even managing to take a game from one of his more experienced opponents. After his shower he went to the shop, bought himself a top of the range racket, booked himself in for a few lessons and vowed he would be the club's top player within six months.

The following day he struggled to walk, even getting out of bed was painful. The tops of his legs steadfastly refused to obey any commands after the punishment he had dished out to them the day before, and his buttocks were in an even worse state. This was not good news. He had planned to learn how to play golf that day. Physical activity – that was what was needed to keep his mind occupied, and he was certainly not about to let a few undisciplined muscles dictate otherwise.

He limped his way onto the golf course, much to the amusement of his friends who knew exactly what he was going through, and why. They had tried to warn him, but would he listen? The man was a killer, he had been so determined to give this new squash game such total commitment that he hadn't given a thought to common sense. But then, this was a man who never allowed common sense to get in the way of his ambitions.

Tuesday evening finally arrived and Toby left the office at 6 o'clock thoroughly wound up. The week had started badly, he was still in pain from the new physical activity when he arrived at the office on the Monday morning to find his secretary wanted to resign, said she couldn't take any more of his unpredictable tempers; followed by two prospective purchasers pulling out at the last minute from buying expensive properties that would have earned the agency downstairs a good commission; he knew that if he'd had his hands on the deals they would never have fallen apart. And today he was in danger of losing the purchase of a prime parcel of land by the skin of his teeth simply because his mind had not been sharp. He had been completely wrapped up thinking about Sally and the promised evening ahead that he had missed the noon deadline for his sealed bid, which he knew from his inside contacts was to have been accepted. The architect's plans were in their final stages, and he had the builder already lined up for the twelve houses – all that time wasted and money down the pan. Now he would have his work seriously cut out trying to rescue it, if it could be done. Damn and blast the bloody woman, it was all her fault.

    The pub landlord could almost see the thunderous black cloud that hovered above his head as he came bulldozing his way into the bar.

    'Hello Toby. The usual?' he enquired, reaching for a beer glass.

    'No, give me a double scotch, Jeff, this is definitely not a beer evening,' he replied, and he took his drink over to a quiet corner to shut himself away with the Telegraph crossword, trying to ignore the door every time it opened. 7 o'clock came and went, as did 7.30. He could feel his blood pressure rising and wished he had opted for a beer, it would have lasted him longer. By 8 o'clock he was in a rage – the fucking bitch had stood him up. Far from calming him the two double scotches he had drunk during that hour had wound him tighter than a drum; the other regulars in the pub watched as he threw his unfinished crossword onto the seat and pushed his way angrily out to the car park without his usual cheery farewell.

    As he drove home at speed he vowed never to allow himself to be put in that position again, it was humiliating and no bloody woman humiliates Havers twice. He'd wasted enough time, money and energy on her, she wasn't worth the fucking bother. It wasn't as though she was all that good looking either, all the right bits in more or less the right place, but not a lot else. She certainly wasn't going to set the world alight in the brain department either. In fact I really don't know what I saw in her in the first place, he thought. She's had it with me, I can do a damn sight better than her.

The next morning he set up a meeting to try to resurrect the land purchase that was going pear shaped and spent the morning at his lawyer's office trying to get a new deal arranged. His secretary answered Sally's call at 9 o'clock.

'Oh, hello, is Toby Havers there, please?' she enquired.

'No, I'm sorry, he's in a meeting at the moment,' Sylvie replied. 'Can I take a message for him?'

Sally wondered if he was now avoiding her, but couldn't blame him. It must have looked as though she had stood him up last night. She felt desperately sorry for the man who had thrown himself under the train at London Bridge station during the evening rush hour, he was obviously very disturbed and unhappy, but his actions had caused a total shut down of the rail service in the area causing chaos for thousands of commuters, including her. She had no way of letting Toby know what had happened since she was stuck on the train for over two hours waiting for the line to re-open.

Sylvie jotted down Sally's apology on a piece of note paper and tossed it onto the pile of papers waiting on the corner of her desk for his lordship when he deigned to come back to the office. He really was getting very unapproachable and unpredictable these days, she was looking forward to Friday when her week's notice would be worked out and she could look forward to her new job in a busier office with other girls to talk to. She was fed up working all alone up here with this unstable bloke for a boss who thought he was God's gift to women; thankfully he hadn't tried anything on with her, she wouldn't have lasted as long as she had if he had made any moves on her.

Sylvie didn't smoke much, but every now and then the urge would take her for a quick puff, especially when thinking of her weird boss. As she stubbed the cigarette out in the ashtray she became aware of how stuffy her little office had become so opened the window to blow some fresh air through whilst she went downstairs to the estate agency to put the kettle on for a cup of tea. She stayed down there chatting to the two agency boys while she drank her tea before settling back at her desk for the rest of the morning, and was pleased to find that the stale cigarette smoke had been blown away from her office as a result of the draught between the window and open door, but so had Sally's apology, the note had blown under her desk and was now lodged behind the waste paper bin, out of sight.

Toby didn't make it back to the office that day. His abortive meeting finished at noon, after which he took his increasingly black mood home and drank himself into a stupor from which he emerged fresh as a daisy at 6 o'clock the next morning. By 7 o'clock he was in the office, took the pile of paperwork sitting on its usual corner of Sylvie's desk and glanced through each letter. Some were quickly signed with a flourish, others amended for re-typing. Now that she's leaving that girl is really becoming quite careless, he thought, then put the whole pile back onto the top of the typewriter for her. He picked up the phone.

'Alex old boy, I know it's bloody early, but how about a game of golf today? The sun's shining for a change and I need to get some aggression out of my system before I blow, not to mention the knots I've still got from last Saturday's game of squash.'

Alex Burton, his next-door rival, had become used to Toby's somewhat unorthodox ways of running his business, and admired his obvious success despite it. Maybe dropping everything at the last minute and taking the odd day off work wouldn't do any harm – it didn't seem to have done Toby much harm, after all. He also had three staff to help run things and there were no important appointments logged for the day.

'Why not?' he grinned to himself, stretching as he fell out of bed.

The office cleaner arrived at 8 o'clock for her usual weekly half-day, passing Toby in the doorway as he left, and tut-tutted over the mess these office people make. What did they think the bleedin' wastepaper basket was for? Why couldn't the lazy girl put rubbish *into* the bin rather than around it? She grumbled to herself as she went around doing her usual thorough job of clearing up and polishing the surfaces before going down to do the same thing to the estate agency.

Chapter 9

March was bitter, England was cold and Sally thought back to her summer of sun last year and felt even colder. As she walked home from the station one evening she felt someone fall into step beside her.

'Hello Sally, haven't seen you for a while, what have you been up to?'

'Colin, how lovely to see you. I saw your mother a while ago and she said you were living abroad somewhere. Where have you been?' Sally was pleased to see Colin Williams who lived a few doors away from her parent's home; he was several years older than her and always very courteous in an old fashioned sort of way.

'I was living in Rhodesia, then I moved down to South Africa,' he replied.

'Where the heck's that?' she asked, geography not being one of her hottest subjects.

'The bottom tip of Africa,' replied Colin with a smile, leaving Sally none the wiser. He chatted away for the duration of their walk home leaving her with mental images of wild animals, wide open spaces, black skinned people and hot sunshine.

Hot sunshine! Those two words melted into her brain.

'Tell you what, why don't you pop over on Saturday morning, I should have my photos back from the developers by then and I can show you what life is like over there?'

'I'd love to, Colin, thanks,' she said as they parted at her gate. 'See you Saturday.'

It had been several weeks since she had left her message for Toby and he hadn't called to accept her apology and arrange to have that drink with her, which was strange, perhaps he was angry and didn't like being stood up by a woman for whatever reason. But, it did solve one problem, at least she was free of his continual bombardment now. She still walked the alternative route home but this routine had become quite a pleasant habit now, it gave her a few more shops to investigate.

Saturday morning dawned and she walked the few doors down to Colin's, spending the next two hours pouring over dozens of packets of photos he had taken in Africa. She had never seen anything like it. Colin had taken some extremely lively shots, and the scenes of dusty elephants, wide-open landscapes and endless skies, African huts, blood red sunsets and the broad, dusty streets of Bulawayo positively shone out of the small squares of glossy paper. She could actually feel the warmth of the sun, she smelt the dust of the plains and questioned Colin minutely about the country. When there had been trouble in the northern part of Rhodesia he had moved himself down to South Africa to where, as he was given to understand, it was possible to emigrate from England for £10.

The time spent with Colin left her bursting with thoughts of Africa, and Jenny listened to her sister's happy chatter as she was talking to her father and showing him some of the pictures Colin had lent her.

'You know what? If Colin is right about this £10 fare thing, I could go,' she said. Jenny looked at the photos and said: 'I could too, we could go together.' The two girls looked at each other and wondered.

Sally rang the South African Embassy in Trafalgar Square as soon as they were open on Monday morning and asked about this £10 thing. Yes, she was told, under certain conditions it was possible to travel to South Africa to live for just £10. She rang Jenny, who was working as a secretary in the City, and the two girls decided to go along to the Embassy as soon as they could and find out more.

One week later and they were full of information. There was an official handbook showing pictures of elephants drinking at waterholes, small black children playing in the dust, Cape Town's Table Mountain, partly obscured by its cloudy white tablecloth and the inside of a small supermarket in Johannesburg. I suppose the wild animals are kept away from the town centres, mused Sally. I wonder if they have things like tights and false eyelashes?

The girls shared a bedroom at home and talked late into many nights about the possibility of living in South Africa.

'We've talked about this for two weeks now,' said Jenny one night. 'I reckon it's about time we made an appointment to see someone at the Embassy and maybe get things moving.'

There were reams of forms to fill in. Questions about

themselves that the authorities wanted answers to. Jenny, as a qualified secretary would be welcomed with open arms, she had much sought after skills, but Sally, as an experienced model, was a less attractive option for the country's economy and would need to secure a job before being granted assisted passage. Back to the Embassy she went and was given listings of fashion manufacturers in Johannesburg to whom she could write. Several days later she had twelve copies of her CV prepared together with twelve small photographs of herself to send to each of the twelve addresses that seemed the most appropriate. Each manufacturer was also given a short letter of introduction and explanation of why she needed to be given a written offer of work before being eligible for the immigration scheme.

The replies seemed to take forever to arrive. Three of them said:

"Dear Sally,
We were very pleased to receive your letter. Please call and see us on your arrival in order to discuss your job application.
Yours sincerely"

Good grief, thought Sally, they obviously hadn't grasped the concept – back to the drawing board, more letters to send.

And then the fourth reply arrived:

"Dear Sally,
We are pleased to enclose an offer of work which we hope will be sufficient for the authorities. Please let us know when you expect to travel.
Yours sincerely"

The 9th of April 1969 was the chosen date, it seemed to be upon them in no time and suddenly the two girls found themselves at Heathrow Airport ready to board a BOAC flight to Johannesburg. The family had all come say goodbye; this was only the third time that each of the sisters had boarded a plane and they were very nervous, but at least they had each other, such excitement. Then they were airborne, southern England was disappearing, the Channel was crossed and their adventure was beginning.

The steps were rolled into place, the plane doors opened, and there in front of them was Africa; all they had to do was walk down the steps onto the tarmac to complete their passage to their new life. The air was dry and crisp, it was wonderfully warm and the girls felt immediately at home. They beamed excitedly at each other as they entered the arrivals hall looking for the immigration authorities that were to house them until they could find a place of their own.

The little hotel in Johannesburg was cosy and clean, and every day the sisters set out together to explore the sights, sounds and smells of the bustling, modern city and soon found their way around. Finding both a job for Jenny and a flat for them to share were priorities, but they took the first few days to acclimatise themselves to the altitude and the newness of everything. It was all so completely different from London. They cautiously sampled exotic fruits; they giggled at hearing that traffic lights were called robots, and they learned how to handle the fierce African sun, even in their autumn. Sally was delighted to find that the stores did sell tights and false eyelashes, and the fact that lions and elephants weren't a problem in the city centre was a bonus.

Sally started work at the factory that had offered her a job, and Jenny found a good secretarial position with a large international company. Colin Williams was back in Johannesburg, and he and his friends were able to help the girls find a large spacious flat in a new block in a quiet residential street. It had all been such a rush – from the decision to leave home in England to finding stable jobs and accommodation in a foreign country on the other side of the world had only taken just a few short weeks.

'She's gone where?' Toby exploded. He had bumped into Sally's mother outside his office and, after politely enquiring as to her health, had asked what Sally was up to these days.

'Oh, didn't she tell you, dear? Yes, she and Jenny went to South Africa last week. Sally has a nice job in a dress factory in Johannesburg and they have just found a lovely flat together, I spoke to them last night and they are really excited about it. I must admit it was a bit of a surprise, she just came home one day full of it, and before her father and I had a chance to get used to the idea they had their flights booked and off they went.'

'Hilda, be a dear and let me have their address would you? I'd hate to lose touch completely, perhaps I could drop her a line from time to time, birthdays and Christmas, that sort of thing.'

What a nice young man he is, thought Hilda. So thoughtful. Such a shame nothing came of anything between them. She resolved to pass on her daughter's address – well, you never know.

Chapter 10

Sally's job was going really well, such a friendly bunch; a father and son business with a factory full of cheery people. The office skills she had picked up over the years were proving to be useful, and she was happy to slot into whatever position was required of her by her new employers. Even lunch was a fun affair, often cooked by the boss who would invite some of his friends round to join him and the office staff. The laughter amongst them would frequently run into the middle of the afternoon before anyone remembered there was work to do. That meant a late evening to catch up but nobody minded.

Travelling to outlying customers meant late nights too as well as early mornings, and the very size of South Africa made every trip an adventure. Visiting a customer in Middelburg meant a journey out of the city in the combi full of dress and coat samples, and Sally sat up front between the son, Roy, who handled the sales, and Samuel the driver. She sat bolt upright, eyes swinging left and right, her excited mind absorbing every detail of the passing landscape.

'What *are* you looking for?' queried Roy looking puzzled. He couldn't see anything worth looking at, but there was obviously something he was missing, judging by the look of intense concentration on her face.

'I don't want to miss anything,' said Sally, eyes glued on the countryside.

'But there's nothing to see,' retorted Roy. 'It's just barren scrub land with the occasional tree.'

'It might be nothing to you my friend, but I've never been out of England before, except for two trips to Spain, and I've never seen anything like the African countryside. I'm afraid of missing something,' she responded with a laugh.

He was right, the landscape certainly was dusty, barren and uninspiring, but that was viewed from the perspective of the hardened South African who was born here, drove this route and saw this view on a regular basis, it was no big deal – but to her it was awe-inspiring. The land seemed to have no end, vast tracts of dry, golden space; there were no houses each piled on top of the other, no traffic jams, no masses of jostling people in grey raincoats, heads bowed against the grey drizzle, she just saw mother nature in all her simple, raw, unspoilt state. Could she really see the curvature of the earth, or was it her imagination?

The customer had wanted Roy to bring the current range to her shop and have Sally there to do the clotheshorse trick that she was paid to do, and as they returned to the factory that evening, driving westwards into the setting sun after taking a successful order, she experienced her first African sunset away from the city and its light pollution. The endless canopy of sky was alive with the shifting burning reds, oranges and yellows of nature's fire, with the dark silhouette of the occasional barren tree outlined against it.

'Roy, let's just stop for a minute. Please, please, PLEASE! This is the most amazing sight I have ever seen and I have to get away from the van to feel it properly, please let's pull over.' She was bouncing on the seat in her desperation to get away from the man-made machine. Samuel pulled into the side of the road and she jumped to the ground, racing away from the proximity of the vehicle. She became rooted to the spot amidst the dust and stones of the African land as the awesome display that nature was putting on just for her in the western sky began to slowly change. The sun continued its journey to the other side of the world, and the brilliant, burning amber shades of the darkening sky slowly turned to powerful burgundies, maroons and purple, each rich colour pierced with the dying golden embers of the setting sun. Surely nature doesn't get any better than this. She felt she had stopped breathing.

Toby's poem arrived a week later:

> *Ah well, my dearest,*
> *Tell me where we are.*
> *Are we in this world?*
> *Or are we just a star*
> *In this universe of ours*
> *Filled with many ivory towers?*
>
> *Our world, it seems,*
> *Is made of dreams*
> *Of sun and sky,*
> *Of moon and stars,*
> *Of green and grey*
> *And night and day.*
>
> *Sometimes blissful,*
> *Sometimes not,*
> *Tell me where we are.*
> *Are we in this world of ours*

Hiding 'midst the ivory towers.
Or are we in another land
Full of laughter, rather grand.

Or is it all just in the mind
This world of ours?
Sometimes loving, sometimes kind;
But always you are there,
Regrets are very rare.
Just to be with you is all I need –
Your love, your looks, your face
Is all I need.

Sally disintegrated. She had only been away from home for a month. The job was great, the people really friendly and helpful in her new country. Their flat was light and comfortable – one they could be proud of. The sun shone warmly as winter approached and she knew she had made the right choice in leaving England, but there were a few thorns in her newfound paradise.

She and her sister were having a few teething problems living together harmoniously; they had never been the best of friends whilst living at home with their parents and had very different ways of doing things. They both knew it would take a lot of effort to make their living arrangement work and were trying hard to get along together without too much friction.

There was such a lot to learn about the way of life in South Africa as well. There were two official languages, and it was going to be necessary for the girls to learn something of Afrikaans in order to fit into their adopted country as seamlessly as possible. New financial calculations in the rand had to be adapted to rather than comparing with sterling all the time. Having Christmas in mid-summer was going to take some getting used to as well, and the crackle dry air 6,000 feet above sea level in Johannesburg's winter was starting to give them serious static electric shocks. Living away from home in Spain for six months was one thing, Sally had already visited the country once on holiday and knew what she was going to, it was only ever going to be a temporary arrangement and she had always had the return ticket in her pocket. But this was different. She was living thousands of miles away from her childhood friends and her parents with an absolute determination to make this new life work, which meant focusing her mind totalling on everything positive about South Africa and shutting out the negative. That formula worked well for her – until Toby's poem landed in her lap.

She was lucky, she had never suffered from loneliness or homesickness and was always happy in her own company, but the poem brought her down heavily. Suddenly the sun's light was not quite so bright, she slept less peacefully, there seemed to be more tension at work, or was it all just her imagination?

After a week of trying to ignore it she knew she was going to have to confront 'the poem'.

The postcard in the shop showed a spectacular expanse of the Drakensburg mountains; mile after undulating mile of the deepest greens and richest of earthy browns bathed in the early morning mist, shadowed by the rising African sun, and she wrote on it: *'See these mountains, how empty they are? I'm feeling a bit like that right now. You would not believe the majesty of this country, it really has to be seen to be appreciated. But, fantastic though it is, I have to admit that leaving home for a new life here is not proving as easy as I had thought it would be, there's a lot I miss, but I know I will settle down soon. Hope you are well – thank you for the poem, it is very beautiful.'* How do I sign it, she pondered? Best wishes? Regards? Love? No, definitely not love, that might give him completely the wrong impression. Damn it, he knows who it's from, I don't need to sign it at all.

What did she mean? Toby wondered, "*… feeling empty … it has to be seen … there's a lot I miss*". Did that mean she missed him, wanted him to come out to her?

'Marla!' he roared at his new secretary. 'Get me on a flight to Johannesburg tomorrow, if there is one, otherwise, get me out there soonest by whatever route.'

Marla's eyebrows shot up to her hairline and beyond. What the hell did he want to go out to South Africa in such a rush for, she wondered, it's nearly the other side of the world.

'Ever flown long haul before boy?' The florid faced, portly gentleman completely filling seat 2A of the BOAC flight to Johannesburg had a full bodied, rather strident voice and was using it to full effect.

'Er, not much Sir,' Toby replied, drawing his face back into the furthest corner of the seat to escape the wall of whisky fumes emanating strongly from his neighbour's breath.

'Ever drunk whisky before, boy?' continued the alcohol laden questioning.

'Has been known, sir,'

'Show you how it's done, boy. Bottle of scotch between us, heads down, see you in Jo'burg!'

Marla had told him the only way to get out to Jo'burg quickly was to go first class, all economy seats were sold out. She was burning with curiosity as she made the reservation, desperate to know why her boss was travelling half way round the world. She wondered whether or not there was another woman somewhere out there, and was disconcerted to think there might be – she had seen no sign of any other female around him, and she didn't want there to be any. He would be a good catch; keep her and her mother nicely he would, if she played her cards right.

Well, why the hell shouldn't I have a little comfort, Toby thought? By the sound of her postcard, if I've read it right, she's going to be so pleased to see me it'll be worth it. Anyway, he reasoned to himself, it's far too long a flight to be squashed up against the great unwashed in steerage. His travelling companion had been right, the half bottle of whisky had worked a treat, and the 12-hour flight had passed in peaceful, dreamless slumber.

It was a Sunday morning and still early as they taxied in to the terminal at Jan Smuts Airport. The early winter sky was a razor sharp ice blue, and if the scented air had been a good Cape white wine it would have been chilled to perfection. As they disembarked into the crystal clear South African morning 2A turned to him and said: 'Nice talking to you, boy,' and sallied forth from the aircraft leaving a wake of whisky fumes behind him.

Toby smiled and nodded his agreement. There was a good lesson learned, the whisky had certainly helped, and he felt refreshed after a full night's sleep.

He asked the cabbie to take him to the President Hotel in Johannesburg where he checked in, unpacked his bag, took a quick shower and vigorously brushed his teeth. All traces of whisky had to be erased from his breath before the next step of his journey – the most important step – the step for which he had travelled thousands of miles half way round the world.

The next taxi took him to an imposing block of light, spacious flats with a large swimming pool that Sally and Jenny were looking forward to making full use of when the weather got a little warmer towards Christmas.

It was still early in the morning so the chances of her being out were slim, fingers crossed. His heart was pounding, the palms of his hands were sweating and he was aware that his knees were feeling rather wobbly as he knocked on the door of the flat. What if she had gone away for the weekend? What if she had a boyfriend? What if – what if – what if?

As she opened the door he watched the look of astonishment spread across her beloved face, then an almost reserved look of pleasure. His heart swelled, it would be OK, she *did* want to see him, she *had* missed him, he *had* interpreted her card correctly, and the journey *was* the right thing to have done. His joy flowed over and he grabbed her, enveloping her in the biggest bear hug, his whole body shaking with relief. When she was able to catch her breath she pushed him off and held his elbows at arms length.

'Whoa there, Toby. What the hell are you doing here?' Her hair was still wet from the shower, and she was aware that she looked an absolute fright standing slipperless in her old dressing gown, but to him she was the most perfect specimen of womanhood in the world, a woman for whom he would travel around the world many times over.

She invited him into the flat and made him sit still for a moment whilst she made him a coffee and warned Jenny that they had company – and who that company was. She quickly got dressed and brushed her hair before sitting down with this wild-eyed man who seemed hell bent on finding her.

They talked for a while about how things were in Jo'burg, about how things were back home, about anything other than the last time they were due to meet that had gone so horrendously wrong. He just wanted to avoid the subject; he couldn't bear to think she had stood him up without an apology, couldn't bear to remember his feelings of frustrated anger towards this precious person; how, fleetingly, he never wanted to see her again. She in turn wondered why it had taken him so long to accept her apology and why he hadn't tried to contact her again, although she had been secretly relieved at the time. But it was nice to see him, she told herself, a bit of home that she was missing. They talked through the morning, and he suddenly realised how hungry he was – he hadn't eaten since his in-flight breakfast several hours earlier, and that had hardly been very sustaining.

'How about a spot of lunch, old thing?' he asked. 'I need to eat something, I'm sure we could get something decent at my hotel.'

'Where are you staying?' she asked.

'The President – where else?' But he immediately regretted those last two words as he saw the flicker of irritation pass across her face.

'Sorry, sweetheart, what I meant was, I didn't know where to stay so I asked the cabbie and he recommended it. It's certainly pricey, I wouldn't want to afford to stay there for long.'

She hadn't eaten at the President before, and found the meal delicious. The wine, their laughter at his final understanding of why she had failed to appear that Tuesday evening all those months ago, and what must have happened to her apology; the pleasure of catching up with happenings from home all made for a relaxed and happy afternoon for her, and he was beside himself with joy but trying desperately hard not to show it. The realisation that she had planned to be with him that evening in Sevenoaks, the fact that she had been delayed through no fault of her own and had tried to say sorry, reaffirmed his belief that there was a future for them together.

'What's Durban like?' he asked suddenly.

'Don't know, I've only been in the country a few weeks and haven't been there yet but I'm told it's pretty humid, although most places have air conditioning.'

'It's your birthday next week, isn't it? How about we take a few days away and have a look at the place?'

'Yes it is, but I can't just take time off, you idiot. I've got a job to do.' She laughed at his bubbling enthusiasm.

'Listen my girl, you've just spent the morning telling me that you haven't even had a full weekend off since you started work – don't you think your boss would be pleased to give you just a couple of days off? I'll ring him, I'll tell him I'm your brother over here just for a few days. I'm sure he'll be happy to let you show me a bit of the country, if he's as good a bloke as you say.' He beamed at his plan.

'You'll do no such thing, Toby Havers.' She was outraged. 'First of all I'm quite capable dealing with my boss, and secondly no one is telling any lies for me under any circumstances. You may have a point about being due a few days off, but you are not to get involved. I tell you what I'll do – the new range is almost complete so most of the fitting pressure is off, and the sample books are up to date so I might be allowed a couple of days off, but only a couple of days. I'll have a word tomorrow, but if there's the slightest hesitation I won't push it. It was really good of my boss to give me this job without seeing me first, and I'm not going to take any sort of liberty.' She couldn't help but be amused at the self-satisfied grin on his face. Does he always get his own way, she mused?

Her boss was in expansive mood on Monday morning when she wandered through to the factory in search of him.

'Course you can take a few days, sweetheart.' he beamed at her, puffing away merrily on one of his perpetual cigars. 'Take the whole week if you want, go and have a good look at Durban, you'll love it. I expect we'll manage without you till then. Just promise me you'll come back.' He waved his arm in farewell and disappeared in a cloud of smoke to check the new delivery of fabric into the bond store.

I don't think I want a week, thank you very much, thought Sally, as she ran to answer one of the phones in the office. A few days with Toby would be more than enough.

'Morning sweetheart, you answer the phones as well as have pins stuck in you, do you?' Toby wasn't going to let her forget to ask for time with him. He had hired a car for the week and was going to make the most of it.

'Yes, I have spoken to David, and yes he is happy to let me go for a few days, so you have got your way,' she laughed. The thought of a few days away in Durban was quite appealing, she had to admit. Johannesburg enjoyed crystal blue skies every day in winter, constant sunshine, but was very cold indeed. Durban, on the other hand, was rumoured to be warmer. A bit of warmth would not go amiss, besides it was a part of this beautiful country she had yet to see.

Toby spent the rest of Monday in a dream. Having no idea where Durban was, the purchase of a map seemed a good plan. Next stop was for some beachwear in readiness for long hours soaking up the warm Durban sun. He was almost skipping with excitement. Sally had refused to see him that evening, she had her own things to see to in readiness for a few days away, and he had arranged to collect her from the flat at 6 o'clock in the morning, so that by the time they arrived at the coast they would still have some sunshine hours left for the beach. It was quite a journey, about 400 miles in total, and the receptionist at the President had told him to expect to be on the road for some seven hours. No problem. He was used to long journeys driving the length of France either for skiing in the Alps or sun in St. Tropez. They were very boring journeys; this one would be different, with his girl beside him and the promise of some uninterrupted time together. If he played his cards right this time . . .

They were very comfortable and relaxed with each other on the journey, and found that they were both enthralled by the changing countryside. As they left the flat highveld on their way to the coast, the barren golden brown savannah began to give way to more undulations in the foothills of the Drakensberg Mountains. At Pietermaritzburg they noticed that the land was much greener, more fertile and the air was becoming softer and more humid. The difference in climate from Johannesburg was very marked; hard to believe they were in the same country.

'I can see the sea, I can see the sea!' shouted Toby, laughing. 'Did you like to be the first to spot the sea when you were a child, he asked? and they both laughed at childhood memories. What a different city from Johannesburg, almost tropical with its lush vegetation and palm trees. They drove with the windows open, breathing in the warm, heavy, balmy sea air,

67

both feeling in holiday mood.

After the long drive he was pleased to get out and stretch his legs. They parked just off the sea front and wandered down to the sand. He thought about taking her hand but then remembered that might be the kiss of death. She had finally agreed to stay till Saturday because of the length of the journey, plenty of time to get her on his side; he also knew he had to bite the bullet with good grace when she had insisted on separate rooms.

They agreed to meet in the lobby of the hotel, and once they had unpacked and got their towels and swimming costumes organised they wandered down to the nearby beach together.

At the dress factory Sally had heard horror stories of sunburn, even in winter, and had bought a good protective cream that she started to rub in liberally. When she was done she noticed that Toby hadn't done the same so offered him hers.

'No thank you, I don't need sun cream. My skin is used to the sun in St.Tropez and skiing, it's as tough as leather. Besides, it's almost mid winter here – how strong can the rays be in winter? No, I'm fine.'

'You might think so, but I've heard that people who live here all year round still suffer sunburn if they don't put sun cream on.'

'Bollocks, do stop fussing, woman. I don't need creams, I know my skin; it has lived with me for 26 years and I know exactly how to treat it.' He would not be told.

As they lay on the beach, side by side, she started to believe that this was going to be the loveliest of birthdays. She was beginning to enjoy his company again, his spontaneity and his silly sense of humour. She began to feel relaxed in the warmth of the afternoon sun, and as she turned to tell him how tranquil she was feeling, he was snoring.

An hour later he woke to find that his skin had turned a gentle shade of pink. Oh good, he thought, this will brown nicely by tomorrow, and I can go back to the UK with a great tan, even though it will only have been a few days.

They wandered back to the hotel to shower before dinner and he began to feel his body glowing warmly, very warmly. The cooling shower water was surprisingly painful, rather like standing under a shower of needles, and he noticed the delicate shade of pink was rapidly turning a rather unbecoming red. Oh well, he pondered, p'raps I'd better cool it in the sun tomorrow and stay in the shade for a bit. Shit, I was looking forward to topping up.

As he sat down to dinner the effects of the sun on his unprotected skin began to make it's presence really felt – he started to feel a little sick and dizzy and his head started pounding. Dinner could not be faced, it was all he could do to mumble his apologies and crawl up to his bed – alone. Instead of it being the night of grand passion that he had looked forward to for so long, it turned into one of the longest and most painful nights he had ever experienced. Fortunately he had fallen asleep on the beach lying on his back, so that part of his body was not affected and he could lie down without pain, but that was almost the only part of him that was not on fire. His face swelled to an alarming size, leaving his eyes mere slits, and the skin on the front of his torso and limbs felt as though it was being continually seared by a blowtorch. He kept the bath full of cold water and spent most of the night gently easing himself in and out of it, allowing the cool water to dry naturally on his skin.

Breakfast wasn't going to happen either, he still felt sick and had a blinding headache, but had at least managed to get an hour or so of sleep between cold baths. Cold baths with plans like he had? – What a bloody joke, he mused.

When he hadn't put in an appearance by 9 o'clock Sally knocked gently on his door.

'Who is it?' he called.

'It's me,' she replied, 'you didn't come down to breakfast and I wondered how you were, especially since you were so unwell last night.'

'Wait a minute,' he called, struggling painfully to put on yesterday's swimming costume, the only thing that didn't touch any burning flesh, and put his head round the door.

'Listen sweetheart, I'm not up to the sun today. You go on down to the beach and I'll get down a bit later – join you for lunch maybe.'

Sally was horrified at the sight that greeted her. That looked like a something-degree burn to her.

'Are you sure you wouldn't rather get back to Jo'burg and see my doctor. That looks nasty, you don't look at all well?'

The thought of spending seven hours driving made him feel physically sick, but he couldn't let on how much he was suffering.

He tried a painful smile, decided it wasn't working so settled for a rather lopsided smirk. 'No ways sweetheart. I'll be fine later – didn't sleep much last night, feeling the heat a little. I'll catch up on a bit of shuteye now and see you on the beach later. If you sit where we were yesterday I'll find you. Just don't worry about me, I'm fine.'

He finally made it out of bed at 4 o'clock and put on the softest shirt and shorts he could find in his suitcase. Shoes were another problem since his feet had swelled too, so he hobbled barefoot down the street, being careful not to tread on anything unpleasant. He found a tourist shop nearby and bought a pair of flip-flops, together with the biggest pair of sunglasses he could find. A large brimmed straw hat completed the picture, and on the way out of the shop it occurred to him that some sun lotion might be a good idea so added a bottle of that to his purchases and gingerly made his way down to the beach. The feel of the late afternoon sun on his bare arms and legs was not a pleasant sensation, and he began to hope that Sally had settled herself near some shade.

One look at his face that morning had told her that shade was definitely going to be required when he turned up, so she had hired a large sun umbrella for the day and settled herself firmly under it away from the burning rays. She had not enjoyed her day, his sunburn had looked serious, and she really thought they ought to head back to Jo'burg straight away. She knew he wouldn't be up to driving so she had better take the wheel, but seven hours made her gulp a bit. He might be used to long stretches across France, but she had never done more that an hour or so at a time. Well, I can always take a break half way, she thought, it will be another of life's experiences. She was amazed at his lack of sense. Here was a man showing the world what a clever and successful chap he was, his decision-making abilities putting him in the top league, yet he was too damned arrogant to take local advice and use a protective cream against the African sun.

But when he finally hobbled onto the beach she felt bubbles of laughter welling up inside despite her annoyance at having their holiday spoilt. He did look a sight. Girl's big floppy brimmed hat, girl's sun glasses on top of this swollen lobster trying not to let the skin between his toes touch the rubber of the flip-flops and failing miserably at each painful step after painful step. She knew she shouldn't laugh, he was obviously in great pain, but he only had himself to blame

'Hello, old thing.' He tried a grin, which felt a little easier than the morning's attempt – thanks in part to the lotion he had just rubbed into his fried face. 'Had a nice day?'

'No, as a matter of fact I haven't, I was far too worried about you to feel at all relaxed. I've made a decision, we are going back tomorrow whether you like it or not, there's no point hanging around till Saturday just for the sake of it. I'll drive and you can enjoy the countryside.'

'No, sweetheart, we'll stay for the extra couple of days, as we arranged. You could do with the break and the tan will make you feel good. I'll just sit under the shade and read a book – Ouch!' he yelled as he bent his body under the umbrella.

'We are doing no such thing, Toby Havers. I am driving back

tomorrow and the easiest thing for you to do is join me, otherwise you'll need to book a flight.'

Oooh, she did sound cross!

By the time they got back to Johannesburg in the evening she had a pounding headache from the strain of the long drive, conversation had been stilted and he was bad tempered, irritable and rude, partly through the pain of his severe sunburn and partly because he had completely screwed up his beautiful, carefully laid plans to get her into bed yet again. She bought him some more pain relief from the chemist and drove him back to the President.

'Come on up for a drink', he had suggested, 'I'm sure you need a stiff one after that journey, I know I do.'

'No thanks. I'll drop the car back to the rental company and get on home. It's been a long day and it's getting late; I'm really tired and am looking forward to a long hot, smelly soak to get this car seat out of my joints. I'll speak to you tomorrow – no doubt.' She waved tiredly as she pulled away.

Even without the pain of the sunburn he could not have felt more devastated and sick. How in the name of sanity had he managed to cock that up so completely? She was definitely not on good form, and his chances of getting her into the sack within the next couple of days before his flight back were less than zero. Not only were his hopes for a week of rampant sex denied him but so was a golden tan, and he still couldn't get a decent nights sleep for Christ's sake. That's two nights on the bloody trot. With both his pride and dignity in tatters as well what was the point of hanging around? He threw his travel bag at the wall in a fit of temper, and the sharp movement made him wince some more. He was a mess.

The next morning the pain had not receded and his skin had started to blister and crack. Even the skin on his scalp was beginning to crack and peel and he was still limping from swollen feet.

Surely something could be recovered from this debacle? So he picked up the room phone and ordered a taxi.

His temper had not improved by the time the driver dropped him at the block of flats, and when he arrived on the eleventh floor his head was starting to thump again. His knuckles pounding on the door did little to reduce all the various pain levels. No reply – he tried again, harder this time. Where the fucking hell was she? After kicking his heels for a few minutes he gave up and returned to his room at the President where he picked up the phone and called the dress factory. Perhaps she had gone into work? No, he was told, she hadn't.

By now his head was exploding so he decided to try and get a few hours sleep then make a decision. No dice, even though he had hardly slept for three nights the pain of his sunburn still kept him awake. He gave up after an hour and called room service for a stiff double scotch, taking more painkillers with the drink. This was obviously not meant to be, nothing in his life had ever gone this wrong at every turn and for so long. This fiasco had cost him his dignity and he couldn't tolerate that, enough was enough, perhaps he ought to take the hint. He picked up the phone once more and called BOAC to get him on the first available flight home. He had never felt this low and close to tears, but he had learnt at a very young age that men didn't cry and he wasn't about to start now. Cut your losses old boy, he thought to himself. Pull yourself together, plenty more fish, and all that.

As he packed his bags in readiness for that evening's flight to Heathrow he ordered another double. He sat on the edge of the bed, holding the drink in one hand listening to the phone ringing out, unanswered in her empty flat, and the tears started to well. 'DAMN HER!' he shouted, hurling his empty glass at the wall.

Reception was concerned. Reception did not like the look of this rather angry, weird looking lobster presenting itself to pay a bill made rather high by quite a lot of double scotches. His clothes were chosen more for minimal contact with his skin than sartorial elegance, and his face was extremely red and puffy with equally red eyes reduced to swollen slits. Reception hoped there would be no trouble over the amount of the bill, and raised his delicate eyebrows when told of the broken glass incident.

'Sorry old boy, slight accident, tripped over the coffee table, don't you know,' was muttered from puffy, cracked and bleeding lips. 'Send me the bill for cleaning the mess – my card.'

The lobster paid the bill without a murmur and limped after the porter to a waiting taxi. 'Jan Smuts airport, my man.' He ordered falling resignedly into the back of the car and closing his tired, bloodshot, swollen eyes.

Sally fumbled for her flat keys, dropping half the shopping bags as she opened the door and reached for the receiver – just as the phone stopped ringing. It immediately started again, that's bound to be Toby, she thought as she picked up the receiver, but it was her mother wanting to catch up with her daughters' lives. When they had finished chatting she began putting the shopping away, so it was some time before she remembered to return what was probably Toby's call a little while ago, and rang Reception at the President.

'No madam, Mr Havers checked out some time ago – I believe he went to the airport. No, sorry madam, there is no message.'

When he landed at Heathrow, the twelve hours of dry cabin air was causing the lobster-look to start peeling with a vengeance, revealing new, raw skin underneath. He hadn't been allowed to even try for sleep on the night flight home; mummy's little darling in the seat behind him made sure of that every time he screamed and lashed out with his feet. The taxi dropped him at his flat and he headed straight for a drop of medicinal brandy. Half a bottle later he fell into bed and finally slept through till the following morning.

When he came to he inspected the damage to his body, then considered the damage to his male pride. His emotions were tumbling around in total disarray. On the one hand every fibre of his being needed Sally by his side – on the other he was being thwarted at every turn, not only by her but also by events. He never lost at anything he really set his mind to, and he had definitely set his mind for her – yet here he was losing out. It was a sensation he could not stomach.

New man – that was what was needed, he decided. New home, new car, new woman, and he spent the rest of the day cleaning the flat and generally getting it ready to go on the market first thing in the morning. With positive actions now firmly embedded he did at last manage to get a good night's sleep.

Marla had not been expecting to see him in the office so soon, he had not been due back for another four days, so had decided to treat herself to a bit of a lie-in with her new boyfriend instead of making a start at her usual 9 o'clock the following morning. But Toby had been in since 8 o'clock, so his temper was bubbling nicely two hours later when he heard her trotting up the stairs an hour late.

'What the blazers time do you call this?' he bellowed. 'I pay you to start work at 9, not the middle of the fucking morning!'

'Sorry Toby,' she stammered. 'I had a puncture. Honestly, I have been here every other morning on time, it wasn't my fault today.' What on earth was the matter with him, she wondered? He had gone off to Johannesburg as happy as Larry last weekend, but look at him now? No, on second thoughts, perhaps she'd rather not. His skin looked a burned mess, and so was his temper. Oh well, thankfully she had got away with the puncture story.

Chapter 11

'What are we going to do for our first Christmas?' Sally asked Jenny over dinner one evening. 'It'll be on us in a few weeks and if we're not careful everything will be booked up.'

'Don't know,' her sister replied. 'It'll be quite boring hanging around the flat, even with the pool to cool off in. Might be a good time to see a bit more of the countryside. One of the girls at the office says it's quite nice in Mozambique; we could always have a look at that, I suppose.'

'Um, why not? Can your travel department get us something, do you suppose?' Sally asked. When they had arrived in Johannesburg eight months earlier Jenny had secured a job as secretary to a department head at one of South Africa's larger companies, and they had a very comprehensive travel section. Since her boss was always off travelling the world Jenny had got to know the girls in that department quite well.

Almost without consideration, the girls took it for granted that they would be holidaying together, they felt secure in other's presence when exploring new territories, but although they didn't always agree, their life together was working out well enough. They were each happy in their respective jobs and had completely separate social lives, only seeing each other on the occasional evening and some weekends.

'Right, decision made. I'll go down to the second floor first thing tomorrow morning and see what there is,' said Jenny.

The sisters boarded the night train for their Christmas holiday in Mozambique and settled into their sleeping compartment full of excitement at their new adventure. Jenny hadn't had an opportunity to leave the city at all since their arrival, and Sally had only travelled around the highveld a little when she was needed to show the range to customers, plus that awful trip to Durban with Toby a few months earlier.

The girls were far too excited to sleep, and lay on their stomachs on their bunks looking out of the window watching the African countryside drift by under the soft, silvery light of a full moon. Neither of them wanted to miss a minute, after all this was Africa proper; they hoped they would get to see elephant, giraffe, lions, springbok, anything at all that might be awake and wandering around just as their train flew by in the night making enough noise to frighten the fiercest creature.

'Phew, this is what I call hot,' said Jenny as they piled out of their taxi at the entrance to the block of flats at which they were staying in the capital Lourenco Marques. 'And humid with a capital H,' agreed Sally. They unpacked in the self-contained apartment on the seventeenth floor that they had booked, then went out for a quick reccy of the area. The rest of the day was spent in acclimatising themselves to the area and the moist heat. They had become accustomed to the dry air of Johannesburg with its total lack of humidity, but going out in Lourenco Marques was like walking into a wall of hot, wet cotton wool. But, hey, it was going to be fun. Their first break since they arrived back in April, and it had been quite a mentally challenging eight months; they were certainly ready for a rest.

Day two and they decided they didn't need to be joined at the hip any more, they could each go and do the different things they enjoyed. Sally went off to have a look at the shops, and after an hour of wandering about and doing a bit of window-shopping she found an air-conditioned department store to cool off in. As she paid for her new supply of sun cream she started chatting to the counter clerk, thoroughly enjoying the cool air-conditioning and in no hurry to leave the store. A very English voice behind her joined in the conversation, and she turned to find an attractive, strongly built man grinning at her. His 6-foot tall ruggedly tanned frame was clothed in brightly painted Bermuda shorts and an outrageously colourful shirt, and as she absorbed the vision before her, Sally noticed that he had loveliest long lashes framing the bluest of eyes that were laughing at her. He was amused by her obvious confusion at his presence, and watched her pay for her purchases before hurriedly leaving the store.

Next stop had to be a spot of lunch, and she quickly found a clean looking bar where she could put her feet up. A straw hat was becoming a necessity; that sun was indeed a monster; her neck and face were already beginning to feel the effects even with sun cream on, and she'd only been out in it for a few hours. A market – that's what I need, she thought. As she made her way to the bar to pay for her lunch she passed a table at which sat the man with the blue eyes and colourful Bermuda shorts from the department store and two ladies, also having lunch. Ah, she thought, he's English, so are those ladies he's sitting with by the sound of their voices – one of them is bound to know if there's a market here.

'Excuse me, I'm sorry to interrupt your meal, but could one of you please tell me if there's a market in town somewhere?' she asked.

Richard Denham introduced himself and the two ladies, both of whom were living in Mozambique through their husbands' jobs, and Sally shook hands all round accepting the invitation for a post lunch coffee with them. In reply to their questions she said that she and her sister had only arrived the day before, were staying at Makatini Court and were getting their bearings before a few days tanning on the beach.

Richard offered to accompany her to the market, but she preferred to go alone, she didn't want to give out any wrong signals, memories of how Toby had misinterpreted her postcard still haunted her. Or did he misinterpret it? Had it been a Freudian thing? Had she really wanted to see him and sent out signals that she had not meant to send? Whatever. He really is past history now. This is my holiday, she thought. I really can't be bothered with men, signals, or anything that might come remotely close to complication.

'Thanks for the coffee and the market directions, I'll think of you all every time I wear my new hat.' And she waved goodbye to them as she left the bar in search of the much-needed head protection.

Her shower that evening was pure bliss. A cooling, cleansing spray on her over heated, dusty skin and hair was just what she needed; Jenny had showered as well and the two girls sat wrapped in their towels drying off and chatting about their respective day when there was a knock at their door.

They looked at each other in surprise. 'Who on earth can that be?' Sally asked.

'I dunno,' said Jenny. 'Open the door and let's find out.' But before either of them could move the door opened and in strode Richard Denham. Sally's jaw hit the floor.

'What on earth are you doing here, and how did you find me out of nineteen floors in this building?' Her voice had gone up half an octave; she was acutely aware that she was only wrapped in a skimpy towel with wet hair trailing down her back and no make-up on.

After a brief introduction to her sister Richard told her that he had spent over an hour searching through the individual floors of the block trying to find which one was rented to holidaymakers. He and some friends were going out for a meal that evening. The two ladies she met at lunch would be there too, together with their husbands. Would she come with him – oh, and bring Jenny too? They would have freshly caught Mozambique prawns, shells like candyfloss melting in her mouth and the best company in Lourenco Marques.

Sally and Jenny grinned at each other and said together: 'Why not?'

The Christmas holiday was over, it had been such fun. Richard had collected her from the flat every day, whether she had wanted him to or not, and they had thoroughly enjoyed each other's company. Christmas Day had been spent with his friends and Jenny, and the girls caught the night train back to Johannesburg on Boxing Day.

By the middle of January Richard decided to leave Mozambique and look for work in Johannesburg to be near her, and quickly found work with an engineering company. He admitted that he had not initially seen her sitting in the bar in Lourenco Marques because he had been so deeply engrossed in conversation with the two women, telling them he had just met the girl he was going to marry, but that all he knew of her was the type of sun cream she preferred, when suddenly there she was, standing in front of him asking for directions to the market. Fate, or what?

He began asking her to marry him on their second date together, but that brought in shades of Toby Havers, it was all much too intense and Sally kept him firmly at arms length. But six months later they had become a very firm item, rarely apart, and she was sure that marriage was what she wanted as well.

'Yes dear, your father and I are very pleased for you, please don't think we're not,' was Hilda's quick apology for her luke-warm reception of her daughter's news. 'I must admit though we were rather hoping something might have come out of your relationship with that nice Toby Havers from the estate agency. Still, I haven't met your Richard yet; I'm sure he's very nice and I shall look forward to meeting him at the wedding next April.'

'Oh, mummy, you're right, you don't know him – I wouldn't be marrying him if he wasn't very nice, would I?' came Sally's sharp response. 'Actually he's lot more than very nice and the total opposite of the Toby that you so admire. I know you're very fond of him, but his overbearing arrogance can be really insufferable at times, certainly not something I could ever live with. I do enjoy his humour, his vast knowledge and some of the silly things he gets up to, but the price of a future with him would be too high. He's a high-flyer and I'm not; he lives in a world I don't understand, and no matter how hard he tries to convince me he lives on the same planet as me, I know he doesn't. His strength of mind frightens me sometimes and I feel overpowered by his resolve – maybe it's just that domineering attitude of his that makes him so successful, but there's a lot more to my world than financial success. I know Richard will make me really happy, he's hard working, and great fun and we share the same views on life, which are completely different from Toby's, so let's just plan for my wedding next year and put Toby out of our minds can we, please?'

Chapter 12

Toby devoted the rest of the year to continuing success. His flat went on the market and was sold within days for a tidy profit, which he immediately put down as a deposit on the purchase of a house in an exclusive area of Sevenoaks. He and Alex played a lot of squash together, and their equal competitiveness made for hard games and furious concentration, neither willing to give the other an inch, and they found the post match drinks they enjoyed together a valuable relaxing counter to the fierce court battles.

'I don't know about you old son, but I'm ready for the sack. Blinding game tonight, but I'm knackered. Can I drop you at your place?' Toby had picked Alex up earlier in the evening for their game, but now it was midnight and he was feeling weary from the exercise, followed by the meal they had enjoyed together.

'Yep, thanks, Alex replied.'

Toby pulled up outside the property and Alex hopped out, immediately beginning a search through his pockets for his house keys.

'Blast, can't find them. I must have locked myself out.'

'Can't you wake Jane up?' Alex's wife could be woken and let him in.

'No, she's taken the kids over to her mother's for the weekend. The house is empty and sodding locked.'

They both left the car and started to walk around the house looking for an open window, or some other means of entry. None. It was well secured.

'Oh hell, I'm going to have to break a window. Jane's not going to be best pleased.'

'No you won't – look.' Toby pointed to one of the upper floor windows, which was slightly ajar.

'That's all very well, but how the hell are we going to get in from down here?'

'You just leave it to Havers.' And off he went in search of a ladder. The one he found was in a neighbour's shed, but that didn't matter. A ladder was a ladder.

'You can't go nicking other people's ladders,' Alex whispered angrily at his friend.

'Bollocks. I'm not nicking it, just borrowing it for a few minutes – you'd do the same for them. Rather smash a window, would you? Bring all the cops for miles around?' And without a second thought he angled the borrowed ladder up to the open window above and started climbing. Gently he eased it open, enough to allow him to fall in. Curses drifted down as he pulled his dripping wet foot out of the open toilet that he hadn't seen in the darkened bathroom, then all went silent.

'Hurry up Toby. Open the front door.' Alex was getting cold and wanted to get to bed now that his friend had solved the entry problem.

'I've had to climb the fucking ladder, now you do it,' came the giggled reply.

'Stop messing about. What the hell are you doing, just open the bloody door.'

The argument continued for a few minutes, Alex getting more and more annoyed. He didn't hear Toby pick up the telephone receiver and dial 999: 'Police? There's someone trying to break into number 44 Westhurst Drive. He's got a long ladder propped up against the wall to an upstairs window that's open – please hurry.'

Just as Alex reached the decision that he would have to give in and began to climb the ladder, so the police arrived.

'Excuse me, sir. Can you tell me what you think you are doing climbing up that ladder?'

'I live here officer, this is my home. My idiot friend had to climb in to open the front door for me because I've locked myself out. He's in there now. Was he the bastard who called you? I bet he was. Havers, you're sick! Open this bloody door at once – you've had your fun, the police are here and want to arrest me for an attempted break-in. Open the bloody door now!' He had started climbing back down while ranting at his imbecilic friend with the wacky sense of humour who was hiding inside. The officers were finally persuaded that Toby was definitely an odd ball and warned him not to waste police time in future. It was all Toby could do to stop himself from curling up with laughter until they left.

Alex couldn't bring himself to speak to him for a whole day after that.

During that summer the two friends partied in St Tropez, and over Christmas drove to Gstaad for skiing. Toby's sports car was totally unsuitable for snowy, mountainous driving, so he lent it to a friend in exchange for an estate car, a vehicle large enough to take some pretty passengers plus skis to the slopes with him.

Alex and Jane with their two young children plus their nanny were in their family saloon car, and Toby, plus four beautiful airline hostesses, were in the estate car, and he had booked them all into the Palace Hotel,

Gstaad's finest, and most expensive.

'We can't afford a week here,' whispered Alex in alarm when he saw where his friend had booked them for their skiing holiday.

'Don't worry about it, we're not. I've got a plan. Trust me.' A Havers plan, why did that sound ominous?

They unpacked their bags, Alex, Jane and family in two exquisite rooms – Toby and girls in two other equally beautiful and palatial rooms.

They each went their own way on the slopes, and wearily returned to the hotel at the end of the day for a bath before finding a small restaurant for their evening meal all together.

'Right, come on Toby, spill the beans. What's this plan you've got going with the hotel? There's no way we can afford to stay there, and I hope you're not planning on us all doing a runner at the end of the week?' Alex had his young family to think about and needed to know what his friend was up to.

'Oh come on, give me some credit Alex. It's easy. I might have booked us in here for a week, but tomorrow morning, after just the one night, we're decamping to another place up the road, a small pension that we *can* afford. Trouble was, when I made the reservations for all of us at the pension they told me they could only take us from tomorrow, so I needed to find somewhere for tonight. Bingo! But the Palace would never have taken the booking if they knew we only wanted one night – this is their busy season. Not a lot they can do about it now though is there?'

At the end of the meal their bill was presented and Toby got his wallet out ready to split it. 'How much? Don't they realise that's £500 before tax? Tell you what, I'll spoof you for it.' he said to his friend, eyes twinkling.

'Oooh, no, not likely, you never lose.'

'Oh come on Alex, don't be such a spoil sport – there's always got to be first time.'

Alex paid the bill.

Management was indeed furious with his ruse when they checked out the following morning, and threatened to charge them for the full week anyway. When he made it clear that they didn't have the funds, management realised that they had been well and truly duped, and had to accept payment for just the one night instead of considering legal action between continents.

Toby had charged each of the girls enough to cover the cost of his own holiday. Well, as he argued, he had done all the organising for them and all the driving – and there had been no charge for the pleasure of his company, either on the slopes or in his bed.

80

Returning to work in January he felt energised and fully focused. Every ounce of his phenomenal energy went into hitting his million pound target. He worked 16-hour days, taking over at a desk in the estate agency when he felt not enough deals were being completed, and immediately the sales doubled; he knew he was king. His hunger for land that he considered had potential for development was well known in the industry. Relying on clever ideas and angles that other developers had not considered he bought anything that came on the market – stretching himself financially tighter than was sensible, but his sort of success didn't come through being sensible or cautious. Some parcels of land had to be sold on quickly in order to allow him to buy bigger and better; he likened himself to a successful juggler, and half the fun was in keeping all his financial balls in the air at one time. He knew that if one were to fall the whole lot would come crashing down around his ears, but the adrenalin burst that success after success gave him kept him on a permanent high.

He'd known his local bank manager for many years and had enjoyed a good working relationship with him, even when he occasionally pushed Bob Grey's professional judgement beyond the limit. Bob became less tense at their monthly lunches together when he saw the occasional movement inwards on Toby's accounts, and became a little more relaxed at backing his rather unorthodox financial dealings.

'Bob, dear boy,' began Toby, as they sat back to enjoy their post lunch cigarettes. 'Have you given any more thought to that million I asked you for the other day? Tempus fugit, and all that, the vendors aren't going to wait forever you know. If I don't close on that parcel of land as I'd promised I'm going to lose credibility, and that won't do my reputation any good. Can't be seen going back on my word.'

'Yes, I was hoping to be able to talk to you about that,' Bob replied. 'Head office are a bit skittish at the amount you want, especially over and above your current overdraft; it's all looking a bit top heavy, and they are rather looking towards a decrease in your position, not an increase. I think this one's going to be taken out of my hands I'm afraid, but I'll certainly let you know as soon as I hear anything.'

Not what Toby wanted to hear. When he returned to his office, feet in their usual place relaxing on the leather-topped surface of his desk, he picked up the phone to Hymie Goldstein, his trusty accountant.

'Hymie, my friend, I need a million, and I need it now. Barclays have just put a new man into the local branch, he doesn't know me of course, and is having to refer my paperwork to head office. You know what those bloody pen pushers are like – not paid to take risks, even though I'm paying their salaries through the nose. Know any of your big boys that might want in on a blinding quick deal? You know me, in and out quickly; anyone investing will make a fast turn around, probably in the region of £25K within two months.'

'Let me have something on paper, I'll go through it and get back to you – might even be interested in it myself,' Hymie said.

'Now I know I'm paying you too much if you can come up with a million just like that,' laughed Toby. 'I haven't got time for all that paperwork rubbish; tell you what, I'll let you buy me lunch tomorrow and I'll talk you through the proposal.'

Hymie had followed Toby's success through each set of annual accounts that he was retained to prepare with growing interest. It looked as though this boy had the golden touch; his property deals in particular were making him a lot of money, all seemingly re-invested in a much larger portfolio. The boy also knew how to spend it, but at 27-years of age could he blame him? Hymie had also done well for himself as a very astute accountant, and through some clever financial dealings had earned himself a seat on the board of Stanhope Bank plc. This was just the vehicle he needed to get in on one of Toby's deals that was being offered to him on a plate. A million was a bit strong though for a first timer; it wouldn't be a bad idea to get the boy to do some of the funding himself, see what stuff he's really made of.

'If I do this it'll be our first venture together, but I want you to come up with at least 25%. Show your mettle to my board, you know the sort of thing.'

What did he have that he could use to raise some cash on, urgently? His house? No, not nearly enough collateral. The office building? Now there's a thought, there should definitely be enough equity in there.

'I don't have that sort of money lying around, and raising it is going to take time – which is something else I don't have. So, will you take a charge on my office block?'

Forty eight hours later the paperwork was in place and Toby was able to tell Barclays that he was going to be running his new multi million pound empire without them. Two months later, over their shepherd's pie, he told Bob Grey of the profit he had just made with his new bankers in London.

'Quickest and best deal I've ever completed, old son, shame your lot wouldn't look after me.' he bragged.

'Congratulations Toby. I'm truly sorry head office declined that

82

proposal of yours, it did go up with my recommendation, you know that, but perhaps, now that you've proved to them what you are capable of, they might look more favourably on your next requirement.'

'Bollocks, I don't need to prove myself to anyone. Nothing personal Bob, but if they don't want to help me when I need funding, they can swivel for my business when I'm on a roll.' he said, emptying his glass of wine. 'In fact, you can tell that lot in head office I'm transferring my business to Stanhope Bank in London.'

'Hmmm, I shall be most sorry to be losing you as a customer, although not as a friend, I hope,' said Bob. 'Are you planning to use some of that new profit to reduce your overdraft with us?'

'Not at the moment, no. I've got plans for that money. Barclays are charging me enough interest on that facility to finance the national debt, so don't worry about it.'

'Hymie! I've got another one for you, bigger than the last. It'll make us a quarter of a bar in six months – you up for it?'

Chapter 13

'Hello Hilda, it's Toby Havers. It's been a while since we spoke, I hope you are well. What's that girl of mine up to?'

'Oh, hello Toby. Well, she's not your girl any more, I'm afraid. She got engaged last week – someone she met in Mozambique last Christmas, they're looking at a wedding in April time next year.'

He put the phone down and his mind went blank. Well, what did he expect? They hadn't spoken for over a year ever since that fateful Durban trip. His mind, which had been kept under such rigid control for thirteen months, began to burn with longing for her. He couldn't concentrate on the architect's drawings in front of him for the new housing estate he was building. He blindly groped for the car keys, stumbled down the stairs and took the back entrance from the office rather than get caught by questions from the estate agency staff on the ground floor.

The journey home was a blur, and once there he opened the drinks cabinet, found a full bottle of scotch and proceeded to drown his sorrows in the only way he knew how. He also knew that if he was to stay sane he had to replace her permanently. That meant a marriage of his own. Right Havers, you're 27 years old, got a nice little empire on the build; you need a son and heir, and you need it now. No more tossing around with that no-hope woman, she's thrown away her chance – time to move on. Tomorrow is day one of operation Mrs Havers.

Samantha Peters didn't know what had hit her when Toby Havers came crashing into her life with his usual style of bravado and joie de vivre, any sadness in his life pushed firmly into the dark recesses of his mind. One minute she was enjoying a drink with three friends in the Six Bells pub at Horley, near Gatwick Airport, a favourite of flight crew like her, and the next there was this bright eyed, bushy-tailed Hooray Henry buying drinks for everyone in her group. Nobody knew who he was, but the four friends had just got back from an overnight trip to Barcelona with British Eagle, and weren't due to fly again for three days, so happily accepted his offer.

As the evening wore on he made it more and more obvious that Sam was being singled out for his special attention, and eventually offered to run her back to her flat. He was instantly smitten but decided not to rush things. Perhaps this will be the one to get Sally out of my head, and I don't want to screw that up by being too pushy, he thought wryly, a lesson he'd learned from a Master.

The poor girl stood no chance. Toby had decided she was the one to give him his son and heir; she was blonde, gorgeous, fun and had a very sexy, throaty laugh that never failed to get him aroused. She was everything he could wish for in a wife-to-be. She also had something of the look of Sally about her.

They were married in the November in Sam's hometown. No bride could have looked more stunning as she gently eased herself from the chauffeur driven Rolls Royce and shook the folds from the exquisite full-length, hooded, snow-white velvet cape, trimmed with white rabbit and softly flowing over her classical white, A-line wedding dress. She took his breath away as he watched her gliding gracefully down the aisle towards him on her father's arm, her slender figure gloriously accentuated by the simple lines of her dress. Her parents arranged for the wedding breakfast to be celebrated at a local hotel, then the happy couple departed for Bermuda for a magical couple of sun-filled weeks.

Life was good. Sam was a delight, she made Toby extremely happy and at last the yearning for Sally began to lessen. Business was going well, and although he still took huge risks, they always paid off – somehow. The property market was booming, he was in at the sharp end and knew he was invincible.

They didn't live at his house for long; now that he had a wife and with thoughts of a family he decided to look for something more suited to his new exulted place in the world. A swimming pool and tennis court would be nice, he decided, and he would find a way to afford it. Hymie?

The deal was done; Hymie's bank had come up trumps for him again. They had insisted on a floating charge over all Toby's assets, private and business, but that wasn't going to be a problem; as soon as the next deal was done he knew he would be able to clear that. Their new home at Little Hammer Farm deep in the Kent countryside was perfect for them. A 16th century converted farmhouse with dozens of old oak beams, low ceilings and centuries of character was just the ticket. Not only did the property already boast its own swimming pool and tennis court, but stables too. He felt every inch the country squire – just the place to bring up a substantial family in style. His first major purchase was a pair of ponies which he and Sam both enjoyed riding out over the local countryside.

Their new home was in a proper English country village with a small green in its centre, where, much to his delight, he was asked to join the local cricket team that played in the summer, and where carols were sung each Christmas. He thought the villagers might appreciate a large Christmas tree for the green for the local children to decorate, and to provide a backdrop for the carol singers. His gift became an annual event, and each year the whole village turned out to rope it down securely and begin draping it with garlands and baubles.

Sally and Richard married in Johannesburg, then spent a fun week travelling round Rhodesia, taking in Bulawayo, Victoria Falls and Salisbury before preparing to cross into Mozambique for the second week of their honeymoon.

'Look at this map, darling,' said Richard spreading the paper out on the bonnet of the car on the outskirts of Salisbury. 'If we go down to Lourenco Marques by the main roads, we've got to go all the way south to Beit Bridge in South Africa, back through the Transvaal then turn east – it's going to be a fairly boring journey, tarmac all the way. The alternative is to go through the Mozambique border at Umtali, then head due south through the bush to Lourenco Marques. Much more fun. I know the area, that's were we used to drill for oil when I was working there when we first met, remember?'

'Oooh yes, I like the sound of that; it'll be quite an adventure, and we'll get to see so much more of the countryside,' Sally excitedly agreed.

The autumn sun shone warmly as they loaded their Renault ready for the journey southeast from Rhodesia's capital. They planned to take two days to reach their hotel in Lourenco Marques, and according to the map, and Richard's knowledge of the local terrain, they would be passing through a couple of large villages that were bound to have some sort of accommodation for them, so they bought a large camping knife in case they should come across any pineapples or mangoes growing wild and set off after lunch, in high spirits, heading for the Mozambique border.

They were hot, dusty and fairly tired as they pulled into the one and only hotel in the border town of Umtali late in the afternoon, and their first chilled beers were extremely welcome. The bar gradually began to fill with early evening trade, and Richard picked up snippets of conversation from travellers around him. Listening half-heartedly to their conversations it seemed as though car journeys through the bush had been rather difficult.

He started chatting to the travellers, explaining that he and his new wife were on honeymoon and were thinking of going through to Lourenco Marques via Umtali – was there a problem with that route, did they think?

'Yes, I'm afraid so,' one of the travellers said. 'There's been some local flooding in this region and some of the trails are impassable, even with our 4-wheel drive. If I were you I'd head further south before going through the border, this seems to be the end of the recent rain belt; it should be OK at, say, Chipinga.'

Richard bought them a beer and waved his thanks as he returned to where Sally was sitting.

'Ummm, slight alteration to the plans, darling,' he said spreading the map out again for her. 'Looks like we won't be going through here after all, flooded trails apparently, so we'll head south for Chipinga and go through the border there. We ought to get there by nightfall, I reckon.'

'That's fine, just a few miles more of Rhodesia and a few miles less of Mozambique but we'll still see the same sort of countryside,' she responded happily. This really was the most delightful way to spend their honeymoon, seeing something of this amazing continent together, and she felt incredibly happy.

After their refreshing beers they continued their journey south watching the setting African sun bathe the whole of the western horizon in a golden haze, turning the world blood red then purple, before enveloping the land in a black velvet cloak of total unbroken darkness. The early evening sky had thrown up some ominous looking clouds to the east that were preventing even any starlight providing relief from the total blackness around them. The route from Umtali to Chipinga became less and less formal the further south they travelled, and the car headlights soon showed them to be on no more than a dusty single track.

As they rounded a sharp left-hand bend, there, in the middle of the track, stood a fully-grown African elephant waving his ears at them. Richard slammed the gears into reverse even before the car had stopped its forward momentum. As they flew backwards, engine screaming, the spinning tyres threw up a shower of sand and dust through which they could make out the ghostly form of the massive creature blocking their way. He lifted his trunk, threw his mighty head back and let out a bellow of rage at the intrusion into his night-time stroll.

Sally shrieked. Richard dealt with it as fast as he could – in reverse.

After a quarter of a mile going backwards he felt they were safe so turned the engine off to listen. All was quiet. The dust gradually settled, and after a further twenty minutes, during which time even their breathing was done as quietly as possible, he idled gently forwards, headlights off, until they had passed the point at which they had encountered the mighty bull. Headlights on again they moved forward a little more quickly, and then they heard him. He was keeping apace with them in the trees to the right; hearing him crashing through the shrubbery galvanised Richard to get out of there fast. A mile later the crashing had stopped and he felt it safe to slow down to a more sedate pace. Just as well. This time it was a whole family of elephants crossing the track just around the bend – first daddy, then mummy then junior bringing up the rear hanging onto mummy's tail with its little trunk.

They felt as though they were caught in a pincer movement – impenetrable bush to left and right, a disturbed rogue elephant behind and a family of elephants with protective parents in front of them. Richard switched off the engine again and they sat very, very still in the darkness. Their hearts thundered in terror and their breathing ceased completely; what had happened to the peace and tranquillity they had planned for these two days? Is this where they were going to end their lives? Messing with elephants out of sorts is not recommended.

Eventually mum and dad decided the dark, silent, immobile intruders were no immediate threat and continued their journey, and the honeymooners shook from head to foot as they continued their journey to Chipinga.

But Chipinga was closed. It was 9 o'clock at night and the railway barrier/border crossing was closed against the road preventing them from reaching the hotel they could see on the other side.

'Never mind,' said Richard. 'If the barrier's down it must mean a train is due soon, and then someone will be able to open the border for us.' So they settled down in the car as best they could to wait for someone or something to happen. They dozed, and at midnight, seemingly out of nowhere, the train came thundering through the darkness, rudely waking them and giving them both a further fright. Richard turned the car headlights on to attract the attentions of the border guards, who jumped down off the train and finally opened up the barrier.

The little hotel looked so welcoming; Richard and Sally invited the border guards to join them for a well-earned beer at the bar and unloaded their cases, looking forward to a nice cleansing shower.

The little wizened old man serving them beers spoke no English, only the local form of Portuguese, but between Sally's Spanish and Richard's hand gestures he understood they wanted a room for the night. Sadly he shook his head and muttered something that sounded ominously like 'no room at the inn.' The guards confirmed that passengers from the train had just taken over the entire six rooms – what a shame the honeymooners hadn't got to the hotel before the train. Oh well, a night in the car it is then – not quite what they'd had in mind for their honeymoon, but all part of the adventure.

At 5 o'clock in the morning the sun's early rays pierced the windscreen of the car then the inside of their closed eyelids like shards of broken glass. They fell out of the car, joints all stiff from the very little sleep they had managed to get whilst sitting upright, and went in search of some clean water to try to freshen up a little. The hotel was still asleep, so since they were parked outside the railway station they headed onto the platform looking for toilets. When they found them they wished they hadn't bothered, the stench told its own tale of other travellers without formal accommodation that had spent the night there having used the toilets with no running water.

Never mind, let's just remember this is our honeymoon, they told themselves. The sun is shining, the air is warm and it can only get better from now on. We've crossed the border, we're in Mozambique now, let the fun of the journey commence, they thought.

Their low fuel supply was the next issue to be addressed, so they searched for, and found, the local petrol pump, woke up the young boy who was responsible for serving the occasional customer, and were amused to watch him operating a very old-fashioned hand pump – until the pump ran out after just a couple of gallons. The boy was quite unconcerned and disappeared into the shack to bring out a large pitcher on his shoulder, and proceeded to pour the contents into the petrol tank through a homemade funnel. Problem solved; at least they had half a tank full and could continue their journey to Lourenco Marques; there's bound to be another petrol station in one of the next villages.

The track out of Chipinga was sandy but firm, and according to the map it improved as it passed through other villages.

The map, however, was seriously misguided as the track disintegrated totally in places, and the monsoon style rains had reached Chipinga during the night, washing away all sign of the trail in places. The honeymooners knew they had the railway line to follow, the one from Chipinga to Lourenco Marques, so every time they were forced away from their chosen route through flooding, at least they had a marker to return to.

After an hour Richard felt the gears getting stiffer and stiffer until he found it easier to stay in third gear rather than grind them in order to change. That plan worked well until they came to a stream that crossed the road forcing them to come to a complete halt. Earlier travellers had found some old, loose railway sleepers and placed them across the road to act as a bridge, but the recent downpours had caused the water to wash them to one side. Richard tried to get the gear into neutral before jumping out to replace the sleeper bridge, but the engine stalled.

The sleepers were easy enough to place into position, and he returned to the car, turned the ignition – nothing. He tried several times more – no spark. They looked at each other in alarm, and Richard opened the bonnet to see if he could work out what was wrong. Nothing looked obvious and he wasn't a mechanic, so he decided the best option would be to try to find some local help with a rope to pull them across the stream, push to get them jump started, then they could hopefully limp into the next village for mechanical help. He set off along the railway line, carefully stepping from one sleeper to another, shielding his eyes from the strong sunlight and concentrating on trying to locate the tops of huts anywhere amongst the bush around him. The snake was not happy at having his sunbathing interrupted and reared up at him, hissing in fury. Richard didn't need warning twice and beat a hasty retreat.

As they sat there in their misery, wondering what to do next, they saw a plume of dust coming towards them; it felt like the arrival of the cavalry. They whooped with joy, praying the travellers would be able to help in some way. The middle-aged English couple were greatly concerned but not able to be of much assistance; they had no towing facilities and didn't know anything about starter motors or gearboxes. Good news though, some friends of theirs would be coming through and they would be able to help – but it wouldn't be for another twenty-six hours. Did Sally and Richard have any water – any food? No. The generous couple passed over a small bottle of water and shared a packet of biscuits with the honeymooners, then went on their way, promising to send someone from the next village, if they could find anyone.

Sally burst into tears; Richard shouted at her that crying wasn't helping. Their first wedded row and they'd only been married a week.

Was it a mirage? Or was that really a truck coming towards them from the other side of the stream? Oh joy of joys, the lovely couple that had passed by an hour earlier had sent someone to help. Like the hotel owner from the night before the elderly driver only spoke his local dialect, but under the circumstances very little language was really required, the problem was fairly obvious. A rope was quickly secured, the Renault was pulled across the stream and jump started, and they were on their way again. There was no mechanic in the next village so they just had to keep going, praying that the car, and Richard's driving skills, would get them through.

Life for the next five hours went from bad to worse; the track deteriorated even further, Richard became unable to shift out of third gear and every gradient had to be approached at a run in order to crest it. The surface became badly rutted and at times it felt as though they were driving over corrugated sheeting, at others axle deep in soft, powder-fine sand. By late afternoon they lost the railway track completely and were not even sure they were heading in the right general direction, but with gritted teeth tried singing to the tapes they were playing in order to keep their spirits up. They blotted out the fact that they not passed a village for several hours and the accuracy of the map was now looking even more suspect.

The evening sun was sinking low in the sky, and just as they were considering another night trying to sleep in the car with the ever present threat of not being able to re-start the engine in the morning, they turned yet another sandy corner and ran straight onto tarmac.

They both had tears in their eyes as they shouted with relief. Richard still couldn't get out of third gear and they were running dangerously low on petrol, so the next ten miles were undertaken at a sedate pace. There was no traffic – hardly surprising really considering where the tarmac ended.

At last, at 7 o'clock at night, after a 12-hour nightmare, they entered a small village that boasted what looked like a bar. Never mind the clutch, never mind the starter motor, Richard let the engine stall outside the little shack, and the newlyweds fell inside gasping for something to drink and eat. They had had nothing but the few biscuits and a pint of water to share, so generously given by the strangers earlier, since the sandwich and beer supper at Umtali the night before, and, combined with the dusty journey they had just undertaken they were feeling extremely dehydrated.

The locals all stopped what they were doing to stare in amazement at the strangers, and nodded sagely as Richard gestured to them that they had just endured the most horrendous journey from Chipinga. 'Ah, Chipinga, si!' Well that explained it all.

They tucked enthusiastically into their meal of lamb chops boiled in oil, washed down by local beer, as Richard tried to explain to the locals the problems he had suffered with the car. Was there a garage anywhere round here that might be able to help tomorrow? Was there anywhere they could stay until the morning?

'Si, senhor. I look you car now. No sleep here,' said a man who had been sitting quietly enjoying his evening with friends. And with that he picked up the keys from the table in front of Richard and walked slowly out to examine the car problem. 'Mecânico,' said his friends by way of explanation before resuming their conversation in the corner.

An hour later the 'mecânico' returned the keys and grunted to them that 'auto OK agora.' Sally thought that meant the 'car was OK now', but the mechanic's continued chattering was beyond her; so they all went out to the dust covered vehicle together, and with lots of pointing and the evidence of burned wires, they worked out the problem for themselves. They saw that the mechanic had made a temporary repair to the starter cable and Sally thanked him profusely, 'Obrigado, senhor, muito obrigado.'

They pressed him to accept payment, but he waved them away, pleased to be returning to his friends in the corner having done his good deed for the day. So Richard left some money at the bar, sufficient to pay for the evenings refreshments for the mechanic and his friends, and taking Sally by the arm, led her back to the Renault so that they could continue their limp to the capital, still two hours drive away. The starter motor was working, but their friend the 'mecânico' had not been able to do much about the clutch. It was still full of sand and dust but Richard did at least manage to get up to fourth gear for the majority of the journey.

The drive through Lorenzo Marques to the hotel became a game of cat and mouse with the traffic lights and roundabouts because of trying to minimise the gear wrenches, but thankfully there was little traffic around at nearly midnight.

They were not expected at the hotel for another two days, the two days that they had planned to spend enjoying the delights of rural life in the Mozambique bush, and they had more visions of having to spend a second night in the car, so approached Reception with some trepidation.

'No problem sir, madam. Your bridal suite won't be available for two days I'm afraid, but we do have a spare double room for you until then.'

Suddenly things had taken a turn for the better, and as they sank gratefully into the huge, comfortable bed that night they both knew that, although they had been looking forward to an adventure through the bush, they had perhaps slightly underestimated exactly how much of an adventure it was to have become, but at least now they could continue with their honeymoon.

Six months later Toby heard the news that he had been longing to hear, Sam told him he was going to be a father. His joy at her news was unbridled; soon he would have a much longed for Havers Junior, an heir for his burgeoning empire. His world was indeed looking rosy.

The whole of the weekend was spent in celebration. They invited her parents and arranged an impromptu party for local friends, and looking at Toby's excited face no one could fail to be thrilled for the couple.

On Monday morning he jumped on a train to share the news with London. The afternoon went by in an alcoholic blur as he dropped in on various friends and business associates, all of whom had to be bought a drink to mark the occasion.

His last call of the afternoon was to Hymie, and they arranged to meet at the Hilton for a glass of fizz at the end of the day. By this time he was beyond excitement, he had already made a lifetime of plans for his son, had short listed some suitable names, designed the nursery, drawn up a list of public schools, even considered the various merits of Oxford or Cambridge. Nothing but the best would be good enough for his son and heir; a daughter wasn't even considered.

Hymie had finished his drink and gone home, and the bar was emptying of its earlier life. The day was done, he was alone, and could feel his exuberant mood slipping away under the furriness of all the Champagne he had consumed that day – Sally – why wasn't it you, he silently pleaded? wondering where she was now and what she was doing with her life, a life that should have been joined with his, the mother for his son.

He had heard that she and Richard had been married in Johannesburg; Hilda had been there for the ceremony and had told him. Tears began to fill his eyes as the sadness began to overwhelm him, and he fumbled moodily inside his jacket pocket for a cigarette, clumsily pulling out his little black book as well, and as it hit the floor the pages opened. He picked it up and started to casually flick through the names, girls that he hadn't seen for ages: Anna, Benita, Clarissa – Clarissa? Now, she used to be something else in bed, and he felt the surge of a strong erection begin to sweep away his melancholy as he remembered her, a completely uninhibited redhead always ready to try something new. He had been faithful to Sam for, what was it - a year now? That's got to be long enough for any bloke, surely? I could just do with a dose of Clarry right now, might make me feel a bit brighter; I wonder if she still lives round the corner, he mused, falling off the bar stool and heading for the nearest pay phone.

Clarissa was in, she was free that evening and, best of all, was looking forward to seeing him. He found out just how much when she opened the door wearing just stockings, suspenders and the fur jacket he had bought her last time they had been together. His brain dropped right down the front of his trousers as he pushed his free hand up between her legs, fingers probing her as he guided her quickly backwards into the bedroom. He had asked the cabbie to stop off at the nearest off licence for some chilled Champagne, and they spent the next hour greedily licking the bubbles off as many erogenous parts of each other's bodies as they could find.

'Bye bye, sweetie. Please don't leave me so long next time,' she purred. 'You're still the best, even though you've married someone else.'

'Clarry darling, we wouldn't last five minutes married to each other, you know that. Neither of us could stay faithful to the other for long enough, and that would be a recipe for disaster, wouldn't it? Just don't change your phone number without telling me though, will you? You never know when I might want to buy you another fur coat.'

Feeling better about the world again, he strolled out onto the street, and considered the logistical complications of getting first to Charing Cross, then to Sevenoaks, then a taxi home from the station. Sod it. 'Cabbie! Fancy a trip to the Kent countryside, my friend?'

His son arrived into the world kicking and screaming, and with much ceremony was Christened George Frederick Havers. His parents were both in awe of this tiny scrap of life that was going to continue the family name and empire; so much was resting on his tiny, new shoulders – he was going to be much more successful than his father; this little man was going to be at the top of a much bigger pile, his father would make sure of that.

Clarissa became a permanent fixture in Toby's life, as did various others when the mood took him. Sam was busy with George, but even with a nanny to help she was still tired at night, and was finding Toby's demands more and more difficult to sustain. If he felt a stab of conscience as he slept his way through his conquests, old and new, he never showed it. He had needs for Christ's sake, and if Sam wasn't going to satisfy them, then he felt no compunction in looking elsewhere for satisfaction.

She became more and more lonely, tucked away deep in the Kent countryside with just a baby and a nanny for company, and Toby was rarely home before midnight; she knew what he was up to and withdrew more and more into herself. She also knew that questioning him would only produce the same vague, lies.

'No, sweetie, nothing's wrong – why ever would you think that? It's just that Hymie/Alex/Bob/someone else wants to meet up this evening to discuss my new land deal at Farnborough/Edenbridge/Orpington. We'll probably grab a bite somewhere – don't wait up, I'll see you in the morning.' But nothing disguised all the different perfumes on his clothing.

Richard was very content working in Johannesburg. Selling building equipment came easily to him, and he was at his happiest swapping jokes after hours in the bars with his customers. He was popular with them as a result and his sales targets were always exceeded. It did mean he was rarely at home in the evenings though, but it didn't matter, did it? He was good at his job, which meant his career ladder was looking steady, all of which was good for their future together, wasn't it?

Well, no it wasn't, not exactly. Sally became increasingly frustrated at being left to kick her heels on street corners after work in the south of the city, whilst Richard was doing his Mister Popular routine fifteen blocks to the north. Since he passed her office at the end of the day it made sense for them to travel home together rather than leave her to the mercies of the local bus.

But not on those days when he was busy selling building equipment over a pint of beer. One afternoon he called her specifically to tell her to be downstairs at 5.15 on the dot – he would pick her up a little earlier than usual that night because he was coming home from a different direction. But by 6 o'clock he still hadn't turned up. The last bus left at 6.10 and she had to run for it. Johannesburg was dark, it was very cold, she didn't work in the safest of areas and was shaking with nerves as she jumped on board, but thankfully managed to get home safely. Waiting on a draughty corner for forty five minutes had chilled her right through, so she ran a hot bath and soaked in it for a while, trying to unwind. She heard him come in, calling for her, finally locating her in the bathroom.

He had had a thoroughly enjoyable session with the lads – what was for supper? She exploded. He slammed the bathroom door in a rage at her unnecessary temper. A few minutes later the front door slammed as well. When she finally left the bath she discovered the plaster around the bathroom door had been cracked with the force of the slam, and a bottle of scotch was missing from the drinks cabinet. He never drank scotch, but apparently he was going to that night because she was being so unreasonable.

Some Saturdays became a battle for his attention too, and there were times when she wondered at the point of marriage and the supposed partnership they should have been enjoying. Telling him of her increasing unhappiness did no good whatsoever. How could she argue against: 'Don't you want me to be successful?'

But he was successful – his selling prowess was well known in the building industry, and eventually he was headhunted to run a ready mix concrete plant in the industrial town of Newcastle.

'Where?' queried Sally, once Richard had calmed down. He had phoned her at work after receiving the offer, and was beside himself with excitement; he had never been headhunted before and was enjoying the feeling.

'It's a small town half way between Jo'burg and Durban. It's where the Government produce a major part of the iron and steel for the whole country. The town is going to explode in growth over the next few years and my plant will be brand new. This is going to be huge for us, darling.' She could hear him dancing around his office with excitement.

'Think I'd better get the bus home tonight,' she said. 'No doubt you'll want to celebrate with the boys and be late in. We'll talk about it tomorrow, but I'm really pleased for you – well done.'

'Cheers, sweetheart!' he whooped, and crashed the receiver onto the cradle.

I wonder if that's going to work out any better than Jo'burg, she thought.

New town, new start, new plans. Rather than sit at home waiting for Richard to put in an appearance Sally decided to open her own business from the spare room at their new home, looking after people's secretarial and accountancy needs. It was time for them to start the family they both wanted, and once the baby was born it only needed feeding every four hours or so, plenty of time for work as well, and they were both delighted when a pregnancy test confirmed the reason for her new morning sickness.

Shortly after their wedding eighteen months earlier she had left the dress manufacturers and began working as PA to an accountant in private practice where she learned a great deal about the requirements of setting up and running a business. She borrowed a typewriter from Richard's new office and began advertising her typing, bookkeeping and credit control skills in the local paper. There was no other service like hers in the area, and pretty soon her little business kept her extremely busy.

All through her pregnancy she burned the midnight oil, revelling in her small success. It also kept her mind occupied as Richard again spent more and more time selling concrete over the bar counter.

'Well, it's a new venture. You don't realise how many customers I've got to keep happy – they're all builders, they all like a beer and I have to be seen to be their best friend. How do you think it will look if I refuse to have a beer with them – I'm doing it for us, for our family – don't you want me to be a success? Things will settle down soon, and I'll definitely spend more time at home when the baby's born, that's a promise.'

Chapter 14

By George's first birthday Sam could not have been at a lower ebb. Things had not improved between them, and she was turning more and more to her mother for support. She and Toby couldn't go on as they were; the more time he spent away from home the more she withdrew, which pushed him further and further away. Now that he had his son he seemed to have lost interest in her completely, and she felt she was rapidly losing her grip on her sanity. She had to sort things out with him, but since he was never at home these days it was going to have to be a showdown at the office.

'He's not in I'm afraid, Mrs Havers,' said Marla, as Sam put her head round the office door.

'I suppose he's over at the pub is he? Don't worry I'll go over and see him there.'

As she pushed open the door to the bar she saw him with his back to her, arm round a blonde who appeared to be revelling in his attention. The landlord was calling him to the phone. She watched as he listened to the caller then spun his head in the direction of the door, where she stood. The colour drained from her face and the ever-present tears welled, Marla was obviously well versed in protecting her boss. She fled from the bar and ran to her car. He didn't follow.

Sam managed to drive home through her tears, packed a few things into a bag and fled to the comfort of her mother and sisters, taking George with her. No note. None was necessary.

'What the fuck do you think you're playing at?' Toby roared down the telephone at her that evening. It hadn't taken much mental effort to work out where she'd gone.

'Toby, I'm sorry but I'm sick of living alone in that empty house, you're never there, always out – and with other women. Don't try to deny it; I saw it today and I smell them on you all the time, a different perfume every day. I can't take your lies any more. If you can't be happy at home with George and me then we need to think seriously about our future together.'

'If you are saying what I think you are saying, that's fine by me. You're no good to me these days, always moping about looking tired and miserable, and if you can't give me the sex I want, when I want it, then I've every right to get it elsewhere, and believe me there are plenty who are only too happy to oblige. But you can forget about George. He's *my* son and he's staying with me. He's going to have the best. I can provide that for him, you can't, and if you try and fight me for him I'll break you! I'll tell the Court you're mentally unstable, not safe to be left with him, that's why I have had to employ a nanny.'

She collapsed sobbing; she knew he meant every word no matter how cruel. George was his world even though he didn't get to see much of him in the evenings – the little boy was asleep then anyway. George's very presence in the world was enough; the plans for his education were totally beyond Sam's means, she was never going to be able to afford a top boarding school and university for him with her resources. She could fight him for custody and force him to pay the fees – yes, that's what she would do. Was that in George's best interests, though? Toby's success would give her son so much more than just education, whereas she had nothing to give but her love, and he had that to give to his baby son as well. How had this happened so fast, she wondered? One minute she was going to try and sort out the mess that her marriage had become – the next she was finding herself on the road to divorce.

She shed an ocean of tears over the next few days as she came to realise that George would have a better quality of life with his father, but she had to see him whenever she wanted. Would Toby agree though, that's the question?

'Yes, sweetheart, no problem. Glad you're able to keep things simple and see things my way, much better for George, you see him any time you want.' As far as he was concerned that chapter was now closed, time to move on.

'Hello Hilda, Toby Havers here. How's my girl doing? Is she still in South Africa?'

'Yes, she is Toby. And she had a baby girl last week, they've called her Sarah. I'm going over to see them tomorrow for a couple of weeks. We're all so excited about it.'

Richard and Sally decided to spend 4-month old Sarah's first Christmas in England, introduce the new family member to the English arm of the Denham clan and arrange her christening. They had been married for over two years by now and Sally had not yet met the rest of Richard's family, so the whole three-week visit passed in a blur of meeting new people, entertaining and being entertained, not to mention all the Christmas festivities. There was also the christening in the local church to organise, and they found they had forgotten just how hard a severe English winter could be after years of living under the African sun. Leaving the warmth of a centrally heated room and venturing outside became one long round of finding enough warm clothing to keep them all from suffering from too much cold. Sarah began teething as they arrived in England and cut her first tooth just as they were leaving, and by the time they had completed their return long haul flight to South Africa Sally was exhausted.

She returned home to find work pouring in, and began to appreciate that perhaps she might be overdoing it. Her day was starting at 5 a.m, trying to get an hour of work done before Sarah woke, and she was often still working at 11 o'clock at night. Her little business was extremely successful for a small town, but it now needed more than just one part timer in order to keep up with the increasing stream of work. Something would have to change, but she didn't want other staff in her home, nor did she want to take office premises pushing up her costs and taking her away from her baby – and to give work out meant she couldn't keep a personal eye on things.

One of her customers noticed that she was looking increasingly drawn and tired. 'That baby of yours keeping you up all night, is she?' he enquired.

'No, it's not that. She's really good; she's been sleeping through since she was nine weeks old so I do get unbroken sleep, just not enough of it. I seem to be typing half the night just to keep up. Don't quite know what to do about it at the moment.'

'Have you thought of selling the business? If it's as successful as you say, you could probably get a fair bit for your client base, you know.'

Now there's a thought. No, she hadn't thought of selling it, but it was certainly an idea. A bit of time off from working, time to spend with Sarah, time to be a full-time mother for a change plus a few extra rand in the bank. That might just be the answer.

Her advertisement in the local paper drew a large response from potential buyers, and she eventually settled on a woman who she felt would give her customers the best service. The deal was quickly done, the cheque was banked and 'The Secretary Bird' was no longer hers.

Since Richard was at his usual post propping up the Holiday Inn bar she celebrated with some girl friends and discussed with them what she could do with the money.

'Why don't you have a holiday?' suggested one.

'Yes, you were moaning about not having enjoyed your Christmas holiday in England. Why don't you go over and see your mum?' suggested another. 'You could stay with your mum, visit your brother, and catch up with all the friends you didn't see at Christmas. It'll be June next month, cold here but a great time to be in England.'

'Do you know that's not a bad idea,' said Sally, mulling the thought over in her mind. 'Mummy didn't get much of a chance to see Sarah at Christmas; we were far too busy for her to spend much time with her granddaughter. I'll ring her tonight, she'll be thrilled to bits.'

Toby bumped into Hilda in the local paper shop. 'Hello Hilda, how are things with you?' he enquired innocently. She knew perfectly well he meant 'How's Sally?' and laughed. 'If you are really interested in how I am, well, I'm fine thank you, as you can see. But if, as I suspect, you mean how's Sally, I can tell you (though I suppose I shouldn't) she's coming over next Tuesday for a couple of weeks. I've no doubt I shall be in terrible trouble for telling you but, there, it's out now, isn't it? I'm really looking forward to seeing her and little Sarah without the fuss of others around. I know it's a bit selfish of me, wanting her to myself, but she's so far away now I don't get much opportunity to see her these days.'

Casually he murmured: 'On her own with the baby, is she? Guess a journey like that will be quite an undertaking without any help.' He held his breath waiting for the reply, whilst casually fumbling for change. His ears strained to make sure he heard correctly.

'Oh yes, on her own. She'll be OK though; Sarah's much easier to cope with now. She's nearly ten months old, you know.' Hilda smiled to herself as she left the shop. If she didn't get a call from Toby in the next couple of days offering to collect Sally and Sarah from Heathrow when they arrived, then Fanny was her aunt.

Whilst doing his utmost to look urbane and unconcerned, he fairly bounced out of the shop and almost ran into the pub for some lunch in the best of moods.

'What'll you have, Toby?' asked the barman.

'Give me my usual half, and I fancy a chip buttie, please Jeff.'

'We don't do chip butties, you bloody well know that, stop messing me about.' The long-standing banter Toby had enjoyed at the barman's expense had never been reciprocated. Jeff was tired of this particular customer's practical jokes and constant need to be the centre of attention.

'Fair enough, squire. In that case I'll have two sausages with chips and two slices of bread and butter instead, if you please.'

When his order arrived from the kitchen he cleared a space around the bar with a flourish, attracting as much attention as possible, and with a sly smile to his assembled cronies, neatly placed the chips onto one slice of the buttered bread, shook a modest sprinkling of salt over them, asked for and was passed the vinegar, a shake of which was added to the plate. He then carefully placed the second slice of bread over the pile of chips, and with a broad smile began to eat his chip buttie.

'Jeff!' he called when he had finished. 'You can send those two sausages back to the kitchen, please, I've had what I want thanks. You really ought to listen to what your customers want, you know.'

'You're bloody barred, Havers!' Jeff yelled at him. 'I'm sick of you taking the Mickey out of me and this pub.' Hearing the laughter from his audience that followed him out of the door was worth being barred for a day or two.

He breezed in to Alex's office, hands in his pockets. 'Say, what are you doing tomorrow? Fancy a ride if the weather's OK? I'll get the ponies tacked up, see if Jimbo can come over on his pony, and we can clear some cobwebs.' Jim Rodway was a mutual friend who was doing well as something-in-the-city, and the three of them had spent many happy bachelor evenings together playing cards. They were all equally competitive, and looked forward to the time they could spend playing squash, tennis, golf or cards together.

Sunday dawned clear, and the three friends raced the ponies across the fields and meadows, laughing as they sped over the sward. As usual Toby's euphoric mood infected the others, and they covered the ground at full pelt, crouched low over their ponies' necks. After half a mile Alex, who had taken the lead, suddenly pulled up. 'Do you realise where we are?' he called to the others. 'We've just ridden across a bloody golf course.'

'Bollocks, who fucking cares?' roared Toby, flying past him. Hilda had been wrong. He had not waited for a few days before calling for Sally's flight details, she had barely got in the door with her shopping before her phone rang.

'My girl's coming home next Tuesday, nothing else matters,' he shouted to his friends, his hazel eyes radiant. 'I'm going to fetch her from the airport, and I'm going to have two whole weeks with her. Nothing and nobody is going to get in my way this time. She's mine – she's mine!'

And he raced away at break neck speed, standing high in the stirrups, defying his friends to keep up.

Her flight was due to land at Heathrow airport at 6 o'clock on Tuesday morning, and Toby had worked himself to the front of the crowd at the international arrivals gate by 5.55 – far too early he knew, she wouldn't be through for at least forty five minutes, but the flight just might have been early and he simply had to be there, in the front row, just in case. His hands were clammy and his stomach churned. He hadn't slept a wink that night, and had finally given up trying. He had downed a cup of strong black coffee and got on the road at 3.30 for the drive to Heathrow where several more cups of strong, black coffee had been quaffed, and he paced. What would she say after so long? Would she be pleased to see him? What was her marriage like? Was she happy? His mind was full of anxiety and he found he was chain smoking to try and maintain some outward show of calm.

And suddenly – there she was. Five years and she hadn't changed one bit. He felt the blood rush to his face and he started to tremble.

Sally was tired. Coping with Sarah and the luggage on her own had been logistically challenging, so she decided to get a taxi into central London and then catch a train to the village where her mother was now living. But when she heard that familiar deep voice close to her right elbow as he leaned over the barrier, she stopped in her tracks, causing something of a domino effect with following luggage trolleys, and lots of mutterings, behind her.

'My God, Toby! It's you! What on earth are you doing here?' she asked, eyes wide in amazement and her colour beginning to rise.

'A little bird told me you were coming in this morning and I thought you might appreciate a lift, especially after a long night flight with your baby. And is this Sarah?' he asked, stroking the little girl's baby-soft, blonde curls. 'How old is she now? How did you cope with her on the flight all on your own? Did you manage to get any sleep at all?' He kept up a barrage of questions as he ducked under the security barrier and began to guide her trolley for her, hoping that his constant chatter would mask his nervousness and make his presence look like the most natural thing in the world. He knew from past experience how easy it was to screw things up with her and was determined to be the perfect gent. No pushing his luck. She was going to have his undivided attention for two full weeks, and he was going to make it a holiday to remember – for both of them.

She had forgotten what good company he could be. He could be really charming when he wanted, and she had to admit he made the journey a lot more comfortable than public transport.

When they arrived at her mother's home he carried the suitcases inside, gave Hilda a wink followed by a quick kiss on the cheek and said he would call later when the dust had settled. He positively skipped back to the car and drove off with the biggest smile lighting up his face with joy. His girl was home and seemed to be in good humour.

'Well, there's a first.' said Sally. 'I really expected he would try to push me into a date within five minutes.'

She and her mother fussed over Sarah who was trying so hard to be good, but was rather over tired and weepy after the long flight, so she was put to sleep in a borrowed cot whilst Sally unpacked their things and had a welcome cup of tea.

Toby drove home and tried to catch up on his lost sleep. Now that she was here, and seemed happy to see him, he felt a little calmer and managed to get a couple of hours rest before going back to the office for the afternoon. But he couldn't concentrate on anything, and finally gave in to the more relaxed atmosphere of the pub. Fortified by a couple of doubles he went back to the office and rang Hilda's flat to see how they had settled in.

'She's having an hour or so in bed,' said Hilda. 'Then we'll have a light meal together. Best leave her till tomorrow.'

He took her advice, and since his regular Mrs Mop wasn't due until Friday, spent the rest of the day cleaning and tidying the house – whisky in one hand, vacuum cleaner in the other, the happiest he had been for along time. When he brought her home to Little Hammer Farm it had to be perfect for her.

Hilda was only too pleased to have some time alone with her granddaughter, and happily agreed to look after her the following morning when Toby arranged to collect Sally and show her his home. They stopped off at a supermarket first and he showed off his skills with a shopping trolley as they whisked up and down the aisles, laughing as he threw what he regarded as various essentials into the basket. He had promised to cook supper for her, and it was going to be a meal par excellence. He enjoyed cooking spaghetti and had got his bolognaise sauce down to a fine art, so as he unpacked the shopping he poured her a glass of chilled Chardonnay and sat her out by the swimming pool, preferring to panic on his own just in case anything should go wrong through his nervousness.

The passage of time had made them both older and a little wiser, and they spent hours talking over the past years. The last time they had seen each other he had resembled a lobster in South Africa, and a lot of things had changed over the last five years. He had been married and divorced and had his two-year old son George. She was married and had ten-month old Sarah. He told her about Sam and how things hadn't worked out between them. She told him that things were not all rosy in her life either; although Richard was good at his job and made sure they wanted for nothing, he was an absent father, and she had been unable to convince him to spend more time at home. Promise after promise was broken; a social life with his male customers was a far more exciting place for him than his home, even though his daughter was there too. No, she was not particularly happy, but things could be worse. Perhaps as the concrete plant became more established he might spend more weekends with them. It had only been a couple of years after all. And Sarah was still a baby; perhaps as she became more of a person it might make a difference. Perhaps. She knew she was making lame excuses for him, which saddened her. Richard was a good and loving man but there was no spark between them anymore, just constant arguments over his time away from home.

As the late afternoon progressed into early evening she began to think about getting back to her mother's flat.

'If you want to get back I'll take you now. But you don't have to go, you know. I've got four spare rooms for you to choose from; you are welcome to stay over, I do a mean breakfast.' he said with a grin. 'Lashings of softly scrambled eggs, crispy bacon and Bucks Fizz to celebrate your visit. The choice is yours, but if you want to go we'll need to get going now before I have any more to drink. I'm much more sensible these days, you'll be pleased to hear.'

He hadn't tried to touch her all the time they had been together. And sharing the last five years with him had been quite cathartic; she was feeling the most relaxed and at ease she had felt for years. What the hell; she was so comfortable, and it was a sneaking joy to have a little time to be herself rather than being someone else's wife or mother, just for a little while.

She picked up the telephone and dialled her mother's number: 'Mummy, Toby has suggested I stay over but I said I'd leave the decision to you. How do you feel about bathing and feeding Sarah for me?' Sally asked as her mother answered.

'I don't suppose much has changed since you were a baby, dear,' said Hilda. 'I'm sure I'll manage. Have a lovely evening and we'll see you tomorrow.'

Something has changed, she thought as she slowly replaced the receiver. Something subtle. A man and a woman, with our history, spending the night together under the same roof. I'm not sure now that I've made the right decision. And as she turned back to the kitchen she was lovingly guided to the cosy looking snug.

Her senses on alert she saw that Toby had drawn the curtains and hurriedly lit a large fire that nestled deep in the huge inglenook fireplace, and a bottle of pink Champagne, with two flutes, rested in an ice bucket on a silver tray. Between the large comfortable sofa and the blazing fire stood the loveliest coffee table made from solid Yew, glowing with its natural life. Although it was early June the evenings were still a little chilly and the room was bathed in the soft glow of the firelight. He had turned the lighting down just a little, and the whole room looked soft, warm and welcoming.

The fire was burning softly, the homely English smell and sound of the crackling logs filling the air, their conversation became even more relaxed and comfortable than before.

After a couple of hours Toby asked if she was hungry. How about some cheese and biscuits? To be waited on rather than doing the waiting was a novel experience – she had never known such concern for her personal comfort, and cheese, biscuits, celery and grapes were conjured up from the kitchen as if by magic.

He placed the cheese board down between them on the sofa, and they began exchanging views on the selection he had chosen from the supermarket earlier in the day. Sally knew nothing about different English and French cheeses, and as they giggled together over the merits of the various flavours, Toby slid himself across to her, asking her to close her eyes and feeding her sweet ripe grapes. Slowly she opened her eyes to find him sitting just a breath away, and the look of total adoration in his eyes swept her along on a sea of elation. He moved a little closer and she didn't resist him. Emboldened, he softly cupped her face between his hands and very gently kissed her lips. Sally closed her eyes again, savouring the first kiss they had ever shared, and gradually felt herself responding to him.

They sat entwined for several minutes, each coming to terms with the newness of what was happening.

'Wow,' breathed Toby, as he sank back into his corner of the small sofa they were sharing. 'All the years I've wanted to do that, I never believed it would feel so good.'

Sally too felt light headed. They both knew that a step had been taken, and they sat gazing into each others eyes for several minutes, each lost in their own thoughts.

'You want some more Champagne, old thing?' he asked, his voice low and full of love for this woman he had fought so hard for. 'Or maybe we could finish the bottle upstairs?' His twinkling eyes said I do hope you are not going to take me up on my offer of choosing any of the other four bedrooms.

She held out her hand to him and together they climbed the stairs to the master bedroom that he had so carefully prepared that morning, hoping against hope that his efforts were not gong to be in vain.

He held her tightly, so tightly she felt she was being crushed and the charge of electricity that fired between them took them both by surprise. He had never known such unbridled joy, nothing he had ever achieved even came close to his need to hold this woman close, his woman, and together they flew on wings of love deep into the night, their parched bodies thirsty for more; then, utterly spent, finally slept wrapped in each others arms until the first gentle rays of the morning sun warmed the inside of Sally's eyelids.

The cold, sober light of day intruded into her mind, and she realised that she had done something morally wrong. Toby watched her as she moved her head and he reached out for her, his arms ready to wrap around her again. But she knew she had to find a way out of a situation she was beginning to find uncomfortable, so sent him down for coffee.

By the time he returned with two steaming mugs she was dressed and ready to leave. He knew then that his hard work with her was not yet over. He spent the rest of her holiday glued to her side, trying to get her to agree to another night together, just one more night with him, but she was adamant. She was still married to Richard and extra marital affairs were not part of her make-up. Put it down to the Champagne and the heat of the moment. Her barriers were firmly back in place again. She was going back to Richard.

He drove them to the airport in the most sombre of moods, trying to keep up some light-hearted chatter; helped her check-in for her flight and fought to hold back his tears as he hugged her goodbye; he certainly wasn't going to let her see his weakness. His formidable mind allowed him to walk away from any disaster with seemingly no damage, but nobody could see inside his mind, and once back in the privacy of his car the tears flowed. She was the ray of light in his life, and now that light had been switched off, yet again. How many more times can he allow this to happen? He had used all his persuasive powers in his attempts to keep her by his side, but to no avail. He just couldn't understand why a beautiful luxury home, expensive cars and a Champagne lifestyle were no inducement? What had Richard got that he hadn't? Simple answer: Sally.

Her flight touched down at Jan Smuts airport and Richard was there to meet his wife and daughter, delighted to have them safely home again and life return to normal. As she unpacked Sally chatted away merrily about her mother and the friends she had seen. She also chatted away about Toby. Richard's antennae were on high alert and he didn't like what he was picking up in her voice.

His eyes narrowed as he stared intently at her. 'Did you sleep with him?' he asked.

She felt herself flush with horror that she had been so transparent. 'Yes,' she said, hanging her head. 'I did – only the once though. He wanted me to stay but I couldn't. It was you I came back to. You I love.'

He turned white, his knuckles bunched and he stormed out of the house in a towering rage, tears in his eyes. For the next week he could hardly bring himself to speak to her. She in turn was fielding distraught calls from Toby, pleading with him to leave her alone. She had made her choice, Richard was suffering, she had done that to him, and it wasn't fair. She told him to stop phoning, it could only cause more anguish and couldn't lead to anything.

A month went by. A month in which Richard couldn't sleep. He paced the floor for hours, every night. Sally stayed up with him trying to soothe him, explaining that she had made a mistake; that no matter what Toby was offering materially she had come home to be with him because that was where she wanted to be.

'This is eating at you like a cancer,' she told him in the early hours of one morning; Richard turned his unhappy, swollen, bloodshot eyes to her and saw the same unhappiness and pain in hers. He saw her love for him too, and as they hugged in their joint misery he turned a corner, took a deep breath and smiled at her for the first time in weeks.

'Yes, you're right. I've got to move on, haven't I? Are you quite sure it's all finished with him? I won't wake up tomorrow and find you've gone?'

'No, I promise, it was a huge mistake, it's over and will never happen again.' And they slept.

Chapter 15

1974 was not a good time to be borrowed to the limit and beyond. Toby was financially insecure, a great number of property companies, including his, were overexposed and collapsing, and for a while his mind went with it. Scotch became his only friend and he leaned heavily on that friend. Everything he had was tied up in a property market that was crashing down around his ears. He had given the bank a floating charge over all his assets: Little Hammer Farm, the Aston Martin, his Hunter powerboat, the lot; then he took a bad gamble just as prices went into freefall, and as a result he was unable to realise enough cash to meet his repayments. The bank called his loan and Toby was fast approaching homelessness – everything was lost except the car, he managed to persuade them that if he could still maintain the right image outwardly he could quickly restructure and soon have the situation back under control.

So, with nothing more left to lose and fired up with alcoholic courage, he booked himself a flight to Johannesburg, hired a car and, armed with a road map, took himself off to Newcastle. She didn't want him when he had been able to offer her the world, would she take him now that he had nothing except a flash car that actually belonged to the bank?

When Sally opened the door and saw the dishevelled mess on her doorstep she was stunned. Losing his empire, just as he had reached his goal of a million, had shaken him to the very core of his being; his mantle of invincibility had been stripped away leaving him bereft and vulnerable, as vulnerable as he had felt at age seven when he had quietly cried himself to sleep in the dormitory at boarding school, in secret. He needed her, God how he needed her; only she could give him back the will to build again, to build for her and their family together.

But just as his crying at boarding school had been kept a secret, so he tried to keep his suffering under control as he stood before her on her doorstep silently begging her. But under his mask of resolve she saw his trembling, wide-eyed helplessness, and her heart broke for him.

'Get your baby, a clean nappy and your passport and get into the car – you're coming with me.' His determination and strength of mind radiated from every pore; his eyes were almost hypnotic and she felt completely transfixed by the force of his will.

'My God, Toby! What are you doing here – how did you know where to find me, how did you get here?' she gasped.

'Sweetheart, I've tried really hard to live without you, but I can't.

I've got a car outside, tickets booked for the three of us to fly to London tomorrow, you, me and Sarah. It's all sorted. Please don't turn me away again.' As the maid walked past the door he called to her to get the madam's passport, some clean nappies and to bring the baby, not giving give Sally a chance to countermand his order as he took her hands between his, staring deeply into her eyes. 'I can't go on without you at my side – you remember the evenings we spent together, just chatting, you know how well we get on, what a laugh we have. You remember that one night we had together? You remember how good it was, for both of us, not just me? We are made for each other, deep down you know that, you're just scared of hurting Richard and unsure of me. Well you don't have to be unsure of me – I've proved my love for you over the last nine years and it's only getting stronger. How are things for you here now? And please don't tell me they are good. Your mother tells me he's started spending more and more time away from home again and I know you're not happy; you told her you are not and she tells me everything – she is my lifeline to you when you won't let me ring you. You're back to square one with him, the abandoned part-time wife. Why do you think I'm here? I'm going to love and protect you and your baby for the rest of our lives together. I will never hurt you, we're going to laugh a lot; you are the heart of my life and the life of my heart. No more thinking about it. Sarah will be a great little sister for George and we can have another child of our own to make a complete family.'

As she looked into his eyes, blazing with his love for her, her brain heard again their laughter, the stimulating conversations; she remembered his silly self-confidence, the way he thumbed his nose at convention and made his own rules, it was heady stuff.

The maid apprehensively handed the little girl to her mother, and the rest of the things were taken from her by the stranger who was saying to her employer: 'You won't need any clothes, we can get you a whole new English wardrobe once I get you home. Come on, you're with me now.'

They climbed into the car, did a U-turn in the street, and headed out of town for the three-hour journey to Johannesburg.

Sally was numb, mesmerised. A couple of hours into the journey and he started to relax, but instead of the man she had shared a beautiful evening and night with three months earlier he became more and more cocky. He had won, he had got his girl and nothing was going to get in his way this time. As his confidence grew during the journey he tried to cover his insecurity with aggression and she was reminded of the unpleasantness he had displayed on their return trip from Durban all those years ago, and she didn't like it. As he bragged about what he was going to buy for her, her mind came out of its trance-like state and went into reverse. What on earth was she taking her daughter into? She told him she needed to stop for a while to get Sarah's milk warmed, so they pulled into a small hotel on the south eastern outskirts of Johannesburg, where Sally asked the receptionist for her daughter's milk to be prepared.

'I need the cloakroom,' she said, starting to head off down the corridor with Sarah in her arms. He looked into her eyes, but instead of love and joy he saw only fear and uncertainty deep within, and he became afraid. 'No, leave the baby here with me,' he said. 'I'll take her to the bar and wait with her for the milk.'

Sally went straight to a pay phone and dialled Jan Smuts airport. There was an outside chance Richard might have called home, wondered where his wife and daughter were, and the maid would have told him that a strange man had asked for the madam's passport and taken the two of them away with only a supply of clean nappies. Two and two would have made a very simple four for him.

'Please, could you page for a Mr Denham?' she asked when the call was answered.

'Is he a traveller, caller?' she was asked.

'No, he's my husband and I need to speak to him urgently,' she said, trying to remain calm.

'I'm sorry Madam, this is an airport, not a message service.'

'Please,' she screamed into the receiver close to panic. 'It's a matter of life and death, I'm being abducted!'

'Very well madam, where are you calling from?'

Her voice shaking, but trying not to cry, she told the operator the name of the hotel, replaced the receiver, calmed down a little and went back into the bar trying to maintain an outward display of calm.

'Rather than go all the way into the centre of Jo'burg for a smart hotel then have to come all the way back out here again tomorrow for the airport, we might as well get a room here,' she said, needing to find an excuse to stay so Richard could reach them if he got the message.

'Good idea, fruit – I'll see to it,' he said, getting up and heading for reception.

What on earth had she been thinking about, why had she allowed her better judgement to be swayed by his persuasive pleas? She had felt a little like a rabbit caught in his headlights, almost hypnotised by the strength of his personality, but this was all wrong. All she wanted now was to see Richard striding in through that door to take her back home to safety, and could hardly take her eyes off the entrance.

'What are you looking for?' Toby asked her when she jumped for the tenth time as the hotel door opened.

'Nothing.'

'Excuse me, sir, do you know that you have been clocked doing 191 kilometres an hour?' said the traffic officer as he pulled Richard over to the side of the road. His motorbike was pulled across the carriageway, blue lights flashing. He had been radioed from the last speed checkpoint, and was looking forward to giving this speed king a good tongue lashing as well as a nice, fat speeding ticket.

Richard's first reaction was to punch the guy out of sight for trying to slow him down, but sanity prevailed through the red mist of his anger.

'Officer, I'm sorry, but my wife is running away with another man and I've got to get to the airport before them – they left hours before me. Please, please let me get on my way!' Richard's eyes were wild and his whole body was shaking – the traffic officer had no doubt about this one.

'Right, my friend, so long as you don't try to overtake me or do these crazy speeds I'll give you an escort, I'll clear you a fast path through the traffic, just stick close behind me and we'll be there in no time, and a bit more safely.'

He heard his name being called over the tannoy as he entered the concourse and raced to the information desk where he was handed a note with the address of the hotel. He left the airport building at a run, jumped back into his car and raced out of the parking area at speed leaving rubber on the road.

He didn't know what to expect when he arrived at the hotel, but as he flew through the doors and saw Sally's frightened face as she sat with a strange man, he knew immediately who that stranger was.

Making introductions seemed unnecessary, but they had to be made.

'I'm sorry Toby, I can't do this; it's all wrong. You'd best drive into Jo'burg for the night, I need to put Sarah to bed right now.' And the last he saw of her was as she carried her sleepy child away from him, then he turned to face Richard.

Richard and Sally stayed at the hotel that night, then began their journey home together the following morning. He refused to tell her what the two of them had discussed, save that Toby had promised him he would not try to contact her again. They talked and talked on that journey. He said he did understand how his late evenings at the bar were upsetting her and promised to make much more of an effort to make time for the family. He knew they had both come very close to the edge.

They were home by lunchtime and Richard went back to work. Sally went out to water the front garden in the afternoon and found Toby hiding behind a parked car on the opposite side of the road. His mask had gone, his nails were badly bitten and his eyes were puffy from crying. He begged, pleaded and cajoled with her to come back with him, but she was adamant. She had been very foolish yesterday, she had hurt Richard yet again, but she was going to make it work with him. Toby had to understand that their one night together had been a mistake and he had to get on with the rest of his life without her.

'It'll be a very short life then, sweetheart. I can't live without you. If you read of a fatality on the road to Jo'burg this afternoon, you will know who it will be.' His eyes, now bleak and haunted, bored into her very soul, and she ran back into the house sobbing but resolute. He sat quietly in his car for a few minutes, head bowed, and after a while he pulled away, and headed back to Johannesburg, alone.

It took a lot of soul searching for Toby to pull himself together after that. He knew now that he would never get Sally out from under his skin, no matter how hard he tried, so he had to find a way to live with it. Work. That was the only answer. It was something he was good at; work could be handled and manipulated to his own ends. Even when everything went pear shaped he could always pull something out of the hat. Work might make him angry from time to time, like when brainless bank managers called in loans, but anger only fuelled his determination to get back on top and beat the bastards. Sally was the only thing in his life that he ever failed at – but he had to pull himself together, his life was not over yet.

First thing was to find a new home for himself since he had lost Little Hammer Farm to the banks; a new place that he could do a deal on and help get himself back on his feet. When he eventually found the right property he knew he was going to have to borrow more than its value in order to have enough money left over to make the repayments; that could be tricky in the current market.

'Hymie, listen, you've had your pound of flesh,' he said, carefully placing his coffee cup on the edge of Hymie's large desk in front of him. 'Some banks have taken a huge hit from this property mess, but you have done all right out of me, got all your money back, so I've got a new deal for you. I'm not going to stick anything into commercial, I've learned my lesson there; bloody expensive lesson too, but I've found a way to get back on top.' And he outlined his plan to buy the magnificent Oakfield Manor with its sixty acres of farmland, block of multiple garages and separate stabling.

'If I guarantee to sell on the garage and stable blocks to you or someone you nominate, will you back me to buy the place? The asking price for the whole lot is a million, but conversion of the outbuildings will bring in nearly that making the debt affordable.'

Hymie doodled some figures on a pad in front of him. 'There's only one way we could do this,' he said. 'If you throw in twenty acres with the garaging and stables I think I can persuade my partners to go with you again. They are a bit nervous so I'm going to have to tie you up in knots, but it could work.'

Toby completed the purchase and could feel his world starting to take shape again. He had made his first million pounds just before the property crash, so he knew he could do it again, it was just a case of focusing.

For now he was a proper Lord of the Manor, and he was looking forward to lording it in style. A few phone calls, get some of the lads round, and they could celebrate together. Havers was humming again.

'Pat old son, fancy a weekend at the old country estate?' he asked as Pat Bennett took his call in Bournemouth. 'Bought this big pad in Surrey, loads of bedrooms, not all furnished yet but good enough for a fun weekend.'

'Yeah, why not, sounds great. Tell you what, there's racing at Goodwood this Saturday, we could use your place as a base and spend the day up there.'

'Better idea old son – why don't we hire a helicopter for the day? He can land right here in my grounds – door to door service.' That is definitely Lord of the Manor stuff, he thought to himself. He was going to enjoy this pad.

A few phone calls later and he had five of his nearest and dearest friends fired up for a proper boys weekend.

The chopper company needed calling. 'Morning old chap – the name's Havers. I wonder if you can sort me out a six-man chopper for next Saturday; take us from Surrey to Goodwood races then bring us home again?' They had a craft to spare and the weekend was on.

'How do we find you, sir?' The pilot would need some pointers to land a helicopter on the right field in the wide-open meadows of the Surrey countryside.

'Ah, yes – tell you what we'll do, old son. There's a large field just

113

to the north of the house, I'll make sure there is a large red 'H' painted on the grass – he won't be able to miss us.'

On Friday afternoon the six friends trooped out to the appointed field carrying a tin of red emulsion paint and a large whitewash brush each, and proceeded to prepare the helipad, as arranged. It was thirsty work, and when they had finished their painting chore nobody was in the mood to cook, so they all piled into Pat's large car and drove down the hill to the local pub for an evening meal and a few beers, full of banter and thoughts of their helicopter trip the next day.

'Landlord – we need feeding, what have you got for six hungry lads?' Toby was in charge and made his presence known to everyone in the bar.

'Sorry, no food tonight. Chef's not well and I've not found anyone to cover for him. What do you want to drink?'

'But it's Friday night. How can you not do food on a Friday night?'

'Because I haven't got a chef, I told you.' The barman was getting a little irritated by this rowdy party who were clearly intent on making as much noise as possible in his quiet little country pub. The regulars were silently watching the entertainment and Toby wasn't about to come second in front of either his friends or the newfound audience.

'Oh, come on landlord. We'll settle for egg and chips all round. How about we look after the bar for you while you nip into the kitchen and see to it, there's a good chap?'

'Don't you "good chap" me. I've said there's no food tonight and I mean no food tonight, and if you don't keep the noise down I'll have to ask you all to leave.'

'We're not leaving till we've been fed, so you'd better get your arse into that kitchen and sort us out some egg and chips my good man. Please.'

The landlord called his two burly sons from their quiet evening watching football upstairs. 'Lads, a bit of help in the bar if you would be so kind.'

The sons were not best pleased at having their evening interrupted and wore heavy scowls on top of their 16-stone frames. The six hungry, thirsty ejectees beat a hasty retreat in the face of such opposition.

Saturday was wet. It had been raining all night, but were the lads downhearted? No, they were not. Breakfast consisted of several glasses of Champagne – some with orange juice, some not, as they listened for the sound of the approaching rotor blades. The helicopter was due at 10 o'clock, but by 10.30 it had not arrived and they began to consider all the various possibilities for its delay. Low cloud? Too much rain (no windscreen wipers. Ha, Ha!)? Got lost? Pilot too drunk to fly?

But by 11 o'clock they were becoming very concerned that they would miss the first race, so Toby rang the company to enquire as to the whereabouts of their airborne carriage.

'Don't know sir – ah, wait a minute, the pilot has just radioed in. Right . . . Apparently he was not able to locate any painted 'H' of any colour in any field in your area, sir,' the operator told him.

'But we spent hours doing that last night – just tell him to hang on up there while I go and check this out. I'll call you back in two minutes,' he yelled down the line.

They all raced out onto the meadow to check their handiwork of the previous evening, only to find a field of contented cows happily licking a vaguely pink area that had been earlier designated as a helipad.

'Didn't know cows liked emulsion paint, did you?' they asked each other.

Chapter 16

Richard's evenings were becoming more and more restless. It had been eight months since the Havers episode and Sally was pregnant again, so why could Richard not be more content and settled, she wondered? He was trying to spend more time with her and little Sarah, rather than the pub, but something was not right. She could feel it. And then it hit her. Richard was having an affair. So one evening she sat quietly in her chair, reading, until he came tiptoeing in at nearly midnight. The shocked, guilty expression on his face when he saw her sitting there waiting for him instead of being in bed asleep told its own story – she did not need to know where he had been. She simply asked, 'What's her name?'

He looked crestfallen. 'Yeah, I'm sorry. How did you know?'

He tried to explain that her affair with Toby had damaged his self-confidence, so he supposed it was just his way of reasserting himself. Sally recognised that he was probably just punishing her.

She asked him, 'Do you want to stay together, or shall we go our separate ways?'

He made them a mug of tea each and they talked into the night, finally putting to rest any lingering doubts over their respective fidelities.

Toby had walked along financial tightropes before and knew he had to do it again if he was going to be able to reverse the damage that had been caused to his little empire through the property crash and start to rebuild.

At least the crash had one positive outcome, there was a good supply of land and properties with potential that could be bought at auction, and with some clever bidding he was determined to take advantage, but he needed to ensure he had the necessary funding first. He had never bought at auction before, in fact the only time he had attended an auction was when Abe Silverman had bought his premises in Sevenoaks eight years earlier

Funding had never been a problem before, but the rules had changed somewhat due to the downturn in the market. Banks were shy, and even Hymie was less enthusiastic than Toby had ever known him, plus he was heavily exposed with him over his purchase of Oakfield Manor. He needed someone with courage to approach, and there was only one man he could think of, his old boss Harry Weston.

'Harry – here's a voice from your past. It's Toby Havers. Wonder if we could have a chat?'

Harry's interest was aroused and he agreed to meet up with his erstwhile employee who had done so well for himself that his estate agency was still the most popular and successful in the area. Toby's property sales far outstripped those of any other agency.

Harry didn't drink so settled for a tomato juice whilst Toby ordered a whiskey, and they found themselves a quiet corner in the London pub he had suggested. Toby didn't want to be seen meeting Harry around the local area, it could be wrongly construed.

'You and I go back along way,' Toby opened. 'And I think I can confidently say that you would be happy to trust my professional judgement. All my funds are currently tied up in a rather large London development that I'm not at liberty to discuss at the moment – non-disclosure agreement, I'm sure you understand. But there's a rather nice potential brown field development site coming up at auction next month that I would really like to get my teeth into but need a partner prepared to fund it for the right percentage. I've got some ideas on the back of an envelope to run by you if you're interested in getting into bed with me on it. I reckon it could make a tidy packet if handled properly.'

Harry had sold most of his agencies and was enjoying his semi-retirement. He had his yacht moored at the Royal Motor Yacht Club in Poole, his palatial home in Bournemouth and a beautiful London flat, but this proposal looked interesting, and he couldn't think of a better partner than Toby. The man's reputation spoke for itself. Through the grapevine Harry learned that Toby had just become the proud owner of the imposing Oakfield Manor, and his Aston Martin with its personalised number plate was as well known in the area as its owner.

'Give me something concrete to work on in the next day or so, and if it pans out as you seem to think it will you've got yourself a deal.' The two men shook hands.

The next few weeks passed in a flurry of meetings with architects and town planners, and Toby's proposals for a small supermarket on the site looked to be promising. This was going to be important, it would kick-start his financial recovery, so ensuring the figures worked in his favour was vital, but the deal he had agreed with Harry needed to be improved on if possible, and the return needed to be fast. He paced the office floor, chewing his bottom lip, as he pondered his various options.

His secretary, Marla, dropped his post onto his desk together with his usual strong black coffee, before going through to her desk to start the days typing. Toby casually flicked through his new edition of the Estates Gazette that lay on top of the pile of envelopes, stopping at an article that caused him to sit up straight in his executive leather chair. He re-read the item that had caused him such interest and a light bulb was switched on in his brain.

More pacing and lip chewing ensued until he picked up the telephone and dialled his accountant. 'Hymie, I need you to set me up a new property development company straight away; just leave your staff registered as nominees for the time being till I get all the bits and pieces in place.'

The day of the auction arrived and Toby wandered into the back of the room, where he felt he had a commanding view of the other bidders. Lot 71 was the only one he was interested in, but he watched the other lots being sold with a keen eye, learning about the process of buying cleverly.

The bids in the room slowed as the price of Lot 71 crept towards what he had agreed with Harry would be their maximum offer, and he waited until the auctioneer said, 'All done?' then raised his finger. 'A new bidder in the room,' the Auctioneer called, pointing his gavel at Toby. Several heads turned in his direction. He held the Auctioneer's gaze and waited, heart pounding, to see if one of the other bidders would outbid him. One did. Toby's finger was raised again to better the offer, but he was quickly outbid for a second time. The other bidder was now offering the maximum agreed with Harry, but Toby couldn't afford to let this deal slip through his fingers. He held his nerve and instantly increased his bid. The other bidder wavered, then shook his head.

At the meeting with Harry the following afternoon Toby explained that although he had paid slightly over what they had agreed there was still a good profit to be made from the development, and he passed over some revised figures.

He then waited for ten days before giving Harry his bombshell. Having recently read in the Estates Gazette about new fears over possible ground contamination within brown field sites he had asked for a report on their new acquisition and, regrettably, methane had been found emanating from an old landfill within the site. Harry knew nothing of the provenance of the report and took it at face value. He was unaware that the report was fictitious, that it had been bought from a colleague of Toby's who had long been looking for a way to ingratiate himself with Toby.

But Harry was not to worry, Toby had found someone to buy it from them immediately. A small brand new development company had approached him and offered to take it off his hands at the price Toby had bid, so there would be no financial loss. It was a new company, probably an inexperienced bunch, and they had clearly not carried out any contamination report. It was not his responsibility to tell them.

118

Harry shrugged. Pity that hadn't worked out, but you can't win them all, and at least through Toby's shrewd abilities it hadn't cost them any money.

Toby's brand new company bought the land from Harry and sold it on the same day to a large construction firm who were happy to pay Toby's inflated price for the new development they were planning on the uncontaminated land.

The large profit Toby made in just a few short weeks did not have to be shared with anyone, and allowed him to take his place back in the world again.

Chapter 17

1962, London
Hilary Savage had always had an eye for the best. An only child born to a professional couple whose lives frequently took them away on business, she had been brought up by a succession of au pairs until her parents divorced.

But once her mother had remarried and the comfortable lifestyle she had become used to dwindled, the teenager became quite a rebel. Her naturally dark hair was dyed raven black, her weight plummeted as she tried to emulate the latest slender look in the fashion magazines of the 1960s, and her temper became fragile and unpredictable.

'Where are you off to at this hour?' her mother wanted to know as she washed up after their evening meal. Although the 16-year old said she had finished her homework, it was still mid-week and she had school tomorrow. She had been forced to take Hilary out of her private school after the divorce, there was no longer sufficient money to pay the fees, but the local state school was quite good. Her daughter was required to toe the family line but the girl was finding life with a stepfather less than easy. Her own father had moved to Italy with his new family where he was learning to take over the day to day running of his elderly father-in-law's vineyard ready for the day when he would need to take over completely.

He enjoyed working in the fresh air and found the world of vines and grapes far more rewarding than his former life as a top barrister and his dealings with warring matrimonial partners in a stuffy courtroom before a pernickety judge. He also had two young stepdaughters to consider and Hilary was finding contact with him was becoming more and more distant.

'Oh, for God's sake, it's only 8 o'clock, I'll be back by 11. Stop fussing,' came the sharp retort.

'I didn't ask you what time it was young lady, I asked you where you were going at this time,' her mother snapped back.

Snapping at each other had become normal, and both were finding life together quite a strain.

'If you must know I'm going over to Wendy's house, we're going to listen to some music together. It's better than listening to you nagging. I'll be back by 11.' The front door slammed.

Hilary marched down the driveway, then sneaking a look back at the house to make sure her mother wasn't watching, and ducking her head against the rain, she quickly turned right and ran to the corner of the road where Anthony was waiting for her in the car he had borrowed from his

120

father.

'Sorry I'm a bit late. My bloody mother is in a right mood tonight. She demanded to know where I was going so I told her I was going to Wendy's to listen to some music. Thankfully she doesn't know her phone number, and so long as I am back by 11 it'll be OK, she'll be none the wiser.' She snuggled into Anthony's arms and they lingered over a deep kiss.

'That's OK,' he said drawing back from her. 'I've got to get the car back home by then anyway, Dad won't be home till midnight but he'd still be furious if he knew I'd taken it without permission. Come on, let's get going to our favourite spot where no-one will see us.' There were few private places in North London but Anthony had located a cul de sac a mile away from Hilary's home that was perfectly screened from prying eyes. He turned on the ignition and the powerful Jaguar engine purred to life.

Aged twenty, Anthony had plans. He was studying law and had designs on becoming a top-notch barrister, ultimately taking silk and becoming a QC. He could see himself in the High Court putting his case before the judge and jury and winning trial after trial for his clients, but whilst his studies continued he had to rely on the support of his parents.

In the meantime he had Hilary to himself for a few hours. Her mother had banned her from having boyfriends till she was 17, and that was nearly a year away, so they had to meet covertly. There was also the danger of them being seen together in the town, which could get reported back, so their time together was mostly spent on the back seat of cars – either his father's or a friend's.

They had been seeing each other secretively for three months, having been introduced by a mutual friend, and had both felt an instant chemical attraction. Hilary had never had a proper boyfriend before because of mother's ban, but she was a willing and enthusiastic pupil.

Their sex was good, and they climaxed together in a perfectly timed peak of passion, bodies writhing in the cramped confines of the car. As they lay curled together sharing a reefer Anthony asked: 'Couldn't you go on the pill thing that I've heard so much about? Save me having to wear these awful rubber things. And we go at it so hard I'm scared one of them will break.'

'Oh no, I couldn't do that. I'd have to go to the doctor to get them and I expect I'd have to get my mother's permission. Can you imagine her face?' Hilary giggled at the thought.

'Well, it was just a thought. Honestly sex is much better without these things,' he mused. 'Listen I think we ought to be getting back now, it's half past ten already, we don't want to be late.'

They straightened up their clothing, zips were closed, buttons were fastened then they climbed over to the front seats and prepared for the journey back.

'Oh no, look at the car clock – it says it's nearly 11, my watch must have stopped.' Anthony was horrified, he knew he would have to get a move on if they were to avoid trouble from their respective parents.

The roads were wet and slippery, and his speed coupled with his inexperience caused him to lose control of the powerful vehicle as they turned the corner into Hilary's street, and the bonnet of the car connected solidly with a lamppost bringing the car to an abrupt halt, sending its occupants sprawling across the front dashboard.

The bruise to Hilary's forehead wasn't serious but was likely to cause problems on the parent front. 'Sorry Anthony, you'll have to sort this out on your own, I can't stay, I need to get home quickly if I don't want to get into trouble.' And she pushed open the passenger door.

'But Hilary, I need a phone. Can't I come in and use yours?'

'Don't be bloody silly. How would I explain you, the damage to your car and the bruise on my forehead to my mother? Use your brains Anthony. Just knock on any door and ask for help.' And she quickly stormed off. What a mess. Now she would have to find some reason for the mark on her face. The patch of damp moss on the pathway gave her an idea, and sliding her foot across it gave out a loud yelp. By the time she had her key in the door and her hand held over the angry welt her mother was easily convinced that she had slipped and hurt herself just outside their door.

'Oh, dear, come into the kitchen and let's put a cold cloth on that dear, it looks painful,' said her mother solicitously.

'No, it's fine, don't fuss, it looks worse than it is,' Hilary croaked. 'I'll just take an aspirin before going to bed. I'm really tired now so I'm going straight up.' And keeping her eyes downcast to deflect any probing questions from her mother she ran up the stairs into her bedroom where she sank down onto the bed feeling really tired and shaken.

The following morning she felt no better. Nausea rose in her throat leaving her feeling flushed and a bit wobbly.

'I'm not feeling too good, I don't think I'm going to be able to make school today,' she told her mother, who had come in to see how she was.

'Yes, you are looking a little off colour,' she replied. Perhaps you had better stay in bed for a while. I'll let the school know, you might be able to get in this afternoon, I don't want your studies to suffer. But if you are not up and about by 12 o'clock I'll call the doctor. Did you eat anything whilst you were at Wendy's last night? Perhaps I had better call her mother just to be on the safe side.'

'No, no, there's no need to worry them.' Hilary couldn't afford for her mother to ring Wendy's home and find that her wayward daughter had not in fact spent the evening there. 'We only had a cup of hot chocolate like we usually do. Maybe I picked up a bug at school yesterday, there was certainly a lot of sneezing going on.'

'Oh, all right then. Do you want me to bring you anything up? A cup of tea perhaps?' Her mother enquired.

'No, thanks. I'll just lay here till it passes. I'm sure it will stop soon.' Hilary curled herself into a ball, screwing her eyes shut against the stabbing pains in her stomach.

Suddenly a gush of warm liquid oozed from between her legs soaking the bedding beneath her. She lifted up the blanket and stared in horror at the amount of blood that she seemed to be losing.

'Mother!' she screamed. 'Mother – help me!'

Her mother ran back up the stairs and burst into her daughter's bedroom. She too stared in shock at Hilary's blood soaked state.

'Mother, what's happening? I know my last couple of periods didn't really happen but I surely can't be having several at once, this can't be right? What am I going to do?'

'How many periods have been different?' her mother questioned her.

'Oh, I don't know, maybe the last two. Oooh, I can't take this pain mother, do something.' And she curled herself up into a foetal position again as another spasm took hold of her.

'Hilary, look at me.' Her mother stood over her, stern faced and worried. 'Have you been seeing any boys? More to the point have you been sleeping with any boys?'

'Mother this is no time to worry whether or not I have been breaking any of your stupid rules. Can't you see I'm in pain here and I need help.'

'I'll tell you why I am concerned young lady. It looks to me as though you are having a miscarriage.'

Hilary rolled over and sat up, eyes wide in disbelief and ready to denounce her mother's accusation as she tumbled to her feet in utter confusion, fruitlessly trying to stem the flow of blood with her hands. Dizziness overcame her and she slid down into a heap on the floor, dark red blood still oozing from her body.

Her mother ran downstairs to the telephone and called for an ambulance to take her daughter to hospital. She opened the front door then ran back to her daughter's room to lay her on her side and stay with her until help appeared in the shape of two burly ambulance men.

'Can you tell us what happened,' they asked.

'Well, I can't be sure,' replied mother, 'but it looks to me as though she was pregnant and is having a miscarriage. She was forbidden from seeing boys, she's far too young. But I think she may have disobeyed me, now look at the consequences.'

Mother was beside herself with worry, pacing the room and wringing her hands, but the ambulance men calmed her. 'Don't you fret yourself my dear, she'll be fine, she's in very good hands now. There may be another perfectly simple explanation for her condition, but if you are right she won't be the first to make such a mistake and she certainly won't be the last, we've all done stuff we later regret.' He smiled at her as they carefully placed their groaning patient onto the stretcher.

'What's happening? Who are you?, Hilary murmured.'

'You've lost a far bit of blood my love,' smiled the ambulance man, wrapping a soft warm blanket around Hilary's bloodied nightclothes. 'But don't you worry, the nurses and doctors at the hospital will check you over and have you back right as rain in no time.'

Hilary closed her eyes against her mother's accusing stare as Anthony's words reverberated around the inside of her head: "*Save me having to wear these awful rubber things. And we go at it so hard I'm scared one of them will break.*" She remembered there had been one time when she had felt particularly wet and sticky inside after one of their passionate sessions, but she had put it down to the intensity of her orgasm. Oh, God, it hadn't been her juices she had felt but his, the rubber protection had broken, she had fallen pregnant and not known.

She kept her eyes tightly shut until they arrived at the hospital where she was wheeled into the Emergency department. The duty doctor asked her mother to wait outside whilst he and the nursing staff did their preliminary examinations. As soon as the curtains were closed around her cubicle Hilary grabbed his arm, whispering. 'Please, please don't tell my mother I was pregnant. She'll go mad at me. Can you find another excuse for all this blood? Couldn't you say I told you I had had a couple of funny periods and this is just my body's way of catching up? Please.' Hilary implored him, her dark blue eyes huge and her forehead deeply furrowed with worry.

'Hilary, I'm sorry. I'm a doctor and doctors don't tell lies, the consequences could be far too serious. We are going to have to keep you in under observation for twenty-four hours, just to make sure that everything has settled down, and from my experience I would suggest you get the chat with your mother over and done with as quickly as possible. It won't get any better by leaving it.' He could understand the teenager's fears, the mother certainly seemed to be rather unsympathetic, but from his experience these things usually worked themselves out after initial emotions had been dealt with and tempers had calmed. The mother obviously cared about her daughter's reputation, as most mothers do, and the daughter wanted to explore life a little further than her mother wanted. All perfectly normal. Except in this case the daughter seemed to be paying an unpleasant price for her exploration. But he found nothing unusual in her presentation; the girl had mentioned the car crash of the evening before and it was likely that the miscarriage was caused by such a trigger.

He smiled at the mother as he left the cubicle, indicating she could join her daughter.

'Well?' mother wanted to know from the doctor. 'What was the cause of that little episode?'

'Perhaps you had better let your daughter explain,' he said as he opened the curtain of the next cubicle to attend to a particularly nasty swollen ankle.

'Before you start mother let me just say that if you had loosened your reins on me a little and given me a bit more freedom and not been so uptight over boyfriends I could have asked you to let me go on the pill and this would never have happened. All my friends are on it and they think I am really stupid for not taking it but I knew you would go mad so I couldn't ask you so this is all your fault,' Hilary exploded at her mother.

'Don't you dare, madam!' Her mother fiercely retorted. 'If you had listened to me this would never have happened. Nice girls of your age do NOT sleep around. Now you know why.'

'I don't sleep around,' came the sharp snap. 'I've only ever seen Anthony Wren, nobody else, so that's not sleeping around. Anyway he's going to be an important QC when he finishes his degree, much more important than father was, so you can't say he's not good enough for me. And another thing. I've decided that when I finish school I'm going to go and stay with father in Terni for a few weeks, he won't keep me locked up like you do.' When backed into a corner Hilary came out fighting.

Visiting her father and his other family was not something that had occurred to her until that very moment, but mother had to be punished for what had happened. It was only an idea, but why not, she thought?

Mother had certainly had the steam taken out of her argument and sank down onto the hospital bed. She was weary of the constant battles with her strong-willed child but she knew her ex-husband was not likely to welcome a new addition to his home in Italy, regardless of the fact that she was his daughter. He had met his new Italian wife, Isabella, whilst she worked as his junior in Chambers in London, the attraction had been instantaneous but they had both worked hard to keep the lid on their emotions for a whole year until it became clear they were going to leave their respective families and move in together. The bombshell had hit Hilary hard and hurt her dreadfully to think that her father would rather have a life with his new little Italian stepchildren than a life with her. Why had he left her, they had always been close, and why did she never hear from him these days? But it didn't take long for her misery and confusion to turn to resentment. Well, if he didn't like her any more as she was then she would change, be more assertive, make more noise in the world, make him notice her. It was her mother who now had to bear the brunt of this new persona, and trying to restrain some of Hilary's more dominant qualities was quite a strain.

'Well, we will have to see what happens when you leave school, won't we? Your father hasn't had much contact with you over the last year other than a birthday card and one at Christmas, and I don't think Isabella will be too pleased to see you there especially after your little tantrum when you met her at their wedding. Like I said, we'll have to wait and see. Maybe try a weekend in the summer holidays. But I'm not going down that route at the moment, firstly we have to sort out the current little mess. Who is Anthony Wren? Where did you meet him? How long have you been seeing him and more to the point where have you been seeing him, and please don't tell me it was in the back of some car.'

'We had nowhere else to go.' Defiance again. 'You would never have let him come to the house because of your stupid rules over boyfriends. His parents' place is too far away so there was never enough time to get there and back and spend time together, and I couldn't risk being seen in public with him because you would have found out and gone nuts at me, so where else could we go? You pushed us together.' She paused for breath.

'You think me going nuts at you, as you so eloquently put it, is worse than this?' her mother asked, indicating the hospital ward around her.

Hilary snapped back: 'I'm not stupid, I made him take precautions, but one of them must have burst or something.' The steam began to dwindle from her argument. 'Look mother, I'm sorry, OK? I don't know what else to say.'

'I know,' said her mother, rubbing her hands wearily over her eyes. 'Maybe when you get home you should invite this Anthony Wren over for a cup of tea and I can meet him. You will obviously need to tell him about this, the implications would have been dreadful for both of you if the pregnancy had continued and he needs to be made aware of his responsibilities. You'll need some clean clothes to come home in tomorrow. Shall I get your grey trousers and pink jumper that you like? and I'll fetch some clean underwear from the cupboard.'

'No, don't worry about all that, I'll be more comfortable in my dressing gown; I expect I'll spend the rest of the day in bed anyway.' The last thing Hilary wanted was having her mother poking around in her underwear cupboard. Anthony had bought her some really racy little red knickers with matching suspender belt for her to wear whenever they were together. His favourite enjoyment was to slowly lick around the edges of the delicate lace until Hilary was squealing with anticipation, then find his way inside, tongue flicking, searching.

Mother realised that a corner she had not expected to encounter so soon suddenly had to be turned. She recognised that Hilary was not a child any more but a blossoming young woman who needed a little more freedom, needed to feel more in tune with her peers. When had it all changed, she wondered? Had it been around the time of her father's re-marriage?

Hilary relaxed back into her pillows and allowed herself to drift off to sleep once her mother had left. Thank goodness that row was over, she thought, and at least mother now knows that I'm going to have boyfriends, whether she likes it or not. And as she began her gentle slide into sleep it occurred to her that it was going to be boring seeing Anthony in the open, in front of mother; half the fun was being covert, sneaking about and enjoying their secretive times together when they could play with each others bodies. It might have been a bit cramped in the back of cars but a lot more delicious than sitting having tea together.

No, it was time for her to move on. It might be fun spending some time in Italy, the Italian boys she had met from time to time in London had been cute.

It had not been easy for Hilary to watch her father vow to love another woman for the rest of his life then place a wedding band on her hand. Hard to watch the glow of love between them knowing that she was being left behind whilst he cared for another woman's children, and she had exploded at the small hotel reception that followed the simple ceremony when he announced his imminent departure for Italy.

'How could you father? What about me? You don't love me any more! Well I hate you, and I hate you too Isabella for stealing my father.' And she had fled to the cloakroom, banging her fists on the doors as she passed through them.

'I'll go to her,' Isabella had said in her gently accented English.

'I'm not sure that's a very good idea,' replied her new husband. 'Perhaps we should leave her to calm down a little – she'll come round.'

But Hilary had been in no mood to calm down and come round, and had sat in a cubicle waiting for something to happen, but nothing did. After a while she had opened the door and looked at herself in the mirror, eyes all red and puffy in an angry face, and decided she couldn't go back in there and face everyone, so she had asked the receptionist to ring for a taxi for her. Mother would have to pay the fare once she got home.

So ringing her father to ask if she could come and stay was always going to be tricky. She heard the phone ringing out at the other end and wasn't at all sure what reception to expect, but he understood what had caused her outburst and was pleased to hear from his daughter. Bridge building would take a little time but his was a warm and happy home; Hilary would be welcome.

Never having been on an aircraft before Hilary felt very uneasy as she boarded the plane for her flight to Italy and was shown to her seat. But the air stewardesses smiled gently at her, assuring her that she would be perfectly safe and would get great pleasure from seeing the earth from above. She sat, fascinated by the calm, elegant crew, and watched their movements with great interest.

She had finished school with good exam grades in English and French and rang her father to ask if she could spend some time with him in order to learn Italian. Her excuse was hard for him to refuse and he was even encouraged to pay for her ticket. She knew she would have to apologise to him and Isabella for her rudeness at their wedding two years earlier, but it was a small price to pay to escape mother's constant scrutiny.

Father met her at Rome airport and hugged her tightly, letting her know that his love for her had not diminished over the intervening years. During the two-hour drive north to the villa on the outskirts of Terni he told her about their life in Italy, how hard he was working, which was one of the reasons he had had so little time spare, and how he and Isabella could help her learn the language. He didn't want to be the first to mention her outburst at his wedding, he wanted her to feel ready to discuss it. But she knew that Isabella also had to hear her apology and didn't want to have to go through it twice so continued a running commentary on her life back in North London during their journey. She told him that she had finally been allowed to have boyfriends, although only two – one a trainee lawyer for a few months last year, and the second one who wanted to follow in his father's stock broking footsteps. Hilary had been impressed by his family's fabulous home in a very expensive area of London, but sadly that relationship had come to an end when he met a girl from an equally luxurious background. Hilary had been devastated; that should have been her lifestyle, and it certainly had been until her father had walked out.

He carried her case into the large airy villa where Isabella was waiting with an equally affectionate hug and a kiss on both cheeks.

'I'm really sorry for my behaviour at your wedding reception,' she mumbled, head hung low, unwilling to meet their eyes and finding her contrition difficult. She still hated coming second in her father's life but recognised it was a situation that wasn't going to change, and if she wanted to have a few weeks in the Italian sun with a degree of freedom she had no option but to eat a large slice of humble pie. 'It was really rude of me. I was young and was just upset at the thought of father being so far away and maybe never seeing him again.'

'It's OK, cara,' said Isabella. 'You are so grown up now, it's all forgotten and we are having a special meal in your honour tonight, you will love it. Now come and see the girls, they are so looking forward to seeing you again and becoming friends.'

That was another thing. The girls. These girls had enjoyed her father's loving attention for two years, two years during which she had been pushed aside.

'Ciao Hilary,' chorused Gina and Pia. They were intrigued to meet their English stepsister again after so long. They had been too young to absorb the trouble two years earlier, but now aged eight and ten they were keen to practise their English from this sophisticated looking sister.

'Hello,' she replied. 'Shouldn't you two be at school?'

They looked blankly at their mother, Hilary's English was rather too rapid for them to follow.

'Scuola,' translated their mother. And addressing Hilary she explained, 'No, they have finished for the day, they start very early and finish early because of the heat in the afternoon.'

'Oh, I see.' That meant they would be around for a larger part of the day than Hilary had imagined.

'They will show you to your room, please take as long as you want to settle in, maybe take a shower after your long journey, and we will eat in a couple of hours. We eat later in Italy than you do in England so I've put some cantuccini and fruit in your room in case you are hungry. Now off you go girls,' and she sent them away with a wave.

The girls silently guided their guest along a passage built from weathered, yellowed stones, the floor of which was worn into soft grooves by the passage of so many feet over the years that the traditional villa had stood at the heart of the family's land.

The room that Isabella had prepared for Hilary was beautiful. There was a large bed with a deep mattress and lots of fluffy square pillows. An outsized wardrobe for her clothes stood by large windows that opened onto rolling hills and were framed by large shutters that kept the room cool during the heat of the day. The paintings on the walls showed what she thought must be local landscapes, maybe even scenes from the villa's own land. The colours were so alive in the Umbrian light she felt as though she was walking along the dusty tracks, following the horse pulling his cart loaded with vines.

Two side tables and a fabulous chest with knotted rope handles completed the picture. Everything seemed to have been fashioned straight from huge trees, all the knots and twists of its growth were on display, an integral part of the furniture.

The cantuccini was awful. Just like trying to bite a lump of really stale bread, how on earth could the Italians eat it, Hilary wondered? But she was hungry and enjoyed the fruit.

Dinner was equally odd. The first course of antipasti was just thinly sliced meats and cheeses, which was followed by a pasta dish with lots of tomato sauce. She was not keen on tomatoes and had never eaten pasta before, it felt rather stodgy in her mouth and she wasn't at all sure what it would do to her weight. So she ate just enough to take the edge off her hunger.

Conversation with Gina and Pia was too difficult to bother with unless she spoke slowly and with care to use simple English words, so she concentrated on asking her father questions about Rome. Did he visit the city often? What were the shops like? The ladies had looked incredibly smart as they had driven through on their way to Terni. Could he take her there to do some shopping maybe?

'Yes, we could do that one day,' he smiled at his daughter. 'How about I show you around here first and we could travel down on Saturday.'

"Around here" quickly became very boring. Lots of fields of vines and talk about grape varieties, not much else. Hilary was fed up and couldn't wait for Saturday.

She and Isabella didn't have a lot in common and father was out with his precious grapes all day, so Hilary spent most of the morning sleeping late then wandering along the sandy tracks alone.

Thankfully her two step-sisters were kept busy at school in the mornings but the afternoons were spent in verbal combat with them, each trying to understand the other's language. Hilary was not minded to help with any teaching, and if they couldn't pick up what she was saying, well that wasn't her fault. Why hadn't father taught them fluent English? And Italian was proving an unnecessary language to learn. She had her French and English, it was enough.

Saturday was raining, but Hilary was desperate to get away from the deadly humdrum of life at the villa.

'Why don't we all go together?' asked Isabella. 'I haven't been to Rome for months, it would make a lovely change.'

'Do you really think that's such a good idea, cara? What if your father were to fall and injure himself, or worse; he's so frail we really ought not to leave him, don't you think?'

Isabella considered her father's fragile state of health and had to agree. Maybe they could get a nurse in for him next time to allow her to have a day in Rome. 'But Gina and Pia could go with you, they would really enjoy the treat,' she suggested.

'And what would they do all day? Two hours in the car, Hilary will want to shop while we're there then two hours back. Besides, it would be good for Hilary and me to have some time together. But I think your idea of a nurse for your father is excellent, we'll organise something for the future.'

Father and daughter skirted the town centre and headed out into the countryside for the trip south. Not much to see, just lots of small villages with small village people sitting around. Hilary was bored after half an hour, father wasn't proving to have much conversation either and she began to reconsider the wisdom of the whole trip. Maybe the shops in the capital will make it worthwhile, she thought.

As they entered the wide streets of Rome her eyes lit up. They passed through piazza after piazza, dodging people strolling arm in arm in the warmth of the air, others scurrying to and fro with briefcases under their arms. Such a busy city. Hilary smiled for the first time in a week. This was definitely worth the trip.

Father seemed to know his way around and parked the car in a side street close to a large piazza.

'Would you like some shopping and sight seeing time on your own?' he asked.

'Yes please,' she quickly replied. 'Can I have some spending money? Where will I meet you?'

'I tell you what. Here's 20,000 lira for you, it's worth about £12 so

131

should get you some nice souvenirs and a coffee, and I will see you at 2 o'clock for some lunch in that café over there.' He pointed to a pretty little bar with a striped cream awning with its seating placed out in the centre of the square. 'You can't get lost, just look for the church spire in that corner and it will guide you back here.'

'What are you going to do while I'm shopping?' Hilary asked.

'Me? Oh, I've just got to see someone about vineyard stuff. I'll see you later.' And he turned, walking quickly away.

This is more like it, she thought, meandering through the smaller streets that led away from the piazza. After a while she stopped at a little café where she could watch the smart Italian women enjoying shopping with their friends, their high heels clicking on the pavements, voices loud and vibrant in conversation with each other, and Hilary felt happy.

She paid for her coffee and looked around for the church spire, but it was out of sight, clearly she had wandered further away than she had imagined. Carefully she tried to retrace her steps but became completely disorientated amongst the jostling people in the narrow streets. Trying not to panic she stood still for a few minutes and looked around her, and to her delight she saw the corner of a tourist information office in the next street. Oh, thank goodness, she thought, they will know how to find the church, and she marched up the two steps into a dimly lit office. There was nobody behind the counter so she wandered towards the back and found a stand displaying various leaflets that she began to leaf through whilst waiting for someone to appear.

The sound of a familiar voice filtered into her brain. It was her father's voice but where was it coming from? She gently pushed open the door that was standing ajar next to her elbow and, to her shock, found herself looking at her father's back. He was growling with passion as he hugged and fondled the tiny woman mostly hidden by the bulk of his body.

'Father! What are you doing?' Hilary demanded.

Her father's head shot round, eyes wide in horror at having been discovered. Hilary's request to visit Rome had been a heaven sent opportunity for him to see his mistress, albeit for a brief moment together.

'Sweetheart – Umm. Oh God. Let's get out of the office and I'll explain.' And with a backward fearful look directed at his mistress that said he was sorry but he had some explaining to do, he took his daughter by the elbow and led her back out into the bright sunlight.

'I'm sorry you saw that,' he began. 'You are too young to understand but things are different here in Italy, everyone has a lover, all the men and most of the women. Things are not discussed in the home of course, it's all done very discreetly, but it's an accepted way of life. Keeps the marriage alive if you like.'

Hilary was stunned and felt a bit sick. She no longer felt the warmth of the Italian sun, no longer wanted to enjoy the city or sit and have lunch with her father. She just wanted to go home. Perhaps he was right, maybe she was too young to understand, but she had seen what his last affair had done to her mother and their family, now he was doing it to Isabella. Maybe Isabella had a lover too, but who cared? History told her this was damaging stuff and she just wanted to get away from it.

She hung her head in confusion and allowed herself to be guided back to the piazza.

'You're right, I don't understand why you have to keep having affairs, and I don't want to sit and have lunch with you. I just want to go home.'

He let go of her arm and pushed his hands deeply into his pockets trying to figure out a way to limit any damage that could be done once Isabella started questioning why Hilary was in such a foul temper after such a lovely day out.

'OK, I understand. I'll sort out your ticket once we get back to the villa, I promise,' he said. 'But it's like I said, having a relationship with someone else is a way of life for the Italians. It's always a short term thing and I'm pretty sure that Isabella is seeing someone too, but it's all kept under wraps. If it gets discussed that's when harm is caused.'

The journey back to Terni was very strained. Neither of them felt able to communicate with the other. She felt completely out of her depth and unnerved, and for the first time feeling the need of the security of her home in North London. And he was praying that she wouldn't say anything to Isabella. Having messed up his first marriage he considered himself to have been lucky when he fell into the vineyard with a villa thrown in when he married Isabella. He couldn't afford to lose it all and start again from scratch just because he had been caught out at one foolish episode.

As he parked the car Isabella came out to the car, embracing him and kissing Hilary on both cheeks.

'I hope you both had a lovely, lovely day together in our beautiful city,' she said. Hilary studied her step-mother's face carefully; surely she could see there was an atmosphere but she seemed to be ignoring it. Perhaps father was right. Maybe Isabella did know what was going on and preferred that such things were best left unsaid.

'Cara, Hilary has decided that although she has really enjoyed seeing our home she has imposed on us for long enough and thinks she ought to be getting back. I've done my best to encourage her to stay for a while longer, but my girl can be pretty stubborn when she's made her mind up, so I've promised to see what I can do about booking her return flight.' Father was completely unflustered, clearly able to handle any awkwardness in the air, and Hilary was allowed to escape to her room for some privacy.

What was it with men, she wondered to herself? Her first boyfriend getting her pregnant through his carelessness, the last one unceremoniously ditching her, and her own father having affairs.

Mother met her at the airport the following afternoon. 'Did you enjoy yourself, darling? How was everybody? You weren't there very long, were you? I don't suppose there was a lot of Italian learned in that short week, was there?'

'It was OK I suppose,' Hilary replied. 'Pretty boring at the villa with only Isabella to talk to. She and father both speak perfect English so I don't know why the kids don't, it was really difficult trying to talk to them. He did take me to Rome last Saturday but that was horrible, I caught him with another woman. He said it was normal for men to do that in Italy but that I shouldn't discuss it with Isabella because these things are always done discreetly. He said she also had affairs, and I must admit she didn't seem at all bothered by the atmosphere between father and me when we got back from Rome. But I didn't like it, not one bit.'

Her mother pondered this information, smiling wryly to herself. Maybe Isabella realised what sort of man she had married and now knew what it felt like to be the cuckolded wife. Maybe she did in fact have lovers of her own. Maybe that was how the Italians lived their lives, but they could keep such ways to themselves in Italy.

Summer was over, no more school to attend and Hilary needed to get a job. She remembered how smart the air stewardesses looked on her flights to and from Rome and was desperate to be like them. But she was only eighteen and was disappointed to find that she needed wait until she was twenty-one before training for such a demanding job.

In the meantime she needed to find something to do, so answered an advertisement for a sales assistant in a local boutique. The clothes were all designer which appealed to her sense of quality, and for three years she enjoyed dressing rich women in very expensive and fashionable clothes while waiting to reach the age required for her dream job. She was permitted to buy some of the outfits herself at cost price, all of which added to her sense of self worth. She cut out photos of air stewardesses from magazines, pinning them onto her bedroom walls, and practised walking up and down imaginary isles offering complimentary drinks and nibbles to her fantasy passengers.

She was careful with her earnings, looking forward to the day when she would have enough money to be able to rent her own small apartment – that would be essential when working for an airline; no self-respecting air stewardess would dream of living with her mother, of that she felt sure.

The day arrived when she was accepted for an interview with BOAC. She was so nervous she could hardly put on her make-up in straight lines. Her written application had obviously been well received as she had been asked to keep the whole day free for interviews.

Mother drover her to Speedbird House at Heathrow Airport and wished her luck. 'Call me when you're ready to leave darling, and I'll come and pick you up. Have you got enough money for something to eat?' She knew she was fussing but also knew how important this interview was to her daughter, it was all she had talked about for three years ever since she came back from Italy. Clearly the flight attendants had made an impression on her.

Hilary was offered a job with the airline, and was beside herself with joy. There was an eight week intensive training programme to undergo, and she loved every minute of it. She also learned that the stewardesses were selected as much on their looks and deportment as their education and abilities. She had clearly passed that test too.

Part of her training was in applying make-up and she was surprised to find that only Elizabeth Arden was considered an acceptable brand. Out went her thick black eyeliner and pale pink lipstick – in came the more elegant shadowing and company red lips. With her new sophisticated make-up and pencil slim uniform she felt extremely glamorous as she practised her new persona on the make-believe passengers in her bedroom.

Her first flight with real passengers was very nerve wracking, she didn't want to make any mistakes, but the Purser kept a watchful eye on her. She had been warned there would always be some passengers who would try to arrange a date with her at their destination, and more than once had her legs fondled by amorous men, but she quickly developed a fiercely sharp, withering look that told them their advances were not welcome.

Hilary loved her job. She worked hard, being careful to maintain her air of dignity and superiority, and was quickly promoted to senior crew giving her the opportunity to work in first class, from where she had no hesitation in accepting an invitation to join a particularly good looking first class traveller for drinks at the Plaza Hotel on New York's Fifth Avenue.

She learned to carve a roast at 35,000 feet, serve canapes and cocktails; to offer small pots of Beluga caviar followed by lobster and smoked salmon to discerning diners, and complete the exquisite five star dining experience with coffee and liqueurs.

But the icing on the cake was the rest days where the crew could party together in exotic locations. As much alcohol as possible was carried off the plane before it was re-stocked for its return journey, and the whole crew could enjoy the temptations offered by the opposite sex on a warm Caribbean or Pacific island thousands of miles from home. The secret indulgences on the island stayed on the island.

Her life was one round of parties when not working. Being a senior member of the crew she was invited to Embassy parties when abroad and always made sure she had an expensive little black dress in her luggage, just in case. The high life was at her feet and she was finding it was exactly where she wanted to be.

1974

Hilary woke to a lovely sunny Sunday morning, and stretching her arms above her head let out a loud, contented yawn. At last, her years of effort had been rewarded by the airline and she had been promoted to Purser. She had her own little rented flat in London and a boyfriend, John, who looked to have a promising career as a financier in the City; life was good. And the following day she was due to fly to New York with Captain Philip Brannigan, a Captain she had flown with many times before. He was fabulous in bed, a really imaginative lover, and they were going to enjoy two days and nights of Champagne filled fun together. On the third day they knew they had to steer clear of alcohol before the return flight so planned to go shopping together, but trying to keep their hands off each other was always deliciously hard.

'Would you like to go down to the Yacht Club, darling?' said John as she rolled out of bed to answer his phone call. 'I've just had a call from Barry Wattle and he's having a bit of a drinks do in Poole at lunchtime.'

'Yes, why not?' she purred, keeping a lid on her erotic thoughts of tomorrows delights with the Captain. She could almost feel his fingers probing her, teasing her, and his huge erection pulsating with unrestrained power. Oooh, that had to wait. 'I have to get back for six though to get ready for tomorrow's flight.'

'Right-ho, I'll pick you up at ten. See you then.' And he hung up, completely unaware of Hillary's struggle to keep a lid on her desperate need for an orgasm.

John and Barry had known each other for years, working side by side at Goldman Sachs in the city of London. Barry had recently bought a modest powerboat that he moored at the Royal Motor Yacht Club in Poole, and he thoroughly enjoyed taking friends down to his club at the weekends where they could enjoy drinks on board during the warm summer months.

Hilary had a leisurely soak in the bath, adding a generous splash of perfumed bath gel. She washed her long dark hair which she wore pinned up in a fashionable chignon, carefully applied her Elizabeth Arden make-up and stepped into a sleek black dress with a low cut bodice, trimmed in glossy black satin.

Humming to herself as she checked her appearance from various angles in the full length bedroom mirror she waited for John to arrive in his saloon car. She would have preferred him to drive something a bit more sporty, but he looked as though he was going to do well for himself with the investment bank, so maybe she could persuade him to buy something more appropriate soon. They had only been seeing each other for two months but already Hilary was beginning to make her preferences known to him, the upgrade of his car would be next on her agenda. Then there was the need for a boat – if Barry could afford one then John should have one too.

They met Barry and his wife in the club car park and walked into the bar together. Hilary asked for a glass of Champagne, her usual drink, and they settled themselves into a corner by a large window giving a magnificent view of Brownsea Island.

Chapter 18

1974

Toby was tired. Sorting out his financial problems, coupled with the Johannesburg fiasco of six months earlier, had completely drained him, but the future was looking more secure now, thanks to the Harry Weston deal, and the way in which his plans for Oakfield Manor were coming together. He felt it was about time he had a weekend away from it all, and a weekend in Bournemouth with his old friends seemed a good idea.

The Yacht Club was still the same; even the bar staff hadn't changed over the years, and the Sunday session was as busy as ever as he and Pat Bennett sauntered in.

'Oh, hello! What's that over there in the corner? Dark-haired bird, black dress? Looks a bit tasty.' His testosterone went into overdrive as he ogled the woman he had singled out for his attention standing in a group of people, sipping from a glass of Champagne. He had stayed clear of women since getting back from Johannesburg six months earlier, but now that his finances were back on track and there was a little more stability in life, his body was starting to wake up again.

'Don't know. I've seen her in here a couple of times but don't know anything about her. Ask the barman, he might know,' replied Pat.

'Jimmy old man,' Toby beckoned the barman over. 'Know anything about the dark-haired bird over there in the corner – one in the black dress with the fizz?'

'No, sir, sorry, she's not a member. But I believe she's a guest of Mr Wattle, gentleman in the grey jacket standing with her.'

'Right, that's a start, what's Mr Wattle's first name?' asked Toby.

'Barry I think, sir.'

'Well done, old son. Thanks very much,' he said, moving in on the group in the corner.

'Barry, old man, nice to see you again,' he said, slapping the total stranger on the back and using his best public school accent. He had picked up enough of the conversation on his way over to the group to know which of his repertoire of accents to use. 'Be delighted to buy you and your guests a drink, what's it to be?' And before poor Barry could gather his wits this brash young man, who he apparently knew but couldn't for the life of him place, was taking an order for drinks from his party. Toby had correctly surmised that Mr Barry Wattle would be too embarrassed to publicly admit that he didn't remember the circumstances of their previous encounter, and there would be no problem in working his way in. He introduced himself to Mrs Wattle, shook John's hand, then made a big fuss over the dark-haired bird in the dark dress; her name was Hilary Savage, and he made his interest in her very plain. Boyfriend John was not amused. By the time Toby had finished dropping hints about his lavish lifestyle her eyes were alight with interest. Since his re-funding exercise he was living in a six-bed manor house in 15 acres, liked skiing in Gstaad, sunning in Bermuda and drove an Aston Martin. She appeared to be rapidly losing interest in the financier boyfriend.

After a while a nose powdering exercise was called for, and Hilary left the group for the ladies cloakroom. Toby swiftly finished his Champagne, told Barry how good it was to see him again, shook hands with everybody and made his exit, an exit that he knew took him past the entrance to the ladies cloakroom. He hovered for a few minutes until Hilary came out and then made his move.

'How about some fizz at Claridges next time you're in town, old thing?' he questioned. Now that she was on her own he was able to get a proper look at her and liked what he saw. Tall and elegant, very nicely turned out. Her dark hair was brushed sleekly back and there was a steely glint in her eye; she looked like just the sort of woman to get what she wants. A bit like me really, he mused to himself.

'Love to,' she replied. 'Give me your card and I'll call you when I'm next in London.'

He thought a lot about her on his way home. He had learned that she was a flight attendant and flew out of Heathrow, just like his ex-wife Sam, so she was likely to be in London soon. He could picture this glorious creature on his arm at smart restaurants; she certainly had an air of sophistication about her – bet she's a tiger between the sheets, he thought, hopefully.

He was nicely fired up when he got back to Oakfield Manor after the weekend; life was definitely beginning to sharpen up a bit. He felt sure Hilary would call quite quickly.

He was right. She revelled in the high life that he offered her, and was delighted to find that he had not exaggerated his lifestyle at their first meeting – Champagne at Claridges was nothing unusual for him; the Aston was definitely the right car to be seen in, but the real icing on the cake was Oakfield Manor. Hilary knew she had hit the jackpot and instantly saw herself as lady of the manor – this was definitely going to be her place in life provided she handled things carefully. She quickly learned how to handle Toby and was only too happy to satisfy his every need, and over the next few months she made herself his constant companion, cleverly pandering to him with just the right amount of reserve to keep him interested.

He buried himself in rebuilding his shattered empire, a delicate job since he couldn't let it be known to another living soul that he had suffered a crushing failure less than a year ago. Only one person knew the truth and she was five thousand miles away. In his early twenties the challenge of each tantalizing deal had been the breath of life to him, but now he was beginning to find the mental strain rather tiring. In the wake of the damage inflicted on the economy by the property crash of the early 70s, financial institutions had tightened their rules, and those rules that he had always enjoyed bending were no longer pliable.

The constant running between Hilary's flat in West London and Oakfield Manor in the depths of Surrey was another strain, but one that he felt he could probably rectify quite easily. She had made it abundantly clear that she enjoyed the life style he lavished on her, and would probably be quite happy to fill his bed every night; she wasn't too pushy and she was certainly a looker. Time to find out.

'Fancy making this your permanent home, old thing?' he enquired over dinner one evening. 'You spend enough nights here during the week anyway, so you might as well move your things in and not have to pay rent on your place in town.'

Hilary was delighted. Her hard work had paid off; and besides, she had grown quite fond of Toby in her own way. He certainly drank far too much, but it didn't really matter so long as she had her Champagne as well, and she easily slid into the role of chatelaine of Oakfield Manor. He asked her to give up flying to devote more of her time to running the house, which she was only too pleased to do, and each evening he arrived home to find her elegantly dressed, perfectly made up and with cocktails and canapés to hand. A beautifully cooked meal followed with sex on tap – what more could a man ask? At last his life was beginning to settle down – he and Hilary could make some really good-looking children to be brother or sister to George, and satisfy his burning need for heirs. Those hiccups with Sally were going to be consigned to the past. Sally.

'Hilda, hi. It's me – I know it's been a while since we spoke but I've been getting my life sorted out; I know you'll be pleased to hear that I've got a really strong relationship going, this bird's moved in with me and I've got Sally out of my system now – that's a promise. Just wondered how she was doing, is she well and happy? Still in South Africa is she?'

'Yes, she's still there, still in Newcastle although they've moved a few times. And, I'm going to be a grandmother again – they are expecting another baby sometime towards the end of July,' she replied. 'I've got my flight booked for the end of the month and hope that I can be of some help to her. She's going to have her hands full looking after two babies, Sarah's not even two years old yet.'

As he replaced the receiver he was surprised to find how totally deflated and empty he felt. If she was expecting another baby soon that meant she and Richard had patched up their relationship fairly quickly after that terrible time on her doorstep last year. She obviously did love her husband, just as she had said. And she had really meant it when she told him there was no place for him in her life. No! No! That wasn't possible; he couldn't allow that to be possible, and his mind began its torturous descent into turmoil.

He picked up the receiver again and dialled home. When Hilary answered the phone he told her he had to go to Bristol to look at a potentially very attractive parcel of land that could be bought on the nod from a bankrupt estate and he would be away overnight. NO, HE DIDN'T HAVE A FUCKING TOOTHBRUSH OR CLEAN UNDERWEAR, BUT FOR CHRIST'S SAKE WOMAN, THAT DIDN'T BLOODY MATTER, DID IT? He needed to clear the build-up of frustration that was starting to cloud his brain and slid his little black book from under some papers in the bottom drawer of his desk. Within minutes he felt the warm comfort of Clarissa's sexy tones washing over him.

'Toby, darling. Come on over sweetness. Don't forget to bring some bubbles for me to lick off you, very, very slowly.'

Two years went by in a blur of Champagne parties, trips in private jets and yet more hard won property deals to pay for them. Toby had regained his touch, everything he bought turned out to be a shrewd investment through which he continued to rebuild his empire. He had paid dearly for his mistakes in 1974, but some clever financial moves had put him back half way up his mental ladder; his crowning glory was being invited to sit on the board of Stanhope Bank with Hymie, from where he could make some serious decisions.

Although she was thoroughly enjoying life with him, Hilary was not happy to consider contributing to the tribe of Havers heirs without a ring on her finger; she felt that Toby was taking her presence a little too much for granted and decided to ratchet things up a bit.

'Sweetie, I'm becoming a little bored being stuck out here in the country without a real role in life,' she said to him over perfectly prepared salmon en croute, lightly steamed vegetables julienne and chilled Sancerre one evening. 'I'm thinking about going back to flying again. I know it will mean I will have to spend more time away from you and George of course, but perhaps you can get the nanny to do some cooking for you when I'm away, just for a few days each month. You won't mind, will you sweetie?'

Yes, he did mind, he minded very much. He had become accustomed to a glamorous lady on his arm, a perfectly run home life and all the comforts that went with it. He was not prepared to give her back to the airline and have her running round the world with all the tricks that he knew flight crew got up to with each other down the line. This was definitely not what he had in mind.

Of course if he married her he would have a bit more control over her, she would also be happy to start giving him more heirs. Certainly he enjoyed the practice but the Havers clan needed to be expanded pretty soon; he wasn't getting any younger, and 34 was as good a time as any to get started. George was five years old and young enough to enjoy a new addition to play with. Marriage to someone other than Sally though – hmmm. He'd already tried that once to Sam, and that hadn't worked out as he'd hoped. What if this one didn't work out either? But it was probably the only way he'd get heirs. Was it a price worth paying, he wondered?

Chapter 19

Richard had been determined to be present at the birth of his second child, but at the last moment couldn't quite face the reality of it. All that screaming and stuff that women did, it really wasn't his thing, but there was a small hatch in the wall of the delivery room through which he was able to stick his head, just far enough to feel that he was a part of the action that was going on inside. As his son was born he punched the wall with his fist in sheer delight, nearly bringing down a patch of plaster. He withdrew his head from the hatch, yelling: 'IT'S A BOY – I'VE GOT A SON! I'VE GOT A SON!' He was beside himself with happiness. His closest friend, JJ, had been dining with them that evening, and had offered to drive them to the hospital as Sally began to feel her first contractions. The two men ran out to the hospital car park together, Richard leaping and jumping for joy, and dragged a case of red wine from the boot, a case that was to have been delivered to one of his customers. They grabbed a handful of paper cups from the coffee vending machine and ran around the hospital offering a celebratory drink to anyone who would join them – nurses, doctors, patients, any passing body was included in the celebrations – which went on until five in the morning. Never had a baby's head been so thoroughly wetted in that hospital.

But a son is still only a baby for the first year or so of his life, and not much use for kicking a football with, so by the time Ben had reached his first birthday Richard had settled back into his normal routine, waiting for him to become a proper boy to have a rough and tumble with rather than change smelly nappies. His evenings at the bar became longer, time spent with his friends became more frequent and Sally felt more and more lonely again with two small children and her circle of friends.

'What is the point of being married if you are always out?' she asked him one evening. 'We are a family, we should be doing things together.'

'Don't be silly, we do loads of stuff together,' he replied. 'I help around the house with mowing the lawn and stuff like that. We go out for a curry together sometimes. Anyway, you know I meet my customers in the evenings, we've been over this so many times before and I know you don't like it, but I can't split myself in half, and being a mate to my customers is part of the reason for my success. Why don't you get the maid to baby sit and come to the bar with me, but I have to warn you it's all bloke's stuff, not the sort of thing you'd really enjoy.'

'Richard, I'm not saying you shouldn't spend social time with your customers, I'm only asking you not to do it *every* night, then roll in after the children have gone to bed leaving me to eat my evening meal alone while yours is in the oven. Why is that so much to ask?'

'Oh for Christ's sake, I've given you an alternative – it's not my fault if you don't like it. I don't need a row at this time of the night – I'm off out.' The windows shook as he slammed the door on his way out.

'Happy? No Mummy, I'm anything *but* happy right now,' Sally complained to her mother during their weekly telephone conversation. 'After that episode when Toby was here two years ago in 1974 I thought Richard understood that I married him for a bit more of his company than the occasional hour he deigns to spare me. On top of that the children need to see more of their father; he just has different priorities.'

'Talking of Toby,' replied her mother, 'I saw him in the square this morning. I must confess he did ask me about you, but then he always does, and I told him Richard was up to his old tricks. Still, he said he has decided to marry that girl he's been living with for the past couple of years.'

Oh well, thought Sally, that's another chapter closed. I really hope he'll be happy this time round.

Oooh – now where did that small pang come from, she wondered?

'Hello, old thing. Here's a voice from your past. How's life treating you these days?' Sally caught her breath as she recognised the deep voice, and he felt as though his heart would burst through his chest as he heard hers and waited for her response.

'Toby, you can't ring me. If Richard answers the phone there will be terrible trouble – you promised him you wouldn't contact me again. Please, don't start ringing, it'll only bounce back on me.' She hung up quickly and tried to stop her hands from shaking. This was bad and she was in a panic; she remembered how persistent he could be once he had her phone number and this was something she didn't need right now.

Richard had decided he had had enough of life in rural Newcastle and wanted to move to Durban to be closer to the sea, maybe get a powerboat and go fishing. He'd had enough of the pressures of selling concrete – trying to meet sales targets that were causing the nagging at home. There was an estate agency advertised for sale in a small town on the outskirts of Durban – now there's an idea. That Havers tosser was an estate agent – anything he can do Denham can do better. I'll show the bastard, he thought, it can't be that difficult to sell a few houses every month, so he decided to investigate it.

A week later Toby called again. Richard was away looking at the estate agency as Sally answered the phone, catching her breath as he began speaking. 'Toby, please, I have asked you to stop this. I can't be deceitful; you are causing me untold grief and I'm sure that's not your intention. My mother told me you are getting married next year, so please settle down with your new wife and be happy. Please, please leave me alone. I don't know how you got my number but if you call again I won't speak to you. I'm going to hang up now – just put me out of your mind for good. Goodbye.'

As she replaced the receiver her eyes filled with tears. What was it with him? Why couldn't he leave her alone? Why did his voice have such an affect on her? As she took herself off to the kitchen the phone rang again, and she was very cautious as she lifted the receiver.

'You sound odd', said Richard. 'Everything all right?'

'Yes, fine,' she said, wondering what on earth she should say to cover her obvious confusion. 'I just thought I heard Ben cry as I picked up the phone, that's all.'

When they finished their conversation she returned to the kettle, but before she had a chance to make her nerve-steadying cup of tea the phone rang for a third time. Now what, she wondered?

'Don't hang up on me this time darling. You don't have to say anything but please just hear me out.' Toby's deep tones flowed down the line to her, making her feel weak at the knees.

'I know you don't want me to keep ringing you, all I ask is that you just listen to me for a minute. You have to understand I cannot get you out of my mind, I've tried and I've failed – the only thing I've ever failed at in my whole life. You are my life, you are in every breath I take – No, don't say anything – Yes, I'm getting married again but only because I have to get on with my life. It's you I want but you have made it clear I cannot have what I want, so I have to respect that. I've never accepted second best in my life, but I need a family so that's what I'm having to settle for now. I hope it will work out for me, it may not and I'm not going to hold my breath. I just have this burning need to tell you how much I love you every now and then. Please don't shut me out totally. I may call you from time to time; just to hear the sound of your breathing is enough for me, but if your husband is home or does answer the call I will make a valid excuse, my South African accent is pretty good you know. Please, don't stop me finding out occasionally if you are still alive. And if you ever need me, I am here for you. 'Bye sweetheart – you'll never know how much I love you. You'll never know.' And he was gone.

She found she was holding her breath.

Richard was really fired up. His offer to buy the estate agency near Durban had been accepted; he could pay for the business in monthly instalments, which meant he didn't have to worry about finding thousands of rands up front. All in all he felt he had done rather well. First things first – he had to find a home for the family then a speed boat for himself; once the agency was open for business he could leave the secretary to man the office while he investigated the delights of deep sea fishing from the back of his boat. He needed to get it kitted out with rod holders, even a fighting chair. The Indian Ocean was full of marlin and shark and he was going to have himself some serious sport. He'd show the locals a thing or two; he could even put up an advertisement in the estate agency window and charge people to come out fishing with him for the day. Oh, yes, it was all coming together nicely.

The weeks sailed by in a blur of settling in to the new town and making new friends. The powerboat was bought on credit and the estate agency secretary was left pretty much to her own devices. Richard was delighted when she sold her first house for him and the deposit from the purchasers was lodged into the agency's special client account to be kept safe until the sale of the property was completed, at which time he would be able to deduct his commission and pay the balance to the vendor. Over the next six months she managed to sell a number of houses while he was busy catching tuna, shark and flat fish, which he either brought home or proudly gave to friends.

But when property sales slowed and the monthly outgoings started to exceed the commissions earned from the efforts of one secretary he became concerned and re-doubled his efforts at getting tourists onto his boat. More staff at the agency – that would solve the problem, but the young lad he employed wasn't up to the job and his salary simply increased the outgoings. The deposit of several thousand rand from the one property still awaiting completion was sitting in his client's account just as the rent for both the office and the house were due for payment. The choice was stark. He had no other money; if he didn't get the rents paid the family would be out on the street and he would lose the business. Borrowing from the client's account might be illegal but it wouldn't be a problem in the short term; the tourist season was coming up, his boat would be full of eager fishermen in no time and he would be able to put back the shortfall quickly, no problem.

Then the property purchaser pulled out, naturally requiring the return of his deposit. Richard couldn't give it to him, he had spent it. The police were called.

Sally sat down with a bang when he told her what had happened.

'How could you do that – you knew you couldn't spend the client's money, it wasn't yours to spend?' she cried.

'I only borrowed it for a couple of weeks for Christ's sake, just till the fishing picked up – how would you like it if I hadn't paid the rent on the house? Just where exactly do you think we would have lived? Answer me that!' he yelled at her.

He was bitterly angry at his fate. Selling properties had to be so easy; why had the stupid bitch in the office not worked harder? Why hadn't that idiotic boy he had employed pulled his fucking finger out and got more properties on the books? And if that wanker of a buyer hadn't pulled out of that last purchase none of this would have happened. Anyway, why the hell did he have to call the police, he'd have got his money back eventually? That really stung.

'Where are you going?' Sally asked as he crashed around the house looking for his car keys.

'I'm going to get drunk, where do you fucking think?' he shouted back at her. 'If you think you could have sorted this out better then you bloody do it!' And he reversed out of the driveway at high speed, taking a small chunk out of the gatepost in his haste.

After a sleepless night Sally drove into the town and called into the local travel agents that she had heard were looking for staff.

'I don't have any experience in the travel business, but I'm willing to learn,' she told the proprietors.

They sent her to Durban on a two-day course to learn as much as possible about the travel industry. She thrived on the challenge; she had Kesaya, her trusted servant, at home to care for the children, and spent every working day at her post in the travel agency. There had been a lot to learn from scratch, but it gave her a varied day with the opportunity of meeting so many new people.

Richard had found out the hard way that writing your own rulebook and hoping to get away with it was a lot more difficult than it looked. His estate agency was repossessed by the previous owner since the monthly payments were not being made. Nor had any payments been made on the boat so that went too – his whole dream imploded and he had to get a job. Gone were his dreams of showing Havers up for the fraud that he obviously was, of having his own powerboat, of living next to the Indian Ocean and thriving on his passion for deep-sea fishing.

Sally became increasingly alarmed as the pile of bills landing in their post box grew to unmanageable proportions as a result of the failure of the estate agency, and Richard's solution to the problem was just to ignore them.

'How many more of these bills are there still to come, and how on earth are we going to get them paid?' she demanded as she opened a new demand for the boat fuel.

'Stop worrying about it, for Christ's sake. It'll sort itself out, it always has,' he yelled as he stormed out.

'We need to talk about this.'

'You want to talk about it? You bloody well talk about it then – I'm off to the bar to get away from your constant nagging.' The door banged hard behind him.

I can't let this go on, she thought, someone's got to deal with it. Out came pen and paper and the list of all their debts grew. The total was horrible and she felt herself becoming quite sick at the prospect of getting everyone paid, but sick or not the job had to be done. Next she listed their net monthly incomes, his from the job he had landed with a construction company in Durban and hers from her job in the town. From that she deducted their necessary living expenses and the servant's wages; she allowed a small amount for a little entertainment for them, and the figure left over had to be used to start paying back all these debts.

'Kesaya, I need to go out for a while,' she called to the maid. 'Please, keep an eye on the children till I get back, I'll probably be a couple of hours.'

'Yes, madam, no problem,' she replied, her round black face beaming with pleasure. She loved Sarah and Ben and was at her happiest sitting on the floor playing with them for hours.

Sally set off to do the rounds of the creditors with her lists. She felt very satisfied with her efforts, and each and everybody to whom they owed money was happy to receive a percentage of the monthly residue until the debt was cleared. By the time she got home she was far more relaxed. But by the time Richard got home he was very drunk, so there was no discussion that night.

Over breakfast the following morning she proudly told him the results of her previous afternoon's labours.

'This will work; everybody's agreed to my repayment plan and we'll soon be back on the straight and narrow again. We just need to be a bit careful for the next six months, that's all,' she told him.

Six months? Shit – I can't wait that long till I get another boat, Richard thought.

At the end of month one of the Grand Plan, Sally asked for his pay

148

cheque for banking, only to find it was less than she was expecting.

'Why is this cheque so small, what's happened to the rest of your salary?' she asked.

'Oh, I had to take some clients out so I asked accounts for an advance. They obviously deducted it from my cheque – sorry, it shouldn't happen again,' he mumbled.

'Well, if you were entertaining clients surely you should have put in an expenses claim, not paid for it yourself?' she asked.

'Are you bloody questioning me?' he yelled at her. 'For fucks sake, I can't take much more of this – having my money dished out to me like bloody pocket money.'

Month one and already The Plan was showing distinct cracks. Month two was no better – this time it was a leaving party for one of his colleagues at work that caused the advance requirement. Month three: 'I just needed some relaxation with the boys – what's wrong with that. I'm entitled to a few nights out and I don't need your permission to do it!' was his rant.

Things couldn't get much worse. The rows between them were getting really bad. He was spending less and less time at home as a result and more and more time and money at the bar drowning his sorrows. She had failed in her promise to honour their debts and was struggling to make ends meet.

'Mummy, things are really bad, we're rowing all the time, even the children are getting nervous when they see us together. You remember I told you about the problems with the estate agency finances, well, do you think you could lend me some money, just so I can get my payments up to date – please?' She begged her mother for a few hundred rand just to get them over this sticky patch, and then try to formulate a Plan B. Perhaps she should have a word with the accounts department where he worked and make sure they didn't give him any advance? No, he'd definitely flip if she did that. Well, what then?

Chapter 20

'Hilary, do you really need to buy any more dresses? We are only going to Mauritius for ten days not a bloody month, and I don't expect we will be dining at the British Embassy while we're there either. It'll be hot, you'll only need bikinis and wraps plus a few light things for the evenings,' Toby asked his fiancée. Their wedding was fast approaching and he had told her to go and buy a few nice things for the postnuptial holiday. He enjoyed the luxuries that his wealth could buy and was naturally generous by nature, but her spending on clothes was beginning to reach epic proportions; he began to wonder what would happen when she was let loose on house furnishings.

'Since you've got all those new dresses and things now, we might as well put some to good use. Let's have some of my friends over this weekend, I haven't seen any of the lads for ages.'

'No, sweetie, I really don't feel like being nice to a bunch of your friends at the moment, I've got rather a lot on my mind. Let's leave it for now.' And that was that. Experience had taught him that when she put her foot down it was firmly embedded. He hadn't entertained any of his friends since he and Hilary had become engaged – she had made it quite clear that she was not keen on encouraging any of his friendships; sad really, he had always enjoyed their company. He would cook for them, and then there would be a few rounds of cards or something, always a good time to let off a bit of steam together. And another thing, she said she was fed up with living at Oakfield Manor now; said it was too cold, too remote, said she wanted something closer to the centre of things. She adored her shopping trips to Harvey Nichols and Harrods in London's Knightsbridge, and would prefer to live closer to those palaces of pleasure. Perhaps she'll settle down after the wedding or when she becomes pregnant, he hoped. Perhaps.

'Hilda, it's your favourite man.' He knew she would recognise his voice, she always did. 'Just thought I would catch up with things in sunny South Africa. Is she well? How are her children?'

'Oh Toby, I don't know. Things are not good. You know I told you Richard had gone into the estate agency business near Durban? Well, that's failed; she is struggling to cope with the fall-out and he's not helping. They've got a lot of problems and she's losing so much weight over it.' Perhaps she should not be telling him all this, but she knew how much he cared about her daughter, and he could certainly have given her a better life than the one she had chosen.

'Give me her phone number, Hilda, I've got to talk to her,' demanded.

'You know I can't do that, Toby. I can't break my promise to her, she'd be really angry.'

'Don't worry, it doesn't matter. You know I'll find out anyway,' he said, his voice thick and heavy with concern and anger. 'I promise you Hilda, I will help her if she'll let me.' Thoughtfully he re-dialled.

'Benny, my dear friend, how's tricks? – we haven't spoken since you were last in the UK. How long has it been now – three years?' Toby was pleased to talk to his South African friend again after such a long time. He and Benny had met during a flying visit to the UK three years earlier when Benny was looking for some international funding, and Toby had been able to help him through his position with Stanhope Bank; now it was time to call in the favour.

He told Benny only what he needed to know. A married woman living in a small town outside Durban and he needed her phone number. He also wanted any local knowledge about the family; failed estate agent in a small town – shouldn't be too difficult. How Benny got the information was not his concern, just get it – please.

'Hello, darling – no don't hang up, I won't talk for long. I heard on the grapevine that you've got problems. You're not going to be able to change him, you know, it's time to get out and start thinking about yourself. Look, I'm supposed to be getting married in four weeks time. You know I'm only marrying her because I need children, but I'll call the whole thing off today if you'll just come home. Hilary's OK but it's not her I love, it's you I can't live without, you know that. We can make a beautiful life for ourselves together. Please, please, let me take care of you, all of you.'

'Toby, I can't just walk out on the father of my children. He and I have got to try and work this out. I'm not in love with you, and you are just obsessed with me, I don't know why and I find it disturbing. I didn't tell you I had moved, so how did you find me? Did my mother give you this number?'

'No sweetheart, she didn't, she promised you she wouldn't – I have my sources, you know that. You can't hide from me, no matter how hard you try.' He was almost in tears at hearing her voice again after so long. 'Please think about it, my darling. You can't go on like this, I can hear the distress in your voice. You've got big financial problems, where are you going to live if your rent is not paid on your house?' How did he know so much? Surely her mother wouldn't have given him this private information?

'Toby, please stop this! Yes things are bad, but running away isn't the answer, I have to try and get it all sorted out,' she answered, close to tears.

'I'm going to call you tomorrow, and I want a different answer from you then. I'm going to arrange for airline tickets to be waiting for the three of you to collect at Durban airport, pick up a connecting flight at Jo'burg and come back to me, safety and security. You and your children will never want for anything else as long as you live, you will be wrapped in my love – just give me the date.'

'Please don't!' she cried, hanging up quickly, and she ran to the bathroom, sobbing uncontrollably. God, this is a mess, she thought, what am I going to do? First things first, cold water on the face and get ready for work – her job was even more important now. Apart from the much-needed income it gave her a way of getting through the day, a diversion from the pressures at home.

She settled behind her counter and began dealing with the first customers of the day, getting a measure of enjoyment from helping to plan holidays for families or trips for businessmen across South Africa or around the world. Customers planning such trips usually had an air of happiness, even excitement, about them, so she was surprised to see a man thundering into the agency just before closing for lunch, his face contorted with anger.

'You're Mrs Denham, aren't you?' he blazed at her. Ooops – this didn't look good – what now?

'Yes, I am. Why, what on earth is the problem?' she asked.

'You live in Freeland Park and own a Great Dane – right?' he was still blazing.

'Right. Yes, we do, why?'

'My name is Blaine, I live on the opposite corner from your house and your bloody dog has just dug up all my Namaqualand Daisies. I planted them at midnight on the last full moon and have been nurturing them ever since, and your bloody dog has just scratched them all out of the ground. You have no idea how much work I put into those plants and how angry I am; if I catch him near my house again I'm going to take my shotgun to him. Be in no doubt – I mean it, I'll blast him to pieces!' And on this Mr Blaine stormed out of the agency, shaking with rage.

Richard thought the world of his dog, but since he was never taken out for walks the hound took it upon himself to have his own fun around the local streets; he wasn't fenced in and clearly had absolutely no respect for other people's Namaqualand Daisies.

When Sally relayed the content of Mr Blaine's ire to Richard that evening and told him that either they would either have to fence in the extensive grounds, which they obviously could not afford to do with the current state of their financial affairs, or his dog would have to go, Richard dealt with the problem through the bottom of a beer glass. He did not take the options surrounding his cherished pet's future too kindly, and Sally was left with the distinct impression that this was going to be yet another situation that would require her careful handling, but would probably prove too difficult to sort out to everyone's satisfaction.

At 4 o'clock in the morning she gave up on trying to sleep and wandered through to the kitchen for a cup of tea. As she sat over her steaming mug, sitting on the terrace in the early spring morning, she asked herself where exactly she was going with all of this. How am I going to get us out of this mess? Can I? Why me? Is this happiness? What more is there? The unanswered questions circulated in her head for two hours until two-year old Ben made his vocal demands for his bottle and a fresh nappy. She felt low, directionless and alone, and a night without sleep certainly hadn't helped.

Toby's call came at 9 o'clock when he judged that Richard would be out of the house. 'Well? When are you coming home sweetheart?'

The flight from Durban landed at Jan Smuts airport in Johannesburg at 4 o'clock in the afternoon and Sally hurried her two young children over to the international departures area for their onward connection to London. Making the decision to leave had been one of the toughest she had ever made. Toby had been insistent, the tickets to happiness were waiting for her to collect at Durban airport, all she had to do was turn up for the flight and all her misery would be over. It really would be that simple. Perhaps running away from all the horrors currently surrounding her wouldn't be such a bad thing, let Richard sort the mess out himself. Someone else was offering to make decisions for her, protect her from her woes and put back some calm order into her life.

There was a distinct sense of déja-vu as she rounded the exit from the customs hall into the public greeting area at Heathrow. The last time she had done this she had only had one child with her, but there he was again, waiting impatiently for her, ready to relieve her of the luggage trolley and guide her to his car. She was exhausted, both mentally and physically. On top of the draining flight the last two years had been an emotional roller coaster with Richard, and now she was going to have to make some more painful decisions for herself and her little family.

They drove down to her mother's; Sally trying hard to avoid any talk of their future, and Toby determined to paint as rosy a picture as possible for her.

'I'll leave you to get sorted out and come down for you tomorrow evening, sweetheart. How about we go out for a meal when we can talk?' he asked.

'Yes, that would be lovely. I need to get some proper shut eye – this is the second night's sleep I have lost in a row and I could really do with a bit of mental peace right now.'

Hilda was only too happy to look after her two little grandchildren while their mother and Toby went out for a meal together. Sally was nervous of giving him any signals that could be construed as indications of a future together, her trauma was still too new and too raw, but he was determined not to let her slip through his fingers again.

He had told Hilary that he was bringing Sally home and he wanted to call off their wedding. She was incandescent with rage, but had been with him long enough to realise that there were some issues on which even she could not budge him, and she was shrewd enough to recognise that this woman seemed to be one of them; she would not get her own way through temper tantrums and sulks this time. This was a situation that needed some careful handling if she was to hang onto the well-padded future she had mapped out for herself. A perfectly prepared romantic dinner a-deux with just the right amount of sexy underwear on display should start things off nicely.

'Sweetie,' she had said, her smile hiding her inner determination. 'I know this woman is under your skin, but look at the way she has treated you in the past. From what you told me she was up for it one minute, then wiping the floor with your emotions the next. You never know, she is probably going to do the same thing again. Whereas you and I have been together for nearly three years now and you know I don't treat you like that; you know how I adore you. We can get married next month as planned – you never know I might even fall pregnant on our honeymoon, wouldn't that please you? – Then, when we get back, I promise I won't mind if you still want to see her from time to time, and when she hurts you yet again, as you know she will, you will always have my loving arms to come back to. I think that would work very well, don't you? That's what we'll do, sweetheart. Now come to bed, I've got some real fun lined up for you tonight.'

Toby could see that Sally was not comfortable as they settled into their seats

154

in the restaurant round the corner from her mother's home the following evening. She hadn't flown into his arms, covering him with her gratitude, as he had hoped, and he was trying hard not to panic. Somehow he had to convince her that Richard would never be right for her; he had to wrench her away from him right now. His wedding was only a few weeks away, Hilary had her claws out and Sally was looking less than convinced that changing the course of so many people's lives, and causing so much misery all round her, was absolutely the best thing to do.

'You know you are so naïve, darling,' he started. 'I can see you have no idea what Richard is really like.'

'What are you talking about? I know exactly what he's like,' said Sally, wondering where this was going.

'Bet you didn't know he was having affairs, did you?' he said, thinking on his feet, although he should have remembered that was never the best of moves around her. 'You know I have my sources in the area – how do you think I got your phone number – and I've had him watched over the last few months. I can give you a list of the names of the women he's been sleeping with.' There, that should do it, he thought, pleased with his inventiveness.

'What on earth are you talking about?' she demanded. 'He's doing no such thing; that has never been an issue. How can you sit there and tell me you want to call off your wedding on the one hand, yet tell me a pack of lies with the other?' She didn't like what was going on inside his head.

'I'm not giving you a pack of lies, it's the truth.' Desperation was digging him deeper into the hole he had dug for himself and he didn't know how to get out of it. He couldn't believe he was screwing up again – why couldn't things be easier with this bloody woman, why couldn't he ever get it right with her?

But Sally was having none of it. She had left Richard a note telling him where she had gone and he called her early the next morning. They talked for an hour and as she listened to his honest misery she understood what had driven him to make so many mistakes over the last few years. She did love him, he was the father of her children, and Toby was blatantly lying to her. Simple choice really.

Toby and Hilary were married.

A few weeks later Richard arrived in England from South Africa and the family rented a home whilst they sorted out a new direction in their life together.

'How do you feel about living in the Middle East?' he asked her one evening.

'Why the Middle East?' she wanted to know, wondering where that had come from.

'Big money, tax-free. We'll be able to get back on our feet really quickly, and have enough to put a deposit down on a house in Brighton within a couple of years. There's a job advertised in the paper, look. It's in a town called Hail in Saudi Arabia, sounds just my sort of thing. Managerial position in construction, family chalet, camp life, swimming pools and a camp shop. What do you think?'

She considered the added bonus that she would be a million miles away from Toby, and agreed to go. There were no telephones at their chalet in the desert.

Things were working out nicely for Hilary. It was obvious that that woman had spurned him yet again, just as she had predicted; Toby had been morose and agitated for a while, but his new aggressive attitude that Sally's latest rejection had triggered was pushing him to support more and more high-risk land deals, the success of which was taking them to dizzy financial heights.

But he still didn't have Sally and now he couldn't even talk to her, hear her voice.

'Come on little ones,' called Sally to the brood of six in the crèche she was running. 'Time for some lemonade and biscuits, and then we'll have a story – a story about the cat that slept in front of the fire. You don't remember what fires are, do you? We have enough heat out here without fires,' she muttered under her breath.

Sally and Richard were enjoying camp life, surrounded by like-minded folk. With their men away at the construction site each day there was little for the women and children to do, but within the community each of the women with a skill used it to enhance the lives of the others. Amongst them they had two primary school teachers, an artist, a yoga expert, someone able to teach bridge and another keen to pass on her needlepoint knowledge. Sally's modelling and bookkeeping abilities were of zero use in the desert, but she found her morning job of running the crèche very satisfying; she could keep an eye on her 3-year old son, Ben, whilst Sarah attended the little camp school with eight others.

Monday was the day when the refrigerated lorry delivered fresh supplies to the camp shop, always an exciting event allowing new menus to be planned for the coming week, and Thursday was Souk day. Before boarding the company bus for their weekly visit to the little desert town of Hail, the women carefully clothed themselves and their daughters in long flowing dresses that left only their heads uncovered in order not to give offence to the local people. They wandered through the various Souks to buy fresh vegetables and exotic fruits that were displayed under cover from the searing heat of the sun, and the sounds and smells of the dusty markets filled their senses as they wandered around the gold traders, the darkened interiors of their stalls hiding their women folk from view. Many of the traders sat outside their stalls together smoking their hookah pipes, their eyes following the transit of the European women suspiciously. Their mode of dress, although respectful, still showed their faces and hair, and this was not something the older men were accustomed to; the women were always relieved to be back within the camp perimeter where they could safely enjoy a modicum of western life.

'Mummy, mummy, come and see the puppy,' called Sarah, running into the villa dripping with water from her swim.

Sally followed her daughter to the camp perimeter fencing, and there was what appeared to be a young Saluki puppy, yapping and pawing at the fence in his effort to find a way in.

'Oh my goodness, where did you come from?' Sally reached through the fencing and scratched his ears. She ran over to the gate, the puppy following her on the other side of the fence, until she was able to walk out of the camp and greet the little flying bundle of fur. He had clearly chewed his way through a cotton collar that had been tied round his neck, but he had to have come from one of the Bedouin encampments that were scattered around the desert, it was their breed of choice. So the puppy was taken in and given food and water until Friday, the holy day of rest, when Richard could drive them around the various camps and return the puppy to its rightful owner.

But it seemed that nobody in the area had lost a dog. The last call of the day was to a very hospitable family who invited Richard and family to join them for chai, a sweet black tea flavoured with mint.

Sally was shown through to the quarters of the first wife where she sat cross-legged on some rugs that had been placed on the desert floor. Conversation between the two women was going to be tricky, the Bedouin wife spoke no English and the only Arabic that Sally knew was limited to pleasantries and numbers up to twenty. But sign language came in very handy during their hour together, and they were able to discuss everything from the ages of children to the price of gold – providing neither age nor price exceeded the number twenty.

Richard sat with the husband in his quarters and enjoyed sharing the pot of coffee that bubbled away on the fire pit that had been dug out of the sand, the beans of which had been ground together with cardamom seeds so popular with the local people.

The local family agreed to take the excitable little puppy until they could find a more permanent home for him, and Richard and Sally took two saddened children back to bed.

Richard was on the move again. He had been offered a job in Jeddah, so the family needed to go back to the UK to apply for new visas before returning to the western coastal city with a new employer.

'Phew, this is hot.' Sally felt she had been slapped in the face with wet cotton wool as they left Jeddah airport.

It's no hotter than Hail, just more humid,' Richard told her. 'Don't worry, you'll soon get used to it and everywhere's air-conditioned.'

Their new white washed villa on a beautifully appointed secure compound was glorious with a squash court and two swimming pools, and Sarah and Ben quickly found several other children of varying ages with whom they could play. It was a very sociable life, evenings having dinner with neighbours or playing squash, and Fridays were spent swimming in the Red Sea then enjoying bar-b-ques with the other residents.

Shopping was more fun too. No more traipsing over to the camp shop looking forward to a new delivery of lamb, or having to cover up when leaving the confines of the desert compound. Life in the cosmopolitan city of Jeddah was more liberal and there were shopping malls to explore, supermarkets with choice.

Then Richard changed his job again. And over the following year he changed it twice more, each time requiring the family to fly back to the UK before returning on a new visa to a new compound with a new school for the children. The last move taking them to Dubai for a year.

'It's a good job the children are still young enough to put up with all this upheaval,' Sally mused. 'But next year we'll have to settle down somewhere for their schooling. What about Australia? You have good skills in construction management and it would be nice to live in the warmth. Surely that would be a better option than cold, wet England.'

'Oh, I don't think so,' he replied. 'I think I'd need to have qualifications of some sort to be accepted. Anyway, I heard that the immigration door has closed now.'

'Well you could ring the Australian Embassy in Abu Dhabi just to ask couldn't you?' She couldn't understand his reticence to at least enquire.

They both enjoyed a warm climate, and the children's favourite toys were sand and hosepipes. The thought of returning to a northern climate was very unappealing, especially when there could be an alternative. Toby was there too.

The talk of Brighton kept cropping up.

'What is it with you and Brighton?' Sally asked one morning.

'Well, I thought we might get ourselves a pub to run in Brighton,' he grinned.

'Absolutely not Richard, I will not be a pub landlady – there's no way you will ever get me living in a pub or pulling pints.' Where did this idea come from, for God's sake? This was not the future she was looking forward to. A stable home, husband doing something managerial allowing him plenty of time at home during evenings and at weekends – that was her perfect family picture. Especially after all that they had been through over the past years, a settled existence for her family was important to her.

'No problem, sweetheart,' he assured her. 'I promise you won't have to pull any pints, that'll be for the staff and me. You can just do the books, save me having to get an accountant in, and you could help with some of the cooking. Anyway, that's a while away yet. You'll see, it will be fantastic. We'll buy a house and rent it out – that will cover the mortgage on it, but at least we will have a property of our own for the future, and we can live for free in the accommodation over the pub and make an absolute killing in Brighton. Then – and this is the best bit – in a few years time we'll have made enough money to be able to retire to Cornwall where we can buy a small country pub of our own, and I can go fishing all day. Just think of it, it'll be perfect.'

She *was* thinking about it and she didn't like it, not one little bit. But he wasn't listening to her.

Toby spent the same five years increasing the Havers family by two sons, William and Simon, and he was persuaded to buy a palatial eight-bedroom villa in southern Spain that Hilary and the children could retire to each time their private schools broke for holidays and half terms.

He was not entirely displeased with his lot. He was becoming known in the financial world as Mr Midas – the dealer with the magic touch. He had sold a large parcel of land to a Japanese consortium the previous year and had been very pleased with the deal that had allowed him to bank a cool quarter of a million pounds.

Mr Hashimoto had been so happy with his purchase that he had invited the Honourable Mr Havers and his wife over to Japan to attend a ship launch. They were treated like royalty during their three-day stay, their generous host providing everything for their comfort, and on their way back they stopped off in Bangkok where Hilary was able to talk Toby into buying some beautiful precious and semi-precious gems to have made up into jewellery for her.

He had his empire, his heirs, two magnificent homes, a fleet of cars including a Rolls Royce and a Porsche, plus a couple of Mercedes Sports and a Morgan. All he had to do now was sit back and enjoy the fruits of his success – but that was the hard part – he still didn't have Sally, and now he couldn't even talk to her, hear her voice.

Chapter 21

The children were growing up and Sally wanted to stop their nomadic lifestyle. They had moved around the Middle East with breathtaking speed, and constantly taking the children out of school whenever Richard changed his job was not conducive to a settled education for them. Sarah had turned ten and Ben eight, and they both needed the stability of a permanent home where they could enjoy friendships that would last more than a few months.

Richard had been right about one thing, though. Through working in the Middle East they had made enough money to put down a hefty deposit on a property, but Sally was not having Brighton. Her foot was going down.

'Absolutely not. I don't know Brighton. I don't like what I have seen of Brighton and I will not live in Brighton. You want to spend at least another year in the Middle East on your own so we will be well set up financially? Fine, you know I don't have a problem with that, but if I'm going to live in the UK alone with the children I want to live somewhere of my choice – for now. We'll sort out the final family destination when you decide to leave the Middle East for good. Until then we'll get something in a town like Uckfield, or somewhere round there.' Richard's family were in the area, mother, cousins, grandmother, people she knew and cared about. She was not going to a strange town and starting again on her own.

They bought number 30 Everest Road, Uckfield. Sally and the children moved in and Richard went back to Saudi Arabia.

'Hilda, my friend. How's my girl doing? Are they still running around the Middle East? What about those children of hers, surely they should be settled in school somewhere by now.'

Hilda quite welcomed Toby's six-monthly calls. She was not happy that her eldest daughter appeared to be heading down the route to being a pub landlady against her wishes, Richard seemed so determined to fulfil this dream of his. Things were looking a little rocky on her marital front again, and no mother likes to see her children less than 100% happy. Shame it hadn't worked out between her and Toby when he had brought them back in '77, he had been very silly, lying to her like that – perhaps he's changed now.

'No, Toby, they're settled in Sussex now, and the children are at school. Oh, bother, please forget what I said; she'll be ever so cross if she thinks I've given away her address.' Hilda wondered what it was that had made her blurt out the county of Sussex.

'Hilda, dear, you haven't given me her address, have you? Listen next time you speak to her, please give her my love and tell her not to forget me – please.'

It was so easy to get information out of Hilda; Toby had been delighted to learn from her that Richard was away for several months. He had a little job for his secretary; it might take her some time to filter through the electoral rolls for all the districts in Sussex, but it would be worth it in the end. Sally would be bound to be registered somewhere.

His Rolls Royce cruised conspicuously along Everest Road, looking for number 3. When he saw that the area between 1 and 5 was just an open stretch of land he wondered how she had managed to swing such a deception.

He drove slowly up and down, looking for any sort of clue as to where she might be living. If her children had been playing in the garden he might recognise them, but it was raining and the gardens were deserted. Still, he considered, if the number was wrong, perhaps the street was wrong too – even the town. She could be anywhere. So close – SHIT!

His failure to find Sally, having got so close, put him in a foul temper, and when he got home that evening he was spoiling for a fight. Hilary's spending was getting ridiculous, and whilst he gave her an extremely generous allowance, he was struggling to reach the same level of enjoyment as her each time she appeared in a brand new and very expensive designer outfit. Today it was not only another new dress but very expensive drawing room curtains as well.

'What the fuck was wrong with the old ones, for Christ's sake?' he yelled at her. 'If you want to keep spending money like water maybe you should go out to work and start earning some, you do fuck all around here all day anyway. You've got a nanny, a cleaner and a gardener, you even get the handyman to drive you around like a bloody chauffeur – why don't you do your own driving and let him get on with the jobs around the place – like he's paid to?'

'Don't you dare shout at me!' she yelled back at him. 'It's not just me that enjoys these few nice little things, you know! You wouldn't want me to be seen in last year's outfits and be a laughing stock amongst our friends; and the old drawing room curtains were looking very tired, they made the room look drab. You're making enough for us to be able to enjoy a few nice things from time to time!'

'From time to time? – I'm talking about your total lack of respect when it comes to spending? And friends – what friends? Ever since we've been married you have made my friends feel they are not welcome. My house always used to be full of friends and laughter. Now, it's just NEW FUCKING CURTAINS THAT WE DON'T NEED, AND MORE DESIGNER DRESSES THAT WE'RE RUNNING OUT OF ROOM FOR!' He was becoming puce with rage and yanked the front door open in answer to the bell. 'YES?' he roared at the taxi driver standing on the doorstep proffering a packet of cigarettes. 'Er, lady called the rank and asked me to buy some cigarettes for her. That'll be seven quid for the packet and the fare please guv.' The pub had helped to soothe him a little on the way back from his abortive trip to Uckfield, but Hilary was starting to wind him up again, something that was becoming more frequent of late. He stormed upstairs, wrenched an armful of expensive designer dresses from the wardrobe, dragged them down to the kitchen and threw them in a pile at her feet.

'There! If they're last year's models that you're too grand to wear again, go and do something fucking useful for a change and start a second hand shop!' And he stormed out of the house, jumped into the Porsche and left the driveway in a shower of shingle.

Now I wonder who's set him off, Hilary mused to herself. 'Mette?' she called to the au pair. 'Tidy these dresses up for me and take them up to the attic, there's a good girl. There are some boxes up there you can dump them in.' And she poured herself a glass of Sancerre whilst considering the two cold lobsters she had bought from Harrods for supper. It was pretty obvious he wouldn't be back for any, shame to waste one of them. She called the cat over and stroked his sleek back. 'Here kitty, kitty, here's a nice little treat for you.'

Richard returned to Everest Road from Saudi Arabia the following summer and it took him a full twelve months of contrived pressure to convince Sally that being a tenant landlord in Brighton was the sweetest of futures for the family. He began his assault by meekly accepting a job and commuting daily to London. Each day leaving home before 6 o'clock in the morning to miss the rush hour traffic, and returning at 9 o'clock in the evening, a frazzled wreck. Work finished at around 5 o'clock, the 40-mile journey home took over two hours in the rush hour, then he needed a further two hours winding down in the pub. By the time Sally got him he was past eating, the meal she had carefully prepared was put away in the fridge/bin, and civil conversation became strained.

'Working in London is not doing it for me, I'm sure you can see that,' he told her after twelve months of it. 'I've given it my best shot, for your sake, but I'm not cut out for this commuting business. I think it's time

I started looking round for something nearer home. But you have to agree that a salary for anything I might be able to do in Uckfield will be much lower than London – we'll have to cut back a lot. And quite honestly, I don't know what I could do around here, other than be self employed.' The pressure had begun.

The pub he found was in a very run down part of Brighton, but it was just what he was looking for. The trade was so low it could only go one way, and that was up. He had big ideas for good home cooked food, loud music, short skirts behind the bar and himself as the genial host, always ready to be the punter's friend but equally ready to sort out fights. The brewery liked him on paper, now all he had to do was convince Sally to appear in front of the interviewers with him as his landlady.

'Tell you what we'll do,' he said to her the evening before the interview in an effort to raise some enthusiasm in her. 'I think you're absolutely right not to want to live in the flat over the pub. It'll be far too noisy, especially when I have the music up really loud, certainly won't be good for the children. How about this for a compromise? You stay here in Uckfield with the children, I'll live at the pub for five nights of the week and come home for two. We won't make as much money as if we rented the house out, but it will be better for you and the children, plus they won't have to move school. I think that's a blinding idea. I get my dream, we make reasonable money, you don't have to pull pints and the children don't get moved around. What do you say?' He was so animated, his whole body tense waiting for her reply. He did love pub life and would probably make a good landlord. What else could he do? Would she mind living without him for a few days a week – she had happily done more than that when he was away in Saudi Arabia. Could she refuse him?

The deal was done. Hands were shaken and The Pendred Arms in Brighton had a new landlord and landlady. With grave misgivings and a heavy heart she had attended the brewery interview with him, and impressed the interviewers with her support of her husband and the menus she planned for bar meals. They did not need to know that she in fact planned to cook these meals in her kitchen at home in Uckfield, freeze individual portions, then transport everything down to Brighton and scuttle back to Uckfield as fast as possible. What they didn't ask, they didn't need to be told. They were also very happy to know that she was more than capable of setting up and running the pub office. The fact that the pub office was also going to be situated fifteen miles north of the Pendred Arms was neither here nor there, another thing they didn't need to know, and pulling pints was definitely not part of the deal.

It was not an ideal way of living, being a part time wife/cook/bookkeeper but they muddled along for a few months. The pub was very rowdy, very noisy and very smoky. Richard was in his element and Sally hated every minute she had to spend there. His routine became fairly set. As Wednesday was his day off he came back to the house late on Tuesday night after closing up, slept until noon on the Wednesday, catching up on some well earned rest, then down to his favourite pub in the next village to unwind for a couple of hours. That took him until about mid afternoon; the rest of the afternoon was spent tranquilly dozing in front of the television before getting ready for the evening drink back in his chosen watering hole. Thursday morning back to work. He had enjoyed a nice peaceful break doing his own thing, no hassle.

But his weekly visits home were becoming a chore for Sally; her children were growing up with a part-time father, and once again she found herself wondering what it was all about.

'Toby, what the hell is this in your jacket pocket? Why have you been staying at the Dorchester while we were away in Spain? And who exactly is the Mrs Havers on this hotel receipt?' Hilary screamed at him. Ooops! He thought he had got rid of any incriminating evidence of the night he spent with a beautiful woman he had picked up at Annabel's Nightclub the week before.

'If you weren't so busy flaunting yourself in Marbella and spent more time being a proper wife to me I wouldn't need to look elsewhere, would I? Besides, how the hell do I know what you're up to out there at night while the nanny's looking after the children, you never answer the poxy phone? You can't have it both ways so mind your own bloody business!' he snarled back. The flying plate smashed a hole in the kitchen window, but that was Toby's fault because he ducked. Hilary ran upstairs in a rage, grabbed an armful of his clothes and tossed them out of an upstairs window. 'There! You want to sleep somewhere else? You'll need your clothes – now fuck off and leave me alone!'

'I'll leave you alone as long as you want, sweetheart; just make sure you include your cheque book and credit card in all that stuff you're throwing out of the window. Life will be a hell of a lot cheaper!' Stupid bitch, he thought to himself, picking up the car keys. Plan. I need a plan. Life's too short to put up with all this shit.

Without conscious thought he found himself on the road to Uckfield. In the three years since he had last driven there he had tried everything he could think of to unearth his woman, but to no avail. Hilda had steadfastly refused to surrender the exact address, admitting only to the county of Sussex. Everest Road in Uckfield was the only starting point he had; it wasn't very long, shouldn't be impossible, just means knocking on every door in the street; but as he sat in the window of the pub on the corner, nursing his beer and considering his next move, she drove past. He jumped up, crashing into the table in his haste to get to the door and see where she turned in.

Number 30 not 3 – so that was where the mistake was made. He sat back with a relaxed, satisfied grin on his face and relished the remains of his beer.

Richard was cleaning his shoes in the kitchen as the lorry pulled up across the driveway; he was getting ready for his usual Wednesday lunchtime session. They had decided to renovate the garden shed and the lorry had a load of timber planking for them – Richard couldn't help, his shoes needed cleaning, so Sally donned an old pair of jeans, some comfortable shoes and started to do the job herself. 11-year old Ben wanted to help her, and between the two of them the planks were gradually transferred from the lorry into the garage.

'Hello, sweetheart.' Sally spun round at the sound of the deep, familiar voice and saw Toby strolling along the pavement towards her, hands in pockets and a huge grin lighting up his face.

'For God's sake Toby, what on earth are you doing here? Richard's in the house, if he sees you all hell will break out. Please go away.' She was in a panic; her face went red and her hands started to shake with the sudden tension.

'I just happen to be building some houses not far away. Came down for a site visit, popped into the pub over there for a heart starter and saw you drive by. What a blinding coincidence, old thing.' He was beaming broadly, outwardly quite relaxed. She had cut her hair quite short – um – don't like that too much, he thought to himself, she'll have to grow it again.

'Please, please go away. Richard will be coming out any second now and there will be awful trouble if he sees you.'

'Tell you what, old thing. I'll just go into that pub on the corner and wait for you there. Come over for a drink as soon as you can, I've got to talk to you.' And with that he turned his back and sauntered off, holding his trembling in check until he was out of her sight.

'Who was that, mummy?' asked Ben. Seeing his mother's confusion had aroused his curiosity.

'Just an old friend, darling,' she replied, trying to stop herself from shaking. Oh hell! Old friend my foot; this was awful.

She carried on hauling the planks into the garage until the job was completed and her pulse had settled into something approaching its normal rhythm. Richard appeared, spruced up for the pub.

'Right, I'm off – see you later,' he called as he drove away.

Sally ran her fingers through her hair and walked over to the pub. She had to find some way of stopping him from turning up whenever he wanted now that he had found her again. She didn't for one minute believe he was building in the area. Mother – it had to be her mother that had let the cat out of the bag. Blast!

He was finishing his beer as she walked in, adjusting her eyesight to the gloomy interior from the sunshine outside.

'What are you going to have, sweetheart?' he asked, rising to his feet and grinning broadly at her.

'Nothing, I don't have time for a drink, the children are on their own in the house. I just need to tell you not to turn up here again. I can't stand the strain any more.' She placed the palms of her hands on the table and leaned over them, staring earnestly into Toby's eyes. 'What will it take to convince you that you have to get on with your life, and leave me to get on with mine?' she pleaded.

'I tell you what we'll do,' he said, covering her hands with his. 'I know you're not happy, my friend your mother told me, and neither am I. My marriage is a bloody sham just like yours. Meet me for a drink just once, we'll each talk without interruption, and if you still want me to leave you alone after that I give you my word I will never try to contact you again. Deal?'

Big breath. 'All right,' she agreed. 'Where do you want to meet?'

'How about the bar of the Grosvenor Hotel at Victoria station? Can you get there tomorrow lunchtime do you think?' His heart was beginning to hammer wildly. He had been given yet another chance to get things right with her, and this time he definitely wasn't going to mess it up.

At least she wasn't going to have to lie to Richard as to her whereabouts. He would be back at his pub in Brighton, the children would be at school for the day and she could get this sorted out once and for all. That's what she told herself anyway.

What to wear? She didn't want to give any wrong signals so no sexy, clingy tops, no high heels, little make-up and no jewellery.

She walked in to the beautifully appointed lounge bar and took in its warm, understated surroundings; deep leather armchairs and couches, wood panelled walls, soft muted tones everywhere and gentle background music. Then she saw him, and saw what the one drink was to be. A bottle of Champagne. She smiled gently to herself, shaking her head slowly as she wondered what made her think it could possibly have been anything else. How long had it been since she had last seen him? It was when he had brought them back from South Africa back in 1977, just before he was due to get married – wow – ten years ago, and he hadn't changed a bit.

'Hello gorgeous,' he said with a smile, rising to his feet to offer a chair for her. 'Champagne?'

Part 2 – And The Shadows That Followed

Chapter 22

Toby and Sally talked and listened to each other for two hours. Their Champagne glasses, with tiny droplets of condensation slowly trickling to the stem, were sitting untouched on the low coffee table in front of them at the Grosvenor Hotel at Victoria Station in London. She was saddened to hear that he was not happy in his second marriage; he was glad to hear that she was not happy in her first. There was still so much unsaid when she had to leave, so many years as yet unravelled, but she had to get back for her children who would be home from school shortly, and she still had a journey of over an hour to get there, but he couldn't let her go just like that. He had promised not to pester her again once they had talked, but the talking wasn't over, so he felt justified in asking her to finish their reminisces before keeping his promise.

'We've still got so much to say to each other, sweetheart, there's so much I don't know about your life, and so much I need to know if I am to feel comfortable at never contacting you again. I know I promised just one meeting, but do you think you could bear to meet me just one more time, just for old times sake – please?'

What was it about this man? He could be so bloody irritating and pushy at times, although not today funnily enough; today he was human and clearly hurting inside. He had certainly been on his best behaviour, but was that just for show? Was he actually calmer and more down to earth than he had been all those years ago? Only one-way to find out I suppose, she thought.

'OK, just once more. But please don't think I am going to make a habit of this. I am still married; we had an affair once but I am not about to repeat that.'

'Good girl, give me a date and I'll fit in around you. We'll have a nice leisurely lunch at a lovely little Italian restaurant I know in the Edgware Road.'

Little Italian indeed. Agreed it was Italian, and yes, it was in the Edgware Road, but there was nothing 'little' about La Loggia when she walked in with him a week later.

'Your usual table, Mr Havers?' greeted the maitre'd.

Their meal was absolutely delicious, no Champagne this time, but a beautiful Barolo Riserva to accompany their meal – a rich red wine, full of fruity flavours and a perfect compliment to the dishes he had chosen for them.

He sipped the sample of wine poured for him, held it in his mouth drawing some air through it, considered it for a moment and finally dramatically declared: 'Definitely from the western slopes.' They laughed together at his pretentiousness, quickly recapturing the relaxed togetherness that they had enjoyed during the night they had spent at Little Hammer Farm thirteen years earlier, and the conversation got sillier and sillier.

They smiled ruefully together as they reminisced over the 21 years that they had known each other – on and off – and the mistakes that had been made. Their marriages were dissected and Toby learned that although she had tried hard to be a supportive wife, she loathed her life as the part-time wife of a Brighton pub landlord. Richard was crashing through life at full tilt, blissfully unable to accept her misery no matter what she said, or how many rows they had. Toby got his knight-in-shining-armour on and announced that she needed a break, and he was the man to give it to her. Leave it to him – he would sort something out for her. Meantime, how about lunch next week – same time, same place?

On her way home she felt she was bubbling inside, and the giggles took a long time to subside. Their lunch at La Loggia had been such fun, a real eye opener for her; he had turned on a light in her unhappy life. There had been no showing off, no bullshit, he had been just a warm, gentle, caring man with a sharp and quirky mind who made her laugh. There was a small family run restaurant in the next village to her home that she had found and adored, but it wasn't Richard's cup of tea and he took her there grudgingly, preferring a late night curry, and she surprised herself with the thought that Toby would probably like it. Obviously her head had decided she was going to see him again.

They met the following week for another La Loggia lunch and enjoyed it every bit as much as the first one.

'Remember I said I'd organise a break for you? Well it's all sorted. How do you fancy three days at a health farm?' he asked. 'I go to Henlow Grange for a few days to dry out every now and then – give my liver a rest.'

'Sounds marvellous, but no,' she replied firmly. 'I can't just drop everything and disappear for three days. I have a family to think about. And what exactly am I supposed to tell Richard? I haven't even told him I have been meeting you, and that's something I'm going to have to put right. I can't live with lies, you know that.'

It was becoming clear that whilst things were moving on between them, she was uncomfortable at what her deceit would do to her husband if he should inadvertently find out.

'So tell him.' Toby sat back in the corner banquette, grinning at her.

Tell him? Tell Richard that Toby had walked back into her life again after all the years in between? Just like that? What would happen? It would break him, that's what would happen. Why would she want to do that? She didn't want to do that. What was the alternative? Stop seeing Toby, no more giggles – rely on his promise never to contact her again. Was that what she wanted now? Push was definitely becoming shove.

'Don't to anything about any health farm. I need to get things straight in my head,' she said. As she looked across at him, his eyes burning with the depth of his love for her, it made her heart miss a beat, and she wondered anew at the obsession he seemed to have for her.

'Just one thing, sweetheart. Whatever you decide to do, just remember one thing – this is not a dress rehearsal; you are never going to have your life over again, this is as good as it gets. I'll call you tomorrow.' And he gave her a quick kiss goodbye, holding her eyes with his until her taxi drove out of sight.

She gazed out of the train window on her way home and watched the countryside flying by. It all looked so tranquil; cattle and sheep grazing meadows, horses nuzzling each other in their friendship. With her chin in her hand she wondered why her life couldn't be as tranquil and trouble free as theirs. She and Richard had shared some good times, had had some laughs, but it had been a long time since they had really enjoyed their partnership. Their time in the Middle East had been good and fairly worry free, but back in the real world of England it was unravelling again, and this time it was because of his need to be a pub landlord. Should she demand he give up his dream for her, or was it better for her to either put up with it or move on? Moving on meant separation, and that was something she hadn't allowed herself to think about up to now. OK, big question to self – do you want to leave Richard? If you do, is it just because of Toby's pressure? That wouldn't be right. Either your marriage is right or it's not. Would you be happy living alone in a little house with just the children, or is Richard as a part-time husband better than no Richard? The questions swirled in her head throughout the journey and she struggled to find a clear-cut answer. She loved Richard but was finding it hard to live contentedly with him, yet living alone was an unknown quantity. Living with Toby was definitely a non-starter, that didn't even come into the equation, but he was the catalyst forcing her to ask herself all these questions. His parting words echoed in her brain, as he had intended. No, her life wasn't a dress rehearsal, was it?

She pulled into the driveway at home and stepped over the timber planking she had unloaded two weeks earlier that was still waiting to be used to repair the shed, and as she walked into the lounge she found Richard waking up from a nap on the sofa, his hair leaving a mark on the sofa arm. There was mess everywhere she looked, he had obviously come home, made himself something to eat then fallen asleep in front of the television.

'Why are you all dressed up? Why weren't you here when I got home – where have you been?' he demanded.

As she looked around at the dirty dishes and clothes strewn on the floor she knew that life alone had to be better than the one she presently had. In a flash of clarity she saw herself living in a small house with a small car, having a small job and not accountable to anyone. The children would be more comfortable not seeing any more of the rows that had been increasing in number and intensity between their parents. It would obviously take some adjusting to in the early days, but she could handle difficulties; after all, she thought ruefully, she had had plenty of practice over the past years. She would talk to the children, they would understand. Dress rehearsal. She took a deep breath.

'I've been having lunch with Toby Havers.' There it was said, it was out.

'YOU'VE BEEN WHAT?' he screamed at her as he fell off the sofa and scrambled to his feet. He balled his fists in his fury and leaned over her, his face purple with his rage.

'I'm sorry, I know this is not what you ever wanted to hear, but I have to be honest with you. This is the third time we have met, and the thing is, I'm finding that I don't want to live with you any more.'

'I'LL KILL THAT FUCKING BASTARD!' he yelled, and started pacing angrily around the room, trying to find a focus for his fury. After a few minutes he collapsed back onto the sofa and buried his head in his hands.

'I don't believe you're telling me this. I don't believe it. I don't WANT to believe it, I WON'T believe it! This is NOT happening! Tell me you're making it up, please; tell me its some sick joke you're playing to punish me for having the pub.'

He pleaded with her to make the awfulness of her admission go away.

'I'm sorry but it's true. He said he is building around here somewhere and just happened to go into the pub on the corner and saw me driving by. I agreed to meet him to try and encourage him to go away, but one thing just led to another I'm afraid; we've had lunch together on two occasions now and I've been doing a lot of soul searching over the last couple of weeks.'

'If you think he's telling you the truth then you're stupid. There's no building going on around here, that was just another of his bloody lies. Have you been ringing him? Is that what happened? I know – it was your bloody mother, she's never really liked me – I was never good enough for her precious daughter.' Richard was going out of his mind with anger and fear. Havers had always been on the periphery of his thoughts, but he had managed to bury most of it – until now, when the terror of the whole situation raised its head; he could feel it sneering at him again and he felt sick.

'Are you going to live with him? What about the children? You're not taking my children away from me. Years ago you told me he was getting married. What about his wife?' Richard was being eaten alive with it all, she had to give him some answers.

'No, I'm not going to live with him. Yes, he is married, but not happily, he says. All that's happened is he has made me see that there is more to life than what I have at the moment. I don't mean materially, but I have found the ability to laugh again. He and I share the same outlook on life, the same humour. Each time we have met I have laughed until I ached, and you and I haven't laughed for years. You have your pub, your dream, and I hate your dream. If I asked you to give it up for me you probably would for a while, just to keep me happy, but you would soon resent me for doing that to you. I am no longer happy being married to you and I want some time apart. I'm not talking about divorce, but I do need to be on my own for a while. And you need to know what has brought this about.'

The terrible anguish passing through his face was painful for her to watch, but this time she could do nothing to help him. She hated herself for hurting this man with whom she had shared 16 years of her life, she wanted to hug him and say sorry, say that it had all been a mistake, that she would settle down and forget all about Toby, bury her head, anything just to stop the pain in his eyes; instead she went into the kitchen to make some tea. As she leaned over the kitchen worktop, trying to calm her thoughts, she heard the front door bang shut behind him, and through the window watched him fall into his car, throwing his face into his hands, and heard his searing pain in the roar that he let out as he sat slumped at the wheel.

After a few minutes he pulled himself up straight, his reddened eyes glistening and his face wet with tears; he started the engine and raced off back to Brighton, to his world.

Chapter 23

Although it was late afternoon Toby didn't feel like going home and facing Hilary. She had been in one of her usual foul tempers at breakfast that morning, ordering him around as though he were one of the servants, and his mood was far too euphoric to put up with her nonsense.

He sat in his office for a while, feet in their usual place on the desk and wondered if Sally would have the courage, or even the desire, to tell Richard about their meetings. He had promised to call her tomorrow and she had not objected. Well, in that case, no reason why I couldn't call her now then, he reasoned.

'Hello sweetheart. Journey home OK?' he asked as she answered the phone. But her voice sounded strained and unhappy and he knew that tone, he'd heard it often enough from her over the years, and his heart sank at the thought that he had done something to frighten her away again.

'Yes, the journey was fine but, well, Richard was here when I got home. Don't know why on a Monday, fate perhaps. Anyway, I told him I had been seeing you and it has really hurt him. He's gone back to the pub now, but I can't bear what I have done to him.' She was crying at the trauma she had caused her husband. 'I'm sorry, I can't talk to you any more right now. Please leave me alone for a bit, I need to get my head round all this, everything's suddenly happened so fast.'

'OK sweetheart, I'll leave you alone for today if that's what you want, but I'll call you tomorrow just to make sure you're all right. Bye bye darling, and just remember, you have a right to happiness. Be strong.' He replaced the receiver slowly and lowered his feet to the floor, sitting up straight in his large leather swivel chair. She'd done it, she really had done it, she'd told him. What had she said to him? How far had she gone? Had she asked for a divorce? He must have got it about right with her this time. One nice drink at the Grosvenor, two meals without going over the top had obviously been about right. After 21 years – at last.

By the time he got home he was so deliriously happy he didn't care what mood Hilary was in.

'Where the hell have you been?' Hilary yelled at him as he drifted past the drawing room door, floating in his own world of sublime happiness that even she was not going to be allowed to destroy. 'If you think I've kept a meal for you you're wrong, the cat's had it.'

'Oh, shut up you stupid woman,' he mumbled as he wandered into the dining room to raid the drinks cabinet for a glass or two of Strega before going to bed. 'I don't want anything, as it happens. Had a blinding lunch today.'

'Well, you could at least have let me know. How selfish can you be? I work hard at preparing nice meals for you and you haven't even got the decency to let me know you won't be in. Who was it this time, another one of your cheap sluts?'

'For fuck's sake you stupid woman, SHUT UP! I know bloody well you do NOT spend your day worrying about MY needs! You get the handyman to do the grocery shopping for you and the nanny to do the preparation. All you leave for yourself is the finishing touches so you can claim credit for a wonderful creation. Don't you dare talk to me about selfishness – how have you spent your day I wonder? Beauty parlour again? Getting yourself tarted up ready to go to Spain on Friday? Looking forward to seeing that Spanish waiter again, the one you were throwing yourself at last time we were in Marbella?'

The row continued as she followed him up the stairs. He put the Strega bottle down on the dressing table and started to prepare for bed as she screamed at him: 'YOU BASTARD! I'M NOT TAKING THAT SORT OF RUBBISH FROM YOU; I'VE NEVER THROWN MYSELF AT ANY WAITER, SPANISH OR ANYTHING ELSE! I WOULDN'T CHEAPEN MYSELF – NOT LIKE YOU AND THE TARTS YOU SURROUND YOURSELF WITH. YOU COME HOME DRUNK AND STINKING LIKE A WHORE HOUSE!' She was completely out of control with anger and picked up the half empty Strega bottle, hurling it at him with as much strength as she could muster.

'Suit yourself. I wouldn't need other women if you were a proper wife. But you prefer spending my money to being a wife in my bed,' he countered, ducking from the flying bottle. 'You used to enjoy sex, I wonder where you're getting it from now. I'm sleeping in the spare room tonight by the way – you can have the draught from the window you just stupidly smashed. Don't forget to get your boyfriend the handyman to fix it tomorrow. It must be him keeping you happy when I'm at work, nobody else would touch you with a barge pole.' And with that he sauntered out to the guest suite with a smile on his face, still buoyed up from his lunch with Sally.

Hilary was white with fury; life with Toby had started out to be all cocktails, exotic holidays, diamonds and smart cars – just what she had been looking for. Where had it all gone so wrong? She'd had enough of his miserliness every time she bought a new dress – everyone buys from Harrods – what was wrong with that? Did he expect her to dress like a

175

tramp, or something?

Toby was ordered to drive her and the three boys to Heathrow airport on the Friday morning for their flight to Spain, and although he was going to miss his boys he wouldn't be sorry to see the back of Hilary for a few weeks. She had become a real pain in the neck recently.

As soon as he got home from the airport he called Sally and told her that the house was empty for a few days whilst his family was away at their home in Marbella.

'Sweetpie, tomorrow is Saturday and the weather is set to be warm and sunny. Bring your two over here for a swim and I'll do us a spag for lunch. I'm dying to show you where I live and the sort of things I like around me.'

So, that was her Saturday sorted then – she'd been told. Following his directions she arrived in Sevenoaks late morning and released her two children into the pool while Toby pottered in the kitchen. He still knew his way around the pots and pans, that was easy to see. Lunch was delicious and everyone was in high spirits. Sarah and Ben settled down to watch a video after lunch while Toby gave Sally a conducted tour of the house; it was certainly impressive. Eight bedrooms, six bathrooms, a formal drawing room as well as a more comfortable family room, servants' quarters and a massive attic, approached by a full flight of carpeted stairs, the floor of which was littered with tea chests overflowing with clothes that had been crammed in haphazardly.

'Hilary spends thousands on designer dresses – wears them once then they end up in here,' said Toby indicating the jumble with a wave of his arms, the annoyance in his voice was obvious.

'Once? Why only once?' Sally was puzzled.

He smiled at her naivety. 'Oh, darling, one must never be seen in the same outfit twice, don't you know? One must never show signs of poverty – dreadful social faux pas.'

Although she was beginning to feel a little out of her depth surrounded by such opulence, she did begin to understand some of his unhappiness. Whilst he had been successful in life and was able to afford to splash out on luxuries whenever he chose, he hated waste every bit as much as she did, and the contents of the tea chests were a dreadful waste. There were probably a lot of other things as well.

He wandered off to check on some paintings that had been stored in the darkness of the attic whilst she poked around amongst the contents of a yellow plastic carrier bag where she had espied Toby's distinctive handwriting on some pieces of paper; she pulled out one sheet, and read:

176

"Hello stranger, can't you see I'm bored.
Meet my fiancé by whom I'm adored.
Gaze into my wicked greeny eyes,
An open book – within no bloody lies.
I'll take you from your chauvinistic view,
Reduce your very arrogance a rung or two!

I'm so used to getting my own way,
I just assume you'll do whatever I say;
Look into my lovely eyes
And tell me that you realise
That everything I want I get,
That till now I've never met
One who can resist my eyes.

I'll pluck you from your perch and cage;
I'll take you to the point of rage.
I'll wind you round my little finger,
Make you sweat and make you linger.
Then when by you I'm adored
I'll just toss you overboard."

I don't believe a word my pet;
There's no way this man will let
You win a battle of emotion,
Will part quite yet with his devotion.
To remain inside a shell,
To remain alone and – well –
Immune from pain that troubles bear
When two people really care.

Don't e'er betray my trust, my dear,
Don't ever place me where I fear
That decisions must be made
If I feel I've been betrayed.
'Til then we'll walk fresh paths of life,
Immune from pain or strife.

Find excitement in each day,

Find another way to say –
"I'm glad we met – hope we last,
Look forward now, forget the past."
And every time I search your eyes
Stay truthful – let me find no lies.

She sat on the dusty floor and read again the poem that he had obviously written about her, the reference to green eyes was a give-away. He saw her deeply engrossed in something and wandered over.

'What have you found, sweetpie?'

She passed the poem to him. 'Is that really what you think of me?' she asked sadly. 'Do I really come across as trying to take you down a peg or two?'

'My God, it was years ago when I wrote this, I do scribble a bit when I'm in the mood – either a very good or a very black mood. This one was probably written after one of my abortive attempts to bring you back from South Africa.'

She held out her hand for the piece of paper and folded it carefully, placing it on the top of the other five poems she had read.

'Come on, darling. I should think your two will be bored by now and keen to get back into the pool – let's get down there and keep an eye on them,' he called to her.

She quickly returned the yellow plastic carrier bag to the place where she had found it and picked up the six poems, carefully hiding them behind her back until she was able to secrete them into the deep recesses of her handbag.

Where are we going to meet today?' Toby asked.

She could hear the smile in his voice through the telephone. 'We are not. Foolishly I thought you were going to exert a little less pressure on me – was I so wrong?'

'Sorry, sorry, no. I'm definitely not in the pressure stakes any more. Those days are over. Please forgive me, I just need to see you as soon as I can and I'm free today.'

'Well I'm not. You may be able to delegate your responsibilities at the drop of a hat, but mine are not so easy to shift around, I'm afraid.'

'Yes, of course, I do understand. Just give me a date – tomorrow perhaps?'

'Toby, stop it. Tomorrow is Wednesday, Richard may decide to come back here. At the moment I don't know, I haven't seen him for over a week, ever since I told him I was seeing you, but it would be wrong of me to plan to be away with you if he needs to talk to me. Give me your number, I will call you in a few days.'

He gave her his office number, and they agreed to talk again a few days later.

Richard did come home that night and they tried to talk, but she wasn't able to give him the comfort that he craved; and when they went to bed that night she found she was no longer comfortable in the strong arms he was trying to wrap around her.

'I'm sorry Richard, this is not right for me any more,' and she ran from the room, confused and upset.

He swore; he had hoped it had all been a bad dream, a huge mistake that she would now be regretting, but her reaction to his warm, loving embrace was crucifying him.

She climbed into bed with Sarah, knowing that he wouldn't cause a scene in front of their sleeping daughter, and a few minutes later she heard the front door slam, followed by the screeching of his tyres as he drove violently away from the house.

He didn't remember the journey back to Brighton, his tears of rage and misery were blurring his vision and his ability to think coherently. He knew he was driving too fast, but he didn't care, and found the dangerous speed an outlet for his anger. As the darkened streets flashed by he wound down the window and howled out into the night, an animal bay of pure pain. He had no idea where this thing with Sally had come from; he hadn't picked up any sign that she was unhappy. Sure they rowed from time to time, but all couples row, don't they? Was it the pub – had she really meant it when she had said she didn't want to run a pub? He carried on driving, past Brighton and out into the countryside, his speed increasing with each mile until he was doing over a hundred miles an hour along the coast road.

After an hour of reckless insanity he calmed down, pulled into a lay-by and lit a cigarette where he sat, lost in thought until 3 o'clock in the morning. His tears were all shed, and the cold night air helped to clear his head a little. He rested his forehead on the steering wheel for a while and considered his options. Give up the pub – and then what? He didn't want to give up the pub, but maybe he would have to if he wanted to keep his marriage. Would she stay with him if he went back to a normal job? Perhaps he could try to talk her round. After all it was great fun running a pub, party time every night, great bunch of blokes to banter with. Darts nights, quiz nights. Why wouldn't she be happy with that? Got to talk some sense into her.

He turned the car round and drove slowly back to Uckfield, climbing back into bed just as the sun was beginning to appear over the horizon.

The sound of his car, followed by his key in the lock, woke Sally and she realised what he had been doing. On the one hand she felt sad that she had pushed him into such unhappiness, but on the other she was looking forward to a new life on her own with the children – no more trips to that awful smelly pub in Brighton. No more late night takeaways that were too late to eat, and no more rows.

They talked on and off for two days. He accompanied her to the supermarket in an effort to show her more support, but it was all too little too late for her. She had made up her mind, and by the time he went back to Brighton he knew that he had lost his wife. No matter what reasons she gave for being unhappy with him he knew Havers was at the bottom of the whole mess – it was always fucking Havers – he'd get the bastard!

She rang Toby later that day and told him what had happened. He whooped with joy, punching the air in his excitement. 'We'll get a place of our own now sweetheart – just get down to the local estate agents and find us a love nest. Something not too far from school for your children. Oh, this is the best news I've heard in a long time.'

'Stop it! That's quite enough of that, and there's certainly no joy in this situation at the moment,' she snapped. 'Richard is still my husband and he's hurting like hell. And don't go thinking I'm moving in with you because I'm not, you have your family to think about. This isn't about you and me, I'm afraid, it's just about me at the moment, I need to be on my own – you just gave me the courage to make the move.'

But nothing could dampen his joy. He drove home that afternoon singing along to the radio, feeling that the world had just dropped into his lap. As he bowled in through the door he was greeted with Hilary's sour expression.

'What the blazers are you doing home at this time of the day?' she snarled.

'Nice to see you too, sweetheart. Sorry, I had this strange feeling that this was my house too – odd that. What's the matter sweetie? Spoilt your afternoons plans have I? Something going on you don't want me to know about?'

Hilary was spitting venom at him by now. 'I resent having my afternoons upset; they've always been peaceful without you around. Tolerating your vile moods has only ever ruined just my evenings, when you design to come home at all, that is – when you're not out with one of your tarts.'

'Well, you needn't worry about ruined evenings for much longer, sweetie-pie,' he beamed at her over his shoulder as he drifted happily into the kitchen, looking for a drink. 'I've been seeing Sally; she's told her husband she's leaving him and we're going to be together, so you can stick that where the sun don't shine.'

She froze, and the blood drained from her face as she absorbed the news. Panic was the next emotion, swiftly followed by fury.

'I'LL SEE YOU IN HELL FIRST, YOU BASTARD,' she screamed at him. 'IF YOU THINK I'M GOING TO LET YOU WALK OUT ON ME JUST LIKE THAT YOU ARE SERIOUSLY MISTAKEN. YOU'LL NEVER SEE THE BOYS AGAIN – I'LL MAKE SURE OF THAT!'

He poured himself a glass of wine and wandered out to sit on the terrace in the afternoon sun and considered the words of a new poem:

> *Garlic odour spreads the scene;*
> *Everyone knows you've been*
> *Out to lunch for a while*
> *Noshing grub Italian style.*
>
> *Was it spag or was it veal?*
> *Everyone knows you feel*
> *Full of garlic, full of wine,*
> *And you think you're so divine*
> *But full of garlic.*
>
> *P'raps it was zabaglione,*
> *Not just the booze, but only*
> *Garlic on the spag or veal –*
> *Gordon Bennet, how I feel*
> *Pissed.*
>
> *And reeking of the meal*
> *As garlic odour spreads the scene,*
> *Everybody knows you've been*
> *Out to lunch for a while*
> *Noshing grub Italian style!*

He knew Sally went to bed early, so wasn't surprised to hear her voice sounding really sleepy when he called her at 11 o'clock that night.

'Hello sweetheart. I hope I haven't woken you. No, actually that's a lie – I don't care if I have woken you, I have some news for you. Since you told Richard about us, I told Hilary this afternoon. As you can imagine she's not best pleased, but you and I are out in the open now and I'm happy about it.'

'Listen you silly man,' Sally responded. 'Please get your head around the fact that there is no "you and me", you do know I am not going to just fall into your arms, don't you? I never have in the past and I'm not about to start now. I need my solitude and solitude is what I am going to have for some considerable time until I've straightened myself out. Do you think Hilary will want to divorce you – then where will you be with your children?'

'What? Divorce her chequebook? No way will she ever want to do that sweetheart, don't worry about it.'

'Rest assured Toby, I am not worried about it. Hilary is your problem.'

'Sweetie, I can assure you this will be very much your problem when you are cited as co-respondent in my divorce petition,' came Hilary's sickly-sweet tones. She had been listening in to their conversation on the bedroom extension ever since she had heard her husband pick up the receiver in the study.

Chapter 24

Still shivering with fury the next morning Hilary rang her neighbour, Fran, for some advice. Fran had got rid of her cheating husband the year before and had well and truly wiped the financial floor with him. She didn't have any children but had still somehow managed to keep their enormous house and been awarded substantial maintenance – her solicitors clearly knew what they were doing.

'Don't bother with any of those little High Street solicitors,' advised Fran. 'The firm I went to are in the West End of London plus they got me a barrister and a QC to make sure I got what I deserved. They are terribly expensive, hundreds of pounds an hour, but Toby will have to pay your legal fees so you make sure you go for the best.'

Hilary had three boys to look after and would accept nothing less than their current home, free of mortgage of course, together with their Spanish home – that would be a necessity. Naturally school fees would have to be paid, and then there were her personal expenses to consider. She licked her lips as she began her list of needs, but even she was surprised at how much she would require to live an independent life. She knew Toby wouldn't like it, so either he would have to put Sally back in the bin where she belonged and start treating the family a bit better, or pay up.

The following morning she picked up the phone and made an appointment to see the London solicitors, and four days later divorce papers were duly served on Toby at his office. He was highly amused, he knew this was just a warning shot across his bows – an attempt to draw him back into line, but he was not so amused at the Mareva injunction that accompanied the papers. Somehow the silly bitch had convinced a judge to freeze all his personal and business bank accounts and assets.

He quickly contacted Sue Jackson, his solicitor, and ordered her to get the injunction removed fast. Such a restraining order on his finances would seriously undermine his credibility, and if he couldn't meet his business commitments he would be finished in the city – the stupid bitch was cutting off her nose to spite her face, that was sure. Then he rang Sally.

'Lunch sweetheart? Got something funny to show you.'

As they sat down to their spaghetti at a restaurant close to the office where Sally was working he pulled out the sheaf of legal papers that had been served on him that morning.

'What's this?' she asked.

'Read on sweetheart; you'll have a laugh.'

183

'Divorce? She wants to divorce you? Are you sure about this? What about your children? You know we are not going to live together – have you really thought this through?'

'Nothing is going to happen; I told you, this is just her way of trying to scare me into dropping you. She ought to know by now that I don't scare easily.'

They finished their lunch and he returned to his office to put a call through to his solicitor.

'Be careful Toby,' Sue warned him. 'From what you have told me of your wife I think she could be very dangerous. It takes some doing to persuade a judge to impose a Mareva so quickly. Besides, the firm she has instructed to act for her are big London boys who have a reputation for going for the jugular as expensively as possible.' Sue Jackson and Toby had known each other for years, and although she had never met Hilary, she had learned enough of her personality through conversations over regular lunches with him, and others who knew her, to be seriously worried for him.

'I'm not worried about her. She's not serious about a divorce – she would have to reduce her living standards, and there's no way she will ever do that, for Christ's sake. This is just her usual way of dealing with a problem – make it as expensive as possible. I suppose I shall have to pay her solicitors' exorbitant fees in any event. All I need you to do at the moment is get that Mareva lifted. Have you any idea what it will do to me in the city if word gets out that I can't pay my bills?'

'Toby, just remember, there are any number of legal tricks she could get up to – be very careful, please.' Sue continued to warn him.

He and Hilary spent the next few days avoiding contact with each other as much as possible, and when their paths did cross they sniped sarcastically at each other; the atmosphere in the house was electric with the tension between them.

Saturday dawned bright and clear and he left the house to drive to the office for a few hours. The slash marks on the two flat tyres of his Porsche looked suspiciously like knife cuts, but the garage would be able to come and fix that later and let him know the cause. He turned to the Bentley to find the bonnet of that had been severely damaged too, and from the position of the concrete flower urn laying upside down in the middle of the driveway it made sense to assume that someone had bounced it across the car bonnet, but of course he could be wrong. He sighed as he got into the driver's seat – what a fucking waste of money, he thought.

Back home for lunch before meeting Sally at 3 o'clock, he

rummaged in the fridge for something to eat since Hilary was not inclined to cook for him these days, and discovered some left over potatoes, which he sautéed with a quick mushroom omelette, and sat down to eat.

Hilary was angry – very, very angry, he had not talked to her about her divorce petition, and even seemed to be taking the whole thing as a huge joke.

'You could have asked me first before raiding the fridge – I was saving those potatoes for the children's supper – how dare you just take what you want!' She threw herself at him and grabbed his cutlery, cutting her hand on his knife as she did so.

'YOU FUCKING BASTARD – NOW LOOK WHAT YOU'VE DONE TO ME!' she screamed, running from the kitchen, wrapping a clean towel round the slice in her palm as she fled, but as she got to the hall an idea occurred to her, and a sly smile spread across her face as she diverted quietly to the study where she picked up the telephone and dialled 999.

'Hello, get me the police quickly please – my husband has just attacked me with a knife.' Replacing the receiver she raced up to the bedroom to await the arrival of the boys in blue.

Within minutes, and much to Toby's amazement, he found himself under arrest. When he learned what the charge was he exploded.

'What the hell are you talking about, you stupid bloody woman? Officers, I swear on my children's' lives I did not attack her – we were having a row and she grabbed the knife from me and sliced her hand in the process. This is fucking ridiculous.'

'All right, sir, we'll have less of the bad language if you don't mind. We'll sort this out at the station, and you'll have to come along with us I'm afraid.'

Sue Jackson's warning came back to him – how right she was.

The one phone call he was permitted to make was to Sally. 'Sweetheart, you'll never guess what that stupid bitch has done!' he yelled into the phone. 'She's only got me arrested. I'm in Sevenoaks nick, and they're going to keep me here till Monday morning, then I've got to go before a judge on a charge of attacking her with a knife. Get up here, please, I haven't got any cigarettes and they expect me to sleep on a hard slab with only a filthy blanket and it's freezing. Please sweetheart, do something.'

When she arrived at the police station with a weekend's supply of cigarettes, a duvet and pillows for him, she found him fuming. 'Sue was right. She warned me Hilary would try something, and since it's Saturday afternoon no judge is going to sit till Monday morning – she's got me boxed in for the whole weekend; oh, very clever!'

There was nothing anyone could do till Monday morning, so Sally spent the weekend doing the 40-mile journey to keep him company and watch him chain smoke, since he wasn't allowed a lighter in his cell.

'Right Mr Havers, out you come,' said the duty sergeant as he opened the cell door on Monday morning. 'You're up before the Judge this morning, let him sort this out.'

'Oh, come on Sarge, I've had no access to soap and water since my shower at home on Saturday morning, you surely don't expect me to defend myself in Court in the same clothes I've had on all weekend, I stink. Can we just stop by my house so I can shower, shave and change – please?' he pleaded.

'We're not supposed to, you know, but if you can be quick I suppose we can make an exception. Mind you, someone will have to accompany you.'

'I couldn't care less, just as long as I can get rid of the stink of this place and clean up. Thanks'.

They arrived at the High Court in the Strand at 10 o'clock to be met by Sue Jackson and David Silver, the barrister she had appointed at the last minute following Sally's panic call to her home on the Saturday afternoon to tell her where Toby was and what had transpired.

'Silly boy,' she said. 'I warned you to watch that woman.'

'All rise,' ordered the Clerk to the Court as the judge made his entrance. After the opening formalities Hilary's barrister rose to make the case that the husband had brutally attacked the wife following an altercation two days earlier, and it was the wife's submission that she considered herself to be in some physical danger from future attacks due to the husband's excessive drinking habits. Her application was that the husband should be removed from the marital home forthwith.

'Mr Silver?' queried his Honour addressing Toby's barrister. 'What does your client have to say to me regarding this disturbing accusation?'

'Your Honour. My client absolutely and categorically refutes such an allegation. May it please your Honour to know that the couple before you have been together for twelve years, married for nine, during which time there have been many heated exchanges between them, and it is no secret that the marriage is presently under some strain. However, my client is not a violent man, and the unhappy incident of Saturday last, the result of which sees him before you now, occurred as a result of a misunderstanding between the two parties. The facts of the matter are that Mrs Havers tried to forcibly remove an eating knife from my client's hand, action that was resisted by him, but which resulted in the slight injury to Mrs Havers's hand. There was, your Honour, no malicious attack upon her person.

'However, as a result of the heightened atmosphere within the matrimonial home, my client is anxious that there should be no repeat of these allegations – howsoever they came about – especially in view of the fact that there are three sons of the family whose well-being must be considered as paramount.

'Your Honour, under the circumstances I feel it is my duty to advise the Court that there is a divorce suit pending between the parties here present, the papers for which were served on my client by the wife just a week ago. If it pleases the Court to deal with this matter today and grant the decree nisi, my client will be content to vacate the matrimonial home forthwith, and save a great deal of valuable Court time defending this present unjust allegation. All matters concerning substantive issues and custody of the children will be dealt with at the earliest opportunity, but for the time being my client is content for his children to remain under the care of Mrs Havers at the matrimonial home, and he gives his undertaking to continue paying the household outgoings, exactly as he has done in the past, until a date for the substantive hearing can be agreed.'

His Honour would indeed like to save not only valuable Court time, but his own as well. The cases upon which he had been required to adjudicate that morning had proven to be particularly arduous, and he knew there was a rather tasty game pie awaiting his arrival at his favourite restaurant around the corner – game that he had in fact shot himself just three weeks earlier and proudly presented to his friend the chef who agreed to hang the bag until they were nicely ripe. If this case was despatched swiftly he could just about squeeze in a quick dry martini before lunch, followed by a few glasses of a good, full-bodied red. His mouth began to water at the very thought of it, and he could almost smell the aroma from the rich port wine sauce, feel the ever-so slightly crispy golden pastry melting on his tongue, but with a supreme effort he forced such tantalising expectation to the back of his mind for the time being – there was this matter before him to be concluded first. He rested his chin on his hand, elbow on the bench, exhaled the remainder of the game aroma from his nostrils and surveyed the angry looking couple before him. I think I can safely say that I wouldn't be doing anyone any favours by stringing this matter out, he thought to himself.

'Mrs Havers,' he addressed Hilary, who politely and demurely rose to her feet. 'The case you are putting before this Court is that your husband attacked you with a knife, cutting your hand in the process. Is that correct?'

'Yes, your Honour, it is,' she replied, trying to look vulnerable with downcast eyes.

'And I am told you have filed a petition for divorce against your husband. Is this also correct?' His features set in a gentle smile; poor woman was obviously going to be relieved to get out of this marriage.

'Yes, your Honour.'

'Mrs. Havers, this divorce application of yours, was it frivolous?' His Honour was clearly not going to muddle the facts.

Hilary panicked. How the hell do you tell a judge you were using the services of the Royal Courts of Justice merely to warn your husband off a certain course of action?

'Er, well, no, your Honour, of course not. It was like this . . .'

The game pie was not going to be easily relegated to the recesses of His Honour's mind, nor was he in the mood to sit through any more time listening to a woman moaning about the shortcomings of her husband – in case that was what she had in mind – it was all he had heard all damn morning.

'Yes, yes, quite so, thank you, I have my notes on the matter. Please be seated.' He turned to address Toby's barrister. 'Well, as you say Mr Silver, in the interests of everyone here I think it would be right and proper to grant the decree nisi – it is clearly what is in the best interests of both parties, and the husband has agreed to remove himself from the matrimonial home forthwith whilst maintaining the existing financial arrangements concerning the support of the wife and children for the time being. A most satisfactory outcome all round I do believe,' and he rose from the bench.

'All rise!' called the Clerk.

'Sue, where did you find that genius of a barrister?' Toby asked as he left the Court with his favourite solicitor.

'I've used David Silver on a number of cases in the past, and always successfully. Thought you'd approve. I gave him the bare bones of the divorce situation and I suspect he took the opportunity to turn it to your advantage.' Sue Jackson smiled at him as he waited with her for David Silver to finish collecting his papers and join them in the exquisitely vaulted main entrance hall of the Royal Courts of Justice. All around them others, who were not hurrying to and fro with bundles of papers and thoughtful or worried expressions, were admiring its majestic Gothic architecture faced with aged Portland stone. There was a feeling of reverence, even subservience, when passing through the Victorian maze of passages leading to 88 different Courtrooms, almost as though the adjudicated affairs of people passing through these hallowed halls were embedded in the very fabric of the walls.

'David old son, you were magnificent. Come on the pair of you, we're going across to the Waldorf for some fizz to celebrate – what a result.' Toby was back on top, the horrors of the weekend were tucked away into the dark recesses of a distant memory.

He ordered a bottle of Veuve Cliquot from the steward and asked for some smoked salmon sandwiches.

'I am sorry sir, we don't serve sandwiches in the bar,' came the quiet reply.

'Fair enough. Could you then perhaps bring us a plate smoked salmon with wedges of lemon, please?'

'Certainly sir. Would here be anything else, sir?'

'Ah, yes. Would you also be so good as to bring us some thinly sliced, buttered brown bread, please?' Shades of DIY sandwiches were creeping in here.

'Certainly sir.'

'Then please do that, my good man. I'm in far too good a mood to argue the point with anyone, and we are hungry.'

'Very good, sir.'

The atmosphere in the bar of the Waldorf Hotel in London's Aldwych was that of a gentleman's club; deep winged armchairs all slightly tired and worn through use by thousands of visitors, who over the years had enjoyed the gentile air that the bar exuded. It boasted large, low coffee tables and the gentle hum of lowered voices, nobody wishing to intrude boisterously on another's tranquillity.

All except Toby of course, who was on a high. Whilst he waited for the ingredients for his smoked salmon sandwiches to arrive he went in search of a pay phone.

'Sweetness!' he yelled at the phone when Sally answered her extension at work. 'I'm divorced! Can you believe it?'

Stunned silence was not quite the reaction he had hoped for.

'Speak to Toby.' he commanded.

'I'm sorry,' she said rather faintly. 'If you're not playing one of your silly jokes just tell me what happened.'

So he did. He talked her through the whole story from the time the police accompanied him to his shower at his house right up to the Champagne and smoked salmon that was waiting for him.

'Come on up, sweetheart, come and join us. This is a huge celebration and I want you here with me. I really wish you could have seen the look on Hilary's face, she was furious and looked as if she could have killed both the judge and me – though I'm not sure in what order.'

'Don't be daft – I've got an afternoon's work ahead of me, I can't just take half the day off – my name's not Toby Havers, I have a boss expecting brilliant things of me. I'm pretty sure this won't be the end of your high jinks – no doubt you'll still be on your pink cloud when I next see you; let's save it till then. Go on back to your friends and have one for me.' He was divorced? She was stunned. Where was he going to live? Did this change things at all, she wondered

He fondly waved Sue off in a taxi, and shook David's hand before watching him stroll back to his chambers just a short walk away. Where on earth was he going to sleep tonight now that he had been kicked out of his home? He caught a train to Sevenoaks station and hailed a taxi giving his home address.

'YOU'RE NOT ALLOWED HERE, I'VE GOT A COURT ORDER. I'M GOING TO CALL THE POLICE AND HAVE YOU ARRESTED AGAIN!' Hilary yelled at him.

'Don't be a stupid bitch, I'm not coming near you,' he sneered at her. 'I need to pick up some clothes and a car.'

'Boys!' Hilary screamed for her two sons, since George was away at boarding school. 'Your father's going to attack me again. If he does you must run away quickly and call the police.'

'What the fuck do you think you're doing? Are you trying to poison the kids against me? I knew you could stoop pretty low, but that is disgusting.' Toby growled at her. He took each of his younger boys by the shoulder. 'William, Simon, I don't want you to worry, I'm not going to touch your mother – I have never hurt her and I never will, that's my promise. She's only angry because she doesn't like me seeing another lady. What she says about me hurting her is all rubbish, you know me better than that, and you know I love you both very much don't you? Well, I'm going away for a little while so that there'll be no more arguments in the house, but I'll ring every day to talk to you and say goodnight. All right?'

Both youngsters looked nervously at him, their hazel eyes mirroring his own, and moved closer to Hilary who was now looking triumphant.

'See, I told you. Don't bother trying to ring them, nobody wants you here, not them, not me. Get the clothes you want, be quick about it and get out before I have you arrested,' she snarled.

His boys, his precious boys – they were looking at him as if he was some sort of monster. His heart ached as he realised what she had spent the weekend doing. Whilst he was incarcerated by the boys in blue, she had been poisoning his sons' little minds against this violent monster who was no longer fit to be their father.

'You unspeakable bitch,' he breathed through clenched teeth, as he went up to his former bedroom, grabbed arms full of clothes and filled the back seat of the Bentley with them, then drove angrily out of the driveway with no clear idea of where to go next. For the first time in his life he was homeless and in something of a state of limbo, so he drove into the town centre to find himself a local hotel for a few nights.

The hotel manager had seen a few strange sights during his career serving the public, but this had to rank amongst the oddest. He observed a man drive into the car park in a fairly new top of the range Bentley Turbo with a personalised number plate and badly damaged bonnet, watched him throw a few clothes around on the back seat and emerge bearing a complete change of attire, then dive back again for a toothbrush.

No, Sir had no idea how many nights he was planning to stay, and no thank you, Sir did not want either a newspaper or a bloody wake-up call. Sir was quite adamant on those points. His day had gone from waking up in a police cell, being watched by another man whilst he showered, the euphoria of the hour in the High Court, then the crushing blow of what the bitch had done to his boys. Sir was probably going to get very drunk tonight, and Sir felt he would not be out of order on this one.

Chapter 25

The lashing rain and heavy, overcast skies did nothing to lighten his mood. He was not accustomed to taking orders from anyone, and being ordered out of his home and leaving his precious boys to Hilary's vicious brainwashing was weighing heavily with him.

He had to sort out some accommodation pretty soon, the hotel was not a long-term option and buying a new home was going to take time.

'Hilary?' he barked down the phone at her. 'There are some more things I need from the house.'

'Like what?' she snapped back.

'I need one of the spare beds and some bedding.'

'What for?'

'Mind your own bloody business. You gave up your right to ask questions when you divorced me.'

'You'll have to get someone else to come round for them, I'm not having you come near us. I'll leave them in the garage tomorrow morning.' And she slammed the receiver down.

A few months earlier he had bought a derelict hotel that he was planning to demolish in order to build a prestigious office block, the top floor of which was secure and in reasonable condition. He decided it could be his home for the next few weeks until he could buy something more permanent, so the next morning he asked a friend with a van to call round to the house and collect the bed and bedding from the garage, as arranged.

'I hope this is OK Toby,' said his friend with the van on his return. 'Only you did say to collect a bed and bedding for you but there was only an old single mattress there. It looks a bit manky to me and there wasn't any sign of any bedding.'

'The bitch!' fumed Toby. 'I remember that old mattress, it's come from the attic and should have been thrown out years ago. She was supposed to leave me a complete spare bed from one of the guest rooms. Do me a favour, take it to the nearest tip, I'll have to buy something and get it delivered.'

Next stop was sourcing a new bed from a bedding shop; delivery was promised for two weeks. Two weeks? What the hell am I going to do for two bloody weeks? he asked himself. He certainly didn't fancy the hotel for that long – too impersonal, no home comforts.

He wasn't in the mood to put in any hours at work – nothing pressing needed his attention, the office could look after itself for a day or

192

two, so he drove down to Uckfield where Sally was busily preparing an evening meal for herself and her children.

'Come in and join us,' she invited him. 'It's only a chicken casserole, nothing fancy, but you're very welcome.'

'You know something?' he said. 'I think that sentence of yours has just solved a life long problem of mine; I think you have discovered how it was I managed to cock up so completely each time we got together over the years. Think back over all the times we have spent together; all the fancy hotels, all the meals we have had together in fancy restaurants. I reckon I must have given you completely the wrong idea of me and the things I really like. You think I only like expensive meals, Savoy, Claridges, all that crap. That's just because I like pushing the boat out every now and again; just my way of enjoying my little successes every now and again, especially when I'm with someone I want to share it all with. But my favourite meal of all time is shepherd's pie – I could eat that every day of the week for months without ever being bored. Bet that's surprised you.

'Did I tell you about the time I went to Spain to stay with my parents, a few years ago now? Full of myself I was, Jack the lad. I was confident my Spanish was pretty fluent and I wanted to address the waiter in his own lingo, so asked him to bring me a plate of "Apollo con patatas". Chicken and chips is easy in Spanish and I couldn't figure out why he kept questioning my order. "Listen my good man", I told him, "I know what I want. Just bring me a plate of Apollo con patatas, there's a good chap". So he did. What I didn't know was the Spanish word for chicken is pollo, and Apollo was a brand of ice cream. But I'm British, don't you know,' he said standing tall with his hands clutching the lapels of his jacket. 'I ate the ice cream and chips pretending it was exactly what I had ordered. Well, what else could I do?' His laughter infected the whole room.

Her chicken casserole did indeed smell good. He tried to remember the last time he had eaten a proper home-cooked meal. Hilary had refused to cook for him since she had been told about Sally. Then he'd been incarcerated all weekend followed by four nights in a hotel. Must be all of a month, he calculated. Her home was so warm and welcoming, something he hadn't enjoyed for a long time.

'Sweetpie, I'm in something of a dilemma,' he said. 'I really don't want to spend any more time in that poxy hotel. It's costing me an arm and a leg and I'm really missing my home comforts. Any chance I could stay here for a while, just till my new bed is delivered, shouldn't be more than a couple of weeks?'

She could see what was coming. Was this the thin end of the wedge

– the start of a new chapter? Yes, probably. Things had certainly moved very quickly this last week and the goal posts had changed somewhat.

'I guess so. It will certainly give us a chance to get to know each other incredibly well.'

After the children had gone to bed they sat curled up together in front of the fire and talked.

'You'll never know how much I love you, but I do hope that one day you will find out,' he told her. 'Ever since that first day you walked into my office looking for a house in 1966 you have been the only woman for me.'

'That's nonsense,' she smiled at him. 'You didn't know me then and you still don't really know me now. Besides, you have married two other women whom you must have loved.'

She felt him sigh as he thought about it. 'I think I married Sam on the rebound from you. You've seen her photo, you can surely see how alike you are in looks, same height, both blonde, plus she had a fantastic sense of humour. She was a great girl, but it wasn't quite right, there was a vital ingredient missing – I needed something more than she could give me which I tried to find in other women – she wasn't too keen on that for some reason,' he said with a crooked smile. 'As for Hilary, well, if you remember I wanted to call off my wedding to her when you came back from South Africa in '77 – that's how much she meant to me deep down. But you wouldn't marry me then and she wasn't bad looking in those days. I wanted more children, which meant I needed a wife, and she has at least produced two beautiful boys and been a mother to George. We had some good times in the early days, but it was never going to work – she wasn't you. You and I could have had better times – and we will, I promise you. In fact I have an idea. How about meeting me for a drink at the Ritz in Piccadilly tomorrow – say 11 o'clock?' Now he was positively bubbling with anticipation; it took more than the small matter of a divorce to keep him down.

And so it was on Saturday that Sally found herself sitting in the bar of the Ritz at 11 o'clock, as arranged. No Toby in evidence, so she ordered a glass of Chardonnay and settled back with her newspaper to wait for him. Five minutes later he came flying through the revolving doors, took the few steps into the bar two at a time and seized a passing waiter. 'Bring me another glass of whatever she's having, there's a good chap – here's a tenner for now – we'll be back in five minutes.' And he grabbed Sally by the hand, positively running her out of the door that was still revolving from his hasty entrance, and once on the pavement ordered her to close her eyes. For good measure he placed his hands over her eyes as well and guided her towards Piccadilly Circus. After a few steps he pushed open a door and propelled her, still sightless, into what felt like a shop.

'No, don't look – just hold your arms out from your sides.' She did as she was bid, wondering what on earth he was up to now, until she felt a huge weight being placed over her arms and realised she was being dressed in a very heavy coat. Her eyes sprang open, and she gazed in amazement at the beautiful platinum fox coat in which she was now encased and that almost reached her ankles.

'My God, Toby – you can't do that – this coat must cost a small fortune, and when on earth would I wear something like this?'

'Don't worry about it, sweetheart, for you I can afford it. I've not been able to spoil you in the past, and I want to make up for it now. This is just the beginning; now come on, we've got a drink waiting for us next door.'

He waved his thanks to the shop assistants, who were grinning widely at the amazement on Sally's face, and he took her back to the Ritz to finish their wine.

Life settled into something of a pattern for them, and after a week they began to feel like an old married couple; him coming back from his office in Sevenoaks, she seeing to the mundane tasks of meals and laundry for everybody, but he wasn't comfortable living under Richard's roof for any longer than was absolutely necessary. He had also taken to parking his Bentley away from the house since Richard had developed the habit of driving past to see if his car was outside. Too much hassle. Although Richard had been to see a lawyer, and their divorce was going through its due process, there was no point in taking unnecessary chances, knowing how heavily Richard had taken his presence in Sally's life.

> *She was blonde,*
> *Incredibly blonde,*
> *And fond,*
> *Incurably fond*
> *Of love,*
> *And you.*
> *I loved her too.*
>
> *Her mind,*
> *Einstein's mind,*
> *Enquiring too;*
> *But fond,*

*Incurably fond
Of love,
And you.
I loved her too.*

*Her body,
Cleopatra's body,
Long legs too;
But she was fond,
Incurably fond
Of love,
And you.
I loved her too.*

*Then she found,
Looking around,
She's my love too.
So now we've found
Looking around,
No hope's too tall
For love.*

*And now she's fond,
Incredibly fond
Of me,
Not you.
You loved her too.*

He had been ringing Hilary constantly trying to arrange to see his children but she was having none of it – she wouldn't even allow them to come to the phone and he was becoming increasingly frustrated by her actions. 'I'm going to see her in Court,' he told Sally. 'I've got to do something. I'm not having my boys growing up not knowing me.'

Hilary laughed when her solicitors told her she was required to attend Court to settle the matter of her ex-husband's contact with his children. If he thinks I'm going to let him anywhere near them he's got another think coming, she thought to herself smugly.

Her lawyer's ruthless reputation was not proving false, and he quickly put her mind at rest. 'Don't worry Mrs Havers,' he purred. 'There are all sorts of ways of keeping him away from your children, just leave it all to us. Perhaps you might like to pop in for a conference. How are you fixed later this week?'

The High Court Judge, Family Division, took a dim view of mothers trying to keep fathers away from the children of a relationship, and made it quite clear that he wasn't going to give her an easy ride. After he had listened patiently to the arguments put forward by both sides he rested his forearms on the bench and pronounced: 'I warn the mother that unless she is more open to compromise, it is my experience that the children will turn against her in years to come, as they will eventually realise their mother may have had another, personal agenda in place that has kept them from enjoying a full and wholesome relationship with their father. I take on board the fact that perhaps the father has drunk too much in the past, and understand the mother's concerns with regard to that particular issue. But the father has given me his assurance that he will not drink any alcohol before or during any access that this Court may see fit to award. The next consideration is: who is to accompany the children on any initial access arrangements? Clearly it cannot be the mother. May I have some suggestions in this regard please?'

Toby put forward the names of various mutual friends, together with some background information on them, that he felt the Court might accept. Hilary rejected all of them – even her former best friend, since she felt the friend now sympathised with the enemy. Hilary provided the names of two women that Toby had never heard of before. One of them being the friend that had suggested the ball-breaking London lawyers – a real man-hater.

'Mr Havers, do you have any objections to the names put forward by the mother?' asked His Honour.

'Your Honour it is difficult for me to object since I don't know either of them – they must be brand new acquaintances of hers. It seems daft to me that she can object to life long friends who the boys know and who get on with both of us, and only trust virtual strangers.'

'Unless you have any objection to either of these ladies Mr Havers, can I assume that we have reached something of an agreement? And although it may not be totally satisfactory to all parties concerned, it may be a way out of this difficult situation,' intoned His Honour, peering over the top of his half moon glasses and smiling benignly at the small crowd arranged in orderly fashion before him. Umm, I do wonder whether this will all work out, he thought to himself.

Toby was delighted. He was at last going to get to see his adored boys on

Saturday afternoon. The Court had arranged specific dates for his access until such time as he and Hilary could work out a more fluid arrangement, and every second Saturday afternoon was going to be his, for now.

He was beside himself with excitement on the Saturday morning, really looking forward to seeing his boys, together with the stranger who was going to accompany them, at Gatwick Zoo. He was desperate to be with them again and try to rebuild the relationship between them that had been so badly damaged.

He kept himself busy by calling in at the office for a few hours in the morning, and as he dropped into his chair the telephone rang.

'Toby – you can't see the boys this weekend,' came Hilary's frosty tones. William's not well enough.'

'What do you mean William's not well? What's wrong with him?' he demanded.

'He has a cold; he's in bed and not well enough to see you. You'll have to wait for another two weeks now.' she retorted icily.

'No I won't,' he replied, seething, but trying to keep calm. I can still see Simon and George.'

'Sorry – I've already told my friend who was taking them to meet you that access is off today, and she's now made other arrangements for the afternoon.'

'You bitch, you're enjoying this aren't you?' he hissed at her. 'In that case I'll see them next weekend instead to make up for today. In the meantime, please give them all a kiss from me.'

'No you won't. I've made other arrangements for next weekend. The Court has ordered the dates when you're allowed to see them, and you can't just change them unilaterally. You'll have to wait another two weeks until the proper date.' Slam.

'Mette!' she called to the au pair as she wandered through to the kitchen. 'Get the boys out of the pool please, it's time for their lunch then we're going to my mother's for the afternoon.'

198

Chapter 26

As much as Toby's dream had come true now that he and Sally were effectively living together, he was not finding it easy to live at Uckfield. He had to endure an extra long journey to and from his office each day, plus there was the understandable nervousness of Richard finding he was staying there and perhaps doing something aggressive about it. So as soon as his new bed was delivered he made himself a temporary home on the top floor of the derelict hotel he had bought, and Sally spent the day helping to make it comfortable for him; she brought over pillows that he had forgotten to buy, a spare bedside lamp, some vases for flowers for him and a small table.

She was also quite relieved that he was no longer under her feet in her small home, his larger than life personality seemed to fill the house to overflowing each time he came through the door, and she had been so looking forward to some space and time on her own with the children after Richard decamped permanently to his Brighton pub. She needed to be clear in her own head about what she was doing, and for that she needed time alone with her thoughts. It was important that she was leaving Richard because their relationship had broken down, not just because of Toby. She still had her bookkeeping job, and found handling other people's affairs for them quite rewarding, plus at the end of each day there were her children to enjoy and some of the solitude that she had been craving.

She could choose when to allow Toby to come down to see her, or when she would go up to him, and life began to settle into a fairly tranquil pattern, but when they were apart she found herself missing him much more than she had imagined was possible. When they were together he inspired and stimulated her, gave her confidence and courage, and she felt herself growing closer and closer to him with each passing week. The more time she spent with him the more she learned about him, the warmth of the real inner man not the brash protective façade he showed to the world. She discovered that the loud insensitive exterior he so often displayed was used to cover his insecurity, and found it hard to believe that he could lack self-confidence. But as he began to believe that at last she wasn't about to take flight again, he allowed her to see the small cracks in his armour that he normally kept papered over with bravado and alcohol. As they lay quietly in each other's arms in the dark of night he talked softly to her about himself; his childhood, his timidity that he had known he had to overcome in order to survive, especially in the face of bigger boys at boarding school. He had learned how to conquer every insurmountable hurdle placed before him, but sometimes had to shut his eyes and call upon resolve in whatever shape and form he had within him in order to achieve it, and never let the outside world know he wasn't fully up to the job. He had to be seen to win whatever the cost. It was survival. When she had first walked into his office that day something told him that she would be the backbone of his life, and together they would forge a brilliant future. But it was not to be; he recognised now that he had been too fanatical, too rash, and each time failure piled on failure he found he was behaving more and more irrationally with her, his desperation to win her blocking any normal behaviour. 'It was no wonder you fled from me in the past, sweetheart,' he said ruefully. 'Looking back I frightened myself.'

'Fancy coming down to Bournemouth with me this weekend, my love?' he asked one evening. 'I'm going down to see some friends and I would like them to meet you.'

As they drew up at the Yacht Club Toby reached into his pocket and produced a small jeweller's box.

'By the way sweetheart, this is for you – hope you like it.'

As she opened the small box she found herself staring at the most exquisite ring. The magnificent rose-cut diamond in the centre winked and sparkled at her, flashing its fire as she slowly lifted it from its setting in the black velvet lining, and the eight emeralds surrounding it were the deepest, purest green and glowed with the deep purity of their colour.

'Toby, this is absolutely beautiful. How did you know that emeralds are my favourite stones?'

'Your mother told me,' he replied happily. She seemed to be delighted by his gift and started to put it on the third finger of her right hand. 'No, sweetheart. Left hand please, you know that's where it belongs.'

As she looked up into the warmth of his smiling eyes she felt the full force of his love for her boring deep into her very core. The power of it was like an electric shock that passed through first her heart, then her stomach and finally turned her legs to jelly. She sat frozen for a moment, staring deeply back at him and feeling that the world had stopped turning for the briefest of moments, and when it restarted everything was going to be different somehow.

'Come on woman, hurry up – I want my friends to meet you.' In order to forestall any argument he got out of the car, and she watched him sauntering happily over the road. She had a choice: leave the ring where it was on her right hand, be sensible, and take more time over her decision, or pay some attention to what had just burned through her whole body, put the ring where he wanted it to be, and let the whole thing sort itself out in the fullness of time.

As she walked into the bar after him she saw him glance down at her hands. 'Just checking, sweetheart,' he said, and gave her the biggest hug, his face bursting with happiness and pride as he saw she had changed the ring over to the third finger of her left hand. He introduced her to Pat Bennett and a whole crowd of strangers that were genuinely pleased to see this crazy man – it had been a long time since he had last visited his old stamping ground. This was a whole new world of his about which she knew nothing. Some of them had known Hilary, so had to be brought up to speed on recent events.

'Serves her right, old chap. Never thought she was right for you, far too much of a madam,' said Pat.

'Well, if you'd been a real mate you would have bloody told me,' snorted Toby.

'Yeah, like you'd have listened.' parried Pat, and the whole bar rocked with laughter.

Toby and Sally stayed with Pat at his beautiful home in Canford Cliffs for the weekend. The two men went out fishing on his boat on the Sunday morning and caught a bucket full of sardines for a simple bar-b-que brunch; Sally and Pat's girlfriend prepared some bread and salad, and the four of them sat laughing and chatting in the Easter sunshine until it was time for the visitors to leave.

Sally had thoroughly enjoyed the weekend, not remembering when she had last laughed so much.

'This is just the beginning sweetheart,' he told her as she thanked him for taking her. 'We are going to have a lifetime of laughs, you and I, just you wait and see.'

A diamond ring upon your hand
Spells love,
And with that very special band
Keep love.

There will be times you will regret,
Keep love,
Because your ring, you may forget
Spells love.

Keep it to your dying day,

Keep love.
Even when your peers say:
"Lose love".

Smile at the glisten on your hand,
It's love.
Ne'er forget that special bond
Means love.
Ne'er forget.

Chapter 27

Life on the top floor of the derelict hotel was becoming a bore and Toby was desperate to move into a home of his own, preferably with the love of his life. And, with her in mind, he attended an auction that included the sale of a recently redeveloped property that had originally been the gatekeeper's lodge of a large estate in the country, halfway between where her children were at school and where his children were living with Hilary.

He had taken Sally round to see the house several days before the auction, and was thrilled at her reaction to the pretty, 4-bedroom, Tudor style property with its masses of exposed old oak beams set in five acres of lawn, gardens and woodland, the nearest neighbour being a quarter of a mile away in each direction. 'How would you like this to be our new love-nest, sweetheart?' he asked.

She was uncomfortable at leaping out of one relationship straight into another, regardless of the new feelings for him that were beginning to well up inside her – that had never been the plan. 'Well, let's see if you are able to buy it first, then we can talk again, OK?' she procrastinated. Progress – she hadn't said no.

Experience at auctions over the years had made him an old hand at bidding, and this one was going to be a piece of cake; he was determined to buy The Old Lodge for her even if he had to pay a little over the odds. He just about had the cash for it, providing there was no hiccup in the property market, although the financial papers were giving credence to rumours of a forthcoming property crash and global recession.

On the other side of Kent things were becoming increasingly difficult with Hilary. She absolutely refused to let him see his beloved boys, regardless of the Court Order that he should see them every second week, and merely made one excuse after another that were hard for him to counter. One week it would be due to illness of one of the younger ones – two weeks later it would be the turn of the other to 'fall ill'. At other times it was an eagerly awaited birthday party to which they had been invited, or perhaps a longstanding arrangement that simply could not be changed without upsetting the boys, and he would surely not want to upset them, would he? When Toby suggested altering the access dates to more convenient weekends she argued that those were the dates stipulated by the Court – it was not her fault that they were not easy to comply with; she was doing her best, but in order that some stability might be retained in their poor, blighted lives, prior arrangements had to come first – and the phone would be slammed down.

But one thing Hilary did not like doing was driving George back to his private school, it was over a hundred miles away, and she struggled to drive herself to the corner shop for her cigarettes, never mind half way across the country, but someone had to take him back to school after the Easter holiday, together with his over sized tuck box.

'Toby? You'll have to take George back to school tomorrow,' came the imperious demand on the answer phone of his office. 'I'll make sure he's ready on the front doorstep tomorrow at 10 o'clock with his trunk. Don't try to come in or I'll call the police, I won't have you in my house. Just make sure you're not late.' Slam.

Toby thought it was about time his first-born met the love of his life, and Sally drove to his temporary home at the hotel whilst he collected George from the house.

'What are we doing here, daddy?' asked George as they pulled up in front of the old hotel.

'There's someone I want you to meet, old sport,' he replied as Sally opened the front passenger door of the Bentley.

'Hello, you must be George. I'm Sally. How do you do?' And she leaned in to shake hands with him. He was far too polite to ignore the outstretched offer and shook hands with 'that woman', although clearly against his better judgement.

'In the back, George!' ordered his father. The 16-year old was too confused to argue against the injustice of being relegated to the rear of the car and did as he was bid.

Sally and Toby chatted amiably for the first few miles, trying to draw George into their conversation as much as possible, but his nose was distinctly out of joint – the front seat had always been his place when they did the school trips. Who was this woman in his father's life that he had been told was the sole cause of all the turmoil and unhappiness at home? Whoever she was, his father was certainly very comfortable and happy with her, and she was making them all laugh – something that was in seriously short supply at home. He was looking forward to getting back to school to get away from his stepmother for a while; he felt he was walking on eggshells around her at home. Very quietly he slipped his hand into his bag and produced a cassette that he was saving for his friends at school. If his stepmother had found it she would have been very angry, she would not have appreciated the sort of humour about to be tested on the two adults in the front of the car. Passing it over to Sally he asked innocently: 'Could you put this tape on, please?'

'Sure George – fed up with listening to your father's choice of Des O'Connor are you? – I must admit I'm with you on that one.' She laughed, pushing the cassette tape into the player, wondering if his choice of music would be anything like the screeching noise that her daughter Sarah enjoyed, and pleased that he seemed to have accepted her presence somewhat.

She wasn't left in doubt for very long as a barrage of blue expletives from Jimmy Jones filled the car. She roared with laughter. Toby roared with laughter, and George sat back grinning, now completely relaxed.

As they were approaching their turning off the motorway, Toby turned to his son. 'Do you want to stop at the Long Spoon for lunch, old sport, or would you rather I take you straight to school?'

Sally was pleased to hear him reply: 'No, lunch would be good, thanks dad.' Had he felt uncomfortable with her he would certainly have wanted to get away as soon as possible. Test number one seemed to have been passed.

'No, test number two,' was Toby's response when she whispered her thoughts to him. 'Test number one was when he put that Jimmy Jones tape on. Hilary would have had seven sorts of hysterics and locked him in his room – you laughed with him and passed his first test with flying colours. Well done, old girl.'

They ordered different starters for lunch, and each offered the other a taste from the dish in front of them, which meant sharing cutlery. George was having no problems sharing with Sally, and even seemed content with her coming up to see his room when they finally reached school.

'It's a real joy to see you two together, you obviously get on well,' said Sally on their journey home. 'What a shame Hilary won't let you have the same relationship with William and Simon. It's really not fair.'

'Umm, I can see I'm going to have to go back to Court on that one – someone's got to show the Judge what she's really like.' Things were no better; in fact it was now some four months since he had set eyes on his two youngsters, and it hurt that they were growing up without him.

'I'm sorry sir, I don't know how I should address you,' said Toby, nervously fidgeting with his tie as he stood before the Judge. His was an urgent exparte application, and he had never been before a Judge before without lawyers to do all the talking for him, plus he hadn't a clue whether this man about to adjudicate on his personal affairs was a "Your Honour, My Lord", or something else.

'Mr. Havers, I don't care how you address me so long as it's not "Guv". Your Honour will do nicely.'

'Thank you, your Honour.' Toby cleared his throat and shuffled a few papers around, then shuffled them back again. He was on top form when it came to dealing with the law where it related to property matters, but this was different, and he was completely out of his depth. His mouth was dry and the brandy he had downed just before the hearing had done nothing to calm him. He was sweating profusely, mopping his forehead, not knowing quite how to start.

'Mr Havers, forgive me if I appear to rush you, but I'm afraid I don't have all day, there is a serious family matter awaiting my presence in Court 32. I have allowed you to come before me this morning in the hope that your application would only take a few minutes, as is the usual case with these ex-parte matters. Please be so good as to be as brief as you can.'

'Yes, your Honour. Sorry, your Honour. Ahem . . . Four months ago his Honour Judge Simmons, sitting in this very Court, ordered that I should be allowed to see my children every two weeks, but each time I'm ready to collect them my ex-wife makes some excuse or other to prevent me from seeing them; sickness, important prior arrangements or something, plus she won't alter the dates to times when they are free and in good health, and I need an urgent order forcing her to comply with that original order. Please, your Honour.'

'Are you saying you have not seen your children at all since that Order, Mr Havers?'

'No, your Honour – I mean yes, your Honour, that's exactly what I am saying. Not once, and I'm becoming desperate,' he replied.

'Before I can rule on this I'm afraid I must hear what the mother has to say about it, Mr Havers. I can't just issue an order without hearing both sides of the problem.'

'But why, your Honour? She managed to get all my assets and bank accounts frozen several months ago at an ex-parte hearing. I had no say in the matter at all and it caused me no end of grief.'

'I'm afraid I couldn't possibly comment on that, Mr Havers. I presume you have legal advisers? Good. Then I suggest you ask them to arrange a suitable date with your ex-wife's advisers for a further hearing before me. Now if you will excuse me I need to be in Court 32. Good day Mr Havers.' And with that he left.

Toby felt he hadn't drawn a breath since he entered the Court. What was it about these rooms that reduced him to a quivering, sweating jelly? He felt in desperate need of another brandy – better make that a double – since it looked as though he wasn't going to get anywhere with the law today, and his boys were just as far away from him as they had been before he put himself through the judicial wringer. Talk about bloody frustrating.

'You did what?' demanded Sue Jackson, his lawyer, when he called her later in the day. 'I could have told you that would be the only result you could have expected – saved you the bother. A Judge can't issue an Order in respect of delicate family matters at one party's behest. He has to listen to both sides of the story for the children's benefit.'

'Then how come she got that Mareva in January, causing me all that financial grief, without me being given a chance to put my side?' he demanded.

'That's completely different. A Mareva injunction has the instant effect of stopping you from hiding or disposing of your assets and leaving your family destitute until you argue your case for having it lifted, which, if you remember, we did just a few days later. But the welfare of children is a different matter and has to be handled completely differently. Now then. I'll get hold of David Silver again for you and try and set up a hearing soon. Try not to get upset, you won't do yourself any good. And please, no more ex-parte applications without talking it over with me first.'

'Thanks, Sue. What's this going to cost me?' he wanted to know.

'Depends how long it takes, but we can't get to the High Court without a barrister, you know that, and they don't come cheap.'

'Well, that's easy then. Get the Court changed to a County Court. We don't need the bloody High Court, for Christ's sake. That's just Hilary's way of spending as much money as possible. How the hell is she managing to pay for expensive barristers, that's what I want to know?'

Sue was very used to dealing with Toby's bluster. They had known each other for years as a result of various legal matters and had a lot of mutual respect, but he could be very naïve sometimes. 'Toby, you're supposed to read the reams of paperwork I send you. She's mortgaged her anticipated award from you to her solicitors, that's how she can afford it. And as for getting the Court changed, I'm sorry, we can't do that. She has brought the action so we have to go to her lawyer's jurisdiction – which is the High Court I'm afraid, unless there are extremely good reasons for requesting a change. But I'm afraid your plea of financial impecuniosity is not likely to be taken seriously because the first thing the other side will raise in argument is your past extravagant lifestyle. I'm sorry, I know that's not what you want to hear, but you're just going to have to trust me and bite the bullet on this one. See me next week, we need to start talking about the proper way to handle these issues.'

'OK Sue, I'll buy you lunch when we've finished as well. I'm glad you're on my side.'

Chapter 28

'This could not be more appropriate,' shouted Toby, happily wandering through the empty rooms of The Old Lodge, jingling the keys to the recently bought property in his hands. 'Do you know what the date is, sweetheart?' he asked Sally.

'Yes, it's the 16th of May – why? What's so special about today?'

He held out his arms to her, and as she walked into them he said: 'It's not just today that's special. It was on the 16th of May in 1965 that I first opened the doors of my estate agency in Sevenoaks – my baby. Now, exactly twenty-three years later to the day, I have bought our first home together. Most appropriate.'

'I don't remember saying I was going to live with you.' she smirked at him.

'No, but you didn't say you wouldn't either, did you? I remember exactly what you said. You said let's wait until I have completed the purchase of this house then we can talk about it again. Well, I have completed the purchase of this house and now I'm telling you to pack up what you want from Uckfield and get your arse over here, girl. You need some serious looking after, and so do I.' He produced two Champagne flutes from the back seat of the Porsche and a bottle of rapidly warming Champagne.

'Cheers, sweetheart. Here's to new beginnings.'

It looked as though events were moving far more quickly than either of them could ever have imagined a few months earlier. They were both free agents now, to all intents and purposes, and both had different choices to make from those they had envisaged for themselves over the past few years. The smiling man standing in front of Sally, offering her a glass of Champagne from the back of the car, was asking her to throw her lot in with him, and sink or swim with him. Care for each other, he had said.

As she reached for the glass he was offering her, the rays of sunlight flitted briefly across the face of the diamond and emerald ring she was wearing on the third finger of her left hand. The bright light caught one of the diamond facets, and in the sudden brilliant flash of fire she saw clearly for the first time some of the facets that went to make up the man standing before her. He was just like the diamond he had given her, so many different sides to him. He could be kind and loving, compassionate and fun-loving, generous, romantic, gregarious, wistful and entertaining, but when turned another way she knew he could be sarcastic and hurtful, childish, hard-nosed, bombastic, secretive, self opinionated, even blatantly rude when things weren't going in his direction. But that was his mix; he asked for nothing more than to be taken for what he was, with all his facets.

When measured in feet and inches he was not the tallest of men, but he was the tallest of them all when measured in thoughtfulness to others and loyalty to his friends, who all clearly adored him. His physical heart, pumping away somewhere in the centre of his chest in the accepted standard rhythm, was probably no different from that of any other male of a similar standing, but she had seen frequent evidence of his loving kindness to his fellow man in need in so many different ways during the time they had been together. His ability to live life to the full seemed boundless, as was his capacity for laughter – as much at his own expense as at jokes, and his favourite pastime of winding people up could be really irritating at times. But there was a vulnerable quality to him as well – she reminded herself of the time he had come out to Newcastle to bring her back to England with him fourteen years earlier in 1974, and how lonely and desolated he had looked when she had turned him away. She knew he was passionate and single minded, and she knew he was genuinely suffering through the loss of his beloved children – a loss that he would not be suffering had it not been for her presence in his life. He was a seemingly very complex man, with a powerful but quirky mind that would take some understanding, but who was asking nothing of her at the moment but to allow him to love and care for her at close quarters.

'Cheers Toby – new beginnings.' she replied with a smile.

He could not have been happier. At night he would climb into bed and wrap her in his arms so fiercely that there were times she had to ask him to loosen his grip a bit so that she could breathe.

On the edge of sleep he whispered contentedly: 'You are my Merlinia.'

'What's a merlinia?' she whispered back.

'Merlin was a wizard, a man of magic. You are a magic woman, so you are my Merlinia.'

'Morning darling, oh good, it's Sunday!' he shouted at her, leaping out of bed.

'Yes, it's Sunday – so what? There's a whole pile of stuff to be done and I'm going to need a bit of help – please. Did you have other ideas, then?' She had hoped for a quiet day with the two of them clearing their little bit of woodland together and bringing in logs for their huge open fire.

It sounded as though he had plans though.

'You have a lot to learn my girl. Sunday is sacrosanct; Sunday is indulgence day, a day for a greasy fry-up and fizz and I'm in charge.'

And so the Sunday routine was set. He cooked large quantities of sausages, bacon, scrambled eggs, mushrooms, tomatoes and bubble and squeak on the open range every Sunday morning, all of which would be washed down with Champagne; after which they sat reading the papers together. Very little logging, or anything else for that matter, got done on a Sunday. The neighbours were frequently invited to join in the ritual, before everyone retired to the pub for a lunchtime beer, and every week that special day became a relaxed, happy blur.

They had no furniture with them; Sally had left everything for Richard to take to his flat over the Brighton pub once the Uckfield property was sold, and Toby had nothing but a few of his clothes from his former matrimonial home. Their new home slowly came together; it was a busy time – buying furniture and carpets, and making curtains for all the windows, which Sally thoroughly enjoyed doing. Then there was the garden. There was an acre of lawn to be mowed plus four acres of woodland to explore and clear. She wanted to see lots of colourful flowers everywhere, so set about digging the beds, and preparing and planting the chosen areas.

A new date in June was set for Hilary to give her reasons for not complying with the earlier Order. The Judge listened to Toby's complaints that he was not being given access to his two younger boys, and Hilary explained that each time an official access date arrived, the precise dates as laid down by the Court, one or other of the boys fell ill. She told the Court that she did wonder whether or not the boys were faking illness because they did not want to spend time with their father, but she had done her best to comply with the Order. Besides, the father had refused to pay for a trip to Spain for them and the boys were naturally upset at his meanness, he always used to be so generous before he left to go and live with another woman.

'Your Honour,' interjected David Silver, rising languidly to his feet. 'Since there is currently an issue surrounding access to the family home in Marbella because a legal dispute, Mrs Havers has asked my client to pay seven thousand pounds for herself and the children to stay at the Marbella Club Hotel for a month, which I am given to understand is one of the most expensive hotels in southern Spain. This my client feels is an unnecessary extravagance, especially since he is trying to maintain two homes.' And he resumed his seat.

None of this was new to His Honour, but there really was a very simple remedy. He ruled that the good offices of Social Services should be employed to appoint a suitable person to supervise each access until such time as the parents could be more flexible and sensible in making their own arrangements. 'I do stress to both parties, it will clearly be in everyone's interests, particularly those of the three children, to resolve matters between you as speedily as possible.'

'All rise!' commanded the Clerk as the Judge prepared to leave the Bench.

A Mrs Barton called Toby at home one evening, and introduced herself as the Social Services member who would be collecting the two younger boys from Hilary on Saturday afternoon, the children's health permitting. What she needed to know was: where was he planning to take them?

His mouth went dry. He was actually going to see his boys this time, he really was. 'How about Gatwick Zoo?' he suggested.

'I would say that was a splendid choice. Shall we say two o'clock at the entrance then?'

His mouth became even dryer when he saw his two precious boys sitting in the back of Mrs Barton's car, and he felt the strong need for a restorative. But he had undertaken not to drink before or during his time with them, and he didn't want anyone smelling anything on his breath and messing it up again.

'Hi kids!' he raced over to give each of them a big hug, but was met with cold indifference from nine-year-old William and seven-year old Simon, who constantly glanced at each other for support. 'What do you want to do first? How about an ice cream to start with?' He wasn't going to let this bad start get to him, he'd soon warm them up.

The boys looked at each other and shrugged. 'Mummy says you won't pay for our holidays in Spain anymore,' announced William. 'So we don't even want to be here.'

'Yeah,' agreed Simon.

'Well, I'm sorry about that boys, but it's not quite as simple as that I'm afraid. You both know how mummy and I used to fight a lot, don't you?'

Two sullen nodding heads.

'There's no fighting at home now, is there?'

Two sullen shaking heads.

'That's because I decided to leave and live somewhere else. It hurt

211

me very much to leave you, but I had to think about some way to stop the awful fighting between mummy and me, and now it has stopped, which must be better for you. I have a new home now that I would very much like you to come and see one day, then you will have two homes to play in. But in the meantime, because I am trying to pay for two homes, there isn't as much money to go around as there used to be.' He thought for a moment. 'Imagine if the front wheel of your bike was broken and you also wanted to buy a smart new saddle, but you only had enough pocket money for one thing – either fix the new front wheel or buy a new saddle, not both. What would you do?' The boys considered that for a moment, then William declared: 'Get the front wheel fixed.'

'Why?' asked his father.

'I couldn't ride it if the wheel was broken.'

'But you could ride it still with the old saddle – yes?'

'Yes.'

'Well that's exactly what's happening to me at the moment. I have to look at what's more important. Right now I am paying for things that you need, like food and all the other things that are important to keep you warm and comfortable, as well as the same things in my new house, but that means there's no money for extra things like holidays in the most expensive hotel in Spain. I promise that as soon as mummy and I get things sorted out between us things should be a lot better, it's just rather difficult at the moment. In the meantime, what about that ice cream, eh?'

The thawing process had begun, but he knew it was going to be a long uphill battle. Thankfully Mrs Barton had heard the boys passing on their mother's complaint, and she was not happy that they were being used in such a way. But other than that the afternoon went as well as could be expected under the circumstances – until they were ready to leave. 'Daddy, mummy said to tell you that you have to pay the phone bill or they will cut it off.'

'Tell mummy I can't pay it if I haven't seen it. Tell her to send it to the office and I'll have a look at it. OK?'

He and Mrs Barton exchanged a look that told him she was going to tell mummy not to ask the children to pass financial messages again, and after waving goodbye went straight to the pub to try and calm his shaking body, and called Sally to tell her how it had gone.

'Phew, that was like pulling back teeth to start with, sweetheart. I've never known them so cold, they always used to like a rough and tumble with their old dad – their mother's done a real hatchet job on them. Still it'll be better next time, I'm sure, the ice is broken now. Mrs Barton was OK –

212

think she's on my side. Every little bit helps. Oh, and apparently mummy wants me to drive them all down to Bournemouth next weekend to see granny. Tell you about it when I get in. See you in an hour or so.'

'Why doesn't she drive herself?' Sally wanted to know. 'She's got a perfectly good car.'

'She's never really liked driving, I don't mind driving them down, at least I'll get to see all the kids for a while, even under mother's jaundiced eye.'

Sally remembered what had happened the last time Hilary had been in Toby's car since she had been told they had been seeing each other. Hilary had conducted a thorough search through the glove compartment and the door pocket of the car looking for anything interesting; she had found a cassette that Sally had compiled for Toby including his favourite songs, and thrown it out of the window. This time would be different.

Sally completely emptied all the pockets of the car, and pasted a piece of paper just inside the door of the glove compartment on which she wrote in bold capitals: "Mind your own business, Hilary" when the little door was opened – and to the top of the paper she securely taped the end of the string of a tampon, allowing it to swing freely. Hilary did not find the prank at all amusing for some reason.

The sun was shining one early July afternoon, and Sally was on her knees to the side of the driveway, planting some new borders with colour, when a car pulled in. She stood up, brushing soil from her old gardening jeans ready to greet the unexpected visitor. Hilary instantly recognised the woman with the trowel in her hand and specks of mud on her nose and a look of shock spread across her face. She had asked at the village shop if a new couple had moved into the area within the last couple of months, and was told she had better ask at The Old Lodge – the couple there would know, and that was exactly what she was preparing to do, but she clearly hadn't bargained for this.

'Hello, Hilary, was there something you wanted?' Sally cheekily asked through the open window of the Mercedes sports car, grinning widely at its horrified occupant.

The car was slammed quickly into reverse and it shot backwards into the busy road at breakneck speed. Stupid woman, Sally muttered to herself, she could have killed herself driving like that.

She and Toby had a good giggle together that evening. 'Her heart must have stopped beating when she realised she had pulled into our driveway. She was obviously being nosey, trying to find out where we were

213

and what we were up to, and she must have been pretty desperate to drive herself all the way over here. Well, she got more than she bargained for, didn't she? Boy, I'd love to have been a fly inside her car when she left.' He was hooting with mirth.

Property deals were getting thinner and thinner and much more difficult to sustain; prices being asked for land were becoming silly, he felt. Solicitors, motorcar dealers, anyone with a little spare cash was getting into the property game, and Toby didn't like was he was smelling. He wondered if perhaps the recent rumours of a property crash were not so idle after all.

He had managed to see his beloved boys twice more, but each time they got out of Mrs Barton's car they were as cold as ice towards him, and he had to work hard at gaining their confidence again. Simon had a plaster on his finger and Toby asked him how he had hurt himself.

'Mummy says you're not allowed to ask us any questions.' came the blunt response. Subject closed.

Summer passed into autumn. It had been a hard year that had started with two nights spent in a police cell and a divorce, followed by three Court appearances and one ex-parte hearing, and Toby felt his system needed a break from it all. He had managed to offload his remaining residential properties for silly money to those unconcerned at the property market rumours, and was sitting with a few spare pennies in the bank. Time for a short holiday.

'Where do you want to go, pet?' he asked Sally.

'I've always fancied a cruise,' she replied.

'Yuk! The thought of being closeted with a thousand strangers night and day for a whole week does not appeal to me one little bit, I'm afraid. What if I don't like them? No, not doing that, sorry love. Leave it to me, I'll sort something else out for us.'

The following evening he came home from the travel agents with an armful of cruise brochures.

'I've found a compromise, old thing. A little cruise liner with only 400 passengers, sails during the night, then each morning we wake up in a new port where we can get away from the punters on the ship and meet the locals – then a week back at the starting point.'

'Which starting point are we talking about here, Portsmouth perhaps, or maybe Hull?'

'No, silly. We fly to Grenada in the Caribbean, stay for two nights, cruise for seven then back to Grenada for the last five. What say you?'

'Wow!' She was stunned. He had gone from definitely no cruising to cruising in zero seconds flat. 'What about the cost? I thought we are trying to keep a lid on expenses,' she asked.

'No probs. Got the whole thing for just over a grand for the whole package. Did a deal with the travel agents I use at Sevenoaks – they owe me one the amount of business they've had out of me over the years.'

So off they went for the most romantic two weeks she had ever enjoyed. And being away from the strain of what was going on at home, namely Hilary, the children and the speed with which the property market was declining, Toby was able to unwind completely and re-charge his batteries ready for the next onslaught.

As they walked into the dining room of the SS Victoria to enjoy their first dinner on board they were greeted by the maitre d' who showed them to a table seating eight others; they dutifully sat in their allotted places and consulted the menu that was presented to them. After a few minutes Toby looked up at his dining companions and froze. The napkin that had so carefully been placed in his lap by the waiter was whipped off, and his chair was pushed sharply back as he spun away from the table. Sally looked up in some surprise at his antics, only to see him disappear in search of the maitre d' who was accompanying another couple to their table, and murmur: 'Excuse me, old chap – I wonder if I might have a word?'

'Certainly sir, is there a problem?'

'Well, no, not a problem exactly. You see, it's the wife – she and I are on our honeymoon and we'd rather be on our own than stuck at a table of ten, if you get my drift.' A roughly folded £20 note was swiftly deposited into the breast pocket of the maitre d' to underscore his point.

'Certainly sir, I do understand, just leave it to me, sir. Samuel!' A click of his fingers summoned the minion called Samuel who immediately rearranged tables in one corner, creating a private space for two to dine without intrusion, and Sally was collected by the maitre d' who deposited at her new table.

'What on earth was all that about?' she wanted to know as she settled into her new seat.

'You're not going to believe this, but sitting directly opposite me at that other table was a Sevenoaks parish councillor. I've been trying to sweeten her for the last six weeks because of a new commercial development I'm trying to get through planning. Thank God she hadn't had time to recognise me, but I'm sure she would have if she'd been given five minutes more. Shit, that was close. Anyway, this is much nicer, I really don't want to share you.'

At each port they called into over the next seven days, most of the passengers disembarked en-masse to follow the umbrella, but he was having none of it. 'Come on old thing,' he'd command: 'Let's get a cab into the town and see the locals.'

'OK, but how can we be sure of finding a cab back to the port before sailing time?'

'Stop panicking. We get one of those cabs into town,' he said pointing at the ranks on the dock. 'But only pay him when he meets us at a designated time and place to get us back.'

'Now why didn't I think of that?' she said with a smile.

'Sweetheart, that's why you've got me around – to look after you.' There it was again, that look in his eyes as he gazed at her; the look that said: "You are my world, my everything. You are the reason for every breath I take – without you there is no point to me. We are going to be as one, the two of us, I shall see to it – trust me, my love, my life." She had never known such intensity; and the bolt of electricity that charged through her was so powerful, just like the bolt she had received when he gave her the diamond and emerald ring, and it turned her legs to water.

Chapter 29

England was cold and blustery when they got home in late October. It had been a magical couple of weeks, but reality had to be faced as soon as they got back. The stack of mail waiting for them contained a command from Sue Jackson for Toby to get in touch with her in order to discuss what offer could be made to Hilary to settle the financial issues of their divorce.

'Shit Sue, you certainly know how to bring a bloke down to earth with a bang, don't you?' he complained as soon as she answered his call. He could picture her sitting in her office, enveloped in a cloud of cigarette smoke and surrounded by active client files covering every spare inch of carpet, save for a narrow channel for clients to access the chair in front of her desk.

'Toby, you need to start getting your act together on this one. The sooner we make her an offer the better – house, maintenance, school fees, that sort of thing, probably around half of your estimated worth. She's not going to accept your first offer, her lawyers won't let her, that much is guaranteed, but we need to talk about it. You must bring me in some figures as soon as you can, and no massaging them – I need to know exactly what you reckon to be worth; bring me in everything you have as accurately as possible, otherwise I can't be held responsible for anything that goes wrong later. And believe me it will go wrong if you start trying to be clever, just give me the proper facts and leave the rest to David Silver and me.

'Yes Sue – no Sue – three bags full Sue.'

'I'm in Court all next week,' she continued as though she hadn't heard his sarcasm. 'But let's try and get together the following week. Leave me Monday to catch up after a week out of the office; how about lunch next Tuesday?'

He was not at all happy with her news. All his life he had made sure he was in control of events surrounding him, it was the only way he could operate; now, all of a sudden other people were taking that control, and he didn't like it, not one bit. Poxy lawyers charging him a fortune to give him bad news; poxy Judges telling him when he could and couldn't see his boys; and poxy Hilary getting away with refusing to comply with Court Orders; and now the final indignity – he was going to have to give her half of his wealth. Ha – we'll see about that.

By the time of their meeting he hadn't done much by way of estimating his wealth. It was quite a simple issue really; all he had to do was ignore it and it would go away.

217

'Oh, for Christ's sake, Sue, how the hell should I know how much I'm worth? Everything I've got is tied up in property, and there's no valuing the market at the moment. I don't like the smell of it. I reckon the whole pack of cards will crash any minute now. I'm out of residential completely and I'm only looking at commercial these days – that's bound to be more solid, but it's a new and unknown area for me. Tell the bitch she'll have to wait, everything's too unstable.'

'You know as well as I do that's not the attitude to adopt. The quicker we get this sorted out the better for all concerned. Anyway, if you are right and market values are falling, your worth will be less now than if you wait for it to become more bullish. So, come on, stop being so negative and give me those figures.'

They finished their lunch and headed back to their respective offices. He sat down heavily into his chair, pulled out his diary and started to consider the approximate, conservative value of the various bits of property he owned, were he to offer them for sale today. In yesterday's market it would have been a lot more, but maybe that's not such a bad thing after all, he considered. If he had to sell some assets today and get rid of Hilary once and for all, he could sell the rest when the market picked up. He reached for the phone. 'Sue, I've followed orders, and I reckon we're looking at a total of about £2.5 million today. So, give me the bad news, what have I got to offer her?' he asked.

'Don't know. Have to get back to you when I've worked it out. Send me what you've got and I'll speak to you soon – bye Toby,' was the only response he got.

He rocked back in his chair and gazed thoughtfully at a photograph of Sally sitting on the corner of his desk.

Christmas was soon upon them, their first together as a proper couple. The garden pond froze over, the ground was as hard as iron, and the frost-covered trees in their little woodland glistened and sparkled in the early morning sunshine. Toby was sad he was not going to be able to see his children over the holiday, but he'd make up for it as early in the New Year as he could. Since Sally was being kept away from them she had no idea of their likes and dislikes, and had quizzed him over the suitability, or otherwise, of presents for them, but since he had only seen the two younger boys just a few times since the beginning of the year he felt he didn't really know them any more either, they were almost strangers, and found it as difficult as she to gauge what the right sort of thing might be.

'What do you fancy doing for New Year's Eve?' she asked him on

Boxing Day.

'I know – let's have a walkabout meal with the neighbours. Nobody will want to drive, so we'll go up the road for the starter course, over the road for fish, here for the main course, then down the road for dessert with coffee and liqueurs before dropping into the pub next to them for midnight. That's what we'll do – I'll tell the others.'

She burst out laughing at his enthusiasm. 'How do you know they haven't made other arrangements for the evening?'

'Bollocks.' he grinned back at her. 'If they have they can bloody well cancel them – this'll be a laugh.' His sense of fun was hugely infectious, and the neighbours dutifully fell into line. Walking the distance between the four properties gave them all a breather between courses, and by the time they fell into the local pub at 11.30 on the last night of 1988 they were all tingling from the frosty night air. The place was packed with friends all waiting to welcome in the New Year together, but when midnight chimed on the radio behind the bar, Toby grabbed Sally's hand and pulled her outside.

'What are you doing?' she demanded. 'Midnight's just struck – we can't go home yet.'

'We're not going home yet, sweetheart. I just wanted to have this moment alone with you, the beginning of a whole new year for us.' His eyes shone with unshed tears of emotion, and glistened in the light shining through the window of the pub. 'I just want to tell you that even with all the problems we've had this year, it has been the happiest of my life, and next year is going to be even better, I promise. I love you so much – you will never know the depth of my love for you. It's as strong today as it was when I first set eyes on you in 1966, if not stronger, because now I know you.'

The surge of electricity that shot through her as she looked deep into those loving hazel eyes of his was becoming familiar.

'Toby,' her voice caught in her throat as she explored every detail in his face as though for the very first time. 'If being unable to imagine a life without you now, and not wanting anything in the world except your love, then I guess it must mean that I love you too, and I suspect I always have.' A mischievous glint came into her eye. 'Why else would I have put up with all your nonsense over the years?'

'I've known that since day one old thing, it just took you a hell of a long time to realise I was right. God, just think of all the grief you'd have saved both of us if only you'd listened to me in the first place all those years ago.' he quipped. She felt his whole body trembling with emotion as he hugged her tightly, rocking her from side to side. His heart pounded through his shirt as they stood together, blocking out the rest of the world for a few minutes as they held each other close, before returning to join their friends in the New Year celebrations.

There was no getting away from it, the financial issues had to be addressed sooner or later, and as Toby opened his mail at the end of January he was horrified. Sue had written to tell him that Hilary was going to need a house appropriate to the standard to which she had become accustomed. There was also the issue of maintenance for her until the boys were 18-years of age, plus maintenance for the boys themselves until that age. Private school fees had to be added to the list, and the matter of the various cars needed to be resolved.

'Bloody hell, Sue!' he exploded when she answered her extension. 'Do you realise what that package is worth? I've just done my sums on the back of an envelope, and unless I'm way off the mark I reckon that's about a million quid. For Christ's sake Sue, there is a code!'

'Will you stop bellowing like a wounded bull for a minute and listen to me. First of all it is more or less exactly what the Court would order on the strength of the figures you have given me. Secondly, I cannot emphasise enough how desperately important your conduct is in this matter. You must be seen to be doing the right thing, so stop shooting the messenger and give me your instructions. Do I put this offer to them in writing?'

'Oh Sue, I do love it when you are dominant with me.'

She heard the smile in his voice as she replaced the receiver and started dictating the offer to be put to Hilary's solicitors.

'You've never skied before, have you my love?' he asked, as they lay comfortably wrapped in each other's arms one morning in early February.

'Nope.'

'Well I think you'd best get yourself a ski suit, because I've decided I'm taking you skiing at the end of March when the kids have broken up for Easter. How about it? We'll take George and some of his mates – do you think your two would like to come as well?'

'Wow, there's a thought. But hang on, pennies are still a little tight at the moment, aren't they?' she asked as she twisted to face him.

'Yes sweetpie, they are, but I need a break from the pressure of Hilary at the moment. Don't worry, I'll get the other parents to cover their own sons' costs, it'll only be us five to pay for – that's a mere drop in the ocean compared with what Hilary wants from me.'

220

'She's what?' Toby was listening with increasing incredulity to Sue the following morning.

'She's refused your offer on the grounds that she knows you have other assets stashed away somewhere and wants an improved offer that more accurately reflects your real wealth. Exactly what assets is she talking about? If I'm to represent you properly you have to be honest with me above all others, I thought I made that clear to you on day one.'

'Oh, please don't tell me you're starting to believe her garbage now, Sue. I am being honest with you. I just wish I had something fucking hidden away. She's completely insane, you do know that, don't you.' He thought for a moment. 'I'll tell you where she's coming from – this will show you how bright she is: I bought a lump of earth down on the coast two years ago for £3 million, all borrowed from the bank, interest rolling up daily, right? After I got consent for change of use and shelled out another million for the infrastructure, Sainsburys was interested in buying it for £6 million for a new superstore. She's still a director of one of my companies, it wouldn't have been difficult for her to find this out because she has had to sign the accounts – up to now. Knowing the way her brain works I reckon she wants the £6 million. The fact that (a) I'm currently indebted to the bank to the tune of about £4.5 million plus interest rolling up, and (b) Sainsburys have pulled out because of the downturn in the economy, has fuck all to do with her, sorry Sue. I'm telling you, she'll settle for nothing less than £6 million.' His eyes glittered with anger at the futility of the situation.

The correspondence passed backwards and forwards between the two firms of solicitors for weeks until Hilary became bored with the "I-don't-have-any-more-money" story, and her solicitors advised her they could serve him with an extremely detailed questionnaire that he would need to complete in minute detail and would easily expose any missing funds.

Sue passed the information to her irate client.

'Bollocks, Sue. My private affairs have got nothing to do with them, and if they think I'm going to spend the next few weeks of my life answering their damn stupid questions, they've got another think coming.' He poured himself another drink to try and calm his anger. It was only 10 o'clock in the morning but he was fuming.

'Come on Toby, you know you need to answer all the questions, and do it accurately. If you don't, not only are they entitled to apply for a Court Order to force you, but it will also look as if you are trying to hide something,' said Sue firmly when he had finished ranting at her.

A couple of weeks later and the forms still sat on his office desk, some of the questions had been answered honestly enough, but he was sorely

221

tempted to be rude in answer to some of the others. In the end he either just left them blank or filled them with a question mark. He was bored, why couldn't the greedy bitch just settle for a million quid while she could; save all this unnecessary expense in lawyer's time. At the rate she's going the whole lot will be gone in lawyer's fees and she'll get nothing. Serve her bloody right.

    He had another drink.

Chapter 30

His Saturday afternoons with the boys every second week were getting a little better; they were taking less and less time to thaw, even Mrs Barton could see that the boys clearly loved their father and were caught in the middle of a very messy situation. As they wandered along watching the boys rolling on the grass together, she told him she was going to suggest to Hilary that she should let him have the boys on his own, she could see how he adored his sons and there really was no need for the presence of a minder. He was so pleased he could have kissed her, but thought better of it under the circumstances, and restricted himself to just giving her his broadest smile of thanks.

The next two weeks dragged by for him, he was so anxious to know if Mrs Barton had been successful in persuading Hilary that her presence was unnecessary. He had plans to take them all to a matinee at the cinema then a nice Chinese meal afterwards – their favourite.

He sauntered happily into the office at 11 o'clock on the Saturday morning, just to tidy up a few loose ends of paperwork before meeting the boys, and turned on the answerphone. A stranger's voice filled the empty office. 'My name is Mrs Matthews. I shall be accompanying Hilary's sons on their access arrangements with you in future. I just want to let you know I shall be at the Hilton Hotel at Gatwick tomorrow at 2 o'clock. The boys may take tea there with you.' And the call was abruptly ended.

His heart sank. Not only could he not have them on his own and enjoy the cinema and a nice meal with them, but Mrs Barton had obviously fallen out of favour with Hilary having dared to suggest that he should be left alone with his children. This new 'friend' sounded like a right tartar. On top of that for some reason today was cancelled and he was only going to be able to see them on Sunday for tea in a cold, inhospitable airport hotel restaurant. One step forwards, two steps back.

His spirits were crushed as he drove home, and he stopped off at the local for a few beers and a chat with some friends whom he hoped would cheer him up.

When he walked in Sally said: 'Hilary has just rung for you, she sounds in a right stew over something.'

'Hilary called here? She only ever phones the office so she doesn't have to talk to you. What's her problem? Bets on how much money she wants?' he grumbled as he dialled her number.

A stranger answered his call. 'Mrs Havers's residence.'

'Put Hilary on.'

'Who shall I say is calling?'

'Oh, for fuck's sake woman, just get her to the bloody phone!' he yelled.

'Don't you dare swear at my friends Toby,' snapped Hilary as she took the receiver. 'If you don't want to see the boys just let me know in advance will you, and stop wasting everybody else's time?'

'What the hell are you talking about you stupid woman. Some tart called Mrs Matthews called the office this morning and left a message saying she would meet me at the Hilton at Gatwick at 2 o'clock tomorrow instead of today. I don't know why you still insist on having a minder for them – I'm their father for Christ's sake, they don't need a babysitter when they're with me.'

'Mrs Matthews is not a tart, so you can stop your petty name calling. And she didn't ring you this morning, she rang you yesterday, Friday, so the tomorrow she was talking about is today, Saturday, and she has just called me to say you haven't turned up at the Hilton.'

'Holy shit – I can't go to meet them now, I've just had a couple of beers and I've given an undertaking to the Court not to drink before seeing the boys. It would have been more sensible if she had had the courtesy to time her message. Can't she make it tomorrow, as I thought she'd meant?'

'No, she can't. And if you don't turn up this afternoon it'll go badly for you with the Court AND the boys – I'll make sure of that!' Slam.

Sally got the gist of the conversation.

'Don't worry, sweetheart. I know what the boys look like, I'll go in your place and see this Mrs Matthews, see if I can't talk some sense into her at the same time. It won't be a problem, I promise.'

When she arrived at the hotel she saw the boys sitting quietly on a sofa in the vast lounge, swinging their legs in time to the softly piped music.

'Mrs. Matthews?' The older woman sitting with them looked up enquiringly from the newspaper she was reading.

'Yes?'

Sally turned to face William and Simon. 'Hello boys, you don't know me, I live with your lovely daddy; my name is Sally.'

The boys looked at each other wide-eyed. Oh no, it was the wicked witch, the one who's name made mummy so angry; whatever would she say about this?

'Mrs Matthews. Can we perhaps sit and have a chat over some tea in the coffee shop? Boys, would you like some orange juice and cake to eat out here while Mrs Matthews and I try to sort a few things out?'

They both nodded mutely, hazel eyes that mirrored their father's as big as saucers.

'Thanks boys. I'll tell daddy how good you've been when I get home, he'll be really pleased. Now, if you stay here we will be sitting just at that table in the coffee shop where you can see us. OK?'

More mute nodding.

She led the way into the coffee shop and ordered for all of them, giving instructions for orange juice and cake for the boys sitting just a few yards away.

'Mrs Matthews, this is the craziest and most unnecessary mess. I'm sure Hilary can't be happy with the present situation; I know Toby isn't, and the children must be so confused and hurt by it all. Isn't there something you and I could do to help?'

The two women sat and chatted their way through a pot of tea, and Sally felt something very hopeful had come out of their meeting. She felt a positive glow at having perhaps achieved a small chink in the battle between these two stubborn protagonists as she drove home.

'It went really well, sweetheart,' she said, throwing her car keys down onto the kitchen table. 'I do hope Mrs Matthews meant all the things she said about talking to Hilary, and I have promised to talk to you.'

'Well, she has already talked to Hilary, my love. She has given Hilary a detailed report of all the jewellery you were wearing, and Hilary has just rung wanting to know how it is I can afford to buy you an emerald and diamond necklace to match your engagement ring when I won't give her any money.'

'Oh, I don't believe it. You gave me this necklace a year ago, long before all this blew up, and you're paying thousands every month just to keep her in that house.'

'You know that, and I know that, but Hilary has only ever been interested in possessions so you shouldn't be surprised. Don't worry darling, you did what you could, and for the best of reasons. It's not for us to fathom the depths of her twisted mind.'

Receipt of his roughly completed financial questionnaire at Hilary's solicitor's office did not produce the desired result and Sue rang to break the news to Toby.

'Because they feel they are not getting the answers from you that they want – think that you are even being somewhat evasive – they want a full and complete investigation into your finances by the Court. They are filing for a 10-day hearing at the High Court, and the earliest date that the

225

Court has ten consecutive days available is in January 1991.'

'But Sue, that's two fucking years away!' Toby shouted down the telephone.

'Oh, for goodness sake, do calm down, that sort of shouting will do no good at all. Did I, or did I not, warn you about the consequences of your actions? Did I not tell you to be honest, straightforward and complete with all your answers? And were you? No, you were not; you made a complete pig's ear out of the questionnaire. I have to tell you I was ashamed to send it over to them. I'm afraid you only have yourself to blame. Come down on Friday and we'll go through it.'

'Right, you're on. And while you've got my file open I would like you to apply for my decree absolute. It's something I should have done ages ago, but now I'm fired up enough. Another chapter closed.'

'Do you know, sweetheart, it's the oddest thing. I had a really civilised call from Hilary at the office today offering me access with the boys this Sunday on my own, providing you are not there of course. Now there's progress. But I only saw them last Saturday, so to get them again this week AND without a minder is double bubble. When I asked her what brought this on she said she was only trying to be nice, but there has to be an ulterior motive if I know her; there's no way she would be nice just for the sake of it. I reckon she must have a hot date and can't find anyone else to look after the boys. Anyway, I'm not complaining. Cinema and a Chinese meal I think.'

He drove up to the house and tooted his horn. The boys cautiously walked out, eyes downcast under the watchful eye of their mother and slowly climbed into the back seats of his Porsche looking very sullen. Oh, here we go again, usual scenario, he thought. Don't want to upset mother by looking happy to see me. And sure enough, within minutes of leaving the driveway the three of them were laughing happily together. The afternoon was a huge success, but as soon as he approached the house to drop them off he noticed their moods darkening again – not even a goodbye as they fled from the car towards mother standing in the doorway, arms folded and looking grim.

He called her on Monday to say that he wanted to see his boys again the following Saturday, and much to his surprise Hilary agreed. He told Sally he was tired of seeing them in unnatural places, always spending money on entertaining them; he wanted to bring them home and show them where he lived now, to try and make their time together more natural, but it would be best if she made herself scarce for the afternoon.

'Sure, darling. I'll go and see mummy for the day. I haven't seen her in weeks. Perhaps we'll go out for lunch or something and I'll get back around 4-ish. Will that suit you?'

'Yes, that'll be about right. Just don't come back before then though, will you?'

She drove slowly back from the day with her mother, and as she turned into the driveway at 4.15 she saw Toby's car still in the driveway. Oh, oh! At that moment the two boys came racing happily out of the house, saw Sally and ran screaming back inside, hiding in the study. 'You said you'd keep that woman away from us!' yelled William. As soon as Toby found them and told them to stop behaving like bloody idiots they fled into the back of the Bentley, locked all the doors and ducked down onto the floor, hiding their faces in their hands.

'Those poor boys,' said Sally. 'I have never seen such cruel brainwashing. What is that woman like?'

As he drove them back to their mother their curiosity got the better of them and they started asking their father about "that woman". Toby told them that she was a very beautiful lady that he loved very much; one day they would meet her properly and they would like her, he promised.

'I have an idea for your next visit with the children,' said Sally when he returned home. 'How about this?' And she outlined her plan to him.

When he saw them again two weeks later he asked them if they would like to go fishing. 'Oooh, yes please daddy,' came the immediate happy chorus once the customary sullen first few minutes were completed for the sake of their mother.

He parked just up the road from The Old Lodge, took the two new rods and nets from the boot of the car, and some bread for bait, and the three of them walked through the woods to the little lake. An hour later Sally took the picnic basket she had packed, and walked past the parked car into the woods, just as they had arranged. The children were really happy and relaxed as she approached where they were fishing. They watched the wicked witch suspiciously from the corner of their eyes as she set about spreading first the waterproof mat, then the rug, then the picnic: chicken drumsticks, scotch eggs, sausages, rolls, crisps, chocolate, fruit and orange juice. She sat quietly watching them with their father, and gradually they became less and less wary of her. Eventually the sight of all that delicious food got the better of them and they asked their father in whispered tones if they could eat something.

'Of course guys, tuck in. Sally did it 'specially for you, so don't forget to say thank you.'

'Thank you,' came the polite but hostile, murmured duet.

'You're welcome boys. I didn't know what your favourites were, except for Chinese of course, I hope you like picnics?'

'Oh yes, I love picnics,' said William enthusiastically, quite forgetting he was supposed to be surly.

'Me too!' said a suddenly cheerful Simon.

Toby and Sally looked at each other and smiled.

Over the next few weeks the boys became less and less distrustful of Sally, and they began to enjoy their times together.

'Fancy a trip to London today boys?' Toby asked as he collected them. It doesn't look as though it's going to stop raining, so there's not much we can do outside.'

'Yes, please daddy,' came the chorus. The afternoon was a great success, except for the lashing rain, which made the roads slow, and they got back to The Old Lodge in time for some tea before being returned to their mother. Toby switched off the engine and ran to open the front door, and Sally quickly climbed out pulling her seat forward for the two boys to follow her. As she got to the front door she turned to see that only Simon had followed her – there was no sign of William, so she ran back to the car to find him sitting in the driver's seat going through the contents of the door pocket, trying to quickly read the papers in his lap.

'What on earth do you think you are doing, young man?' Sally demanded. 'Don't you know that going through somebody else's private papers is terribly rude? Now, please put everything back where you found it and get into the house quickly.'

No guesses as to who put him up to that, she thought as she closed the front door behind them all.

The month of March came around quickly. Suitcases were packed with the warm clothes needed for their skiing holiday and Toby, Sally, Sarah and Ben all piled into the Bentley to drive to Dover for the ferry to Calais. When they arrived at the seaport Sally took a taxi to the local station to fetch George and his four friends who had come down from London by train. Toby took the car onto the ferry waiting area whilst Sally and her seven charges went through the foot passenger's terminal. Then the unthinkable occurred to her – she had all of their nine tickets in her bag, meaning that Toby was not going to be able to board and she couldn't get to him. After what seemed to take an interminable amount of time she managed to raise an uninterested voice through a telephone line accessed from the Help desk.

'Please, can you help me?' she started.

'Yes madam, what seems to be the problem?' From the tone of his voice he'd obviously already had his fill of passengers and their problems, and the day had hardly started.

'Well, my partner is waiting to board the ferry with the car, but the rest of our party is up here with all the tickets – including his. How can I get his ticket to him?'

'Can you describe the car is he driving madam?' Bloody women.

'Yes, it's a cream Bentley and the registration number is . . .'

'Thank you madam, I think Bentley will do. We'll find him and give him a pass allowing him to board'. Yawn.

They all met up on board and her nerves settled down a bit.

As they disembarked at Calais Toby and his boys used the vehicle exit, and Sally and the others used the foot passenger exit – then spent twenty minutes trying to link up with each other because none of the exits seemed to converge. The trip was turning out well so far, and was about to become even more interesting.

They discovered that, due to a French strike, the snow train was not now leaving from Calais and they were all expected to make their way to Boulogne. Still too many of them to be squashed together into the car, so Toby drove with some of the boys, and Sally took the rest of the party on the train. He and the car ended up at Boulogne Maritime station, and she at Boulogne Ville station.

Neither of them knew there was more than one station at Boulogne and each thought the other had got lost. After two hours Sally's French was becoming less and less coherent as her jitters and frustration got the better of her, but finally she found someone who explained that there were in fact three stations in Boulogne. The authorities telephoned to the Maritime station on her behalf and someone there said Yes, there was a cream Bentley waiting patiently in the queue to board the snow train. She needed two taxis to get everyone across town, and finally the convoy set off, with great relief, through the customs gates where passports were required to be produced. But the passports were all in the glove compartment of the Bentley. Enough was enough, and as the tattered remnants of her schoolgirl French completely deserted her, she burst into tears.

'Ah madam, pas de problem, pas de problem. Allez! Allez!'

'Merci beaucoup, monsieur.' What a nice chap.

And so they finally all arrived together at the snow train destined for the Alps and their holiday could begin.

The train journey was an event on its own. One of George's friends had brought his guitar and none of the younger members of the party bothered with any sleep as they partied through the night. Sally was far too excited to sleep and watched the darkened French countryside slip by. Recalling memories of her last overnight train journey from Johannesburg to Lourenco Marques for Christmas in 1969 where she had met Richard, made her smile.

When they woke at six in the morning it was to find themselves speeding through the twists and turns of Alpine valleys and surrounded by the awesome sight of snow-capped mountains and spectacular winter scenery. Tiny glimpses of blue sky between towering peaks reinforced their feelings of insignificance when compared with the majesty of nature all dressed up. Snatches of excited chatter about black runs, moguls, ice fields and off piste could be heard all around them as their co-travellers, all seasoned skiers, buzzed with excitement.

Toby had insisted on bringing a picnic for breakfast – smoked salmon sandwiches, hard-boiled eggs, Champagne and orange juice, which was shared with who ever was up for Champagne at that time of the morning.

The train disgorged its passengers at Moutiers at 8 o'clock in the morning; the car was unloaded from the train and they were met by the chalet owners who helped transport the entire team and their luggage up to the pretty little resort of Meribel in the Three Valleys. The town sparkled brilliantly with its covering of freshly fallen snow, and the new arrivals could hardly contain their excitement as they gazed at the dazzling white vista of the snow-covered mountains of the Alps that surrounded them.

Toby and George and his friends were all accomplished skiers, but Sally and her children had never touched a pair of skis before.

'Weeeee, look at me mum!' shouted Ben, sliding past, arms over his head, poles waving dangerously in the air. Sarah was also managing to stay upright, much to her delight, but Sally had no chance. Even before fixing her second binding she had crashed down onto the hard packed snow of the reception area.

'Stop laughing you two. I'll get the hang of this if it kills me!' she shouted at her two teenage children who were hooting with laughter at the sight of their mother sitting in a tangled heap of skis and poles.

Day three and she was still struggling. She had managed to get half way up a gentle slope using the draglift, but came a cropper as she went over a small lip and sat back. That clearly was a bad move – apparently one does not sit back onto a draglift – it dumped her onto the hard-packed snow.

'That's it! I'm not doing this stupid skiing any more, I'm too old to learn a new sport. I've had three days of lessons and obviously haven't

230

learned a blind thing. My feet hurt, and my legs are rubbed sore from these hired boots. I'm never going to get the hang of it. I'm going to spend the rest of the week on the ice rink and sun bathing.' She threw off her skis and poles in frustrated disappointment, and released the clips securing the boots to her ankles.

'Well, I don't know how you think you're going to get down the mountain old thing,' Toby said with an amused grin on his face. Not often you saw Sally in a real strop and he was thoroughly enjoying the entertainment. 'It's a hell of a long walk back to the town centre. Alternatively, you could just put your skis back on like a good girl and follow my tracks. Look, watch me – just pretend you are walking, transfer your weight from one ski to the other and you will automatically traverse the slope. Couldn't be simpler if you copy my tracks exactly.'

What exactly were her options here? Stick with her pride and go for the two hour long walk carrying skis and poles, or trust him and give it one last go? Well, if it didn't work, which it wouldn't, she would have a shorter walk back to town.

'Right – lead on.' And she banged her boots angrily back into the now all too familiar bindings.

No one was more surprised and elated than her when she arrived back at the start of the draglift, having skied all of 500 yards in a surprisingly competent manner.

'I've done it – I can ski, I can ski! Whoopee! Oh sweetheart, thank you!' she gave him a huge hug.

'One more time on the drag?' he suggested.

'You bet! But right to the top this time, I'm determined not to fall off half way any more.' And she was away before he could turn around and get into position for the next drag behind her. Achievement, that's what it was all about, and he was damned if he was gong to let her fail.

Only two more days left and it was proving difficult to get her off the slopes for lunch. 'Just one more run, darling. You go and get us something to eat – I'll be back in fifteen minutes.' And she was off again, the wind throwing her blonde hair out behind her.

She walked into their favourite mountain restaurant fifteen minutes later, her cheeks glowing and eyes sparkling from the exhilaration of the new-found sport, and saw him sitting in a corner half way through a bottle of red wine and entertaining the couple sitting next to him at the table.

'All right darling? Had enough for one day yet?' he asked

'Enough? Are you mad? It's only lunchtime. I want to do that run again loads more times till I feel really confident. And I think you should be doing some more skiing and less drinking – that's nearly a whole bottle of wine you've got through – how on earth are you going to get down the mountain?'

'I get down better after a bottle, silly girl,' he chuckled, pouring them each a glass.

Saturday, and it was time to pack up and go. One last quick mountain run, then shower and change ready for the journey back to Moutiers and the snow train to return them to Calais for the following morning.

'I wish I could tell you how much the children and I have enjoyed this holiday, Toby. Thank you for not giving up on me. I'm so glad I didn't spend the rest of the week moping around, a skiing failure. It's all down to you, and I love you so.'

She was in her bunk on the train again, gazing out of the window as they sped northwards through the starry night, whilst he went into the corridor to have a cigarette and allow the warmth of her words to gently caress his mind.

Chapter 31

A copy of the questionnaire that he had partially completed with such bad grace several weeks earlier was returned to him by a process server one Friday morning in early April, together with several new pages of more questions added. He was also handed a Court Order requiring him to complete it properly this time, and threatening a term of imprisonment if he didn't.

'God, she really knows how to turn up the heat on this, doesn't she?' he complained to Sue.

'I'm not going to say I told you so, but I did warn you. I've also had a letter in today from her solicitors asking why you haven't paid the mortgage on the former matrimonial home for the last two months.'

'Sue, I don't know from which particular orifice she expects the money to appear just to keep her in that eight-bedroom mausoleum. I've told the mortgagees that they won't get another penny out of me merely to keep her in luxury while the financial world is in a state of collapse. If they want their money they are going to have to get her out so the place can be sold. She obviously wants to play hardball, well I can play that game too. Repossession, that's the only way to deal with her, then she can have a much more reasonable place of her own – unencumbered – and we can split the rest of the equity which will give me enough liquidity to keep my companies afloat for a few months till I can work out which way the market is going. Yesterday I had to agree to give the bank a floating charge over all my assets, including the cars. They are getting as jittery about the state of the housing market as me, and they wanted to call in some of my loans. That would really finish me. Contrary to Hilary's opinion, I am *not* made of money, nor do I have any stashed away – I only wish I fucking did.'

'I'll tell them what you said, but I don't think they'll believe us. She will think your financial difficulties, and the floating charge, are just another of your scams. It's clear that she wants the value of the property she's currently living in, unencumbered, and I get the impression she won't settle for anything less.'

'What about the state of the property market? Even I can't make that up – surely they read the fucking papers.'

'Don't bank on it. Don't forget I know which firm of solicitors we're dealing with and they go for the jugular every time, which is presumably why she instructed them in the first place.'

Sue's predictions turned out to be painfully accurate. Within the month the mortgagees applied for a Court Order to have Hilary removed from the property, but she and her solicitors fought the move on the strength of the award she expected to receive from her ex-husband. She just needed a little more time and he would be forced to pay her demands, she knew that for a fact.

Her bitterness and her solicitor's determination to uncover the whereabouts of the missing millions that Hilary told them he had stashed away, and Toby's equal determination to let the whole thing wash over him and appear totally unconcerned and unco-operative, made any contact between them extremely difficult.

He dis-instructed his solicitor. 'Sorry Sue, I can see her dragging this out for years, and I'm damned if I am going to run up legal bills of thousands which I don't have.'

Sally was bored. The house was complete; they had bought enough furniture to make it comfortable and she needed something else to do now. She had given up office work when they moved in together to devote more time to putting their home together, and a new project was now urgently required.

'Why don't you go back to modelling, sweetheart?' Toby suggested.

'What house modelling? No, I couldn't do that. It would mean commuting to London every day, coping with the rush hour at both ends of the day, and working in a dress showroom from nine to five every day – that would drive me nuts. It's all right – I'll think of something.'

Lucie Claytons – her old model school – that's the answer; they were also an agency, they'll know what she could do in the fashion world that did not involve the grind of daily commuting.

After Toby left for his office the following morning she drove to the station and caught a train to London, then the underground to Bond Street. Lucie Claytons – Lucie Claytons – I know they're around here somewhere. Good grief, she thought to herself, it has been thirty years since I last entered their doors. Either they've shut up shop or just moved – either way they are definitely not in Bond Street any more. Shit! Now what? She began wandering around the back streets of the West End that had been so familiar to her in the 60s. There was the showroom she had worked in for a time, and they were still selling ladies wear, so on impulse she walked in smiling at the house model.

'Excuse me, do you know where there's a model agent around here I can talk to, only I can't find Lucie Claytons in Bond Street any more – it's been so long since I worked in London?'

'Yes, it must be. They've been in Gloucester Road for donkey's years now. What a pity my friend is so far away; she has a model agency in

Brighton and I know she's looking for women for fashion shows.'

'Wow, now there's a stroke of luck. I don't live all that far from Brighton, I could go and see her. Have you got her number?'

The girl scribbled the phone number down for her and grinned at Sally's infectious excitement. She could hardly wait to get home and make the call.

'Hello, is that Irene? A friend of yours, Mandy, gave me your number. She said you put on fashion shows and might be looking for models? I used to be a model in the 60s and am looking at getting back to some sort of modelling now, but not the house modelling I did then.' She held her breath and squeezed her eyes shut whilst waiting for the reply.

'My God, yes I am. I am desperate, one of my usual girls has gone down with a bout of 'flu. How old are you?'

Oh blast, this will blow it for sure, I bet she's not looking for my age. 'I'm 44.' she said.

'Fantastic. What size?'

'I'm a size 12 and 5ft 7inches tall.' More breath holding.

'You angel, you sound perfect. Are you free next week, and can you come down and see me this afternoon?'

'Well, yes, on both counts.' And she carefully wrote down the address in Brighton, had a quick shower to get rid of London's grime, and drove down to the south coast. The premises were easy enough to find, and she was surprised to find herself really nervous as she opened the door of the agency and popped her head round.

'Irene? Hello, I'm Sally – we spoke on the phone,' she said, cautiously entering and closing the door behind her.

'My darling, my saviour.' Irene was rather a large, ample bosomed lady with a loud, booming voice, and when she threw her arms around Sally they were both in imminent danger of ending up in a tangled heap on the floor.

'Let me see you walk angel, and do a twirl for me – perfect, I can see you've done this before. Now, I need you to go to Allders in Sutton for me first thing tomorrow morning for fittings, they are expecting you; and then on Monday morning I want you to be there at 9 o'clock sharp to start rehearsals. You'll be doing three shows on Tuesday, Wednesday and Thursday then an extra Champagne gala show on Thursday evening for the account customers. All right my angel? Any questions?'

'Er . . . No . . . Um . . .'

'Good. You will meet the other girls who you'll be doing the show with on Monday morning – oh, and take a pencil and pad of paper with you.

235

Bye angel – enjoy, enjoy.'

And she found herself back on the street again. Rehearsals? Well that will be to sort out the order everyone is going out in, I suppose. Pencil and paper? Surely it wouldn't be that difficult to remember a simple running order? She hadn't even asked what the fee would be; still, it wasn't really important, she could sort that out next week, it would be good just to work again.

The fittings went well. The fashion manageress had put aside sixteen outfits for the model that had pulled out, and the sizing was now wrong, so everything had to be tried on and refitted; but by lunchtime all her outfits and accessories were on a rail with her name on it ready for Monday morning.

She arrived early and sat quietly in a corner as the other girls trouped in, noisily greeting each other like long lost sisters. She watched all these extremely tall and slender young things in micro mini skirts leaping around, chatting excitedly amongst themselves, it seemed like a club from which she was currently excluded. Never mind, she was going to enjoy this show, she told herself, mentally practising the walk and turns she hadn't done for eighteen years.

That was until Julian the choreographer introduced himself and started outlining some of the routines he was expecting them to do. What? No, please, I'm not a dancer, Sally wanted to screech out. She felt decidedly unnerved when she realised that this was what the pencil and paper were for. The music started thudding out its modern beat and the first pair of girls began slinking down the catwalk that had been marked out with white tape on the floor of the room set aside for them at the store.

'No, no, no, no, no – for God's sake! Don't you girls ever listen? I said: mark the first four beats with your left hip, then four steps forward leading with the right, then a washing machine, four more steps THEN two to the side before you turn back to cross each other. Do try and pay attention – I'm not here for my health, you know!'

Sally sat frozen listening to the hysterical outburst, and it was only 9.15. How on earth was she going to do this – and where did "washing machine" come from? If these girls were used to dance routines and were still getting shouted at, what on earth was he going to do with her who had never done a dance routine in her life?

Her turn came soon enough. She had been paired with another woman of similar age, and Julian minced over to them ready to walk them through their steps. The music blared again and the two of them were rigid.

'It's all right ladies, don't panic. No need to be so tense, just loosen up a bit. I'm not going to get you to do anything like the other girls, I know it's probably not what you're used to. Just follow me. Now, cross at the top, four steps to the middle, cross again, four to the end and cross. Now on your way back to the top you will be meeting the next pair coming down, so follow each other through the middle, you go first sweetie. Cross again, two steps together, do a twirl, and leave one at each side. Got that? Good, let's do it after the fourth beat. One, two three four .... No dearie, I said cross at the top BEFORE four steps down to the middle.' The heel of his hand hit the top of his forehead as he turned away, eyes raised to the ceiling in despair. Far from being kept simple for them, the next routine was different again, as was the next. In fact all sixteen routines turned out to be different and she was never following the same pair of girls twice. This was going to be a nightmare.

By 6 o'clock she was physically exhausted and mentally drained. Thank God she could go home in a minute and practice in the kitchen on her own.

Wrong!

'OK Girls, there's some sandwiches waiting for you for you in the canteen. Sorry there's no hot food but there is a tea and coffee machine as well if you want. Back at 7 o'clock for the dress rehearsal on the real catwalk in the store, if you please.' Surely Julian was some sort of a masochist. The other girls seemed to know not only their sixteen different routines, but also the punishing schedule of the day, and were sitting contentedly, feet up on the empty chairs, munching through the tray of sandwiches left for them by the canteen staff.

The dress rehearsal turned out to be plural, and by the time she got home at 10 o'clock she was dizzy, her head thumped and it was now too late for any clear thinking or practice for the next day.

She quickly learned the meaning of manic changes: sixteen complete outfits, accessories, hats and handbags in 50 minutes. Trying to look cool and serene in winter coats, scarves and boots, with the temperature in the small changing corridor somewhere in the 80s, and tempers fraying as girls tripped over garments flung onto the floor in their haste to get changed ready for the next routine, was not proving easy. She pinned her routine notes up on a wall where she could remind herself what she was supposed to be doing just before going out, only for someone else to knock them off as she went flying past. Shit! Oh well, try and get a clue from the music, she told herself watching her partner's every step.

The girls were all dripping with perspiration and Sally was shaking with nerves as the show finally closed. One down, still nine to go. But by the gala performance on the Thursday night she had pretty well got the hang of her routines and the frenetic changes, and started to relax and enjoy it. Last show, what a shame. The younger girls had all become very friendly towards the newcomer, and offered advice about modelling agencies and the industry in general. Next step – more work. Within weeks she found an agent prepared to take her onto their books, had a variety of photos taken and produced her first index card. Toby was very proud.

George phoned to ask his father if he and Sally planned to attend the annual cricket match just before school broke up for the summer. 'You bet old sport, wouldn't miss it.'

He parked the Porsche along side all the other parents, and George wandered over to inspect the picnic.

'Picnic? What picnic? Why wasn't I told about a picnic?' Sally wanted to know. Never having attended a public school sporting event before she was completely unaware that parents usually brought a boot full of delicious food for their offspring and friends, whose habit it was to drift en masse from one car boot to another, collectively sniffing out the most succulent spread.

'Bollocks,' said Toby, swiftly thinking on his feet since he had forgotten to tell Sally to arrange it. 'I decided we weren't going to do the usual boring bullshit this year. I thought you might prefer fish and chips and saveloys instead. I'm going to the local chippie – how many cod and chips, George?' George cringed at the thought.

Half an hour later the aroma of freshly fried fish and chips drifted over the playing field, and George suddenly found his circle of friends had increased by 500%.

Christmas was upon them again, and Sally was enjoying a pretty good relationship with the boys, so Toby asked them if they would like to come over with George for a few hours on Christmas Day, and be back with their mother again for a late lunch.

'Yes please, daddy,' came the chorus, so Hilary was outvoted without sufficient warning to have made unbreakable plans preventing the visit.

Sally was determined that this should be a real family Christmas, especially after all the trauma they had suffered over the last few years. During the summer they had taken a drive to the south of France to visit Toby's sister in the Dordogne, a sister he had not seen for fifteen years.

'Why did you lose touch with her?' Sally had asked him.

'Dunno, Hilary wasn't interested and I just went along with it for a quiet life,' he replied.

His sister was delightful, a slightly more stable version of Toby, and since her two teenage children had wanted to meet the rest of the family that they had never seen Sally decided to invite them all over for Christmas. Sally's mother, Hilda, was collected and Toby's mother made the journey from her home in Spain. Toby's brother and wife arrived bearing gifts together with their three children and an aged aunt. Sarah and Ben had been awake since very early and were put in charge of preparing the table for the festive lunch, and the house overflowed with the sights and sounds of happiness.

It was a real Christmas at last with all their children together and getting along well. Sally had spent two days decorating the house; the tree glistened with its twinkling lights and red and gold baubles, and the greenery from their little woodland filled the house with the lovely Christmassy smell of freshly cut pine, which mingled with the aroma of the slowly roasting turkey. When Toby got back after returning his children to Sevenoaks, the rest of the family sat down together to a sumptuous feast, and everybody felt the warmth of the family coming together.

'Do you know, sweetheart – that was one of the happiest Christmases I have enjoyed for many years. All the kids had a good time, and best of all I didn't have to put up with rows and tantrums from the ex-Ayatollah.'

The next bombshell arrived at 5.30 one morning two weeks later when the legal system returned to work after the Christmas and New Year holidays.

Noises emanating from the darkened driveway roused them from sleep, and as they peered out of the window to see what was happening, they saw a rather large man climbing into Toby's Porsche as another approached the front door. Toby dragged his dressing gown on, raced downstairs and yanked the door open.

'What the fuck do you think you are doing?' he yelled. 'Get away from my car or I'll call the cops!'

'We've got instructions to remove three cars from this address, sir. A Porsche 911, a Porsche 924 and a Bentley Turbo. You'll save yourself a lot of trouble if you just give us the keys and let us get on with our jobs.' And they handed him a legal looking document with a Stanhope Bank heading, the bank from whose board he had been asked to resign when Hilary's brief Mareva injunction made some of his loan repayments unstable. Now that the property market was floundering, and he was missing even more repayments, the bank were exercising their right to remove his assets through the floating charge they had insisted on, and which he had been happy to give at the time in order to stay in business.

'Fucking banks!' he roared. 'When the sun shines they all rush to lend you umbrellas by the bucket load, but when it rains they want them back again! You lot can go to hell – get off my property – I'm calling the law!' And he stormed indoors, puce with rage. The two police officers that eventually turned up were not particularly happy at being called out at 5.45 on a freezing, damp morning. Their night shift was due to end in fifteen minutes and there was no way they were going to let this minor matter escalate into something that would mean hours of paperwork and being late to bed. They looked at the document and asked whether or not Sir was actually indebted to the bank, and had Sir really given a floating charge over his assets?

By this time Sir was shaking with anger and completely beyond reason. 'That's beside the point. You lot need a Court Order to remove my property. What would happen if I turned up on the chairman's driveway at 6 o'clock in the morning and started driving his cars away without proper authority?'

'How about you two blokes coming back after the owner has had time to speak to the bank when it opens at 9 o'clock?' suggested the sergeant.

'No ways mate. Our orders are to come back with the cars, and we've got a transporter waiting outside for that very purpose. We can't hang around for over three hours, and if we push off for breakfast and come back at 9 o'clock he'll be long gone with the bank's property.'

The officer turned back to Toby. 'Look Sir, as far as I can see this is only going to end up in Court, which will cost you a packet. Since you don't seem to be disputing either the debt or the existence of the floating charge, why don't you just let them take the cars, then you can sort it out when the bank opens?' And the two officers left the kitchen.

'Where the hell d'you think you're going?' Toby stamped after their retreating backs.

'Sorry sir, doesn't seem as though any laws are being broken and there's nothing more we can do to help. You'll have to sort this out with the bank.'

'Sweetheart, stop it! Just let them take the cars and you can talk to Hymie Goldstein later, as the policeman suggested.' Sally tried to calm him down, but he was too busy ranting at the two drivers waiting patiently in the kitchen to listen to her. She fetched the various keys, handed them over, and watched their cars being loaded onto the transporter.

'You know there's no way you can legally fight the bank if you have given them a charge over the cars and have been missing payments. Will the sale of the cars clear your arrears?'

'No, it will hardly make a dent.' He felt as though all the stuffing had been knocked out of him, and sat down with a bump into one of the kitchen chairs, putting his forehead into his hands.

'Well, don't look so glum, why don't we use some of the money I got in my divorce settlement and we can buy two cheaper cars for now? We don't need all the bullshit of Porsches and Bentleys, and we certainly can't afford them at the moment, can we?'

What a fucking way to start the day, and a New Year, he thought. 'I need a drink.'

'Hymie! What the hell are you playing at? For fuck's sake, we've had a blinding relationship for nearly twenty years now, and you've been my accountant for a lot more than that. Why did you have to send two bruisers round to lift my cars this morning? Why the hell didn't you tell me you were going to get heavy with the repayments?' He was fired up again.

'Toby, calm down. Several things. Number one, we have been sending you letters about this, but if I know you they've ended up in your usual filing basket – the one on the floor by your desk. Secondly, not only are the repayments on your business loans not being serviced, but because you're also not reducing the mortgage on the house your ex is living in you're costing us a fortune; and thirdly your ex is fighting to stay put. She's being bloody minded and her solicitors know she'll have to get out eventually, but they're just ratcheting up their fees and the legal costs are going through the roof. The board are getting very hot under the collar about our exposure with you. And on top of all that, as your accountant, I am not at all happy with the last set of accounts that we've just done for you. You don't have any liquidity to meet your obligations unless you sell some assets, but even the commercial market is as flat as a pancake and going to get worse – nothing is selling. I've been telling you this for six months now, but you only hear what you want to hear. I know this is unpalatable but if you want your cars back you're going to have to come up with some cash from somewhere, and pretty quickly. The cars are going to auction after the weekend, so you've only got a couple of days. Sorry, old son, but a deal is a deal.'

Toby sat cradling his fourth glass of wine and considered his options. Hymie was well aware of the reason he had stopped paying the mortgage on the old house, originally he had wanted to force the bank's hand in re-possession. But if the truth were told he couldn't make any payments now even if he'd wanted to – the property market had seen to that. He had never relied on anyone to help him out of a hole before, but he was going to have to go with Sally's suggestion to get the cars back. Best they were in her name anyway which would remove them from the floating charge.

'OK, we'll go your route,' he finally told her. 'Ring the number that bloke left and find out how much is needed to get the two little ones back.'

'Why do we need Porsches? Why don't we get cheaper cars – ordinary Fords, or something?'

'Because I'm not letting the world see me going down,' he growled. 'What the hell do you think it would look like next time I need a couple of million if I turn up for a meeting in a clapped out old banger? No, we are getting our Porsches back; I've got an image to preserve. Besides, I've had those two personalised number plates for over twenty years and I'm damned if I'm going to lose them as well. We'll soon be back on top again sweetheart, I promise. Havers doesn't stay down for long.' He filled his glass again.

Sally managed to buy their two Porsches back within the week, and regretfully had to let the Bentley go – what use did they really have for such a large car anyway? Three years earlier Toby had bought a vintage soft-top Mercedes sports car in poor condition and had placed it with a small back street body shop to have the rusted parts replaced. The garage was not known for speedy repairs, but they had finally been completed and Toby arranged to collect it; so now they were a three-car family again, and thoroughly enjoyed taking the old lady out with her hood down for a spin on a sunny day.

The property market started to pick up a little by the autumn, and he was able to sell one of his commercial sites, releasing enough equity to buy some more land and continue planning for his recovery.

'Let's have a few days away,' he suggested to Sally one evening. 'My nerves are stretched to breaking point with all this and I need a rest.'

'Where do you want to go that won't tax our delicate bank balance?' she wanted to know.

'Henlow, that's where we'll go. We'll drive up on Monday and come back on Thursday – it's cheaper during the week than at the weekend. How about it?'

'Before I agree, what happens at Henlow?'

'Henlow Grange – it's a health farm. I used to go there quite a bit in the past. We can have facials, massages, gentle exercise, swim, sauna, steam room. It's not at all posh and bullshitty like some of them are, it's very laid back and we can spend all day in swimsuit and dressing gown being pampered. The bonus is there's no booze there and I need a detox, my liver is starting to argue with me. Come on, let's book it.'

By the end of the year Toby counted that he and Hilary had faced each other in Court a total of twenty-eight times since the legal battle had started two years earlier, and he was now becoming quite used to supporting himself at them, provided he had been sufficiently fortified by the now regular glass or two of wine beforehand. Mixed in amongst the usual household reminders on the kitchen calendar there was also a scattering of remarks such as, "Court 10.30"; "possession hearing 2.30"; "10.30 house hearing"; "10.30 Court – financials"; "July 5th committal proceedings". He was bemused by the fact that he could stand up in the High Court and spout whatever he liked, and be given indulgence by the Court, yet his solicitor, who would be far better versed at saving Court time, was not – only an expensive barrister would do. What an odd state of affairs.

Chapter 32

The two years of waiting for the financial hearing were nearly over. Sally had been kept fairly busy with her new modelling career, and Toby spent his time trying to keep his business together and handling his inner demons the only way he knew how – with a glass in his hand. The two years of stress and continual Court appearances had taken it's toil on him, and Sally was concerned that he was drinking far more than was healthy, but when she tackled him about it he dismissed her fears with his standard reply: 'You know I've always been a heavy drinker so stop trying to change me. All this rubbish that's going on around me doesn't hurt so much when I've had a drink.'

Late on the last Friday afternoon before the hearing was to commence on the Monday morning, a motorcycle outrider delivered twelve bulging lever arch files, labelled A-L, to The Old Lodge. Each page was numbered and ran into several hundred per file. These were apparently the legal bundles upon which Hilary's lawyers were going to depend for their case against her ex-husband, and they were giving Toby just 48 hours to absorb it all. He also had to arrange to take all the files up to the High Court with him on the Monday morning ready for the hearing to start at 10 o'clock.

They spent the weekend trying to read through some of the papers, and gradually it dawned on Toby why Hilary had been so co-operative about letting him see the boys for an extra weekend, and on his own for the first time, two years earlier. It was certainly nothing to do with 'being nice' as she had put it. It was clear that she had gone up to his office in Sevenoaks and photocopied virtually every piece of paper she could find. There were copies of pages from his diaries, notes from private files. It must have taken her all day, but she knew she wouldn't be interrupted since she had him well tied up with the children, and the Sunday staff in the estate agency would not have questioned her presence since they knew nothing of the marital problems.

Sally had kept her modelling diary free for the next two weeks to allow her to be at Toby's side, and each day they journeyed together to the Law Courts at the top of the Strand, and into Court number 32.

Just entering the portals of the imposing edifice was unnerving, and Toby only felt able to cope after a large brandy from a hip flask on the train.

Sally was permitted to sit just behind him in the Courtroom with a large pad and pencil ready to try and write everything down, as she had seen the clerks to the lawyers do.

The other side had gone from barrister right up to QC, although quite why they felt the need for such a senior member of the judiciary was a mystery, they were not exactly up against any heavyweight opposition. The QC had his clerk; the instructing barrister had his team, as did the lawyers, in fact at times there were up to ten people in a huddle – against Toby and his note-taking partner who didn't even do shorthand.

The QC's opening speech to Her Ladyship droned on for the whole morning, outlining what an unmitigated swine Toby was, and how badly treated his client had been. My God, is this what it's going to be like for two whole weeks, thought Toby? I shall go potty – I could murder a decent pint.

For the lunch recess the two of them adjourned to a nearby Italian restaurant for some pasta and a bottle of wine. The afternoon session was taken up with more legal boredom and Sally tried to stare out of the window between bouts of scribbling, but the angle was wrong from where she was sitting and there was nothing to see, so she watched the hands on the Courtroom clock instead.

Day two and they got down to the nitty gritty of Toby's dastardly behaviour. The wife, Her Ladyship was told, was used to a very expensive lifestyle that included flights in helicopters and private jets. Expensive jewellery and designer clothes were an every day need for her. In the list of her absolute essentials was a huge sum to allow her to buy copious quantities of fresh flowers every week; there was a large amount required for donations to charities; when the children went to parties they would be expected to take an expensive gift. Sally felt her eyebrows collide with her hairline at the list of 'absolute essentials' required by this woman, and Toby had long given up any hope of this being a sensible hearing.

By the end of the first week they were both mentally and physically drained. The journey to and from London each day, together with the noise and dirt of the capital, rendered them almost insensible by the Friday evening, but at least they had the whole weekend to freshen up their minds and bodies, and the Sunday ritual of Champagne and a greasy fry-up brought a measure of light relief to the week.

That first week had pretty much been taken up with describing to the Court the lifestyle that Hilary was used to, and should be entitled to continue as the wronged party. It was well within the husband's means to continue to provide the lifestyle that he had so greedily snatched away in order to live with another woman. It was well known that he had millions of pounds hidden, probably off shore; in fact the husband had been heard to admit to a mutual friend that he had a secret bank account in the Cayman Isles.

Sally's had not been the only eyebrows to levitate skywards at that remark – both Her Ladyship's and Toby's did too.

'Listen sunshine, if you really do have secret funds stashed away in the Cayman Isles, pray tell me why exactly we went through all that rigmarole when the cars were repossessed? Why didn't you just pop over there and collect some?' Sally wanted to know over lunch, with a twinkle in her eye.

'Shit, if you start believing the garbage that woman spews out all hope is definitely lost,' he replied. 'I've been thinking about that, and I think I know where that rubbish came from. I remember talking to that Mrs Matthews woman; you remember, the one you went to meet at the Gatwick Hilton? She told me once that everybody could get on with their lives in a much more pleasant and friendly fashion if I would just give Hilary what she wanted straight away because she would get her own way in the end. I then said to her something along the lines of: "I suppose she thinks I've got millions stashed away in the Cayman Isles, or something." It wouldn't surprise me in the least if that irritated, throwaway remark of mine has been translated into hard admission that I do have hidden millions in Grand Cayman.'

'Well, how are you going to disprove it, sweetheart?'

'You tell me. It's easy to prove what you HAVE got, but nigh on impossible to prove what you HAVEN'T, so I don't know, is the answer to that. They've got all the company accounts, including the ones she copied at the office. I tell you what I'll do – I will give Hilary any missing millions she can find, all of it; anything I have not declared she can have, the whole fucking lot.'

Week two and they stripped him bare. Sally felt quite cold watching him struggle in the witness box. The QC was working hard to get him to trip himself up, and he succeeded when Toby admitted that many years earlier, when William was tiny, his accountants had advised him to open an offshore trust fund in the Isle of Man to enable him to reduce his tax liabilities.

Sally put her head in her hands and her heart sank. Even she was beginning to question her unwavering support in the light of such an admission.

'Mr Havers, I would direct you to bundle M, at page 47.' Much page turning as everybody in the Courtroom turned to the indicated page. 'Would you agree that this is a photocopy of a page from your diary? According to this entry, which appears to be in your own handwriting, you went to Ireland on the 12th of June last year. Pray tell the Court the reason for your visit.'

He was momentarily puzzled; he had never set foot in Ireland in his life. 'Ah, yes, I remember, I had been invited to a golf match, but in the end

I turned it down – didn't go.'

'We stay with bundle M, m'lady, and I would now ask you to turn to page 238, a copy of your bank statement, where we see a purchase made on your debit card at Geneva airport, in Switzerland. Please tell her ladyship the purpose of such a visit to Switzerland.'

'Skiing. We had a skiing holiday in Meribel. We could just as easily have gone to Lyon, but the Swiss flight was cheaper; and since they are not known for putting airports anywhere near ski resorts on top of mountains we had to fly to the nearest airport then take a bus.'

Ignoring the sarcastic outburst, the QC continued: 'A further entry in your diary, at page 53 shows, again in your own handwriting, the word "Gibraltar" and the figures £100 followed by a double headed arrow. The Court would be most interested to know your reasons for visiting Gibraltar in June of 1988?'

'Good grief, I can't remember, that was three years ago.'

'But you admit visiting Gibraltar, Mr Havers?'

'I may have done, I really can't remember – it obviously wasn't important.'

'Wasn't important, Mr Havers? Wasn't important? M'lady, I am sure it will not be lost on this Court that destinations such as Ireland, Switzerland and Gibraltar are all tax havens.'

Toby groaned, Sally sighed in despair. How could you argue against such innuendo?

'I suggest, Mr Havers, that in as much as you have admitted hiding funds off shore in the past with the intention of declaring reduced wealth to the Revenue authorities, the same ruse is being applied here and now for the sole purpose of denying my client her rightful entitlement as your former wife and mother of your children,' shouted the QC, leaning forward to accentuate his point. Toby was confused, it was just before lunch and he desperately wanted to top up his alcohol levels so that this time and money-wasting fiasco wouldn't hurt so much.

'You're on completely the wrong track!' he bellowed back. 'I've never used that Isle of Man trust fund which was set up when my son was born, and your client is well aware of it. On top of that she has twisted a stupid sarcastic remark I made once about the Cayman Isles, which she now believes to be hard fact. Here's my offer – I will give you anything in writing, anything at all, that will help you uncover any undeclared funds suspected of being mine anywhere in the world. Anything and everything that you find – no matter how many tens of millions of pounds – I tell the Court I gift to my former wife. Just let me know what you want me to sign and you can have an open authority in my name.' He was punctuating his words by angrily thumping the wooden surround of the witness box in which he stood.

Her Ladyship leaned towards him. 'Mr Havers. I know this is difficult, but please do try to be a little less aggressive in your attitude, it's not helpful. It is most important that we get to the bottom of these matters as quickly and, I hope, as painlessly as possible.'

'Yes, Your ladyship. I apologise, but he is spouting such garbage, there's no truth to any of it and it makes me really angry to see how everything I say or do is being twisted out of all recognition to reality.'

'Yes, well please just remember what I have said to you, Mr Havers. Please continue.' she commanded the QC.

His accounts for the past ten years were examined and dissected, and Sally lost the plot completely when they tried to unravel the complicated pyramid structure of his companies. There were so many; some had ceased trading, some held shares as nominees, whilst others owned shares outright, and some had made healthy profits the whereabouts of which needed to be discovered. Surprisingly all were. She gave up trying to make sense of it and just scribbled what she heard – they could sort it out later, if necessary.

'What was all that about hiding money offshore? My heart sank when you admitted that.' They were having lunch round the corner from the Law Courts trying to calm down after such a traumatic morning, and Sally was seriously concerned.

'I've never paid taxes in my life. Hymie sees to all that for me, and he arranges things in such a way that I simply don't have to pay taxes.' He was shaking with relief at getting out of that bloody witness box, and his beer was hardly touching the sides. Only the afternoon to get through, then tomorrow was Friday, last day, thank God.

'That wouldn't be the Hymie Goldstein that repossessed our cars last year, would it? Because I'm not sure whose side he's on. Nobody can get away without paying taxes in my world.'

'You are just too squeaky clean in your dealings with authorities; you'll learn, you just have to be cleverer than the next guy if you want to survive in this world. The reason for the complicated structuring of my companies is that profits from one can be moved around through others that made losses, once those losses are offset against profit, hey presto – no tax to pay. When those companies had served their usefulness they were either wound up or liquidated, depending on which was the most tax efficient method, but my name remains associated with them for years. It's not illegal, not complicated, just tax efficient,' he said tapping the side of his rapidly reddening nose.

As they walked back for the last couple of hours of purgatory, he felt a light being switched on in his head. 'Ha! I know what that Gibraltar business was all about? Remember when I went to Marbella in June 1988 to sort out the legal problems with the house there, and Hilary refused to give me the paperwork I needed? The police threw me in jail – remember?'

'How could I forget' she replied, it had given her a huge fright. He had gone to Spain to try to recover his large residence from a former business partner who was trying to take possession of it; there had been an altercation on the doorstep and both men had ended up behind bars for the weekend. It was the only time since they had started seeing each other again that Toby had not called her in a twenty-four hour period. Alarm bells had rung, and she had needed to draw on all her rusty Spanish to try and find out where he was. Guardia Civil, local police, Marbella hospitals, anywhere she could think of, including the British Embassy presence. She finally found him being held by the local police for causing a disturbance on the doorstep of the villa, and was eventually released on £50 bail. Being a squirrel, Sally still had the bail notice.

Friday, the day of reckoning, had arrived.

But before anyone could say a word, Toby jumped up, waiving the Spanish bail receipt in the air. 'M'lady, I can prove why I went to Gibraltar in 1988. All that rubbish about tax havens – I have a bail notice here from the local police in Marbella with the same date on it as in my diary.' He explained why he had gone to Spain, the £100 followed by the double headed arrow doodled in his diary was the each way fare, and he had found Gibraltar to be the cheapest route. No expensive first class tickets or private flights.

The other side was on his feet within seconds. 'With respect m'lady, there is no way the Court can accept this piece of paper as evidence. It is written in Spanish, and unless there is a Court appointed interpreter present, which there clearly is not, we have no way of knowing that what Mr Havers is claiming is accurate. It could be anything, anything at all.'

The hearing had taken precisely ten full working days, just as anticipated two years earlier. Her Ladyship sat with her chin resting on the heel of her hand, and surveyed the company assembled before her for a full minute whilst she collected her thoughts on such a complicated issue. She had heard all she was going to hear, and now it was her job to try to make some sense out of it all.

She did not like Toby's testimony. She found him to be unreliable, cynical and at times downright devious. She considered that the companies were deliberately structured in such a way as to thwart any attempt at discovery of assets. The wife had been sorely done by and deserved to be treated fairly by the Court against such an arrogant former husband. Her Ladyship knew nothing of the insecure man with the laughing eyes who used any route at his disposal to disguise his shortcomings. But Sally did, and she wanted to cry out to the Judge that she was wrong, so very wrong; she had been manipulated by an expensive firm of legal sharks determined to boost their own fee accounts.

The other side had totalled the list of their client's needs, and submitted that the husband be ordered to pay the wife £753,449 within 28 days, together with all her legal costs totalling £249,000. She was also to keep the entire contents of the former matrimonial home together with both the recently restored vintage Mercedes sports car and the Morgan sports car which had been brought back from their home in Spain. Toby was fairly languid by nature and not in the habit of moving quickly, but he did this time, and shot onto his feet. 'Your Ladyship, that's outrageous. I demand leave to appeal!'

'Denied. Please sit down Mr Havers. You've had your say and were not able to convince me that anything other than that sum should be paid to your former wife.'

'Excuse me m'lady, I understood that anything that was mine before our marriage remains mine, like furniture given to me by my mother from the place where she was born, things like that?'

'Your understanding is correct Mr Havers, unless the ownership of those items is overturned by an Order of Court, which is just what has happened. Are you saying there are some items you would particularly like?'

'Yes m'lady. On top of the furniture given to me by my mother there are a couple of paintings as well.'

Sally whispered in his ear.

'Also, m'lady, I would like the Yew coffee table I had in my bachelor flat and a yellow plastic carrier bag in the attic which is full of my poems.

There was a short whispered conversation between Hilary and her supporters.

'M'lady,' intoned her QC. 'My client will permit Mr Havers to take the furniture he mentioned and the Yew coffee table. He may also have the two paintings, but they will only be handed over once my client has had them valued. However, she knows nothing of any yellow plastic bag containing any poetry. Apparently none exists.'

Toby turned to look at Sally and shrugged his shoulders; she wondered what was going to happen next, and Hilary beamed with delight and smug satisfaction.

They all had to wait whilst the Order was prepared for signature by the Judge, so Sally joined Toby in the passage for one of his perpetual cigarettes. He didn't seem particularly concerned at the Order that had just been awarded against him, he had already written it off in his mind as a load of worthless rubbish and a complete waste of everyone's time and money; he was much more concerned by the fact that he hadn't been allowed to smoke in the Courtroom. A few minutes later Hilary emerged, grinning triumphantly, and waved her Order in Toby's face as she swaggered by, ecstatic in her victory. She clearly had not realised it was almost a quarter of a million pounds less than the sum he had offered her two years earlier, which she had considered insufficient for her needs, and she certainly had no idea at that point that she was never going to see a penny of it.

As she sauntered by, Sally's hackles rose at her smug haughtiness. 'You are nothing but a parasite, Hilary,' she called to the retreating back.

'Oooh, that was bitchy sweetheart – not like you at all.' Toby smiled at her anger, crushing the remains of his cigarette into the ashtray provided.

'Well, that bloodsucking creature makes my blood boil,' Sally said. 'I don't know how you could have put up with her for so long.'

'I needed a wife, and she did give me two lovely boys. But now that I am officially broke, and up the proverbial without a paddle, I think it's about time you became the next, and last, Mrs Havers. What do you say, sweetheart?'

'If that's a proposal of marriage, it has to be the most unromantic I've ever heard,' said Sally laughing at his grinning face.

'Bollocks, you haven't answered my question.'

'Of course I'll marry you, silly. But let's get the dust of this out of the way first.'

'Um, I wonder how many other people have been proposed to outside Court 32.' He chuckled as they wandered slowly, arm in arm, towards the stairs and a final escape from the Royal Courts of Justice.

Two months later a cloud of real and ferocious wrath settled over Hilary as the mortgagees refused to accept any more delay from her after four repossession hearings, and an eviction notice was served on her. They had given her four weeks grace after learning that her ex-husband had indeed been ordered to pay her sufficient money to allow her to clear the outstanding mortgage repayments within twenty-eight days, but since nothing had been forthcoming during that time they had no option but to foreclose. The property was sold at auction for just enough to cover the outstanding mortgage, and she now had the task of finding somewhere for her and the children to live. A large and rather run down house became available at the edge of town; there was no phone line to the property, and she had no money to get one installed, so the phone box at the end of the drive became her only contact with the outside world. Her car had been returned to Toby, as the Court had ordered, and both the vintage Mercedes sports and the Morgan in his possession were ordered to be given to her, but were immediately seized by her lawyers as assets being recoverable from her against their unpaid costs. So it was the bus into Sevenoaks twice a week for shopping. Social Services were covering her rent and she was receiving income support to cover food bills, but nothing else.

The dust was settling very badly for all concerned. Sally watched Toby struggling to come to terms with the fact that all his private affairs had been made so public and ripped apart in open Court; he felt as though the vultures picking over his private affairs had torn him to shreds with their vicious talons. He was a man who guarded his privacy jealously, revealing nothing about himself to others, especially by way of business, and to have to suffer ruthless strangers dissecting the private and personal aspects of his life was total anathema to him.

One glimmer of justice pierced his black mood when he learned that Hilary's grandmother had died just before the hearing leaving her over £60,000, but being an asset of hers was immediately sequestered by her lawyers against their costs. Her decision to mortgage any award in order to encourage her lawyers to continue to fight him, whatever the cost, was coming back to bite her, and Toby was thunderstruck anew at her stupidity and greed.

'I'm beginning to believe there may be some justice in the world after all,' he wryly told Sally on hearing the news of Hilary's lost inheritance.

His drinking levels had increased significantly during the two weeks of the hearing; he had always been a heavy drinker, but he had been getting through a lot more recently. How much damage was it doing him, she wondered.

Chapter 33

The date and venue for their wedding had been chosen. They decided on the beautiful Caribbean island of Grenada. Just the two of them on the beach, steel drums playing and no nightmares over guest lists.

The hotel manager agreed to escort her, arches of exotic flowers were arranged, the steel band was booked and the Archbishop of the Windward Isles was asked to conduct the service.

Archbishop indeed. 'Nothing but the best for my girl,' Toby exclaimed at Sally's surprised expression.

Newly made friends staying at the hotel agreed to be witnesses, and the small group enjoying the Champagne reception following the service were in high spirits. Sally had decided that no shoes were to be worn for the beach ceremony, and the general air of informality made it a really fun occasion.

Toby sat quietly watching the merriment going on around him. Now he really felt he had everything worth having; he had finally achieved what he had set out to do when he first saw her in 1966, and at last was at peace with himself. Nothing more was important; no matter what life was preparing to throw at him in the future he had won the biggest battle of his life. Making a vast amount of money had been easy compared to finally winning Sally. He stood up, Champagne glass raised. 'Ladies and gentleman – a toast to the most amazing lady in the world. She's finally where she should be, at my side and wearing my ring. I've had a long and hard fight for her, but she's been worth it – she's mine now, at last. No matter what happens to me from now on I can cope knowing that my beautiful lady is waiting at home for me. She'll never know how much I love her – she'll never know.' His eyes were moist with unshed tears as he swallowed the contents of his Champagne glass. Sally's were too. 'Oh sweetheart, that was lovely. Come on, sit down or you'll have me in tears in a minute.'

When the new Mr and Mrs Havers returned home they arranged a party for all their friends. The wedding finery was trotted out again and Toby positively glowed with pride. He was a popular man – all one hundred and fifty invited guests turned up to share in the new couple's happiness. The summer skies were kind to them, and the sun shone all afternoon, allowing the festivities to spill out of the house onto the lawns where the steel band could be appreciated.

Demands from Hilary's lawyers were received on a regular basis throughout the year, and were just as regularly ignored. Finally they lost patience with him and issued a summons threatening that they would apply for a prison sentence if he continued to ignore the demands of the Court. More time was spent while a new date was set for the whole lot of them to go back to Court for Toby to plead continued poverty, and he found himself back before a new Judge just before Christmas. Once again he was not believed, and was given another final twenty-eight days in which to produce the goods or suffer serious consequences. Hilary was not looking quite so sure of herself any more, and the effects of her impecunious state were clear for all to see, she looked bitter, drawn, puffy and very angry.

They had only been married for eight months, and Sally knew she had to tighten the housekeeping belt because things were looking so bleak again. After the small lift in the property market the previous year it had nose dived again, and the prediction of a crash had been realised, affecting not only residential sites but commercial properties were standing empty too, and agency sales were still not being achieved often enough to generate sufficient income to meet office and home outgoings. Toby had told the Judge a year earlier that things were bleak and he was not going to be able to comply with any order made against him, but nobody listened. As far as the Judge was concerned the man before him was a thoroughly disreputable character who not only didn't take the matter at all seriously, but clearly did have substantial funds hidden away, probably in the Cayman Isles; the ex-wife's case had been very compelling, and he was going to have to produce the required funds in order to provide for his poor benighted ex-wife and get himself out of trouble, or else. Threats of a prison sentence for non-compliance were continually made, but withdrawn at the last moment.

On the day he came home with the news that Stanhope Bank were repossessing The Old Lodge as a result of his continuing failure to meet his business commitments, he was very drunk. He had driven home very drunk, and had reversed his Porsche straight into the side of the house. He headed straight for the wine cupboard and poured himself a large glass. 'Want one sweetheart?' he mumbled.

'No I don't, thank you. What on earth has happened? Please don't tell me you drove home from Sevenoaks in that state.'

'Oh, for fuck's sake, don't start. You sound just like Hilary. If I'd wanted to be nagged I would have stayed married to her.' He was maudlin and very distressed. 'If that stupid bitch hadn't been so fucking greedy and had agreed to sell the Sevenoaks house as I suggested, I would have had enough fucking money to pay her off and get out of this fucking hole.'

There was clearly no point in talking to him in this mood, so Sally began their evening meal.

'Don't do anything for me, sweetheart – I'm not hungry,' he mumbled from the pantry where he was pouring himself another large glass of wine.

Sighing, she put everything away again, it was no fun eating alone, instead she went to sit quietly with him and listened to his rantings.

'Don't worry about it, darling,' she tried. 'We have each other and things will pick up soon, I'm sure. We can rent somewhere for a while – I've still got a good income from modelling, that'll keep us going till you're back on your feet.' She reached for his hand, but he continued to look dejected.

'You don't understand. It's not just that they want to repossess any old house, I bought this love nest for you and now someone else is taking it away. It makes me feel like I've let you down, and Havers doesn't fail at anything. On top of that the Revenue have been after me for four months as well, they want £157,000 in back taxes from me. Where the fuck do they think I'm going to get that sort of money from?'

'How on earth did that happen?' Sally asked him, rather more worried now than before. 'You've repeatedly told me that Hymie Goldstein had your various company accounts so well tied up that there was never any tax due.'

'Yeah, well, that's just the point.' He was starting to slur his words now. 'It seems that Hymie had me tied up tighter than I thought. The agreement I thought I had with the bank was that they had released The Old Lodge from the floating charge because of the network of shares owned by various different nominees. But you know what I'm like with all that fine print rubbish, and now the bank is trying to recover some of its losses by attaching any scraps they can find – including The Old Lodge.' He got himself another drink.

Over the next few days he continued to drink to excess and Sally couldn't persuade him to moderate it.

'You've no idea how fucking hard I've worked over the years to build what I had. Now, all because of Hilary's fucking greed and stupidity, it's all gone down the fucking pan! The only fucking winners are her fucking lawyers, and now the fucking Revenue are after me because of a fucking bent accountant!' he yelled, his focus becoming less and less sharp.

'You know, there might be a way out of this. What if you were to be declared bankrupt? I've heard that all your debts are wiped out in a

255

bankruptcy. How would that work?' she wanted to know.

'I haven't the faintest idea. The only thing I do know is I wouldn't be able to be a director of my own companies any more, so it wouldn't work.'

'Yes, it could. I could hold the directorships for you, and it wouldn't have to be for long – I think someone said the restrictions fall away after three years. Sweetheart, from what I've read in the press you wouldn't be alone, some of the biggest developers in the land have suffered badly because of the state of the construction industry today, I don't think there can be much of a stigma attached. You can surely take some comfort from knowing that this is not your fault; you wouldn't be in this mess if Hilary hadn't been so greedy, but you had your control taken away when she kept her claws into the only asset that could have got you out of trouble.'

His gaze was distinctly bleary and his eyes looked bloodshot; his hair was awry from constantly running his hands through it and his whole demeanour was that of a beaten man. But after a moment's quiet thought she could see a light being turned on in that agile brain of his as he sat back and folded his arms.

'You know, you might have hit on something there, sweetheart; it might just do the trick, and the best thing about it would be shafting Hilary's lawyers and putting a stop to all that rubbish they keep sending me with threats to put me in prison if I don't cough up. On top of the three quarter of a million I'm supposed to find from thin air to pay to keep her in luxury, that stupid Judge wants me to pay her lawyers fees as well – £249,000. If the Revenue can be persuaded to bankrupt me, her lawyers' fees will go into the melting pot as creditors. So, not only do they *not* get paid for all their years of work, plus all the reams of paper they've had to produce, but they will already have had to pay the barrister's and QC's fees themselves because they instructed them, so they will be seriously out of pocket. Ha – nice one, sweetheart.' He was becoming quite excited at the thought of getting his own back, and a glint was returning to his bloodshot eyes.

He knew Sue Jackson wouldn't be able to help him with this one, she only dealt with family matters. Besides he needed a legal mind that wasn't averse to finding a way of persuading the Revenue to bankrupt him, and he knew just the man.

All his directorships and remaining shareholdings were transferred to Sally and a few days later he found himself declared bankrupt. It was a strange feeling, not being in legal control of his own affairs any more, and one that he found he didn't care for very much. But the counter balance to that was the way Hilary's lawyers must have been feeling knowing that the golden goose was no longer going to give them their expected golden egg. He would love to have been privy to their conversations when they received the news of his bankruptcy.

Nothing much was happening at the office, the property world was completely upside down. People had become very nervous of the volatile housing market, and many were unable to move since their house was currently worth less than the amount they owed on it. The few sales that were achieved kept most of the office expenses paid, but nothing to help reduce the company's overdraft.

They had the balance of Sally's divorce settlement to prop them up, plus her growing income as a model. Toby had another drink. His days began to blend into one. There was nothing for him to do at the office, but he couldn't just sit at home. At least in Sevenoaks he had the pub over the road where he could meet his friends, have a laugh and pretend that everything was OK. After all, he had his Porsche 911 with its personalised number plate sitting outside to prove it.

No money to buy land, and legally unable to borrow any. Nothing coming in to the estate agency. About to lose his home. He needed one good deal, just one, to put him back on his feet again. He went over to the pub to consider the matter, and drove home that evening more sober than usual. 'Sweetheart? You know that friend of yours you talk to on the phone sometimes, the one in South Africa – JJ isn't it – the one who was at Ben's birth? Do you think he would be up for a deal to help us put a bob or two behind us?'

'Probably. But I'd rather you run it by me first.'

'You know the bank is going to take the proceeds of the sale of this house against my business loans? Well, I've worked out a way to collect a slice of the action. Don't worry about it. It'll work, trust me.'

She called JJ that evening.

'Sally, my skattebol. Hoe gaan dit met jou?'

'I'm really well thanks JJ,' and she ran Toby's question by him. 'As I understand it, all you will need to do to help is send us a series of faxes, Toby will explain it to you – you won't have to buy the house, I promise.'

'My skattebol, if by doing that means you and that man of yours get out of the financial mess you say you're in right now, I shall be more than happy to help,' her friend replied. They had known each other for over seventeen years, and the thousands of miles between them hadn't lessened their friendship.

'So he tells me JJ. Knowing him there's bound to be something less than straightforward about it, so if at any point you have any reservations please say so and he'll have to find another route.'

'Listen sweetheart, who's going to trouble an old Dutchman like me living on the other side of the world? Of course I'll do it for you. You just send me my instructions now.'

'JJ you're a real friend. I do hope you'll be able to come over to the UK soon and we'll find a proper way to thank you.'

'No problem, skat. I'll wait for your fax. Tot siens.'

Hardship or no hardship, nothing could persuade Toby to give up his bottle of Champagne on a Sunday morning together with the greasy fry up that made the week worth getting through.

'How about we go down to Bournemouth for the day, my love?' he asked after their special breakfast. 'It's been ages since I've seen my old friends at the Yacht Club.'

'Yes, OK, but we'll have to leave it for an hour or two. We've both had Champagne so we'll have to wait for it to clear our systems before driving.'

'Rubbish. I've only had just over a glass. Look – there's over half a bottle left, and I can drink a hell of a lot more than that before it has any effect on me.'

'That's not the point and you know it,' she argued. 'They say it takes over an hour for one unit of alcohol to clear your system, and you've only just finished maybe two units. Let's leave it for an hour or so before we go.'

'Bollocks. I've had a huge breakfast to soak it up. I'm going whether you come with me or not. Don't worry about it, I'll be fine, I never get stopped. You coming or not?' and he picked up the car keys ready to leave.

She sighed and dragged out washing the dishes for as long as possible, but not so long as to encourage him to have another glass while he was waiting for her.

The flashing blue and red lights on the police car close behind forced him to pull over to the side of the road. Sally looked at him in horror and her heart started to pound.

'Don't look so worried darling, nothing that can't be sorted out.' But he was going to need more than bluster and bullshit with this one.

'Morning sir,' said the sergeant. 'Mind telling me what speed you were doing back there?'

'Oh, about 30 I should think, officer. I live around here; I know it's

258

a 30-mile an hour zone, and I never speed. Dead against it myself.'

'Would you mind stepping out of the vehicle for a moment, please sir?'

'Why?' Toby wanted to know. He felt he had been all smiles and reasonableness itself. Why would this young copper want to waste more of everyone's time?

'I have reason to believe you've been drinking sir, and I need you to take a breath test.'

'Oh that. Yes, I forgot, I had one glass of Champagne this morning, wife's birthday you know. It's that you can smell I expect, but it was only the one.'

'Yes sir. Just breathe into this tube.'

'Look here my friend, you can't be serious. One measly glass of Champagne and now you want to wreck the wife's birthday? I'll have words with your superintendent!'

'Very well, sir, I'll give you his details when we're through if you like. Now, just blow in here as hard as you can till I tell you to stop, if you please.'

The law of the land 1, Toby 0.

The breathalyser had turned bright red, and never wavered. The alcohol he had taken the night before, and probably several weeks before that as well, was obviously still in his system and making its presence known.

Next stop another Court hearing, this time to take his driving licence away for eighteen months and a £200 fine.

Sally stood in the public area listening to it all, he was clearly rattled but his blustering manner told her he was trying desperately not to show it.

There were only two things he needed when he left the Courtroom. Firstly, a cigarette, because that could be smoked on the move, and secondly a stiff drink at the first pub they came to in order to calm his shaking.

She drove them back with only half an ear listening to his rantings about the unfairness of it all: Her aging mother with half a glass of sherry inside her would have been a far greater danger on the roads than himself with only one small glass of Champagne; they obviously only targeted him because he was driving a Porsche with a personalised number plate; it was just envy on the part of the fucking coppers; he was going to appeal; he'd go to the House of Lords if necessary; it was so unjust. His ravings went on and on. But Sally was more concerned with the logistics of moving him around for the next eighteen months, her load was going to be doubled with driving him to and from the station to take the train to his office, and since there was no direct connection he was going to have to go up to London from Sussex in order to catch a train down to Sevenoaks. How would he manage when she was away on a modelling assignment? Oh, well, that was a bridge they would have to cross on a daily basis.

Against his solicitor's advice he insisted on lodging an appeal against the ban, which was heard at the beginning of August, a week before the sale of The Old Lodge was due to complete. He lost.

'Fancy a heart starter, old girl? He asked at 11 o'clock one morning.

'What? It's still the middle of the morning. It's not a Sunday and if I start drinking now I'll never get through the day.'

'Nonsense, great way to start the day.' And so his pattern was set.

JJ was as good as his word and followed Toby's instructions to the letter, but two days before the completion date Toby said to Sally, 'I want you to fax JJ with these new instructions, it will make us an extra £20,000.'

'No, please don't do that. What you're doing can't be right. You've potentially made £70,000 and you've got away with it so far, please don't push your luck, it will all collapse.' Sally was getting a headache, this whole business was worrying her sick.

'Don't worry about it sweetheart. I know how their minds work, the bank won't want to lose the sale at this late stage – all they're interested in is getting some money back for their shareholders. Trust me; when have I ever let you down?'

Well, the drink driving fiasco for one thing, and the Inland Revenue bill for another, she thought. But she said nothing.

The day before the sale of The Old Lodge was due to be completed, Toby rang his contact at the bank with the bad news that the offer had been reduced by £20,000 because of the depressed state of the property market.

Sally headed for the bathroom feeling sick.

'Sweetheart, will you please stop panicking, it's going blindingly. They are coming back to me – they haven't said no. Come on, have a drink – calm yourself down, this works every time. Trust me.'

The phone rang.

'Hello, yes this is Havers. Yes. I see …….. Got it…….. Right, OK. I'll get back to you as soon as I've spoken to my buyer in South Africa. I'll call him right away. Thanks. Bye.'

'What happened?' Sally was curled over the sink feeling quite faint. 'Bad news I'm afraid, sweetheart.' His face was solemn and downcast while she wrapped her arms tightly around her waist, preparing for the worst. 'I'm afraid they won't drop the price by £20,000 – but they will drop it by

£10,000, so as the place is going to be sold by JJ on the same day to the real buyers who are paying £80,000 more, we just made another £10K in one phone call. Now you tell me Havers has lost his touch. Crack open a bottle of bubbly sweetheart. We're back in the game.'

Champagne in hand he called JJ and gave him his new instructions.

'My friend, you have saved our lives. When are you coming over so I can meet you and we can thank you properly?

'How about next week ? I want to meet the guy that has made Sally so happy.'

'Great, your ticket will be waiting for you at Jan Smuts airport – I shall really look forward to meeting you. Sally's spent the last few weeks packing everything up and we haven't found anywhere else to live yet because of all the uncertainty over this place, but she'll pick you up from the airport and we'll make space for you somehow. We'll have some hard celebrating to do, old son.'

Surprisingly everything sailed through without a hitch, and a few days later Sally's bank account was looking very healthy. Cleverly he had bought them some time to re-establish a firm financial footing again. Together they had stared into the financial abyss – Sally had been terrified and Toby had poured himself another drink to help him work it out.

The little farmhouse that Sally had found for them was not far from The Old Lodge, but most of their furniture and possessions had to go into storage because the place was so tiny. Access to the bedrooms was not large enough to take the bed base, so they had to be content with sleeping on a mattress placed directly on the floor. But it didn't matter, they were together, they had a little security in the bank and a lovely open fire to sit by at night as the summer days drifted into autumn.

'I've got something for you, sweetheart,' he said one afternoon, home early from his office, hands behind his back. 'I know I put you through a lot when we sold The Old Lodge, and this is a small token of my gratitude. Close your eyes.' He placed the small packet on the table in front of her, together with a single sheet of folded paper. 'OK, you can open them now.'

He watched the joy spread slowly across her face, her eyes growing huge and moist with as yet unshed tears of emotion, but he knew it would not be long before they tumbled down her cheeks as her happiness overflowed. She shook an exquisite emerald and diamond eternity ring from the velvet packet and turned it around in her fingers, allowing the light to play across the facets and bring life to each separate stone.

'Here, let me put it on for you.' He drew her left hand towards him and gently placed the ring on her finger, next to her wedding band. She did her best to see through the blur of tears as she picked up and unfolded the sheet of paper:

For you this is forever,
As love grows.
For you this is forever,
As blood flows
Through every single vein;
Throughout the ache and pain
That love can give.

From here to Eternity
Love grows.
From here to Eternity
Life flows
Through every single vein;
Throughout the ache and pain
That love can give.

You are my little diamond,
My emerald, my gold.
And all I give is love, my love
Throughout the ache and pain;
And all I give is love, my love,
Through every single vein.

Chapter 34

'What's happened to those lovely scotch eggs you used to make me? You haven't made any for ages,' he complained to her one Saturday afternoon.

'Because my sausage meat source has dried up. You know the depot I used to go to in Farnborough to get the sausage meat packets, rather than having to break open sausage skins? Well, they've closed down and I haven't found a new supplier yet. Sorry, you'll just have to wait a while.'

'Was it that place by the roundabout that I went to for you once?'

'Um, it was.'

'What are they doing with the land there – did they own it?'

'How should I know,' she laughed. 'I only bought sausage meat from them, not land . . . Ah, I see where you're going.'

'Get the number of the sausage meat people and ring them. Ask them to give you the name of the people that own the land then find out from them what they are doing with it – it's right in the middle of a residential site, but tucked away at the back. It may be that no-one else knows about it, so be quick.'

'Yes sir!' she saluted.

The land was for sale and it could take six small homes. Without sufficient funds, though, it was far beyond Toby's current means. He rang Alex Burton, his old friend from Sevenoaks.

'Toby, my friend, how the devil are you? I haven't heard from you since your wedding party last June. How are things going? Heard you'd moved – did you get a good price for The Old Lodge?'

'Blinding Alex, full asking, and in a shrinking market. Couldn't be better. Listen. Got any spare funds you want to turn a quick profit on? It's just that I've got all my readies tied up in a quarry I'm looking at, but there's a small residential site just come available, nobody knows about it and it hasn't been advertised. I can get planning for six terraced on it then sell it on. I'm not looking to build them out myself, got too much else on at the moment, but it could be a nice little earner for someone.'

'Might have, might have,' said Alex thinking. That was the first he'd heard about a quarry. He'd heard on the grapevine that Toby had some financial problems with a bank; perhaps that was why he wanted a quick turn on the land, not waiting around to build. Still, have to allow a chap his dignity.

'Let me have something in writing, Toby. I'll look at it and get back to you.'

'Don't hang about Alex; it won't belong before someone else comes across it.'

The deal was done and the site was quickly sold on with the benefit of planning consent for six new homes, just as he had predicted.

'£35K for a few weeks work is not bad.' Toby was smiling. He and Alex were both well satisfied with the shared profit, and he was pleased that he hadn't lost his touch.

As she collected him from the station one evening he was looking less than chirpy.

'What's up?' she wanted to know. 'Please don't tell me it's more bad news.'

'You could call it that,' he replied. 'I've had a final demand from the estate agency bankers. They want me to clear the company overdraft. How the hell do they expect me to do that in one go? Don't they read the bloody financial papers? Don't they know what's happening in the property world?'

'Maybe that's exactly why they are asking for it to be cleared. They obviously had their fingers burned in the last property crash and don't want to expose themselves too much any more – especially with property related customers like you.'

'I wish you weren't so fucking logical,' he mumbled. 'As far as I can see we have a brace of choices,' he continued. 'One, we can use some of our funds from The Old Lodge sale that you've got tucked away in the building society, or two, put the company into voluntary liquidation and continue trading, but you're the boss since my bankruptcy, so you decide.'

'What does voluntary liquidation mean?' Sally asked. Certainly the idea of pumping their hard gained security into the agency didn't appeal.

'Not a lot really. Pretty much like my bankruptcy, all the creditors lose out and we start trading again under a different company name.'

'You mean the bank has to write off the overdraft, and then we carry on as though nothing has happened? That doesn't seem very fair.'

'OK sweetheart, your choice. We'll need to use £20,000 of our funds to make the bank happy. If that's what you want, we'll do it.'

'How much?'

'Listen, £20K to a bank is a drop in the ocean, petty cash. It's what they spend on light bulbs every year.'

'Oh, right. Yes. I suppose so.'

'So, we're agreed on voluntary liquidation are we?' he asked.

The company was declared insolvent, the bank was the only creditor, and the substantial overdraft was wiped out at the stroke of a pen.

264

The new company, still under Sally's directorship, continued to trade as Havers Estate Agents, and the business limped on.

Funding the monthly outgoings of the office without an overdraft facility was not easy. The staff salaries still had to be paid, but often there were insufficient property sales to generate the income even for that, and Sally found it was becoming increasingly necessary to dip into their capital to meet these commitments. She spent more and more time working in the agency learning the secretarial ropes in order to reduce the number of staff required.

'Don't worry, sweetheart, something will turn up. It always does. Trust me.' Toby was full of optimism.

Two weeks later his prophesy turned out to be accurate and he found a small plot of land right in the middle of a residential area.

'We're going to build us a home, my love,' he reported, well pleased with himself. 'But you're not going to like what I'm going to say next.'

'Why? What won't I like?' Eyes narrowing, heart sinking, feeling of a headache coming on.

'We've got enough in the Building Society to buy the land, but I've done some figures on the back of an envelope and I reckon we're going to need to borrow another £80K to build. I can't borrow because I'm bankrupt, but you can.'

'*I've* got to borrow £80,000? Why won't I like it?'

'Since we are going to ask for stage payments they will want to know the name of the building contractor, and we're going to use Diamond Construction.'

'That's OK, that's our own development company, what's wrong with that?'

'Before they agree to lend they will research the company and discover that you are the director of Diamond Construction as well as the borrower and you're obviously doing an own build, which they might not be too happy about.'

She sat down with a bang. Nothing was ever simple with him.

'You bending the rules and talking yourself out of trouble is one thing, but I cannot get involved in anything dodgy because I can't talk myself out of it if it goes pear shaped.'

'No problem. I've managed to get the land for an absolute song, but if you really don't want to do this for us and our future I'll just let someone else have it, shall I?'

'Oh shit, you're doing it to me again. I don't have a choice, do I?'

'You always have a choice sweetheart.'

265

The little 3-bed house was ready for them to move into by the beginning of November.

Toby stood in the empty kitchen, surveying the new plaster with his hands on his hips, and said: 'You know something, my love? Other than the flat I had in Farnborough when I was a bachelor, this is the smallest place I have ever owned.'

'Well, I love it, it's like a doll's house,' she replied, running her fingers over the brand new work surfaces. 'It was fascinating watching it go up, and I've learned a lot about building as well. But I still don't understand why you wouldn't agree to some nice landscaping; that overgrown garden land at the back looks such a mess.'

'It's not what you put into a property that makes your profit, sweetheart – it's what you leave out. We won't be here for long, and anyone buying it will want to do their own thing with the garden. You've made the front of the house look great with all your pots and climbing things – it's enough. You'll see.' She had a lot to learn.

Chapter 35

It began with little things at first. Because they were living in a remote country village it was awkward getting him to the office; more and more time was spent at home, and home was two hundred yards away from a lovely country pub. He was popular with most people, always ready with a joke, even an old one that could be adapted to suit an up to date situation, and never at a loss for an entertaining story. Full of tales of his cosmopolitan past and the famous people he said he used to socialise with, he bragged of how he was able to turn each failure into yet another success, proud of the fact that he had been able to bounce back every time; nothing keeps Havers down for long.

At the end of each day his eyes looked a little less focused, and his speech a little more slurred. At home he was becoming more argumentative and confrontational. Tensions were starting to arise in their daily conversations and small issues were becoming more and more difficult to resolve. Having to be tied to each other for daily journeys wasn't helping either; Sally was finding having to fit her life around his schedule a huge strain, plus she was becoming really concerned at the heightened level of his drinking.

'Bollocks!' was his usual response. 'You know I've always been a heavy drinker. Bloody women, they marry you for what you are then spend the rest of their lives trying to change you. You don't have to worry about me. I'm fine.'

'Darling, if you want a lift to the station we'll have to leave by 9.30 absolute latest. I have to be in Cheltenham by 12 o'clock for a shoot, and I don't want to be late,' she called up to him as he finished shaving.

'Yeah, yeah, don't nag woman. I'll be ready,' he grumbled.

By 9.30 Sally had the car running outside the front door, the wardrobe she needed loaded into the boot. She hooted. She waited, and eventually she got out of the car and ran back to the house. 'Toby – what the hell are you doing? – I'm in danger of running late,' she called up to him.

By 9.35 he still wasn't down. Furious now, and concerned about her journey, she stormed upstairs to find him still wandering around the bedroom looking for trousers.

'You've got exactly two minutes to get your backside downstairs and into the car before I leave without you,' she yelled. 'You've had over an hour's warning of when I needed to leave and I'm not going to make myself late because of you. Two minutes or I'm gone.'

Two minutes later he heard the car accelerate up the lane and shrugged his shoulders. Bloody women. Still, never mind, he'd be getting his licence back in a month.

She was becoming more and more worried at his lack of interest in anything but the pub. He needs a project to occupy his mind, she thought, something challenging. Maybe he'll drink less and work more when he gets his licence back. He wasn't even playing his regular games of golf anymore since there was often a problem getting him to a golf course, so the only exercise he had was wandering all of the two hundred yards to the local pub then back again for an afternoon nap. He had long ago stopped paying the regular annual subscription to his old golf club; it was a luxury he knew he should not afford at the moment. He was proud of his fourteen handicap and had an impressive array of small silver cups and tankards to prove his ability, which he happily cleaned and polished every week, looking forward to the day when he could stride purposefully around a challenging course again, and maybe when things picked up he could rejoin his club. The one thing he did miss were the society meetings; his three playing partners used to arrive at his house before dawn where they would all pile into the Bentley, bags of golf clubs were thrown into the boot and he would drive them to the nearest transport café for a Champagne breakfast. The guv'nor of the greasy spoon couldn't let them be seen drinking Champagne, so they poured it into the café's mugs under the table. He also missed wearing his bright red golfing trousers, everyone would make fun of him because of them, which was one of the reasons he wore them; it also meant everyone knew he was on the course. But all that fun was a thing of the past, for now.

The manager of the estate agency was reporting continued doom and gloom, so he found no enthusiasm for going in, and his office on the first floor was simply collecting dust. He hadn't employed a secretary for several years since the slump, and Sally had become accustomed to doing any office typing for him, together with the agency accounts, at home.

As he sat browsing through the local paper one week he noticed an application being made for planning consent on a piece of land in a pleasant residential area close by.

'Write to them sweetheart. Don't tell them we are developers, just say you noticed their application and wondered if they would consider selling to you – you are a private individual and you want to build yourself a home. They'll prefer to deal with you rather than a developer, you see if I'm not right.'

He was. The asking price for the land was £90,000, providing planning consent was granted, and according to Toby's calculations any property built on it should sell for a large profit, so they proceeded with the paperwork to set up an Option Agreement to secure the land.

Several weeks later Sally opened the morning post to find a letter from Anna, their conveyancing solicitor, asking whether or not the Notice to Complete had been served on the vendors, as she had advised them to do a week earlier.

'What's all this about?' Sally asked her husband.

'Nothing. Don't worry about it.'

'Stop saying "don't worry about it" – I am worried about it. Anna is saying that if the Notice to Complete has not been served we have probably lost the land. What's this week old letter she mentioned?'

'I don't know what she's talking about sweetheart. Do stop panicking, it'll be fine, trust me.'

Sally picked up the phone and dialled Anna's number. 'What's all this about Anna? Toby's telling me not to worry, but I know nothing about any Notice to Complete; he must have opened the mail and dealt with that letter you are referring to whilst I was away on a modelling trip to Paris last week.'

'Ah, yes. Because of clause 7(b) of the Option Agreement, if the notice of your intention to complete the purchase has not been served on the vendors by yesterday you are effectively out of time, and they are no longer obliged to sell to you. The option agreement between you is null and void, I'm afraid, unless they agree to waive the notice.' Sally went cold.

'Shit!'

'Don't worry about it, I'll speak to them this afternoon, it'll be fine,' said Toby pulling on his coat.

'Will you please stop telling me not to worry about it. And what's wrong with phoning them right now, this is urgent?'

'Oh, do shut up woman. It's nothing that can't wait till I've had my lunchtime pint. I said I'll call them this afternoon and I will. Do stop nagging, for Christ's sake.'

No, the vendors would not agree to waive the Notice. They said they had received another offer of £95,000 that very morning, and if the Havers still wanted the plot they would have to better that. Toby could almost hear the glee in the vendor's voice.

'We don't have a choice. We have to go to £100,000 if we want to be sure of getting the land,' said Sally, nervously running her fingers through her hair.

'Garbage. It's a bluff. He hasn't got another offer. I'll just slap a caution on him.'

269

'What's a caution?'

'It's a legal thing. The Land Registry is told that there is a legal issue surrounding the land, and won't allow the sale to be made to anyone else till I lift the caution.'

'But from what Anna said we're out of time, so we don't have any legal right to stop him selling to anyone else.'

'Oh, do stop going on about it, I know what I'm talking about. It'll be fine. I'm going up for a kip. Wake me at 4 o'clock, I'll call Anna when I get down.' She had no choice but to sit fuming and worrying until 4 o'clock.

'No, Toby,' came Anna's calm, reasonable tones. 'You can't apply for a caution on that land – I've already explained you are out of time. It is now as though the agreement you had with the vendors never existed. You have no more right to put a caution on that piece of land as on my back garden. I'm sorry.'

'Fuck!' He was now in trouble. According to his calculations on the back of his usual envelope, the house he was planning to build on the site should net them about £200,000, if the market was buoyant enough by the time they wanted to sell. He couldn't afford to lose it. He called the vendors. They were out. He called them several times during the evening. They were still out.

The next morning he insisted on having a shower and spending some time with the newspaper before trying that all-important call again, by which time Sally was nearly tearing her hair out with worry. But she was learning not to keep on at him when he was in one of his ever more frequent stubborn moods.

'Hello Taylor, Havers here. It seems I don't have any option but to agree to your raised price. We'll close the deal at £100,000.

'Sorry Havers, we had another offer last night. It seems that plots of land around here are at more of a premium than I thought – if you still want it you will have to better £100,000.'

Sally was sharing the receiver and signalled him to go to £105,000. Whether Taylor was bluffing or not he held the whip hand.

Neither of them was happy that it had cost them an extra £15,000 to be back at square one, but at least the purchase was back on line and she had learned an expensive lesson.

Sally picked up the phone. 'Hi Anna, I'm sorry to say I think Toby's losing the plot a bit, so in future please deal with me so that I can keep tabs on what's going on.'

Early in the New Year he applied to have his driving licence reinstated and was pleased to be independent again. His Porsche had been sold long ago, no sense in keeping two cars with only one driver, and Sally bought him a small family saloon, much to his disgust, but it was at least affordable.

Tensions at home eased only slightly because his drinking levels were not being reduced; she had to find some way of getting him to address the drinking issue without being confrontational. 'How about we go to a health farm for a few days, darling? I should think your liver could do with a break right now, and I've just been paid for that cruise shoot, so I can treat us. Please say, yes. I'm dying to get some proper pampering as well. What do you say?'

A health farm? Yes, why not. They'd had a few tough years without much of a break. Good idea.

As they approached reception the wonderful aroma of soothing massage oils and creams greeted them. Oh, this is going to be so good, thought Sally. And the bonus is I can leave him alone without worrying about where he is.

Dinner was the lightest meal of consommé, followed by steamed fish and a buffet table groaning with fresh, crisp salads. They both decided against any dessert and wandered through into the smoking room for him to enjoy his other habit. He had a glass of lemon water constantly by his side, and she was spoiling herself with the large array of different herbal teas permanently on tap.

Breakfast the following morning became a bit of a problem. He was shaking quite badly, and was finding it difficult to feed himself without spilling everything.

'Don't worry sweetheart, it'll pass by lunchtime. I'll be fine.'

The morning passed in blissful pampering for Sally. Facials, massages, sauna, steam room, swimming in the huge pool completely devoid of any other human presence, all to the strains of softly piped music and the most relaxed of atmospheres. She was in heaven.

But Toby was in real trouble by lunchtime. She hadn't seen him during the morning and was alarmed to see how much worse his shaking had become. It was now so violent she had to spoon-feed him. It also explained the damp patches all down the front of his dressing gown where he had spilled his lemon water when trying to drink.

'I think this is alcohol withdrawal. I think you had better have a glass of wine quickly – this could be dangerous.'

He didn't argue, so she ordered a bottle of red wine and had to hold the glass for him as he sipped, and made him gradually drink the whole glass. After lunch she sent him off to bed for a few hours sleep, and tried to concentrate on the various activities around her. She went to a yoga class, but couldn't relax. The gym couldn't hold her attention, nor did she find the pool as soothing as she had during the morning, so she finally gave up and spent the rest of the afternoon sitting beside her sleeping husband, trying to concentrate on her book.

The next two days were no better, and even with half a bottle of wine a day he was still having difficulty feeding himself, but at least he was getting no worse.

'Does this tell you anything, my love?' Kneeling at his feet and holding his hands Sally spoke gently to him, she didn't want him to think she was nagging but there was clearly a problem here that had to be addressed, whether he liked it or not – and she was pretty certain he would not.

'I suppose if I don't cut down a bit you'll keep reminding me about this, won't you? I'll never hear the end of it. Anything for a quiet life.'

As she drove them out of the health farm she knew there would be no point trying to drive past the pub in the lane. He needed his heart starter.

The estate agency manager asked for a meeting with both of them when they got back. 'Sounds ominous,' remarked Sally.

'Got some difficult news for you both. As far as I can see the agency is going further and further down the pan. We're not generating any new business, and the office looks tired and scruffy. The carpet is threadbare and the woodwork looks shabby. It needs some serious money spent on it to bring it up to date. A new lick of paint, give it a whole new image, new modern display in the window instead of those dreadful old wooden things we currently have.'

'I'll have you know they were state of the art when I put them in. And another thing, I was the first to have them in the whole area.' Toby was smarting from the criticism of his baby.

'That's exactly my point. They might have been modern in the 70's but that was over twenty years ago and now they're just tired old hat. Everyone else in the area has a much cleaner, brighter image. We have to get rid of the old grey paint, the place looks like a very run down railway station.'

Sally could see Toby was starting to get wound up. Nobody criticises his beloved agency and gets away with it, sparks were bound to fly.

And fly they did. 'You know how tight things are at the moment, old sport; so exactly how were you proposing I get such an injection of capital, may I ask?' Toby was at his most dangerous when he was quiet and still.

Much embarrassed clearing of throat from the manager. 'Well, I happen to have some funds put away and would be able to raise enough to take it off your hands and bring it up to date. I don't suppose an outsider would want to get involved in estate agencies, the way business is at the moment. Believe me I really want what's best for the agency.'

'Best for the agency, my arse. Who the hell do you think you are, talking about buying MY company and telling ME what's best for MY business. I opened these doors in 1965, that's exactly thirty years of successful trading, and I'm not about to part with any of it now so some jumped up two-bit manager can get his foot in my door. You can clear your desk and fuck off right this minute. Sally will send you your P45. Close the door on your way out.'

Sally hadn't opened her mouth and didn't plan to, but she had to agree with the principle of finding at least £10,000 to get the agency out of trouble. Toby couldn't see past his baby, couldn't see the difficulty it was in, or didn't want to, and he clearly wasn't going to be told.

'That explains why business is so bad. He's obviously been deliberately running it down to undervalue the company so he could buy in cheaply. Fucking arsehole!' No, he definitely wasn't going to be told.

The new house was finally completed and they were able to move in. It was a large and spacious home, and some of their furniture that had been in storage since they left The Old Lodge could be unpacked but the rest remained stored in boxes in the garage.

Toby had been true to his word and had cut back on his drinking, making it a rule not to start until lunchtime, then only a pint and a half before driving home from the estate agency where he was back in control.

A state of calm prevailed.

Chapter 36

It had been a lovely Friday evening spent with friends, getting home after midnight tired but happy, but it became known to Toby and Sally as Black Friday.

As she passed the telephone answering machine the following morning she noticed the red light was blinking, they had a message, so she pressed 'Play' whilst the kettle was boiling for early morning tea.

'Hello? Toby, Sally? This is Jan, your Saturday staff. It's Friday night; I've just been to pick up my daughter from a friend's house and came past the office. I noticed all the lights were on and the windows and door were boarded up. Can you tell me what's going on and whether or not I shall need to go in tomorrow? I'll stay at home in the morning till I hear from you. Bye.'

Sally couldn't have heard right, must have missed something. She pressed rewind and listened more carefully.

'Toby, can you come down please? There's something you need to listen to.'

'For Christ's sake woman, let me have my water first before you start on me.'

'It's not me starting on you – please just come down – there's a message on the answering machine that you need to listen to right away.'

He grumbled but did as she asked. He also asked her to rewind so he could hear it a second time.

'That must have come in while we were out last night. What the hell is it all about?' she asked.

'I don't know but I'm going to bloody well find out.' And he plodded back upstairs to get showered and dressed whilst Sally called Jan at home.

'Thanks for your message Jan. No, we've no idea what's going on either. Maybe there was a break-in or something, but if it was it's strange the police didn't call me. Toby's on his way down there now and I'll let you have more news later.'

The news could not have been worse, and he was wound up tighter than a drum when he returned home. The landlord had locked him out on a legal technicality, happy to replace him with another firm of estate agents willing to sign a new lease at a vastly increased rent.

When the regular agency staff had locked up at 6 o'clock on the Friday evening the new tenants had immediately moved in, using a key given to them by a former disgruntled employee of Toby's who had begun working for the new people. They put up boards at the windows immediately, and systematically began copying all the details of vendors and purchasers they could find, their customer database improving by several hundred percent in one evening's work.

The landlord wasn't answering his phone, and Toby could only sit and stew for the weekend.

On Monday morning he went back to Sevenoaks to see what else could be fathomed, and Sally went grocery shopping. When she returned home there was a light blinking on the answerphone. A message from the landlord.

'Hello, my dear,' came the oily tones of the elderly man to whom Toby had sold the premises when he had needed to raise funds 25 years earlier. 'I imagine by now you will have discovered the changes we have made at the office over the weekend. I'm so sorry things had to work out this way my dear, but you never told me your company went into liquidation, did you? Now that was very naughty of you. You see, it means the lease is invalid now, doesn't it? And since your rent has often been so late recently, I'm sure you will see that I had no choice my dear. I must say the new people seem very nice, and tell me they are going to continue as an estate agency; that's nice, isn't it? So sorry my dear. Bye bye.'

Toby wanted to sue. He wanted to commit murder. He wanted to put bricks through windows. Instead he had a drink – then another. His baby had been thrown out with the bath water to die, and all because he couldn't support it. If he'd had access to funds to get it through the tough times he could have saved it, and his mind began the torturous path around the financial damage that had been done to him and his empire over the past few years, all precipitated by Hilary's greed. It would have worked out so well for both of them if she had accepted his original offer. She could have had her million pounds, her mansion with its indoor swimming pool that she thought she deserved, and he could have continued trading. He got very drunk that night, and for once Sally didn't try to curb him.

The next hard part was bringing home all his records and office stationery. The furniture wasn't worth anything, but the thought that it would all just be appropriated by the new people without so much as a thank you, really churned him up. Perhaps a brick through the window was not such a bad idea. But he didn't, he went over the road into the pub to cry into his beer. Everyone wanted to know what was going on.

'Oh, did a good deal on the agency. Getting too long in the tooth to carry on, you know.' But he couldn't stay and keep up the façade for long, and sadly headed for home with his car full of telephones, typewriters, fax machine, folders; anything that could be removed, he took. Not that he needed any of it, but it meant they couldn't have it.

Most of his time was spent sitting in his favourite chair in the kitchen, phone in one hand and drink in the other whilst talking to friends and colleagues, the telephone becoming an extension of his arm. He had nowhere to go, no reason to get out of bed in the morning; and as the weeks of inactivity turned into months of apathy Sally felt they had lost the entire tunnel, never mind the light at the end of it.

Then one day came a small glimmer. 'You know what, sweetheart? I've been thinking. Each time we've flown to Jersey the flights have always been pretty full, right?'

'Right – and?'

'I reckon there's room for another airline to fly between London and Jersey. What about a small airline from, say, Biggin Hill? It's an up and coming airport, the landing fees won't be as much as Gatwick. Could make a killing there I should think.'

Over the past three years they had flown to Jersey to visit his old friend Ray Milne a couple of times for odd weekends. Ray had done well for himself and owned a beautiful palatial home to the north of the island. Always so welcoming, Ray and his family made them feel really at home.

At last Toby had found a plan in which to plough his mental energies. He had been discharged from bankruptcy earlier in the year, and felt that he had regained a little of his self respect, although he was not interested in running bank accounts or limited companies any more, he was more than happy being absolved of any responsibility, and Sally was quite capable of handling all that boring paper stuff.

He spent hours on the telephone, sourcing the leasing of planes, calculating costings, and working out the logistics of how he could quickly set up and run a small airline and make millions out of it. The tricky bit was going to be funding.

His new dream, Diamond Air, was going to need a bond of over a million pounds with the Civil Aviation Authority, as well as a couple of million for start up costs.

'What we need is a presentation pack, sweetheart. Get your computer thing out and let's put something together.'

'I've promised mummy I'll take her out for lunch today. Can't it wait till tomorrow?'

'No, it can't, don't stop me when I'm on a roll. Let's get down to it now. Hilda will understand, I'll call her, you know how much she loves me.

The sooner this is put together, the sooner we can get our backers on board and have lift off.' He was really enthusiastic and fired up about his new project; the CAA had granted him the route, now he just needed to pay for it all. Shouldn't be difficult to clear over a million a year for the investors, and that was based on an average of just 50% of the seats sold.

He discussed his proposals with friends in the airline business, even stewards and stewardesses, any information was useful, and he paced the floor in the mornings as he racked his brains for the right formula.

The forty brochures were ready, coloured inserts, costings, contingencies and estimated profit, all beautifully and professionally laid out and properly put together. He had met the owner of a small airline who already had the infrastructure of an airline set up, together with his CAA bond paid, a ready-made partner.

'Now we just need ten people to each put in £100K, and we're away.' He beamed happily as he hawked the idea round as many people as he could think of, running it by friends in Norway as well as Ray's friends in Jersey, but it seemed nobody wanted to invest in Diamond Air at the moment.

'Let's put the house on the market, sweetheart. I've found a piece of dirt for a song. If I can time the purchase right we won't have to borrow to buy it, we'll have enough from the proceeds of this place. We'll just rent somewhere to live whilst I get planning for two houses, sell the whole thing on and all the profit will be ours.'

For six months the house was advertised for sale without success, so they took it off the market rather than have it go stale with the agents, and the plot was lost. Christmas was lost too. Belts had to be substantially tightened that year, but they didn't mind, they had each other and knew they would somehow get through the mountains of problems that life was choosing to throw at them.

'I've had another idea. I know I'm a blinding estate agent, in fact I know I'm still the best in the land and there's no reason why I shouldn't start up again from home.' He positively preened with anticipation.

'How could that work? You don't have a shop front.' She would back him to the hilt on all his various harebrained schemes, but they did need to have a modicum of possibility about them, and this one didn't seem to have that essential ingredient, as far as she could see.

'I'll only take top of the range properties and advertise in top papers like The Times and Country Life. No problem, it'll be blinding, make us a fortune, trust me.' The idea lasted for three months before being laid to rest.

Chapter 37

As the year progressed Sally noticed that his interest in golf had dropped off completely even though he was driving again. She couldn't remember the last time he had picked up a club or cackled with delight when putting on those awful red golfing trousers for a round with friends. Although he was constantly receiving invitations from various societies for matches, he always found a valid reason not to join them. Games with friends were being turned down too; he couldn't even raise enough enthusiasm for the practice ranges, there was always one excuse after another.

'What's the matter love? Tell me the real reason you don't want to play golf any more. It's beginning to worry me, you were always so stimulated by it, you loved playing, yet these days it's hard to prise you out of that chair unless you're going to the pub.'

'My leg hurts too much.'

'What's the matter with your leg?'

'It's these damned varicose veins, they make my leg throb and I can't walk very far. Certainly not round nine holes, never mind eighteen.'

'Right. I'm making an appointment for you to have them seen to then, your golf is too important for you to lose over a simple thing like that. It's off to the doctor tomorrow for you my lad.'

The doctor took a blood test, the results from which came in three days later and the patient was referred to a specialist, who took more blood tests, the results of which meant that he could not be operated on.

'But why not?' he wanted to know of the specialist.

'Mr Havers. The state of your blood is such that if I were to operate, you would in all probability die on the operating table. I could not take the risk of cutting into your veins – your blood has lost its ability to clot and you would bleed to death.'

'With all due respect, doc, that's the biggest load of bollocks I've ever heard. Every day of the week I cut myself shaving and I'm still here. I've got the constitution of an ox.'

'When you shave you cut a tiny capillary under your skin, Mr Havers, not a major vein carrying vital amounts of blood through your body. I can assure you, there is no doubt – there is every chance you would die.'

'Well, just give me something for it, doc. There must be a pill I can take that can make it clot again?'

Doc sat back in his chair and pyramided his fingers as he surveyed his patient's rather red nose. 'The results of your blood test show that you

279

enjoy more than just the occasional drink. Would you say that was a fair assessment?'

'Yes, but nothing excessive, and only beer and wine these days, no spirits any more. I can hold my drink, you know.' He was quite indignant at the suggestion that his personal drinking habits were, for some reason, to be brought into question by this quack.

'The reason your blood won't clot is because it is missing a valuable component called platelets. Amongst other things platelets help to coagulate your blood, and one of the factors that can destroy platelets is an excessive intake of alcohol. Mr Havers, if you regularly take more than the recommended amount of any sort of alcohol, that is more than likely to be the major cause of your low platelet count. I'm not surprised you are in pain, the veins in your leg are in a very bad way indeed, but if you want me to operate on them you will have to abstain totally from alcohol for several months. Then your GP will need to take a further blood test to establish whether or not your platelet level is back to normal, which is more than possible, and we can proceed with the operation. Please consider seriously what I have said. A low platelet count is a serious condition, and can be the cause of many other ailments. Good-day Mr Havers.'

Abstain from alcohol – no more beer or Champagne? The man was mad. Good grief, his leg wasn't that bad.

'What happened at the hospital? When's the op to be?' Sally wanted to know when he arrived home from the pub.

'Oh, he didn't give me an exact date, he's pretty busy at the moment, lots of far more urgent cases. Apparently my leg's not that much of a problem so he'll probably want to see me some time next year. He'll let me know.' He reached for the wine box. 'Want a glass, lover?'

'No, I don't. Now sit down and tell me what he really said, because I don't believe what you've just told me. You don't have to be a brain surgeon to see that those veins in your leg look like a massive bunch of purple grapes. I'm not stupid, I know yours is a bad case.'

'Oh, all right then, I never was any good at lying to you, was I? He said I've got to pack up drinking for a bit before he can operate. Apparently my blood needs a bit of a rest from booze, or something. Don't worry about it, it's not a problem.'

'You? Stop drinking? That would be impossible. You used to be able to stop drinking for a period of time, but I don't think you could now; I'm afraid you have to admit that alcohol has got the better of you. Look what happened when you went twenty-four hours without a drink at the health farm two years ago, you couldn't even feed yourself – you were half a step away from the DTs, and you've had two more years of drinking on top of that. If anything should show you that you have a real problem that should. You'll go to your grave with your varicose veins, my friend, and it could be an early grave if you have an accident and knock them badly, you'll bleed to death.'

'Garbage, I could stop drinking if I really wanted to. It's just the first couple of days that'll be hard, after that it'll be a piece of cake.'

'Well, I don't believe you could do it. I think your drinking problem is bigger than you,' she taunted him, concerned that she might be pushing him too much, but she knew he needed goading before he would rise to the challenge.

'Listen, sweetheart, nothing is bigger than Havers; I'll show you it's not a problem. Today's Friday – I'll have my last drink on Sunday night and go on the wagon from Monday, then you'll see a difference in my next blood test, you wait and see.'

'Yeah, well, we'll see.' Please, please God, let it happen. Let him beat this thing, she prayed.

It was rather odd seeing him sitting in his usual chair in the kitchen with only a glass of lemon water to hand. This was going to be a walk in the park, he assured her – he was absolutely fine. But by Monday evening the shakes had started to settle in and he was barely able to feed himself. Tuesday and Wednesday became more difficult and he needed help with everything, feeding, bathing, dressing, and Sally stayed glued to his side determined to help him get through this.

By Thursday he seemed a little calmer. 'See, I told you I could do it, didn't I?' he told her. 'No probs, sweetheart. The worst is over, you go off to work. I'll manage on my own today. I'll be OK – I promise, now go.'

She was nervous at having to leave him for the first time, but ten days earlier she had accepted two days filming a television commercial and didn't want to let her agent down, besides the money was really good and they needed every bit of income she could bring in.

'OK, I'll go. I've left you some stew to heat up for lunch, if you want it, and please be careful not to slip in the shower.'

'Do stop fussing woman, look, the shakes are a lot better this morning. Just go; I'll call you later.'

He did – around 11 o'clock. She was in a break between takes when her mobile phone rang.

'Hello, sweetheart. You OK?' she asked.

'Yes, I'm fine, but there's something very odd going on here.

'What sort of odd?'

'Well, when I went to put my slippers on after my shower there were dozens of little black worms crawling around in them, and I don't know what to do about it.'

She went cold, this looked to be serious, potentially more serious than the shakes.

'Right, darling. No problem, nothing to worry about. Put the slippers into a plastic bag, tie the neck really tightly and put them down in the garage. I'll see to it when I get home. Try not to worry, it'll be fine.'

The first thing she did when she returned home was to look at the slippers. They were fabric slippers, sewn with black thread, and a couple of the ends had pulled free and were visible, which to his unstable eyes were obviously the dozens of black worms.

She made supper and they sat cuddling together to watch the evening news. He was calm and relatively shake free, but suddenly growled at her: 'You can tell that son of yours it's no good hiding – I can see him, and he can fuck off right now!'

'What do you mean you can see Ben? He's in Germany.'

'No he's not, he's hiding behind those curtains – look – over there. FUCK OFF BEN!'

'Darling, I promise you he's not there,' and she put out her hand to try to comfort and calm him. 'I think you are having withdrawal problems, you're starting to see things that aren't there, like your slippers this morning, it was only a couple of loose ends of black thread you saw – there were no black worms. Come on, let's get to bed, get you some sleep – perhaps you'll be better in the morning.'

But after an hour of winding down quietly, side-by-side, he suddenly sat bolt upright and started swearing at all the people he saw hiding around the room. She did her best to calm him again, to persuade him to lie down and try to get some sleep. He hadn't enjoyed a good night's rest since Sunday night, and it was important to break the habit of broken nights.

But the outbursts of ranting continued till 4 o'clock in the morning. She was exhausted and doing her best not to lose her temper, that would not have helped the situation at all, but she was due back on the film set again in four hours time and desperately needed some sleep.

'Please, darling. Just lie down. I promise there is no-one in the room and we both need some sleep. Please.' She had resorted to begging.

'Oh, I'm sick to death of your constant nagging. I'm not getting any sleep with you going on and on at me all the time, I'm going downstairs for a cigarette.'

282

As she laid there with her eyes closed she heard the front door open. In a flash she raced down to the hall and found him struggling into his sheepskin jacket, a lighted cigarette dangling from the corner of his mouth.

'Where are you going?'

'I'm sick of your constant chattering, I'm going over the road to the pub,' he shouted at her.

'Darling, please, there isn't any pub over the road – look – it's just open countryside. Come on, let's get you back into the house.' And she tried to guide him gently back into the warmth and help him out of his jacket.

'What the hell do you think you're doing? Get off me, woman.' His face contorted as he tried to stab her in the eye with his lighted cigarette, and he gripped her arm so fiercely that she cried out in pain, then just as quickly he let go, his eyes becoming glazed and he slumped into his favourite chair, staring at the floor.

She quickly grabbed the phone, trembling with fright at his condition, and dialled 999 for some professional help. The two ambulance men were quickly on the scene and strode into the kitchen.

'What's the problem, old chap?' they asked.

'Problem? Me? Nothing sport, it's the wife, there's definitely something wrong with her, she's kept me awake all night with her constant talking and whinging. Can't you give her something to knock her out? Oh, for God's sake, all I want is a bit of peace and a good night's sleep.'

'No, no. It's not me that has the problem.' Sally was really alarmed now and explained the whole story of the withdrawal problems he had been suffering.

But he looked fine; he sounded lucid and was clearly in strong spirits – not apparently at all unwell. The ambulance men stood up to leave, saying: 'We're really sorry, Mrs Havers, but he looks as if he's OK now and there doesn't seem to be any need for us – nothing we can do I'm afraid. But if you do have any more problems please feel free to call us again.' And they began to leave the kitchen, heading for the front door.

'And while you're going you can tell that lot in the hall to fuck off as well!' blurted Toby.

They two professionals looked at each other. 'And what lot would that be then, Sir?'

'That noisy bunch having a party in my hall – tell them to clear off, I need some peace.'

Sally heaved a huge sigh of relief as the two men returned to the kitchen and sat down again. They called the duty doctor for her who recommended she give him some alcohol since he appeared to be de-toxing far too quickly and without any medical support, which could be potentially serious, she was told.

'I don't want any wine, you stupid woman. I don't drink, you know that. What are you trying to do to me? You trying to turn me into some sort of alcoholic or something?'

'Sweetheart, it's not really wine – it's medicine to help you get some sleep. The doctor has told me you must have it, it will help you. So, please drink it up – all in one go if you like.' She held the glass to his lips and tipped the contents gently down his throat.

'Right you lot, I've had my medicine. You satisfied now – can I get some sleep please?'

'Get hold of his doctor tomorrow Mrs Havers, he's going to need some medication.'

'I will, and thank you so much for your help. Thank you.'

As the sun rose they found they had both enjoyed a good hour's sleep, and he was behaving in a much more lucid fashion, but she knew she couldn't leave him, and had the task of explaining to her agent what had happened the night before and why she couldn't get to the film set; she wasn't sure if she was believed, but the tale of the night's activities had been too distressing to make up. Then she rang Doctor Lincoln and asked for his advice.

'Oh, dear, what a silly chap. When I saw him last week to discuss his veins he told me he was going to stop drinking and I warned him not to try and do it on his own, it would be too dangerous. Keep giving him small regular amounts of alcohol for now and I'll leave a prescription with my secretary for you – it's a muscle relaxant that he needs, and he must start taking it immediately. What on earth induced him to ignore my advice?'

'He doesn't see that he has a problem with alcohol. He says he has always been a heavy drinker and has always been able to stop whenever he felt the need. He didn't see any difference this time and he wants to get his blood straight in order to have his varicose veins operation.'

'I think we both know that he does have a problem, a serious problem. Please make an appointment for him to see me on Monday, meantime continue with regular small amounts of alcohol for the rest of today, combined with the muscle relaxants, then tomorrow he should be able to leave the wine and just take the tablets.'

The rest of the day went reasonably well, he even had a meeting with a builder and managed to make sense, although he was looking pale and pasty. He ate well at lunchtime, took the small doses of wine and the tablets as prescribed, without a fuss, and by the evening Sally was feeling far more relaxed about it all.

She fell into bed, totally exhausted, in desperate need of a good's night sleep, as on the Saturday morning she had been booked for a fashion show, and at the moment her face was looking less than fresh and glowing. But by her side he was tossing and turning and snoring loudly. She finally gave up at 1 o'clock and went to sleep in the spare room to try and get some rest.

'GEORGE, GEORGE!' His bellowing crashed into her slumber at 4 o'clock and she shot downstairs to be met with a scene from a horror movie. The whole house was a blaze of lights and he was sitting in his favourite chair in the family room covered in blood, his face ashen and his foot displaying a large and very deep gash from which blood was gently oozing all over the carpet. It looked as though he had tried to staunch the flow with his hands then run his hands over his face, neck and hair, unless he had done more damage to himself as yet unseen. She checked him over quickly and strapped the bleeding toe as best she could, putting his leg onto the coffee table to try to slow the blood loss.

'It's OK sweetheart. I know what's been going on and it's all sorted out,' he mumbled, running his blood soaked fingers through his hair again. 'I know you've been having an affair with Will Carling, and I've got him and the whole English rugby team penned into the garage downstairs. I've locked them all in, so your honour is safe now,' he rambled. The week before she had told him she had met Will Carling and the English rugby squad who had been watching her photo shoot, and it had obviously stayed in his tortured mind.

She ran quickly down to the garage and found both outer doors standing wide open, all the lights were on and he had unrolled a spare rug in an attempt to make a bed for himself. Her eyes widened with apprehension as she followed the trail of blood out of the garage and up the steps to the front door of the house where there was a pool of fresh blood in front of the window by the side of the door.

When she returned to the kitchen he was shakily smoking a cigarette, looking glazed and ashen. Obviously the combination of alcohol and tablets were having the wrong affect, the whole thing was spiralling out of her control and she was extremely worried about his sanity.

'Right, my darling. That foot of yours looks serious, it needs stitches which I can't do, so we have to make a trip to the hospital. Stay put for a minute while I get the car open.'

'I'm not going to any fucking hospital, all I need is a good night's sleep – help me up to bed, there's a good girl,' he slurred, trying to stumble to his feet.

'Your foot is bad. You're losing a lot of blood and you could pass out if we don't stop it. Come on, no more arguments, up you get,' she ordered. 'Don't worry, you won't have to drive, I'll do it.'

She brought some clothes down for them both and managed to get him looking a little more presentable before driving as quickly but gently as possible to the hospital, his drugged and sleep deprived body crashing from side to side in the passenger seat as she rounded corners on the journey. She asked the doctor for a quiet word outside where she explained about his withdrawal problems, and asked if he could be kept in for observation for a couple of nights after his foot was stitched. But the hospital was full to overflowing and the medical wards were not the place for mental problems, such as alcohol withdrawal. She had her work cut out trying to persuade the overworked staff that he had a life threatening condition, mental or otherwise. Eventually they agreed to admit him and she was able to leave him in the care of someone capable of helping him. By the time she got home dawn was breaking and it was time to get ready for her day's work. She was dead on her feet with eyes that were puffy and red after two sleepless nights, not exactly looking her best for a fashion show.

Her phone rang after lunch. It was Toby. 'Hello sweetheart. Are you planning on coming up to the hospital after your show? If you are, could you please bring me some more cigarettes and hankies, I seem to be running out?' It was bizarre to hear him sounding normal, in no way stressed or concerned, as though going to the hospital in the middle of the night with an unexplained split toe and rambling incoherently was quite the norm, and she was pleasantly surprised.

'Yes, of course. I should be with you late afternoon.'

She found him sitting up in bed with strange looking plugs stuck to various parts of his chest. 'What on earth are those for?' she wanted to know.

'Dunno, you'll have to ask the nurse, they were there when I woke up,' he mumbled.

She stopped the nearest nurse hurrying by. 'Excuse me, nurse, could you tell me what these things are for?'

'They are to monitor his heart.'

'His heart – why? He only came in with a split toe and suffering from alcohol withdrawal. Why do you need to monitor his heart?'

'Apparently your husband was withdrawing too quickly without any medical supervision – it's really a very dangerous thing to do. He could have had a heart attack, a stroke or a fit, so we had to monitor his heart, but he's OK.'

After a good night's sleep she was back at the hospital to see him the following morning.

'Hello love,' he looked pleasantly surprised to see her. 'How did you know I was in hospital?' His voice was a little slurred again but at least the heart monitor connections had been taken off.

'What do you mean "how did I know"? Don't you remember anything of the last thirty-odd hours?'

'Obviously not. What did I do to end up in here? And why is my foot all bandaged?'

So she gave him an update of the various activities since Friday night.

'Hmmm. Seems I've got a bit more of a problem than I thought, eh sweetheart? Been a bit rough on you, sorry. So, what day of the week is it now?'

'It's Sunday, see I've brought you the Sunday papers.'

'No way I can read them. I don't know what they've given me but I don't remember a thing since Friday evening and all I want to do now is just sleep. Probably best, so you go home – maybe you can come in again tomorrow? And thanks darling.'

He was monitored for a few more days as his dosage of the muscle relaxant was gradually reduced until they felt he was stable enough to be released, and Sally was pleased to finally have him home again. Doctor Lincoln had been brought up to date, and he called in to see his patient, reading him the riot act about behaving in such an irresponsible fashion. Perhaps next time he would listen to the medical advice given.

'Next time? You've got to be joking, doc; this has given me one of the biggest scares of my life, and I've had a few of those over the years I can tell you – I'm off the booze for life now. Guaranteed. Plus I've got my minder, and she isn't going to let me near a pub,' he said taking Sally's hand and smiling up at her.

'Don't put the responsibility for this onto your wife, Mr Havers. It has to be your choice, not hers, or it won't work.'

'Sorry doc. Only joking. I'm totally reformed – promise.'

'Good news mummy. Toby has knocked drinking on the head and he seems to be quite content without it at the moment. It's only been three weeks, so it's early days yet, but I'm really hopeful he can do it – he has such a strong will and he really went through the mill, I think he scared himself. The other thing I need to talk to you about is money. Since we left The Old Lodge we've had a couple of minor successes, but today we're coming perilously close to running out of money. We ploughed all our cash into building this house, which I'm putting on the market again next week. I need a short-term loan that I promise I will repay with interest once it's sold, but at the moment we've nothing to keep us afloat. Could you help us, please?'

Chapter 38

The letter from Hilary's newly appointed local lawyers landed on the doormat. Messrs Copeland & Copeland understood that Mr Havers was now discharged from his bankruptcy, and they would therefore be most pleased to hear from him as to his proposals for settlement of their client's outstanding claim of £750,000, as ordered by Her Ladyship five years earlier, plus interest on the late payment, of course.

But Mr Havers was having none of it. He was only just beginning to struggle to the surface of the financial mire caused by her last attempt to crucify him, and he was not prepared to let her get a foot in the door again. On top of that he could do without any of her aggravation whilst he was trying to come to terms with his new teetotal state. His life was finely balanced for recovery, and who knew what might happen if that balance were to be upset.

'Write to them, sweetheart,' he growled. 'Tell them to fuck off. Tell them their client has got a screw loose. The woman's more doo-lally than I thought if she still believes I've got millions stashed away. I've already told her she can have the whole fucking lot if she's able to find it anywhere in the world, but she didn't bother to take up my offer. Tell her to just leave me alone. I'm willing to bet a pound to a penny the London mafia mob she employed last time have had enough and refused to represent her anymore, which is why she's had to change lawyers.'

Sally, however, felt that telling Messrs Copeland & Copeland to fuck off was somehow unlikely to do the trick. 'Don't worry, I'll write something for you. You just sign it when I'm done.'

"Dear Mr Connor

I am pleased to note that your client has decided to instruct a local firm with whom it is hoped I may correspond in a spirit of co-operation.

I must advise you that, contrary to what my ex-wife has probably told you, I do not have any undeclared funds. If she has the slightest suspicion as to where any such funds may be secreted, I will be only too pleased to assist her in discovering their whereabouts. I am happy to repeat the declaration I made in open Court in January of 1991 that any assets found to be undeclared are unequivocally gifted to her.

Furthermore, you have probably not been made aware that I offered her the equivalent of £1 million in 1989, which she refused, preferring to "take me to the cleaners". She also refused to sell the former matrimonial home, the proceeds of which would not only have provided her with security, but would also have allowed me to meet my commitments and continue trading, thus avoiding bankruptcy.

As a direct result of her actions, I have now lost my estate agency after thirty years of trading, and which also used to provide a modest income.

I must further advise you that, whilst I have indeed been discharged from bankruptcy, I am in no financial position to make any offer to your client. Nor do I envisage any time in the future when I might be in such a position, since the bankruptcy petition has seriously impacted on my ability to raise the funds necessary to invest in income producing ventures.

Yours sincerely"

'Read and sign if you're happy, please darling,' she said placing the letter on top of the newspaper he was reading.

'What does it say?'

'I've told them to fuck off, just a bit more politely.'

'Gimme a pen then.'

He was quite oblivious to the continuing correspondence, and Sally answered all the accusations from Copeland & Copeland on his behalf. Just as well, really. Had he become involved in his fragile teetotal state, all attempts at civility would have gone completely out of the window. It was clear from their correspondence that Hilary had indeed convinced her new solicitors that he definitely did have millions of pounds stashed away, no matter how much he refuted the allegation, and she wanted them, as the Court had decreed was her right.

As the teetotal weeks progressed Sally marked them off the calendar, and it was a joy to notch up his successes. He stayed away from the temptation of pubs and he didn't feel up to driving anywhere, so most of his time was spent sitting in the kitchen, a glass of lemon water within easy reach, and he ate more healthily than ever before.

After six weeks she was beginning to feel that he had got over the worst, and Sally's daughter Sarah asked if she would join her on a short break. Her shift work as ground crew for British Airways was arduous and she felt in need of a little sun on her face, so Sally rang her mother-in-law in Spain to ask if she and her daughter could impose on her for a week.

Toby's mother was a magical lady, of whom both she and Sarah were incredibly fond, and they enjoyed a glorious few days of mother and daughter fun and tranquillity, leaving Toby alone with the telephone for company.

> *Fear lurks as*
> *Floorboards creak*
> *At home.*
>
> *Light through every*
> *Crack appears*
> *At home.*
>
> *What can it be,*
> *This lurk, this fear*
> *At home?*
>
> *A flash, a roar*
> *Key turning in the door*
> *A bark, a scream,*
> *For me*
> *Alone –*
> *At home?*

She found all his good intentions had gone out of the window when she returned a week later and saw him in the pub, cigarette in one hand, pint of beer in the other, and her heart almost stopped beating.

'What are you doing? What happened to your "no more drinking" rule?' She was devastated.

'No problem, sweetheart, keep your hair on. I had a blood test yesterday and the results were almost back to normal, so I've decided I can have the occasional social drink, and that's what I'm going to do, I can handle it. Besides, you weren't here and I was bored.' His eyes were looking a little less than focused again and his speech was a little slurred, this did not look like an occasional social drink, this looked like trouble. The good intentions had lasted exactly six weeks.

A death in the family is an emotionally taxing time, and when Sally's younger brother died that summer she found she was alone with her grief. Her mother was now frail, her sister Jenny was still living in South Africa and her husband was no help; displays of emotional trauma were signs of weakness in his world. However, the modest inheritance from her brother's estate allowed her to repay the loan to her mother and keep them afloat for another year.

But only a year; after that it had all gone – they were running out of money again. Income from her modelling wasn't enough to support her mortgage and she was beginning to panic, she had never defaulted on any commitments in the past and was not about to start now.

'I've thought of a great way to make money, sweetheart.' Toby announced, raising his eyes from the magazine he was reading. 'There's an advert in here for a book all about how to make money, well, that's a subject I know something about. I'm going to write a book called "Want To Make A Million?" If this bloke can afford to take out a full-page advert his book must be making him a bomb. Come on darling, get your typewriter out.'

The book kept him alert for a while and allowed him to use his ability to verbally entertain, and he stretched ten pages of common sense into seventy-six. He calculated they only had to sell fifty-five copies to break even, after which it would all be profit, and he rubbed his hands with glee as the orders came in after his first advertisement. They stopped at thirty orders, seven of which asked for their money back. It clearly wasn't going to make them millions after all.

Her mother came to their financial rescue yet again until the sale of another small plot gave them enough to repay her and survive for another six months. Their very existence was becoming a struggle.

'Alex, old son. Want a piece of this action? A petrol station closing down in Crowborough – perfect for a terrace of five houses. Land will need contamination reports, but it's right in the middle of a residential area. Can't fail.'

'Got a buyer lined up for the site yet?' Alex wanted to know.

'Nope – I want to build this one out. It's about time Diamond Construction was back in business. You up for it?'

'Same deal as before – 50/50?'

'You're on, my friend. I'll get Sally to call you to discuss the fine details.'

He was excited. His first proper project for years, it felt quite like the old times.

At last they could afford to take a holiday together, and Toby promised William and Simon he would take them skiing to Andorra where the skiing wasn't too taxing for beginners. Sally hadn't skied for so many years she was beginning to feel like a beginner too, but Toby was unlikely to have lost his touch. 'Bit like riding a bike, old thing, you never forget how.'

They were all looking forward to it enormously. In a couple of months he would have the first holiday with his beloved boys for years.

A week before they were due to travel he stumbled through the front door, his face ashen, and dropped into his chair in the kitchen.

'Christ, darling – what ever's the matter? You look terrible. What's happened to your arm, your wrist looks all swollen? And you've done something awful to your eye too.'

'I slipped on some fucking black ice when I came out of the pub. It's all your fault – if you'd given me my car keys and let me drive this would never have happened.'

'Pack it up. You know I won't let you drink and drive. Just get in the car, I'm taking you to the hospital to get your arm seen to whether you like it or not, it looks as though it might be broken.'

'I don't need the hospital. Just get me a glass of wine, sweetheart.'

'CAR – NOW!' She stormed out of the house. How dare he blame her. She seemed to spend most of her time either running errands for him or mopping up after him. These days he appeared to be incapable of doing anything for himself, even some of his money-making ideas could be considered suspect.

He had a Colles fracture to his wrist, which put his left hand into a sling and out of use for a few weeks. More driving for Sally.

He became intimately acquainted with most of the bars in Andorra since he was unable to ski, and Sally divided her time between helping the boys in the afternoons, when they had finished ski school, and trying to keep Toby occupied with walks rather than eight hours solidly sitting in bars. So much for the family holiday.

The builders were cracking on at Crowborough, and Sally was constantly on site, learning a little more every day about the building trade and making decisions where necessary. Toby spent most of his time on the phone talking to people about it, networking he called it – running up a hefty phone bill she called it, but he was happy with a watered down glass of wine in one hand and the phone in the other. At least it was something he could do with his wrist in plaster and a seriously swollen black eye.

The little houses proved to be popular and were quickly sold.

'Fancy changing the cars sweetheart? I've just been talking to Alex and he's has got a blinding deal for me,' said Toby one Sunday morning.

'Why do we need to change the cars?'

'Well I'm driving that poxy little family saloon that we bought when I got my licence back, and it's not doing my image any good. Imagine what it looks like when I drive up to meetings in that sort of car. I need something more prestigious and Alex's 500SEL would be just right, plus his mother is also selling her little Mercedes sports which would be nice for you. On top of that we'd get more for our present two cars than the cost of the two new ones, so we'd be a few quid in plus having two nice cars. What do you think?'

The 500SEL might be a monster of a car and a bit of a gas-guzzler, but then he wasn't planning on doing any real mileage – Sally was the one clocking up the miles with modelling around the country. She had to admit it was a glorious car, and although it was quite old Alex had kept it beautifully maintained. Driving around in it gave Toby's spirits quite a lift, he felt that he was getting back on top. The little sports car was an equal joy for her to drive, plus there was the bonus of having some spare cash from the exchanges.

'I'm going to put this place on the market again,' decided Sally. 'The property market's looking quite strong at the moment and I would like to get some funds behind us ready for any interesting deal that might come along, at least we will be able to fund it ourselves, not permanently relying on Alex.' Their house was proving difficult to sell because of the dual issues of the flight of steps up to the front door and the railway line running quite close to the back garden, but there was bound to be someone out there that wouldn't mind.

But the property seemed to be more blighted than she had realised, and although potential purchasers loved what she had done with the house with its light and airy rooms, and the imaginative way in which she had used pastel colours to create the feeling of spaciousness, it just wouldn't sell.

Four months later she took it off again; having people constantly wandering through, being really enthusiastic but not wanting to buy was becoming demoralising.

'Right.' she said, heading down to the garage. 'I'm going to re-paint it. We've been here nearly three years now, the paintwork could do with a bit of freshening up.'

'Oh, give it a rest, sweetheart. Sit down, have a glass of wine and talk to me,' he complained.

'You might have nothing better to do with your day than sit and drink at 10 o'clock in the morning Toby Havers, but someone's got to do all the maintenance jobs, and we can't afford to get a man in, unless you are offering, of course?'

'Oh, come on, sweetheart. You know I don't know one end of a paintbrush from another.'

'Right then. Leave me alone to do what I'm good at, and you do what you're good at. Come up with some sensible ideas to make some money. We're OK now for about another year, but you need to start a new project to keep us going otherwise we're going to run out of money again.'

Sally opened the morning mail.

"Dear Mr Havers

We appreciate your continued stated financial predicament, but must reiterate our client's position in that she is in possession of an Order of the Court that must be complied with, as you are fully aware.

Correspondence between us has been continuing for some considerable time now, and we must advise you that, whilst our client has given you every opportunity to settle the matter, her patience is not boundless.

Please be so good as to provide us with your proposals for settlement forthwith, to avoid further unnecessary Court action.

Yours sincerely"

Sally sat down at the word processor.

"Dear Mr Connor

I fully concur with your sentiments with regard to the length of time this correspondence has continued between us.

As I have continually repeated, I have no assets, and clearly it would be inappropriate for me to ask my wife to risk any of her assets in order to satisfy your client's excessive requirements. So we would seem to be at something of an impasse.

May I make the following suggestion? Were your client to be encouraged to moderate her demands, I feel sure we could arrive at an amicable agreement.

I look forward to considering any suggestions you might care to make.

Yours sincerely"

'What's this?' asked Toby, looking up from his diary at the paper Sally was pushing under his nose.
'Another reply to Hilary's lot. Do you want me to read it to you?'
'No, I can't be bothered, I'm sure it's fine.'

'Hey, I've had another blinding idea.' He was really fired up again. 'Tell me what you think of this, sweetheart. Tourists coming into the UK usually have a destination organised and some idea of what they want to see. Right? Well, imagine if you arrived in a foreign country with a hotel booked in one city, wouldn't you like to be given a free magazine containing information about the rest of the country as you arrive at the airport? Train information and timetables, sights of interest around the whole of the country, divided into the four quadrants, not just the area you are visiting; emergency telephone numbers and contact details in, say, English, German, Spanish, Italian and Japanese. I've calculated we would need to print a magazine of about forty pages three times a year to accommodate the changing places of interest in different seasons, and we could pay students to hand them out at airports and sea ports. We could fade the national flag under the text of each country to make it more identifiable, filling it with advertising which pays for it all. By my calculations I reckon we could clear about a million a year. Is your husband still brilliant, or what?'

'Oooh, welcome back your lovely mind my darling. You've kept that idea very quiet although you've obviously spent some hours thinking about it.'

They had great fun putting together the basics of a tourist magazine, and advertisers seemed keen to become involved, providing the rates were reasonable, of course, but Sally did wonder why someone else, already in the tourist industry, had not come up with such a logical idea before; still, it wouldn't be the first time something so obvious had been overlooked. They took the concept to the British Tourist Board, and met with a very friendly and helpful member of staff who told them that such an idea had already been tried some years earlier, but eventually failed through lack of interest on the part of the tourist. Besides, travellers were now beginning to use the information available on the new World Wide Web. Another dousing of cold water.

Diamond Air still continued to occupy his mind, regardless of the total lack of enthusiasm from potential backers; he was like a dog with a bone and he considered it far too good an opportunity to give up on. Running his own airline? The world would know that Havers was still king. That would give him some lovely tales to tell in the pub.

'I tell you what's worrying me,' said Sally one afternoon. 'According to your travel agent friend, the fact that we have been granted the route from London Biggin Hill to Jersey has become known within the aviation industry?'

'Well, he would know, wouldn't he? He sells thousands of airline seats a year, and he keeps his nose to the ground.'

'My point exactly. He didn't get the news about the route from us; therefore he must have picked it up from others within the industry who know about it. My question is: if there's good money in it, why haven't one of the big boys picked up on it and snapped the route from under our feet, it's been months since it was allocated to us and I worry that it's because they know a bit more about it than you do, and know there's no real money in it.'

'Don't worry about it. Anyway, I've had another idea that'll make us an absolute fortune. There has to be a way to beat the odds at a racetrack. I've been thinking about it, and I know just how to do it.' He ran a complicated process of races multiplied by the number of horses divided by the race number of the favourite, or something, by her, but she was completely lost after the second equation.

'Yeah, right. Whatever. Any particular preference for supper?'

'Give me my car keys, sweetheart, I want to go to All Saint's Road,' he demanded, his outstretched hand accompanied by much clicking of fingers.

'You've just had two glasses of wine and can't drive so I will drive you to All Saint's Road, and will you please stop snapping your fingers at me,' she replied sweetly. 'What do you want to go there for anyway?'

'Questions, questions always fucking questions. If you must know there's a piece of dirt I want to look at. If you have to drive, you can drop me at the pub when we're finished and pick me up again at 7 o'clock.'

'I'll certainly drop you at the pub if that's what you want, but you can bloody well walk back, it'll only take you ten minutes and I've got supper to see to.'

He got a taxi home, his varicose veins made it far too painful to walk.

The land at All Saint's Road turned out to be quite an interesting proposition. A homeowner was selling 50% of his garden for development, and a large firm of house builders had agreed a deal to purchase it, but had finally withdrawn in the face of stiff opposition to the design from other neighbours. But Toby came up with a clever, stepped design for the house that didn't impact on anybody in the vicinity. He penned his original design first thing in the morning, but by lunchtime he was creating ever more outlandish ideas. Sally sent the early morning design to the architect.

'Hi Alex, it's Sally. Feel like another funding deal? Good. Toby is asleep at the moment . . . Yes, I know it's the middle of the afternoon, but that's how it is these days, I'm afraid, which is why you are talking to me, not him. We want to buy a single plot of land in All Saints Road that we don't expect to have any trouble getting planning on, then build it out and sell once completed. I've been promised 60% from a local building society, but I'm going to be short of the final 40%, which is where you come in. If you feel like plugging the financial gap, with only a second charge, I would be happy to pay you an agreed percentage over base rate for the duration of the loan. What about it?'

'I have to say, Sally; when I saw Toby the other day I did not like what I saw,' said Alex. 'It was only lunchtime, but his eyes were bloodshot, his nose was red and he looked like an old man. What is he doing to himself? He looks as though he's drinking himself to death.'

'That's about the size of it, I'm afraid Alex. And if I dare to raise the subject I get told to mind my own business in no uncertain terms; that I knew he was a heavy drinker when I married him and I shouldn't try to change him now. He doesn't seem to understand, or perhaps I should say doesn't want to understand, that his liver is so damaged by so many years of abuse it is no longer able to deal with the volumes of alcohol he is continually throwing at it. I am desperately worried about him. There's no point trying to do anything before Christmas is on us, but I am going to try to encourage him to do something about it in the New Year.'

'Good girl, he needs you more than he knows. I tell you what though, and I'm sorry to have to say this, but I wouldn't want to get into any deal with him in his present state. If I know that you are in the driving seat I shall be happy to support the All Saint's Road project. Fax me a line with your proposals and we'll get something moving.

She wanted to cry for her Toby, she loved him so much and it hurt her to be so helpless in the face of his drinking problem. Looking at the whole picture from a distance it seemed as though everything had started to slide badly when he lost the estate agency; his baby had been taken from him and he didn't seem to have much of a purpose to his life any more, his fight had gone. If one of his oldest and closest friends saw it as well it certainly wasn't her imagination. If only there was someway she could just get him to ease up his drinking without him flying off the handle.

The doctor – perhaps he could help. She made an appointment to see him.

'You remember the lump in my neck that you sent me to have aspirated twice this year?' she began as she settled into the surgery chair. 'I was told it's a cyst, and if it fills up again I will need to have a piece of my thyroid removed. Well, it has. Surgery is certainly the last thing I need at the moment, but I guess it's important, so could you arrange an appointment for me, please. That's number one.

'Number two is Toby. I don't have to tell you he's drinking again, you would know through his blood tests anyway, and it's causing all sorts of problems. He drinks and drives, which I try and stop, but not always successfully; he's already had one ban, if he gets stopped again it's going to be more than 18 months, and apart from anything else it's a huge strain on me. But most importantly it's his mental health that concerns me. He used to have such a sharp, clever mind, especially in the property market. He used to run circles round his competitors and had an awesome reputation in the industry – he even sat on the board of a bank at one time, but he's lost his touch now; he spends hours on the phone, but only finds the occasional small deal – just enough to keep us afloat and stop our home from being repossessed. We're living a very modest lifestyle, but even that is way beyond what I can earn from modelling, and we're struggling, constantly borrowing. I am having to make all sorts of decisions in his industry that I feel ill equipped to make, though I'm learning all the time. The last straw was yesterday when one of his oldest and dearest friends refused to do any form of business with him any more. He used to be so smart, such lively, wonderful company with a wicked sense of humour, but it's all gone now; the tragedy is he can't see it. Every time I raise the issue with him I get told to stop trying to change him, that I knew he was a heavy drinker when I married him. It's an endless cycle and it's getting me down.' She lost the battle with her tears, and they began to trickle down her face.

Doctor Lincoln sat quietly listening to her outpouring of distress and making his notes. When she sat back, tissue in hand, drying her eyes, he reached for the telephone and asked his secretary to bring in Toby's notes.

'Did he tell you that he has almost no platelets in his blood? This means that if he were to sever either a vein or an artery through surgery, or even an accident, he would, in all likelihood, bleed to death. I'm sorry to be so brutal since you've obviously got more than enough on your plate, but he clearly does need help, and if anyone can help him, you can. Alcohol abuse is responsible for his condition, and if he is drinking as much as I think he is, and for as long as he has been, it is definitely abuse. You may remember he came to see me about his varicose veins. The reason I sent him to see the specialist was because I had blood tests done here, at the surgery, but your husband refused to accept those results and said he still wanted to see the specialist. Perhaps he was hoping the results would be different.'

She was numb with the horror of what she had heard. Something had to be done, but how on earth was she going to get him to take it seriously?

Let's get Christmas out of the way first, she thought.

Toby brought George, William and Simon home on Christmas morning, and Sally made them all walk the ten minutes to the pub for their Christmas drink, then walk back again whilst she was busy with the preparation of their festive meal together. She considered how she would tackle the problem of his drinking in the New Year, and found her thoughts drifting to others who had problems, especially over Christmas – all the unhappiness and difficulties that there were in the world. Christmas Day would have so much more meaning if such things could be put aside for the day, just like the English and Germans did when they had their game of football together in the First World War before going back to their trenches to try and kill each other.

She dialled the number. 'Hello Hilary, it's Sally. I just wanted to wish you Christmas greetings on Christmas Day. Just a Christian gesture, nothing more.'

'Thank you, that's very kind of you,' came the soft reply.

The receivers were quietly replaced.

Chapter 39

In the New Year she saw the specialist about the cyst in her thyroid, and an appointment was made for the operation at the end of May; meantime she had been booked for a week's modelling in Mauritius, which was a small break in the ever-darkening cloud that was looming on the horizon – that of bringing his drinking under some sort of control.

Back from Mauritius and she found one of the garage doors hanging on just one of its hinges as she pulled into the driveway, and his big Mercedes was parked askew across the driveway, half in, half out of the garage. Oh God, she thought, he's obviously completely out of control now.

'I need to talk to you Toby. I've been waiting to get Christmas and the New Year celebrations out of the way before telling you this, but I've got to go into hospital for surgery in a few months. This lump in my neck has got to be removed. It's not life threatening, but what you have is.' She let that sink in for a moment.

'What do you mean? What have I got that's life threatening?'

'You weren't quite straight with me after your visit to the specialist last year were you? When I saw Doctor Lincoln just before Christmas he told me the real results of your blood test, and it's so serious that you could die by simply falling over because of the damage your long term drinking has done to your blood.'

'Oh for Christ's sake, you're not starting on that again. Can't you give it a fucking rest?'

She could feel a row brewing, but had to plough on. 'It's your drinking that has to have a rest, not my nagging. Look what you've done to the garage door – you've been drinking and driving again while I was away and it has to stop. Either you cut out drinking or you cut out driving, one or the other – which is it to be? For my money it has to be the drinking. Remember how positive you felt about giving it up three years ago? You've done it once, you can do it again.'

'Bollocks! I'm not drinking nearly as much as I used to, and when I hit the garage door it was just because my foot slipped off the brake pedal as I turned round in my seat to judge the distance I had left. You know how close I have to get to the garage because of the length of the car. So it was nothing to do with drinking, but if you're really worried I promise I will cut down a bit, OK? Now, what's for supper?'

And so we drink and drive,
No care for others on the road.

We're drunk, we are alive –
One more for the frog and toad.

And then – fate casts it's weary line,
We do not care, we do not see
That all around can find a sign
That shows that we're a touch malign.
We don't appreciate we're drunk.

In sober light of dawn you find
Others of a same, like mind.
Some are sober, some are drunk.
Some just stink like a skunk.
But you, of course, were never drunk –
You will of course deny it!

Sally's mother had been unwell for some time, but although her death came as something of a shock shortly after her return from Mauritius, the modest inheritance gave them yet another financial lifeline and kept the Havers going again. Toby was right about one thing – just as things were looking economically bleak for them something would turn up, but her brother's and mother's death were not at all what she would have wanted.

Some fucking bastard shopped me!' Toby yelled, storming through the front door and throwing his car keys down on the hall table.

'Which fucking bastard are we talking about exactly? For what did he shop you, and to whom?' Sally was amused at the screwed up indignant expression on his face.

'How the hell should I know who it was, the cops wouldn't tell me. I'd only had a pint at The Spotted Parrot, just one, good as gold I was. Saves an ear bashing from you when I get home. I came out, got into the car and the bastards nabbed me round the corner, they wanted me to take a breath test; 'course I refused, I'm not being done for that again. I told them I was asthmatic, they could have a urine or blood sample if they wanted but I couldn't breath into that machine of theirs, but they wouldn't take either, so there's nothing they can do me for – I offered, not my fault if they refused. I want to know who shopped me to the law – I'll kill the fucking bastard.'

Sally rubbed her forehead in frustration. 'Listen, you may be very popular with some people, but although winding people up is one of the joys of your life, there are a lot of people who don't take as kindly to your particular style of humour as you would like. You have been known to wind some people up into a state of active dislike, and they are quite capable of going out of their way to cause trouble for you. Besides, why should some people take great care not to drink and drive, then watch others like you flouting the law? How do you think it makes them feel? Anyway, you can't simply refuse a breath test and expect to just get away with it, otherwise everyone would do it. They'll need proof from your doctor of any asthma and you're no way asthmatic.' For a seemingly clever man how could he be so stupid?

"My man, I'll have another double."
"Sir, you'll be in real trouble"
"I haven't had enough to drink!"
"I think you've had more than you think,
If you go home to see the wife
You'll be into loads of strife!"

*"It's just that now the day has ended
The consequences can be mended.
Just pour me another double,
I'll sort out the real trouble.
When I get home I'll have more wine,
Believe me, I can walk the line."*

*And so six more were bevied down.
Then on driving back through town
I saw blue lights far behind,
Flashing madly –* "Never mind
*I haven't had a serious drink.
That is what I liked to think.*

*The breathalyser showed up red,
The booze had now gone to my head.
Three years I'll get, and quite a fine,
I'm sure if I'd to walk the line
I'd have known that I was drunk –
More drunken than a drunken skunk!*

'Darling, please sit down and talk to me, just for a minute – please?' She sat on the floor at his feet, her tear filled eyes pleading with him as she held his hands. 'I can't bear this any more. Are we only to have 11 years together after all we have been through? We lost over 20 years because of mistakes made; please let's not make any more. I can't take the repercussions of your levels of drinking any more; your liver is so damaged by years of abuse that you could easily die without warning. Your mind has lost its edge, your clever reasoning has gone. Your humour is only alcohol fuelled rubbish. You are just a shadow of the man you used to be, even Alex has noticed it. You have stopped caring for me, now it is just me caring for you. I will continue to care for you because you need help and I love you so, but there's a certain amount you simply have to do to help yourself. If for no other reason, think of what your drinking is doing to me, to us. If you won't help yourself how can you expect me to – do you want me to just walk away with a broken heart?'

He knew his resolve had to be mustered again. He'd done it once, he could do it again. Doctor Lincoln pulled a few strings and found a bed immediately for him in the mental ward of the hospital; an overnight bag was packed and Sally drove him over.

Once in bed he was given a heavy dose of diazepam and quickly fell into a deep drug induced sleep. She knew there would be no point visiting for 48 hours, he wouldn't be coherent or able to stand, but once the dosage was reduced a little she went to the ward as often as she could, taking a fresh dressing gown each time to replace the one he wore in the only area where smoking was permitted, and where he spent most of his waking time. He didn't bother to shave, his posture became stooped, his hair was a dirty mess and he stank of stale cigarettes. He was going to have a long fight to regain his self-respect.

She refused all modelling for the first two weeks after his return home so that she could keep an eye on him, he was very fragile, but soon perked up once the effects of the diazepam cleared his system. She pampered him and did her best to make him feel that life was far better without booze, and gradually life settled into a pattern of it's own without regular visits to the pub. Ironically, now that he had stopped drinking, he was still going to get a serious driving ban when he finally got to Court in May. Oh, well, that's life.

Chapter 40

William told his father and step-mother that he wanted to get married, but privately he told Sally he was worried that his father might embarrass him if he got drunk at the ceremony, and could she keep an eye on him please? But William was delighted when she told him his father had decided to have another stab at drying out and hadn't had a drink for a month. The boy was only 21 and rather young for such a commitment, but he and his girlfriend Gemma had been together for over two years and she had recently found that she was pregnant, so the announcement was given parental blessing all round.

Sally fretted over the coming together of both William's mother and stepmother in the same room at the celebration of the happy event. If this wasn't handled carefully it could turn the wedding into a disaster.

She decided to take the initiative:

Dear Hilary

Toby and I are delighted to hear that William and Gemma are to be married next month, and will do all that we can to help the day go smoothly.

With that in mind, it occurs to me that, as the mother-of-the-groom, this is almost as much your day as theirs, and I would be loathe for anything to mar your joy.

How do you feel about meeting up before the event, for a quick drink perhaps, in order to take any potential strain away from a first meeting on the wedding day?

I should be very pleased to hear from you if you think the idea has any merit.

Best wishes - Sally

But as things turned out there was not enough time to organise a meeting between them. Hilary had taken a job selling furniture that required her to travel across the southeastern region of England, Sally was busy with modelling, and before they knew it the day was upon them.

Sevenoaks Registry Office had been chosen for the hurried wedding, with the small family reception to be held at a local hotel, and a state of almost friendly calm prevailed between the three adults, each aware of the need to make it a day to remember for the right reasons.

Sally went into hospital at the end of May for her thyroid operation, and this time it was Toby's turn to visit his wife in hospital. The day following surgery they sat together on a bench in the grounds of the hospital and chatted. He was doing fine, he was starting to get some colour back into his cheeks again and the missing sparkle was slowly beginning to find its way back into his eyes.

'Your drink driving charge is coming up tomorrow, isn't it?' she reminded him. 'Just do me a favour, I'll still be stuck in here and won't be able to drive you, but please, please, please don't drive yourself. If you drive to the Court and do get banned the car will be stuck in Bromley and will give *me* the problem of getting it back. Take the train, it's not as though you have the busiest of schedules at the moment, so the extra time it will take won't matter. Please?'

'Yeah, don't worry about it. I'll be fine, they can't ban me because they didn't get a breath sample and they refused to take blood or urine. All they can do is fine me.'

'Toby, look at me. I am asking you as a favour to me not to drive there. Please, if you do nothing else just do this one thing for me.'

'Yeah, yeah, whatever you say, sweetheart. You'll be home the following day though, won't you?'

'Yes. I'm home on Saturday morning, so I'll see you again then. Please remember what I have asked you.'

'Bye, darling. See you Saturday.' And he was gone.

She was still feeling a bit tired from the effects of the surgery as she drove herself home on the Saturday morning, and was surprised to see Toby's car parked at an angle across the driveway blocking her access and forcing her to park in the street. She put her overnight bag down in the hall, and her car keys onto the hall table to go in search of her husband who was staggering around the kitchen, hardly able to stand, waving a glass of wine in the air.

'Oh, hello sweetheart, come in and have a drink. Everything OK? How was the op?'

'I don't believe this! What the hell are you doing? What happened to your promise to stop drinking?' The tears spurted unbidden.

'I never promised. I said I'd give it a go, and I did – I went into that bloody awful hospital for a week, didn't I? Fucking bastards banned me from driving again yesterday, gave me three years this time for failing to give a breath test. Bloody doctor wouldn't back me up on the asthma story, but at least they couldn't do me for drink driving, so I won there. They also want me to pay a £500 fine, so I told them I had no money and can only pay in monthly instalments – got the bastards on that one too.'

'Why is your car half across the driveway?' A nasty suspicion was crawling through her mind.

'Dunno. The way I parked last night I s'pose. It was late, it was dark.'

'Last night? Are you telling me you drove last night, after the Court had banned you in the afternoon? How did you get to and from the Court?'

'Fucking drove, what do you think? Stupid woman,' he muttered as he went to refill his glass.

She was in despair and went up to the bedroom to unpack and lie down for a while. After a few minutes she heard her car being started – he was driving away in her car. She ran downstairs to find the keys to his car so she could follow him, but they were nowhere to be found, so she locked the house and began the 15-minute walk to his favourite pub, still feeling rather unbalanced by the recent anaesthetic and operation. When she finally arrived at the car park, feeling utterly drained, she found her car with its keys in the side pocket, which was where he usually left them, and drove herself home.

His car keys finally appeared the following morning in the bowl of pot pourri in the downstairs toilet where he must have thrown them on his first port of call after returning home on the Friday night. That explains why he had taken her car – he had been unable to remember where he had put his keys. She took both sets and kept them securely hidden from him.

There was no point in keeping both cars with only one driver. Since hers had more value and was too small to be practical for a one-car family she let it go, and got back what she had paid for it, which was a bonus, and Toby's cherished registration she had used on the car went onto retention for now.

His friends were starting to become really concerned at his state now. Their constant remarks were enough to make him think that perhaps he should think seriously about his liver. Did he really look a bit yellow? He didn't think so, but more than one of his drinking mates had commented on his colouring. Maybe he ought to have another go at this detox lark. But there was no was he was going back into that poxy mental ward. Dreadful place that was.

'Right – I've made a decision. I've decided I'm going on the wagon again, for good this time you'll be pleased to hear, but I'm not going back into that awful place. Find out from the doc if you can give me the tablets at home, sweetheart. Shouldn't be too hard, that's all they did in hospital, just gave me a bunch of tablets and I slept most of the time.' Toby sounded committed, he was making all the right noises, but Sally could do no more than keep all her fingers and toes crossed; his teetotal record wasn't that good.

She was instructed to give him 60 milligrams of diazepam a day, gradually reducing the dosage over the period of a week. 60 milligrams made him totally incoherent and as limp as a rag doll, but at least it helped to stop him from suffering the DTs. It became rather tricky and time consuming for her to give him his first knockout tablets at breakfast, take the train to London for some television work she had been booked for, race back in time to wake him for a light lunch and administer his next lot of tablets. Next train back to London, then return to wake him for supper and more tablets for the night. After three days she was exhausted, but he was holding together. They were both pleased with his progress and gradually he returned to a state of normality.

After receipt of the last letter from Copeland & Copeland, who were wondering where the negotiations were taking them, Sally suggested to him: 'Things seem to be a little calmer with Hilary since the wedding, how about we meet up with her and try to discuss how we could help her get a property in return for squashing the Order?'

'You're mad, there's no way she'd ever agree to scrapping her precious Order. I'm surprised at you, Sally – I thought you'd got her measure.'

'That's exactly my point. Listen, she clearly won't accept that her Order is a worthless bit of paper; but if we can persuade her to drop her ridiculous demands in return for something she can actually have, and explain that such a compromise might give you the incentive to get back into the stirrups, she might well see the logic. How about it?'

'Sorry love, I'm afraid you'll find that words like logic and compromise aren't in her vocabulary. But if you want to have a stab at it I'll tag along with you.'

Following their successful meeting at William and Gemma's wedding Hilary cautiously agreed to meet them both for a drink to try and agree a way out of the stalemate that had arisen over the last three years since she had instructed Coleman & Coleman. She was really quite disappointed with her solicitor, for some reason he didn't seem to be getting anywhere, almost as though he agreed with her ex-husband's stupid statements about not having any money.

The meeting took place at a pub next to where Hilary was living, where she and Sally had a white wine and Toby had a limejuice and soda. The two women chatted in a cordial enough fashion until he returned with the drinks, but he wasn't looking at all comfortable with the situation. Give him a boardroom of directors to win round or a pub full of blokes any day; this was not at all his cup of tea.

'Well now,' Sally started, addressing Hilary. 'Let's try and get this sorted out as simply as possible, shall we? Our problem is that we are struggling for money because I'm handling everything, and I'm a very cautious person – safe pair of hands, if you like. The only person who can make any real money is Toby, and he has no incentive to do that whilst he has an unattainable £750,000 axe hanging over his head. Our suggestion is this: if you will agree to quash that Order we will agree to enter into a new, legal agreement with you for something that will be possible for us to achieve. For example, we could buy a plot of land and build you a house somewhere, if you would like that. Then you would at least have your foot back on the property ladder. How does something like that appeal to you?'

'How about the property you are building in All Saints Road? You could give me that?'

Sally wondered how on earth she knew about All Saints Road; but of course, William or Simon would have mentioned it. Hilary also made it clear she was keeping a regular eye on their company accounts filed at Companies House as she talked about the board of directors.

'No, not All Saints Road I'm afraid, the spec on that is too high and the expected equity is all we will have to keep a roof over our heads for a while, but if you were to agree to an outline proposal for a new build, properly drawn up by your solicitors of course, then we can start looking for somewhere for you.'

Sally deliberately didn't mention the church hall Toby had found in Bickley; in any event the six little semis planned for there wouldn't have suited Hilary's tastes. Once planning consent was granted there would hopefully be a tidy profit, but that would be at least a year away, if not more. It was all finely balanced at the present time. What Hilary didn't know, she didn't need to be told.

'Why were you out in Jersey two months ago?' Hilary demanded. Such knowledge could only have come from Simon or William.

'I don't see that that has anything to do with tonight's issues, but I'm sure you remember Ray Milne? His wife was rushed to hospital after a stroke and Toby went over to support him. But to get back to the matter in hand ...'

'What about the Cayman Isles?'

'What about the fucking Cayman Isles, for Christ's sake?' Toby was starting to lose his temper, a temper that was becoming more and more fragile without the cushion of alcohol. 'You keep banging on about the Cayman Isles, and I've told your solicitors that it was just a stupid throw away line donkey's years ago. Do me a favour, get yourself out to the Cayman Isles with an open letter from me and from Sally, that will allow you to access any bank account anywhere on the island in either of our names. If you find any money you can have it – it's all yours. Just get off my fucking back woman!' And he stomped off to the toilet.

Sally needed to pour a little oil on increasingly turbulent waters. 'Hilary. There are no hidden funds. If there had been I would not have needed to continually borrow from my mother and rely on others for support. Really, those constant allegations are not helpful. Plus, he's trying to stop drinking and he's not finding it easy to deal with emotional situations like this. All I can ask you to do is think about what I've said, run it by your solicitor and get Mr Connor to give us your thoughts.'

Toby returned, Sally stood up. 'OK, I think we're done, Hilary has agreed to think about what we've said and get in touch, through Mr Connor, as and when.' And they each departed to their respective homes.

Chapter 41

At the end of June Sally received a call from her mother-in-law who had decided to leave Spain and return to the UK for good. Her health was failing, and as a former matron she knew exactly what was wrong with her; she had an idea roughly how much time she had left and she needed her daughter-in-law's help in sorting out her Spanish affairs whilst she still had time. Sally was a little concerned at leaving Toby on his own after what happened the last time she had left him to his own devices, so he decided he would go to Jersey and spend some time with Ray whilst she was away. Ray knew his friend was drying out and wouldn't encourage any drinking, so it was all arranged. She took him to the airport to catch a flight an hour earlier than hers and arranged his return flight to coincide with her return four days later.

Ray's home was quite remote in the northern part of the island, and Toby was bored after two days wandering around the house. So the following day he asked Ray to drop him in St Helier on his way to work, he would do a bit of shopping and catch the bus back later. Which he did, via the pub where he stopped for a limejuice and soda, which was followed by a half pint of beer. Just the one mind you. One would certainly be OK, he was on holiday after all.

His flight arrived at Gatwick an hour before Sally landed with his mother, so he wandered into the airport pub for a limejuice and soda, which was necessary to try and disguise the smell of the beer he had first.

But there was no disguising it, she smelt it instantly and felt so angry. How are you supposed to help someone who doesn't seem able to help himself? she asked herself. All her tireless efforts at the home detox had been wasted. What the hell were they going to do now? She tried to hide her feelings from his mother, the old lady had enough on her mind, and they only had to get through this evening before taking her down to her friend in Gloucester the next day. They arrived home from the airport, Sally settled her mother-in-law into a spare room then took their bags up to the bedroom to start unpacking and sort the laundry. Toby was annoyed at her for being angry with him so went to the pub to drown his sorrows and was quite drunk when he got back two hours later. She was in tears and sent him to sleep in another room. Their brave new world was collapsing again.

Simon called round a few weeks later and found the mental mire into which his father and stepmother were slowly sinking; the atmosphere was not good and he didn't stay long. An hour later the phone rang. It was Hilary.

'Sally? I'm so sorry to hear that things are not good – Simon told me Toby has gone back to drinking, but he seemed to be doing so well when we met the other week. How are things, are you all right?' Someone being nice to her was like opening the floodgates; Sally started crying and found she couldn't stop. As she sobbed, Hilary was at her most solicitous, providing a shoulder, offering help, asking questions. By the time the call ended Sally was a crumpled mess, Toby was drunk again and Hilary had learned all she needed to know.

At bedtime Sally found she couldn't bear to be anywhere near him and banished him to the spare room. But he was frightened, he knew he was out of control again; was scared of where all this was going to end and terrified of losing her. As she sat on the edge of the bed he told her in no uncertain terms that he was not going to sleep in the spare room again, his place was next to her in their bed. 'I've been faithful to you for 11 years,' he shouted, leaning his whole body closer to her, trying to dominate her with his presence. 'I've never been faithful to one woman for so long, so don't you dare tell me I'm not sleeping with you.' But after all the years of frustration her temper finally cracked, she screamed at him to get out and leave her in peace – when drunk he was repulsive. He panicked, his right arm took on a force of its own as he lashed out at her, and his hand dealt her a massive blow to the side of her head, knocking her right across their king size bed where she fell to the floor on the other side. He turned and left the room to get some support from a glass of wine in the kitchen.

As she sat curled on the floor gasping and holding the side of her head, she wondered if the bottom had now totally fallen out of her world. How was she ever going to get everything back in control? He needed a short sharp shock. Then she remembered Hilary's answer to such a problem and dialled 999.

The police arrived within minutes and saw the red welt across the side of her rapidly swelling face. The two officers were angry, wife beating was taken very seriously and he was hauled of to the local police station, protesting violently that it had only been a little tap because she wouldn't let him get to bed. 'Anyway, what's wrong with that?' he continued to mumble. 'It's only the wife.' But that just made it worse.

Neither of them slept much that night; he because he was locked in a cold police cell with only a hard shelf and light blanket for warmth. She because most of her night was spent sobbing in abject misery at the loss of her adored husband.

When she collected him from the police station the following morning he was contrite, and said he realised that he had to do something about his drinking, yet again. Having the occasional drink was obviously not going to work out; he needed to see the doctor again.

Doctor Lincoln agreed to put him back on the detox programme, but warned him he couldn't pull any strings for him this time, it might take a few weeks.

'For Christ's sake doc, when a bloke decides he needs help, he needs it now, not in three months time.'

'Yes I do know, but you've probably heard how stretched the NHS is. Have you thought about going privately?'

'That would cost thousands, and we haven't got thousands. No, just get me on the NHS programme ASAP, please doc.'

'Doctor, how about giving him that pill that makes him sick when he drinks?' Sally wanted to know.

'You probably mean Antabuse. No, I couldn't give him that if he is still drinking. At best it would make him very sick indeed, at worst it could prove fatal.'

'No, I think it could be OK doc.' Toby thought he could see an easy solution to the problem, another prop that might help get him through. 'I'm only drinking a bit, and it's only been for a couple of weeks – it won't be difficult to stop completely again without taking those awful muscle relaxant things. I should know, I've done it before. Sally will keep an eye on me and the Antabuse would stop me cheating.'

'The Antabuse won't stop you cheating, it will just be dangerous if you do, and you're putting a huge burden on your wife, you know.'

'Yeah I know, but she'll do it for me.' He took his wife's hand between both of his, and his love for her glowed from his eyes as strongly as ever. He looked deeply into her heart, and said: 'When I'm through this completely we're going away for a nice long break – she's had a rough time with me, doc, and I owe her big time.'

'All right, here's the prescription. I'll leave it in your wife's capable hands then, but please remember, even one drink could be very nasty indeed.'

'Thank you doctor. He'll be fine, don't worry, I'll look after him,' Sally assured him.

'Have you thought about Alcoholics Anonymous?' suggested Doctor Lincoln. Sally looked at her husband in pleasant surprise when he replied: 'That's a good idea, doc. I'll find out where the meetings are and pop along one day.' Was there yet a modicum of hope?

He was as good as his word. He took the Antabuse under Sally's watchful eye – it was worse than giving a child unpleasant medicine, insisting on checking under his tongue each time he was given a tablet to swallow; but he took it in good spirits and the lack of alcohol was having no adverse affects on him this time. Quite the contrary, he seemed bright and bubbly, very much like his old self.

He started to go to local meetings of Alcoholics Anonymous, and for the first time in his life had to stand up and say: 'My name is Toby, and I'm an alcoholic.' The meetings were pretty boring, he had to admit, and as he walked home after each session the lights and laughter coming from the pubs he passed became more and more inviting as the weeks went by. Going to the meetings was the only time he was leaving the house these days and he was becoming starved of entertainment. Just the one wouldn't hurt, would it? He had taken the Antabuse that morning, hours ago, and he calculated it would have worked its way out of his system by now. Anyway he knew he had the constitution of an ox – always needing more aspirin than others to cure simple headaches. Just a half pint then.

Then at lunchtime the following day he had just the one glass of wine at home from his hidden bottle.

Two days later Sally thought he was dying when she walked into the kitchen and saw him sitting in his chair with sweat pouring down his face; a face that was chalk white, and he seemed to be struggling for breath.

'What's the matter? What the hell's happened to you? Please tell me you haven't taken alcohol on top of the Antabuse?' He could only nod mutely. 'Just the one, though.'

'Here, drink this water, try and flush your system through while I ring the chemist for advice. Are you trying to kill yourself, you stupid, stupid man?'

It wasn't working. He was really struggling to stop drinking and nothing seemed to help.

He stopped taking the Antabuse, and asked her to help him monitor his drinking, and keep it moderate, until he could get onto the detox programme at the hospital again. Each day she measured out a one-litre jug of wine mixed with water, gradually increasing the water and decreasing the wine content, as he had asked her to do, and he seemed to be managing with that, which was encouraging.

Sally had been in bed for an hour. She had finished reading her book and realised that Toby hadn't come up, all the lights and the television were still blazing downstairs, which was odd for this hour of the night.

She went to investigate and found him lying flat out on the kitchen floor, moaning about the pain in his back, seemingly barely conscious and covered with foul smelling liquid, as was most of the tiled floor. She bent over to try to help him to his feet and realised the smell was urine mixed with wine, and it made her gag. He couldn't lift himself without a stab of pain, and she couldn't help unaided. She had to call 999 again.

The ambulance men were not as gentle as his wife, and Toby found himself being manhandled by two burly men when they realised he had been drinking. They hauled him to his feet when their examination revealed there was nothing wrong with his back, and plonked him into his chair, having first thoughtfully covered it with a large sheet of polythene to protect the upholstery.

'I'm so sorry to have called you out for nothing.' Sally apologised when she realised she should have been tougher with him.

'No, don't worry, it's not nothing. It could have been serious if he really had injured his back when he fell, and it's quite normal for heavy drinkers to lose control of their bladders at times of stress like this. He's obviously had a hell of a lot to drink, does he have a problem?' they asked.

'Yes, a big problem, but I thought he was trying to sort it out. Obviously I was wrong.'

They left her with a copy of their report and bade her goodnight. The next step was to help him get undressed, place his soaking wet, soiled clothes straight into the washing machine, and lead him up for a quick shower before putting him to bed.

When she had finished washing the kitchen floor she checked the supply of wine, and found that there was a lot less in the bottle than she had noticed that morning – there was her answer.

The episode gave him yet another fright; he was less invincible than he had thought, and in the cold light of day realised that he was back at square one.

'I'm out of my depth aren't I?' he asked her sadly. 'I always used booze to help when things came apart at the seams, but used it too much to help me cope with Hilary and her lawyers, and now it's using me, isn't it? You know, there are times I want to shout and scream till I'm hoarse, but I can't – it's not the done thing. I've never let my failures show, never admitted to them – just had another drink. Please help me sweetheart,' and he broke down, sobbing in her arms, a broken shadow of a man. 'You're the only one I can let my guard down in front of, the only one that I can turn to when I'm in trouble and I know you'll understand and help me.' They held each other tightly in their mutual pain.

The doctor had kept him listed for the detox programme at the local hospital, and Sally drove him over on the appointed day. The ward was every bit as grim as she remembered, and the smoking room, where he spent most of his time, was worse. His dressing gown had to be changed daily, he was usually unshaven and unwashed, and Sally wondered what he must have thought of himself, if anything. His self-respect seemed to have gone out of the window with the alcohol. Patients with all sorts of mental problems were receiving help in the ward, consequently there were no single rooms, only large wards with each cubicle curtained from the next providing a minimum of privacy. His lunch was a pre-prepared meal on a tray taken from a trolley containing other identical luke warm meals, and eaten in solitary silence at a Formica topped table. As she watched him slowly eat the plain, tasteless offering, her mind wandered back to the meals they had enjoyed at the Savoy, and all the other beautiful restaurants where he appreciated the finer points of a superbly cooked meal with the finest of wines to complement each perfectly presented dish. Because he could never enjoy a fine wine again, did that mean he would not be able to enjoy an exquisite meal on its own, she wondered?

Four green walls surround you,
The room is really shit.
How I wish and how I rue
I had no wounds to lick.

You look at all around you –
Some perhaps are due,
Some just make you tick,
But mostly, mostly, mostly
You just want to take the mick.

Take your pick of those who're here.
Some are straight
And some are queer.
Whether it is Tom or Dick
A lifetime here would make you sick.

Some depressed and some just bicker.
The green, the paintings make you sicker.
Not just day one, all the time
Let's get out before we're sad.
Let's get out before we're mad

'I had a look round a card shop today, sweetheart. God, what a load of rubbish. I could write better cards better than that.' He was in good spirits, and had been for a couple of months now since his release from hospital, and she was daring to hope that the worst might really be over this time.

He began composing his cards, and spent hours on the poetry, she spent equal hours producing prototypes for him. They looked like fun. Next step would be to get them properly printed and marketed.

'I've got a plan for you,' she declared one morning. 'I remember you said you used to enjoy acting at school. How about I introduce you to some of my modelling agents, see if we can't get you some work that way. You'd really enjoy it so long as you don't try and take over directing the shoot. Come on, let's do some happy snaps for the agencies.' She took photographs of him sweeping leaves, trying to fix a car, relaxing in a bubble bath, cooking – anything that would show some diversity, and was very pleased with her results. Two agents were happy to take him on their books and they began to ask him to go to castings. He didn't get booked though, and eventually his enthusiasm waned; perhaps it wasn't as easy as it looked.

Chapter 42

Another Christmas was fast approaching and Sally was a little concerned as to how Toby would be able to handle his new found teetotal state over the festive holiday, but it had been three months now and it was looking good. Together they would just have to handle each day as it came. Christmas holidays were always a serious alcoholic period, but this one was going to be particularly heavy because of the Millennium celebrations, and she knew she would have her work cut out keeping him occupied and content at home without getting drawn into all the various parties. But seeing the new man that was starting to emerge from the drunken chrysalis was making the effort all worthwhile.

The evening before Christmas Eve and there was a violent, thunderous knocking at the door.

That's a bit strong – something must be wrong for someone to want to bash the door down like that, Toby thought. It was a process server, and Toby was forced to receive a large parcel of paperwork, which he brought through to Sally. They opened it up to find two bundles of legal papers, one for her and one for him. She felt her hackles begin to rise as she realised that Hilary had gone on the attack again. All that comforting shoulder and sympathy stuff she had offered a few months back had merely been a ruse to get as much information from Sally as possible whilst she was in a traumatised and emotional state. What a first class bitch!

Right – she wants to do things the hard way? So be it then. Sally got fired up with anger and began her plan of counter attack. She carefully read through all the information from the Court. It seemed that Hilary had made yet another ex-parte application to the Court, this time to block the sale of both their home and the new property in All Saints Road in order to secure all the equity in both assets for herself. As Sally read through she became more and more incensed. Hilary had convinced the Judge to grant her demands because her ex-husband and his wife were living a life of unashamed luxury whilst she was suffering in abject poverty. They were driving around in two Mercedes motorcars, each with a personalised number plate. Furthermore the ex-husband had made absolutely no attempt whatsoever to provide her with any financial assistance, not withstanding the Order of 1991. And another thing, the only reason the couple's assets were in the wife's name was to ensure it was all kept well out of reach of the Court, the wife was just a paper front, but in reality it was the ex-husband's money and Hilary wanted it – all of it.

Although the papers had been stamped by the Court on December

20th, they had only been served on the 23rd, so the 14 days they were given in which to respond – or face a potential jail sentence – was reduced to 11, and those 11 days were over a 14 day national holiday to celebrate the new Millennium.

Sally hadn't been this angry since she watched Hilary waving her worthless Court Order in her face back in '91. But her anger made her totally focused and she spent hours at her word processor assembling what she considered to be a suitable rebuttal; there was no way she would not be ready.

Toby couldn't stand the thought that all they had worked for over the past few years was going to be lost, it was just inconceivable. He saw the huge black hole of financial ruin yawning before him again and had a drink.

There is no greeting in the street,
No meeting of the minds.
It takes no effort to be sweet,
But there are other kinds.

The kind that always lacks the manners,
To give and not to take.
The kind that's rude and throws the spanner
To the lawyers, not the lake.

A world of compromise is easy to behold.
It takes no real effort
Just to give and not be cold.
It takes no real effort
To give – not go for gold.

There is no greeting in the street,
Just bitter, twisted sneers and sighs
Of your distaste.
It takes no effort to smile and greet
Others who can see new lines
Upon your face.

He couldn't be a part of Sally's paperwork; he made no sense whatsoever and relied on pure emotion, bent on telling the Court that Hilary was a lying, fucking, greedy bitch, which would not have served him too well before the

Judge. He was feeling completely useless and surplus to requirements, so had another drink to try to blot out thoughts of another hearing back at the High Court. By the time he went to bed he was less than steady on his feet. He staggered up the stairs – and slipped. Sally was reading, ready to try and get some sleep, when she heard his body crashing down the stairs. Shooting out of bed to see what had happened to him seemed to be becoming something of a habit, and she found him in a heap at the foot of the stairs with blood dripping from a large cut over his right eye and from another cut below his lip where it appeared his tooth had broken right through the skin. The cuts were deep and she was concerned at the platelets thing. Off to hospital again.

They were in Court number 46 of the Queen's Building of the High Court two days after the holiday finished and Sally was steaming. She had given up all hope on his drinking problem for the time being; the most important thing right now was stopping this vicious woman, the architect of all their present problems. She had also packed an overnight bag for Toby to present to the Court; she was fed up with the constant penal notices attached to everything served on him and wanted to call their bluff. They had been threatening him with jail for non-compliance for years and now she wanted to force them to show their hand and either exercise their threat – since he still refused to submit to Hilary's demands – or withdraw it.

She listened to Hilary's Barrister droning on, thinking how daft it was that he should be able to pass off such unsubstantiated rubbish as fact and be taken seriously. When it was her turn, she first apologised for the bloodied and stitched state her husband was in, explaining that he had fallen on the stairs two days earlier, then continued with her prepared rebuttal of Hilary's ludicrous and greedy claims, but was interrupted, very gently by the lady Judge, who told her: 'Mrs Havers, you are very erudite, but I'm sorry to have to tell you that you cannot continue with your present line. You seem to be basing your argument upon issues raised during the hearing of 1991, and I'm afraid they cannot be raised again here. I can only listen to matters pertaining to the latest Order granted on the 20th of December 1999.' She turned to Hilary's team and suggested perhaps more time should be given for a fuller presentation. Could they perhaps suggest a likely date, bearing in mind the Court's busy schedule? Indeed they could, m'lady. Knowing that the ex-husband was not to be professionally represented today they had anticipated such an outcome and had taken the precaution of enquiring of the Listings Clerk the next available date for a full seven day hearing, which was their estimate of the time likely to be required. It was to be the 9th of May – if that suited everybody? Hilary was smirking. Sally was deep in thought, and Toby wanted a drink.

He sat and worked on his cards idea. He picked up the airline plan again and spent hours on the phone chasing potential backers. He tried to find another site for residential development. Anything to fill his day with hope, to lessen the fear of the future.

Sally sat and typed, it was her turn to drone on now, and she was going to drone for England. If Hilary thought Sally was just a clueless fluffy bunny she was going to be in for a shock – this fluffy bunny had just had her fur rubbed up the wrong way for the last time; beware Hilary – bunnies have sharp claws and can deliver a nasty kick!

She wrote first to the hospital to ask for copies of Toby's outpatient and inpatient records, then to the ambulance service for copies of their two visits to the house. Her next letter was to Doctor Lincoln to ask for a report on both their medical histories, and was delighted to read his responses. Concisely laid out for all the world to see were details from his notes showing her state of mind and distress over their financial worries; did that sound like someone with millions stashed off shore? She gained proof that the value of their one car, not two, was negligible, and made it clear that the ex-wife was fully aware that the two personalised number plates she had tried to draw to the attention of the Court had been owned for over 25 years – the Court could draw their own conclusions from that. Affidavits were offered by various colleagues swearing that they will no longer deal with Toby because of his unstable state, and provided proof that it was only through Sally's efforts that they had held together financially over the years. Twenty-five points over nine pages of droning, and every fact backed up with evidence. Her bundle was quite impressive when she had finished.

She had been told she needed to file her response at Court within 28 days, with a copy to Hilary's advisers. But first she needed to ensure that it would pass scrutiny, that she had not gone too far off at any tangents and would have her paperwork thrown out at the first step; she needed Sue Jackson's advice, Toby's lawyer friend, who knew their case intimately.

Sally talked Sue through the paperwork that they had received just before Christmas, and told her what had happened when they went to Court in January.

'What I would like you to do, Sue, is cast your eye over my Affidavit with all it's supporting paperwork and just make sure I haven't strayed too far from the narrow points. What I don't want is for you to try and change anything that doesn't need changing or try to introduce any legal speak. This is my personal, unprofessional Affidavit and I want it to remain so. By the way could you please tell David Silver, that lovely barrister that got Toby his divorce, that we're due in Court for a week from the 9th of May, and see if both you and he can make that time free in your diaries for me? Could you both also find a few days at the end of April to run through everything? At the moment you are not instructed Sue, neither is David Silver, I just need a proper eye over my Affidavit – please.' Sue was happy to oblige and whilst there were a number of things in Sally's Affidavit that a solicitor simply would not say, on balance it would probably do the job and would certainly raise a few eyebrows.

Her papers were filed within the required time, and Hilary now had another 28 days to respond. Her advisers clearly felt they did not need to bother.

Chapter 43

Both the houses they were selling were attracting interested buyers, which raised their spirits, and Sally found she was showing people round one house or the other most days. The front garden of the property in All Saints Road had been turfed and she needed to visit it regularly with the hosepipe; then the weeding and mowing started on both properties. Modelling was keeping her quite busy as well so there weren't too many spare hours in the day.

The 9th of May was rapidly approaching, and Sally smiled to herself as she pictured Hilary and her advisers imagining that they were going to enjoy a repeat of Sally's amateur performance at her Court appearance at the beginning of the year, imagining that their barrister would be able to trample all over her. Hilary was no doubt feeling very pleased with herself and looking forward to grabbing her financial rewards.

'I'm willing to bet any money you like she's already rubbing her hands with glee and planning how she's going to spend all the money she expects to get from those two properties,' Toby remarked.

Towards the end of April Sally rang Sue Jackson and put her on the record, asking if she could arrange a conference with David Silver. Sue's first task was to advise Mr Conner at Copeland and Copeland that she had been instructed by her client, and that they would be instructing a barrister by the name of David Silver, who would be well known to their client.

'I wonder what's going on in Copeland and Copeland's office now that they know we are going to be legally represented, and by the same barrister that shafted her when you went for your divorce?' Sally smiled at her husband, feeling very smug and hopeful for the first time in years.

She went off to a photographic assignment, where she was to be a patient receiving medical help from a colleague at work following a heart attack, and had to look very solemn.

As she started applying the appropriate make-up her phone rang – it was Sue Jackson. 'I've just called Mr Connor to let him know we're on the record. You're never going to believe what he said.'

Her heart missed a beat: 'Oh shit Sue, what?'

'He said to me – and this is verbatim: "Can't you get your client to offer my client something, anything, just to get her off my back? The woman's driving me crazy".' By the sound of things I reckon we could get away with offering her £100,000.'

Sally put her phone down, finished applying her make-up and assumed the correct position slumped against the wall. The photographer said: 'Sally, would you mind wiping that silly grin off your face, you're supposed to have just had a heart attack.'

'Sorry. I've just some rather good news. Can we start again, please?'

She and Toby met with Sue at David Silver's chambers the following week, and went through every item in fine detail. Most of the morning went by in a blur, sandwiches were called for lunch and more detail was further examined during the afternoon. When they had finished, David Silver put his elbows on the desk and tapped the tips of his fingers together. He sat quietly, thoughtfully peering over the top of his rimless spectacles for a minute or two before he spoke.

'You know that I am well acquainted with their barrister don't you; matter of fact we did our degrees together. I propose to ring him first thing in the morning and make them an offer to settle.' Pause for dramatic effect, glasses removed.

'Do I have your permission to go as high as – say – £50,000?'

Sally took one long blink and one deep breath, her scalp prickling with delicious anticipation.

'Yes, indeed you do, David. I shall leave it in your very capable hands, and wait with bated breath to hear from Sue when you have reached a settlement figure.'

Sue rang Sally the following morning and reported that settlement had been agreed at £28,000. Sue was clearly finding it hard to remain professional and detached and keep the glow of satisfaction out of her voice, but she knew just what her friend Toby had been through over the years at the hands of that woman he had been married to, and was delighted to be the bearer of such good news.

Sally didn't object to his Champagne celebration that evening.

They all appeared at Court on the 9th of May to have the agreement ratified by all parties and rubber stamped by the Court. The seal was finally set and the Order of January 1991 was finally consigned to its rightful place on the scrap heap.

'Come on Sue, David. Over to the Waldorf for a final bottle of bubbly. When we get some decent pennies together from the sale of the two houses, which I have to say are both looking promising, I'm going into the Priory to get some proper serious help with my drinking; we'll be able to afford it now. Come on my friends – job brilliantly done!' The paradox of Hilary's lost inheritance of £60,000 in 1991 plus the two cars, all sequestered by her lawyers, and her final acceptance of just £28,000 was not lost on any of them.

Both houses sold within a week of each other, and at the end of July Sally was finally released from the strain of running two gardens during the hot dry summer, and they had sufficient funds to pay for Toby to spend a month at The Priory Clinic.

His large private room was light and airy, a far cry from the NHS ward, and once the effects of the diazepam had worn off towards the end of his first week he was kept busy in various group discussions on the subject of addiction.

On her second visit to him Sally was surprised to be asked if his personal counsellor could have a quiet word with her. The three of them sat together under a parasol in the elegant, relaxing grounds, and the counsellor said: 'I'm afraid we feel we are not going to be able to keep Toby here, Sally. I don't think we are going to be able to help him. I'm so sorry.'

'But why, what on earth's happened?' She could see the grand plan going out of the window again, and she found she was pleading with him inside.

'You know we have group meetings where everybody opens their hearts in their search for self help? Everybody talks very openly about themselves; they all say things to each other that they probably wouldn't admit to anyone outside the group. The whole purpose of this open honesty is to get each patient to admit their individual problem to themselves, but Toby spends most of his time at these meetings trying to crack jokes; his humour is most inappropriate, and I'm afraid his presence is upsetting some of our more vulnerable patients.'

She was stunned. He had always been a very strong character with very outspoken views – never caring two tuppenny damns what anyone else thought of his opinions, but this thoughtlessness was dreadful and had to be nipped in the bud, it was his last chance to get the help he needed and she was not going to allow him to screw it up with his silliness.

'What the hell do you think you are playing at?' she demanded.

'Well, I was only trying to lighten the mood, it was so bloody serious and depressing.' He did at least have the grace to hang his head.

She knew she had her work cut out trying to get him to toe the line – he had never toed someone else's line in his life, he had always drawn the lines himself and others toed them. Eventually he apologised to the counsellor, and agreed to apologise to the group. He began to realise that if he didn't he was in grave danger of losing not only his last chance at sorting out his drinking problem but his wife as well, then his life would truly be at an end. The counsellor agreed he could stay on the course, for now, and Sally felt she had crossed yet another abyss – how many more were there going to be, she wondered. Although her love and support for him were unquestioning she was getting very tired.

The sale of their home meant another move, everything having to be packed up again and prepared for removal to another rented property.

Following the estate agent's directions, she turned off the quiet country road and took the long winding driveway down to the main manor house, then turned right into a small courtyard, and there in front of her she found a tiny converted coach house. It was a bit scruffy, but really quaint, and she fell in love with it immediately. Only two bedrooms, but the rooms were large enough that one could serve as a storeroom for all the things they had no need of during their stay, until they found a home for themselves.

She told Toby all about it on her daily visits to The Priory, and he was looking forward to the end of his month's incarceration when he could get back to his own bed again.

The pub was only a short walk away from the little coach house, but he avoided it for the first month, happy to see Sally content with his sobriety, and they both felt they could at last perhaps try again to build their future. They had money in the bank for the first time in years, and Hilary was off their backs for good – she had bought herself a former council flat above a shop on a busy main road and had no more claim on him. Although she had a home to call her own now, Toby couldn't help but gloat; to think she had turned down a million quid in 1989 because she had wanted more – oh, how are the mighty fallen.

His pub visits began again in October, but he felt absolutely no need for anything stronger than lime juice and soda, which pleased him. He was actually finding it quite refreshing, and allowed himself to enjoy the camaraderie of the pub that he had missed with no-one trying to encourage him to drink anything else. He began to search for land or properties to buy, and the telephone was once again surgically attached to his hand as he trawled through the names of friends and contacts he hadn't spoken to for months; everyone was thrilled to hear from him, and wished him well.

Various brochures and property details fell through their letterbox over the coming weeks, most were discarded, but one caught his eye, March Hill Farm, just outside a small Kent village.

'Let's go and have a look at this one sweetheart. It sounds lovely, plus there's loads of land and potential for developing some of the outbuildings. I reckon this could be the one to really get us back on our feet again.'

As they turned off the little-used lane onto the private driveway of the farm, the sight of a large pond fringed by swaying reeds greeted them; the island in the centre boasted a graceful weeping willow tree, and a family of ducks waddled from it into the water, looking for lunch. As they continued down the long curving driveway they were spellbound by the beautifully manicured wide grassy lawns on either side, bordered by dense, mature woodland where rabbits and squirrels scampered in their haste to escape the approaching car – the whole vista was one of rural peace and perfect tranquillity.

'This is it, sweetheart; this is for us. It might have taken a bit longer than I had hoped but I've kept my promise to you; I told you I'd find you a new love nest after we lost The Old Lodge.' Toby felt good; he was back on the roller coaster of property developing and he liked the feel. The farmhouse, privately tucked away half a mile from the lane, turned out to be Medieval in part, and although it needed a bit of tidying up here and there, otherwise it seemed to be in pretty good order with a swimming pool close to the back door. The agent's details said it included 60 acres of farmland and there was a small 2-bedroom cottage in the grounds as well. Two more lakes emerged on their walk around, each more beautiful than the other, and Sally felt her breath being taken away – to own this would be beyond her wildest dreams, but the owner wanted over a million pounds for it, and she couldn't see how they could ever borrow such an amount, given their financial history.

But Toby did, he had a cunning plan, as he always had when apparently insurmountable obstacles appeared to challenge his chosen route. Drawing on his legendary store of property and planning knowledge, and happy to be back at the helm of a burgeoning new empire with his loyal lady by his side, he set out his plans to the building society. He convinced them that obtaining planning consent to convert one of the oak framed barns into a residence wouldn't be a problem, and the proceeds from its sale would be sufficient to repay almost their entire borrowing. The agricultural land could not be built on, but he showed them the clever route he had devised around the restrictions, and of course he would want to use the same lender throughout the multi million pound development that could be planned. They were happy to support the project.

Being secure in the knowledge that Hilary had had her pound of flesh and could no longer use the Courts to force him to expose his affairs to the world gave him back his dignity, and they bought their little corner of paradise.

Thursday the 14th of December, moving day, could not come quickly enough for Sally, she was beside herself with excitement. She scrubbed and cleaned the little rented coach house that they had enjoyed for five months, and piled herself and Toby into the car for the trip to their new home.

The crooked white walls, interspersed with old, weathered oak beams and crooked chimney seemed to welcome them as they parked in one of the four garages and waited for the removal van to appear. The little cottage in the grounds was rented out to a delightful elderly couple, who came out to greet them, and the sun shone. All was well with their world at last. It had been a rough few years, but now they knew that, hand in hand, they were well on their way to a secure future together.

That night they slept soundly in their bed on an old oak floor that was less than level. Most of the doorways needed some careful head ducking to avoid grazed foreheads, and the huge Aga exuded a cosy warmth that filled the kitchen. The rooms and passages were heaped with overflowing packing cases, but nothing mattered, they had their home and would be settled just in time for Christmas.

Friday morning they set to and began unpacking the boxes. Toby was in charge of the kitchen and Sally the rest of the house. Fair division of labour somehow.

There were so many things in the packing cases that they hadn't seen since they left The Old Lodge in 1992; he was constantly calling out, looking for instructions. 'Sweetheart, what do you want to do with this – it looks like a specimen bottle?' He was hooting with laughter as he held up a rather plain, narrow necked vase. 'We've managed without it for all these years, I think I can live without it now. It is rather ugly, isn't it? Just bin it,' came her happy response. And so the morning progressed.

'Oi, excuse me, where do you think you are going?' she demanded as he turned on the shower and started to undress.

'It's the Croydon businessman's lunch today. I've been going every year since I can remember, and just because I don't drink any more doesn't mean I have to give up my social life completely. I'll be back in time for supper, though I probably won't be very hungry after having had lunch.'

Ouch! If she reminded him not to drink it would sound like nagging. If she didn't . . . Well, it's a decision he does have to make for himself, she can't sit at his shoulder all day every day. This needs to be his decision, but these lunches were always raucous, boozy affairs, filled with men who would regard a teetotaller as something of a wimp. They would have no conception of what he's been through, and he wouldn't want to enlighten them. She really felt that four months was a little early for him to put himself back in front of such temptation. Oh, well.

The afternoon was awful for her; she couldn't concentrate on anything, and as the late afternoon turned to early evening found herself constantly wandering to the window with a nervous heart. She wasn't going to bother to cook, her twitchiness made it impossible for her to eat and he would probably only want one of her special, spicy welsh rarebits, if anything.

His taxi pulled up in front of the house, and she waited with bated breath as he remained in the car, sorting out change to pay the fare. Finally the door opened and he fell out, immediately steadying himself, then rolled rather shakily up the path to the front door. His eyes were a little glazed, his focus a little slow and his speech a little slurred.

'Hello, sweetheart. Did you have a good day?' he managed to get out.

'You bastard – you're drunk! What the hell have you been drinking?'

'Me? Nothing. Come on sweetheart, don't be so snappy, you know I don't drink. I only had about six of those low alcohol beer things. It's not my fault if I seem drunk, 'cos I'm not, honestly. You can ask anyone. I am a bit tired though. Think I'll go straight to bed. Night, night darling.' He aimed a kiss in the general direction of her face, and missed as she slammed the front door and ran sobbing into the kitchen. That was the precise moment that the light from their fragile dream exploded into a million tiny pieces, and as she sat at the kitchen table it finally died; the fading embers of the fire that had warmed and cheered them for a little while had at last been extinguished. She was losing her strength to keep rebuilding that fire and he just didn't seem to have the willpower.

He was contrite the following morning. Swore he had only drunk low alcohol beers, but maybe it was the quantity he'd had that was wrong. He'd be more careful in future. Yeah, maybe.

Having only moved into their beautiful home a few days before Christmas, she had not had time to decorate the house properly, so instead of buying a tree for just a few days she had twined ropes of twinkling fairy lights into a huge pot plant, which now glowed cheerily in the corner of the dining room. She had planned for all the various children to join them for Christmas lunch; it was a really happy occasion, Toby's boys were pleased with their father's progress, and he seemed content as he sat chatting quietly with his sons around the huge open fire when they had finished eating, his glass of lemon water constantly to hand. His lapse of ten days earlier wasn't mentioned, and there was always an outside chance it wouldn't happen again.

As Gemma and Sarah helped Sally to clear the table and load the dishwasher, Gemma said: 'I've been so looking forward to seeing this house, I'd heard so much about it and how old it was.'

'Who told you that?' queried Sally, since the boys had not seen it to the best of her knowledge.

'Hilary,' replied Gemma innocently. 'Apparently she came up here to see it just before you moved in.' Sally didn't let her see the look that passed between her and Sarah.

'Anybody want anything more to eat?' asked Sally during the evening.

'Oh no, thanks,' came the groaned chorus.

'Tell you what, I'd like some fruit salad,' said Toby, rising to his feet. 'No, don't worry, sweetheart, I'll do it.' And he gently pushed Sally back down into the chair she was beginning to rise from.

'Anybody else for some fresh fruit salad?' he asked.

'Oh, go on then, but not too much.' they all replied. It would be a nice clean way to finish the day.

He passed the little bowls of freshly chopped fruit around, and as they each took a mouthful they felt their eyes begin to water. It was obvious that he had poured a large quantity of brandy over the fruit, and the rest of the family watched him happily tucking into it seemingly oblivious to the atmosphere around him.

Chapter 44

Early in the New Year Sarah and her fiancé Tony were to be married on the Caribbean island of Grenada, where her mother and Toby had married exactly ten years before. The dress had been bought, the hotels booked, everything was in place and Sally had arranged for the same archbishop to perform the service as had presided over her own wedding. Sarah and Tony were travelling out with family and friends, but Sally and Toby were going out a few days earlier.

The wedding party were all to stay at the Rex Grenadian Hotel, where the ceremony was to take place. All except Sally and Toby. Sally wanted him kept as far away as possible from Sarah's father Richard and brother Ben, who were both aware of the problems she was facing, so she arranged to stay with him at the Blue Horizon Hotel on another part of the island, and would transfer herself to the wedding hotel to meet the incoming wedding party and stay with her daughter until after the wedding. Toby was to come over just for the wedding itself, and she would return with him after the ceremony. A tricky arrangement, but achievable.

As Sally looked around the house for a final check before locking the door and climbing into their taxi at 6.30 on the morning of their flight, she noticed that the decanter on the dining room drinks trolley, which had been half full of whisky, was now nearly empty. His breath smelt of it too, but she was determined not to have a row about it before checking in. Sarah was working as an aircraft dispatcher for British Airways and was on duty at Gatwick airport the morning her mother and stepfather were due to fly out to Grenada, and had arranged for them to be upgraded to the first class cabin for the eight-hour flight. The last thing Sally wanted was let her daughter know anything was wrong and upset her just before her wedding.

But she knew her daughter's face so well, and couldn't fail to notice Sarah's darting eyes and tight muscles around her mouth when she looked at her stepfather. Sally held her anger in check for a few minutes more until they had cleared security and were well out of Sarah's sight and hearing, then she let rip at him for his lack of control, today of all days. He swore at her, threw the hand baggage onto the floor and kicked it across the airport lounge, leaving her to pick it up and follow him to the pub, where he sat and read the paper with a limejuice and soda.

They boarded the flight in silence, each angry with the other, and much of the joy of the first class service was lost.

They tried to talk to each other over the next two days and find some common ground, but the air between them was scratchy and glacial. He was adamant he had only had one nip of whisky, just to take off the chill of the early morning start. She no longer believed him, but somehow had to keep the peace for the sake of her daughter's wedding.

The wedding party were due to arrive on the Sunday evening, so Sally packed her bags after lunch and took a taxi over to the Rex Grenadian, where she was to share a room with one of the bridesmaids. Her unpacking finished she slowly walked the half mile to the airport to greet them.

The flight landed bang on time and she found she was really looking forward to seeing her beautiful daughter's excited face, the bride-to-be. Everybody was jumping around with joy, suitcases were being collected and counted, bags were being passed around, happy chaos reigned. Some of the party decided to travel in the minibus that was taking all the luggage, others wanted to walk the short distance to the hotel and stretch their legs after eight hours of being cooped up in an aircraft.

Sarah was feeling a little disjointed; on boarding in London she had asked the stewardess to hang her precious wedding dress, but was refused since she wasn't flying upper class, staff or no staff, and was forced to try and deal with the dress as best she could, keeping creases out but not allowing Tony a glimpse. Not an easy task, she found, and was feeling less than charitable when she disembarked.

Never mind, drinks all round when they arrived at the hotel. Quick head count, all had arrived. Quick bag count – no, granddad's suitcase was missing. Hand baggage? No, Sarah's wasn't there. This was the little bag that contained all their legal paperwork without which they could not be married, together with their wedding rings. Three of the boys ran all the way back to the airport, located granddad's missing suitcase but Sarah's bag was nowhere to be found. Enough was enough and Sarah became hysterical when they came back without it. Sally hugged and rocked her, assuring her that the island people were the most honest she had ever come across, and her bag would soon be found. Friends tried to soothe her but she was inconsolable. What with the wedding arrangements, organising sixteen people plus the episode with the dress and the emotion of the occasion, it all got too much for her. Finally, an hour later, the taxi driver found the small black bag tucked into a dark corner at the back of his minibus where it had become wedged under pressure from the larger cases. His smiling face as he walked into the hotel reception area holding her bag out to her was the best wedding gift Sarah could have asked for, and at last she was able to enjoy the island speciality of rum punch and begin to unwind. So could her mother.

Toby rang Sally that evening to say goodnight, and he sounded fine, much to her relief.

Sarah, Sally and Tony's mother spent most of Monday checking the arrangements for Thursday afternoon's ceremony, and meeting with the archbishop. When Toby rang that evening she wondered if she could detect a little slurring – yes, she thought perhaps she did. What could she do about it? Nothing, except hold her breath and hope. He said he wanted to come over the following afternoon and see his lovely stepdaughter before her wedding day.

'By the sound of your voice I know you have been drinking today. Please, please, stop it, for me. You will be hurting me, my daughter and most of all yourself if there is the slightest suggestion of drink about you tomorrow. Richard and Ben are both here, and if they think there is any chance of you spoiling Sarah's big day there will be trouble. And I don't think you want that to happen, do you?'

'Don't worry about it, sweetheart. I promise you I haven't been drinking. I probably sound a bit slow because I've only just woken up, I had a bit of a kip after lunch. See you tomorrow, love you.'

Tuesday was spent unwinding on the beach, the sun was hot, the breeze was gentle and everybody began to relax properly. Sally waited in reception to meet Toby at 3 o'clock, as planned, and as she watched him climb rather unsteadily out of the taxi she wanted to cry. He made a great effort to walk carefully and smile, but the smile was crooked because some of the muscles in his face were more relaxed than others.

'Honeshley sweetheart, I promise you I haven't had a drink. Must admit I do feel a bit odd though. Sat next to some bloke in a bar where I had my lime juice and soda, the bastard mussed a spiked my drink.'

'Go back, Toby. Get back in that taxi and go back to the Blue Horizon, I'm not letting Sarah see you in this state.'

'Get me a lime juice and soda first, please love. I'm parched. I'll go when I've had that, promise, then I'll go straight to bed, I don't feel great.' She watched him slowly sip his drink, and then arranged a cab for him. He went uncomplainingly. Wednesday was not a happy day for Sally. She tried to keep her spirits up for Sarah's sake, but she was desperately worried about her husband and what was going to happen when he came over the next day for the wedding. She kept herself busy in the late afternoon by putting her photographic experience to good use. The bridal arch needed to be placed at the correct angle to maximise the soft late afternoon light for the photographs; then she wanted to make sure that the exotic locations she had chosen would be bathed in the early evening light at just the right time for all the post ceremony shots.

Toby didn't ring that evening, which was ominous, but she had to put it out of her mind and went to bed early; she needed a good night's sleep to be bright and fresh ready for the next day's ceremony.

The room telephone trilled rudely at midnight.

'Hello, is that Mrs Havers? This is the manager of the Blue Horizon Hotel, madam. I'm sorry if I have woken you, but I must tell you that your husband had a slight accident this evening. I'm afraid he fell into one of the storm water drains in front of the hotel, which is full of black, stagnant water, and he smells very strongly of alcohol. The police were called to fish him out, but it is not fair to ask my staff to deal with such things. I would be obliged if you would come over and deal with it straight away, if you please.'

She felt the scream bubbling up in her throat, but instead of crying out she suppressed her throbbing pain and calmly took a taxi to the Blue Horizon to find him sitting on the side of the bed, glassy eyed and filthy from the stagnant water with his stinking, grey, soaked clothes strewn all over the floor. She rinsed the filthy water from them and insisted he take a shower before getting into bed. No point trying to get a taxi at this time of the night, so she resignedly got into bed with him at 2 o'clock in the morning. So much for her early night.

He woke her at 6 o'clock with a cup of tea. 'Morning, darling,' he chirped brightly. 'Dunno what happened last night, must have slipped or something. Where are my clothes, love?' She couldn't believe that he seemed to think all was well with the world, she was angry and confused. How can he have been so drunk just a few hours earlier, but bright eyed and bushy tailed now? It didn't make any sense, if she had been that drunk she would be feeling like death four hours later.

'Listen, I've got to get back for Sarah's wedding but I can't take the risk of you turning up later as drunk as you were last night, and since you seem to choose drink over common sense you're going to have to miss it I'm afraid, it's not fair on Sarah, me or anyone else. If you're going to drink then drink, but you do it here, in this hotel, on your own then go to bed.'

'I'm coming to the wedding, whether you like it or not,' he growled darkly. 'I'm not going to miss seeing my stepdaughter married. If you try to keep me away there will be trouble, blood will be spilled I can assure you of that!'

'I'll compromise with you,' she said, thinking furiously. 'Sarah knows why I was called back here last night and she is very angry with you too, but I'll ask her if she will accept you coming just to the reception and I will ring you with her answer. But if you sound to me as though you have been drinking the answer will be no, and I will ask the hotel security to prevent you getting through. Your choice – fair enough?'

'I don't drink, sweetheart, honestly. I don't know what happened last night. I'd been out for a walk – it must have been just a silly accident.' He looked the picture of small-boy innocence. 'I'll wait for your call then. Kiss goodbye?' It was all she could do to allow him to touch her, she was feeling very shaken and upset.

The wedding was perfect, the soft golden light from the late afternoon sun shone on the happy couple standing under an arch of exotic, tropical flowers. Cameras clicked, videos whirred softly, and the archbishop looked splendid in his mitred hat with his red and gold robes billowing gently in the soft breeze. The whole party moved around to the various locations that Sally had selected the day before as suitable backgrounds for the various group shots, and more footage was taken of the newly weds.

Back on the pretty white terrace overlooking the ocean that the hotel had provided as the venue for the reception, the Champagne corks popped, confetti was thrown and everybody crowded around Sarah and Tony to congratulate them. Toby arrived unnoticed, and sat himself quietly in a chair away from the celebrations taking place on the opposite side of the terrace; he ordered a grapefruit juice and waited. Sally was surprised that he had slid in so silently, he wasn't known for quiet entrances, and she made her way over to him, assessing his demeanour as she slowly walked towards him. His focus seemed reasonably sharp, his eyes looked bright enough and his smile didn't look too crooked. She sent a silent thank you to whichever guardian angel was watching over her daughter's special day.

'Hi,' she greeted him. 'Thank you.'

'For what, sweetheart? I'm always sober these days, you know that. Anyway, doesn't she look stunning – how did it all go?' She sat down with him and chattered happily about the whole day. She watched Sarah's father wander over and wondered what he was going to say, but Richard just smiled, shook Toby's hand and welcomed him to the reception, but her brother Ben stood as far away from him as possible and just glowered, feeling fiercely protective of the two women in his family that this man had upset. Toby stayed just long enough to give Sarah a kiss of congratulation, shake Tony's hand and swallow a second glass of grapefruit juice before taking a taxi back to his comfort zone, whichever bar that was.

The following morning she packed her bags, as arranged, and took a taxi over to the Blue Horizon to spend the remaining five days of their holiday with her husband.

He wasn't in their room when she arrived, so she unpacked, donned her costume, picked up a beach towel and went in search of him. She quickly located the sun bed he was using by the sight of his shorts and coloured shirt hanging from the back of it, and was pleased to see that he had prepared one for her as well. As she looked around she saw him in the distance, strolling happily along the beach, ever present cigarette in his hand, and she began a swift walk in the same direction to catch him up. She glanced out over the sea, thinking what a magical place it was, and when she looked back he had disappeared from view. She quickened her pace and realised that he must have gone into a local beach bar, it was the only answer; so she walked off the beach and approached the bar from the back, feeling very sneaky but needing to catch him unawares. She stood and watched for a few minutes as he drank from his bottle of beer, then approached noisily, but on catching sight of her he pushed the beer away, saying it was someone else's and they had just left. Her heart sank. Again.

'I've actually been standing here for several minutes, watching you drinking from that bottle. Why can't you be truthful?' She was beginning to lose her self-control.

'Oh fuck it! I've decided I can just be a social drinker. I knew you wouldn't understand, that's why I didn't tell you. You stay and finish it if you want, I'm going back to the hotel for a kip, I'm sick of your bloody nagging.' And he wound his way back along the beach.

She made her way back to the hotel swimming pool and watched him emerge from their room just after lunch. His face was pasty white and he was beginning to slur badly. 'Just going up the road for some cigarettes, sweetheart. Shan't be long.' Two hours later she broke down, alone. A decision had to be made.

With the key in her hand she slowly walked back to their room and began to pack her bags. When she had finished she took one last look around, and with tears rolling silently down her face walked through the beautiful hotel grounds to the gate, pulling her heavy suitcase behind her; she turned right onto the road and began her journey towards the main road where she would be able to find a taxi. Her head was bowed and her tears splashed onto the dusty surface of the road as she dragged herself along. A large 4-wheel drive vehicle pulled up along side her, and an American female voice asked her: 'Excuse me – are you all right? Can I give you a lift somewhere?'

'Oh, yes please. I need to get to the main road up there to get a cab.'

'Sure, no problem, hop in, are you going to the airport?' she asked.

'No, the Rex Grenadian.' And the whole sad story tumbled out as she sat with her rescuer.

'Don't worry, I'll take you to the hotel, it's not that far. Been in a similar situation myself, and I'll be pleased to help you.' Sally sat back in gratitude and allowed herself to be driven right to the door of the hotel that she had left only a few hours earlier.

'Oh, hi mum – what are you doing back here?' Sarah was surprised to see her mother walking through the reception area with her suitcase, but one look at her distraught face and it didn't take too many guesses to work out why she had come back. She ran to her mother's arms and the two of them rocked together as Sally sobbed out the story. This was the one thing she had feared, that her daughter's wedding should be marred, but Sarah was dismissive. 'Don't worry mum, it's OK. The wedding was perfect, this is just a holiday from now on; we've got to think about you now. What do you want to do?'

Sally thought she was going to be sick, and walked around for a few minutes, taking deep breaths with her arms wound tightly around her waist. Her whole body was shaking and she knew she had to get away as soon as she could.

'How many are going home on tomorrow's flight?' she asked. Sally wasn't due to leave for another five days but had no wish to stay now that the holiday had been so completely ruined. 'Do you think I could change my ticket for a stand-by on tomorrow's flight?'

'Yes, I'm sure we can. Try not to worry mum, I'll ring the local office and see what the flight's looking like.'

The Saturday departures swelled by one, and they all took the mini bus to travel the short distance to the airport. The atmosphere was a little subdued because of Sally's trauma; she was still shaking and praying that she would be able to get on the flight, and they all stood in a huddle together, Sarah looking worried for her mother, Richard and Ben trying to comfort her as they waited to hear whether or not there would be a seat for her on the plane. She turned away from the group and took a large lungful of air, trying to calm herself, and as she looked up she found her eyes were locked with Toby's who was standing alone, slightly behind one of the large pillars. Over the distance between them his eyes spoke to her of his love for her, his pain, his loneliness, his terror and his sorrow. One look, then he turned and melted away into the darkness and she boarded the flight home.

Over the next two days he bombarded her with telephone calls until she nearly went crazy, hanging up each time to curtail the ramblings. In the end she unplugged the telephones and merely left the answerphone to field the calls in case of emergencies, then she could decide what she wanted to listen to and delete the rubbish. On Tuesday morning she saw there had been a message left for her during the night – it might be Sarah – it might be important:

> *Just one last kiss to*
> *Say goodbye.*
> *Just one last kiss before*
> *You cry.*
> *Just one last kiss before*
> *I die.*
> *I loved you so – just didn't*
> *Try*
> *Enough.*
>
> *If I could live my life*
> *Again,*
> *Some things might change, just*
> *Now and then.*
> *But my love will never*
> *Die,*
> *However hard I might*
> *Try*
> *To change.*
>
> *Your love is such a*
> *Special thing*
> *That can't be bought by*
> *Diamond ring.*
> *But in many, many*
> *Ways*
> *You were just my treasured*
> *Days.*
> *My love.*

He looked sober when he appeared in the arrivals hall at Gatwick airport, and seemed to be walking fairly straight much to Sally's relief, but she still found it hard to be natural with him. She no longer had any idea where her life was going, and it made her feel very vulnerable. Their journey home was mostly in silence, neither found it easy to talk to the other.

The simple shepherd's pie she had made for supper was one of his favourites. After a few mouthfuls he put his fork down and grasped her free hand. 'Sweetheart, I'm really so sorry for what I know I've put you through. This drinking thing is obviously a much bigger problem than I thought, but I won't let it beat me; you know I've never been beaten by anything in my life – for starters look at the fight I put up to win you, and I won in the end didn't I, no matter how long it took? And believe me you didn't make it easy for me.' She smiled sadly at him. 'I'm not about to start losing now, my love, I will beat this thing, I promise you. I will.' He clenched his hands around hers. 'I know I've got a hell of a fight on my hands but I can't do it on my own, I need your help, your support. Together we'll win, I know we will, please don't give up on me just yet, please.'

Chapter 45

The winter turned into early spring, and Toby was trying hard to cope on his own without medication; staying away from pubs, refusing all invitations where alcohol was likely to be served, keeping clear of temptation, but it was an uphill struggle. He started attending the AA meetings again, and took a taxi straight home afterwards without passing the temptations of a pub. One of George's friends went to meetings in London and encouraged Toby to join him there for a change. Then Sally was booked for a trip to Miami, she would be away for five days in all.

'I'll go back into the Priory for a week.' he offered.

'OK, good idea.' It would be worth the expense.

She brought him home from the Priory on her way back from the airport, and they settled back into the hard work of his abstinence. Just four days later she was booked for a week's work in Johannesburg. They couldn't afford another week in the Priory but she was nervous of leaving him at home, alone. 'I know, I'll go and stay with Ray in Jersey again, but this time I promise I won't go into St Helier, I'll stay in the house; I can do all the cooking for the family, take some long country walks, and Ray will be home each evening as company. That's what I'll do.'

What he hadn't reckoned on, though, was Ray's unlocked drinks cupboard. When Sally picked him up from the airport after her trip she could see he was less than sober. Back to square one. How many more times did he expect her to pick up the pieces?

Back at home he apologised again. Said he knew it was inexcusable, said he knew he was weak, but now that she was with him again he would be strong – for her sake, for the sake of their future together.

He began taking the Antabuse tablets that were left in the medicine box after his last attempt at drying out, and insisted she watch him so she could be sure he was swallowing them – that he was really serious about conquering his problem.

He didn't leave the house, he read books and newspapers, he slept a lot – even during the afternoon, which she found odd. His focus began to show signs that something was wrong, and yet he was definitely taking the Antabuse but not showing any signs of distress. She was puzzled by the smell of his water glass as well. Every morning she washed the few glasses and cups from the night before, but the residue of liquid in his glass smelt vile. She put a tiny drop on her tongue and immediately gagged – it was as she imagined the raw elements of vinegar to be. He had to be drinking on top of the Antabuse and this was the chemical his body was producing.

Her worst suspicions were confirmed as she began a search of the house and grounds. In the old greenhouse that they were planning to demolish she found what she had suspected. The old vase that he had uncovered when unpacking, the one that resembled a specimen bottle, had not been thrown away after all, it had been filled with whisky and covered in cling film then secreted away against the day when it might be needed. She felt as though she had been hit by a stun gun, no wonder he was sleeping a lot.

Ray phoned from Jersey. He just thought she ought to know that there had been a few problems with Toby when he had stayed with them whilst she was in Johannesburg. There was the matter of the smashed window – it seems that he had locked himself out of the house one day and found a sledgehammer to get back in; later he had taken himself off to bed after downing a whole bottle of red wine. Then there were the red wine stains and cigarette burns on the carpets and furniture. Although he was deeply worried about his old friend, there was no way he could ever invite him into his house again under the same circumstances.

The whole thing had become an impossible nightmare. She had heard that an alcoholic could not be helped by others, they have to accept that they have a problem and want to fight it themselves. But she thought he had wanted to do just that. Obviously, it had all been just words, no real commitment, but how do you watch someone you love head down the road to self-destruction without lifting a finger to help? At what point do you stop helping?

She rang a local firm of estate agents the following morning and asked for someone to call round with a view to putting the whole property back on the market. They had only been there for four months, the home of their dreams, but at the age of 55 she was quite incapable of taking on the management of 60 acres of land, several outbuildings, the large old farmhouse with it's swimming pool, plus care for the various gardens and lawns as well, the responsibility was awesome – then there was her photographic work too. Modelling was something she was good at and enjoyed, she was well paid, had some lovely friends in the industry and it had helped to preserve her sanity by getting her out of the house from time to time over the last few, traumatic years.

The estate agent called round the following morning and pointed out that she didn't have to sell it all, it was easily possible to divide the property. She could either sell the cottage, outbuildings and three of the meadows and keep the farmhouse with some land, or do it the other way round. Now that was an exciting idea; she didn't want to leave the farm, so nervously agreed to go with his suggestion and see what offers were received. This would be the first time she had made such a major decision on her own, she and Toby had always discussed important issues together in the past, his experience and ideas were invaluable, but this time he was fast asleep, even though it was 2 o'clock in the afternoon, and she was on her own. She had finally taken back control of her life.

Having realised his subterfuge had been rumbled he stopped making excuses for his inebriated state, but didn't want to run the risk of having his supplies confiscated, so when she was at work he called a taxi to do some off-licence shopping for him and buy some bottles to be secreted around the house and gardens.

Spring had turned into early summer and Sally was trying to spend as much time away from him as possible. Late one evening she assumed he was in his usual position in bed and went round the house locking up for the night, but looking out of the upstairs bathroom window she saw him staggering across the darkened lawn with a bottle and glass in his hand. She watched him try the back door, realise it was locked and stagger round the house to the front, where he rang the bell. She opened the door to find him empty handed, but on looking round the side of the porch she found his empty glass together with a half empty bottle of brandy hidden behind a garden urn.

She followed him into the kitchen where he was trying to stand straight, using the sink for support, and ran at him shaking the rest of the contents of the bottle all over him in her rage.

'You stupid, stupid bastard. What the hell do you think you are doing? You have no intention of trying to stop drinking, have you? HAVE YOU?' She was screaming at him, beside herself with rage. With every shake of the contents of the bottle over his head she screamed: 'You have no courage. You have no strength. You are worthless, a coward. You are not worth my love. You don't deserve my help. I have no more time for you.' And she ran sobbing hysterically from the kitchen, taking her night things up to the spare room as she passed their bedroom. He followed her up. 'Never go to sleep on an argument, love. Kiss, kiss?' He closed his eyes and puckered his lips as he unsteadily tried to lean over the bed to kiss her.

'Get away from me!' she screamed at him. 'I don't want you ever coming in here. This is my sanctuary. You have yours in a bottle – you can have it, just leave me alone with mine. You've made your choice and you've chosen drink over a loving wife. You can't have both.' And she pushed him away.

'Why can't I have both?' he murmured brokenly, half under his breath, as he stumbled back to his lonely bedroom.

Potential purchasers were enchanted by March Hill Farm, and within a few weeks a family decided to buy the farmhouse with its pool, multiple garages and 25 acres of the land, so the process of saying goodbye to their dream home was started. That left the cottage, the outbuildings and the remaining 35 acres, now that would be more manageable.

Sally was making her bed in the little bedroom that she had made her own under the eaves of the old farmhouse; the sun was shining and the air was warm, such a morning couldn't fail to lift her spirits, no matter how bleak their life together was looking, and her gaze drifted out over the lawns. Hmm, the grass will need cutting soon, she thought, and found herself looking forward to the time when she could move into the cottage and the lawn maintenance would be someone else's responsibility. At that moment Toby appeared from the front door, still in his dressing gown, his usual early morning glass of lemon water in hand. From the shaded room she watched him rest his elbows on the 5-bar gate leading to the meadows where the sheep grazed contentedly, he was clearly enjoying the clean morning air too. If only moments like this didn't have to end, she thought, feeling her eyes start to prickle with tears. He turned away from the gate, stood looking at the house for a moment, then moved quickly into the passage between two of the barns and disappeared from view. She stayed quite still and waited. Two minutes later he reappeared, nonchalantly wandering towards the house again, empty water glass still in his hand.

By 10 o'clock he was back in bed, looking very much the worse for wear, and she began her hunt, tracing his walk between the two barns. She didn't have to look far. Under two large paving slabs that had been placed against a wall to create a small cavity, she found a bottle of brandy that was half full and a bottle of vodka two thirds full. The by now familiar feeling of despair swept over her as she picked them up, walked back to the house and placed them in the centre of the kitchen table – the first thing he would see when he came down.

The feeling of emptiness was overwhelming, she felt totally crushed. The sale of the farmhouse was going through, although it wasn't proving easy. The buyer knew that that Toby was a property developer by trade, and was nervous that his newly bought piece of paradise might be damaged by housing developments on the land that Toby was retaining, and he became very demanding in his need to protect himself and his family from any such ideas. Sally agreed that housing on their very doorstep was not a pleasant option, so was happy to go along with the covenants and restrictions that the buyer wanted. Toby was asleep for most of the day, so she made all the decisions, but when he found out what she had agreed to he lost his temper.

'Christ, you stupid cow! Why have you agreed to so much? We could have made millions on developing that land. There's no way I'm agreeing to any covenants that prevent me from doing what I want on my own land. For fuck's sake!' He poured himself another glass of wine and went back to bed.

The following morning he acted as though nothing had happened. 'Morning sweetheart. When are you coming back to my bed? I really miss you, you know.'

She sat down opposite him at the kitchen table, watching him drinking his early morning water and puffing away on one of his interminable cigarettes. 'Listen to me, Toby. Several things are happening here. Number one, you have decided to drink again, and in your occasional moments of sobriety you do admit it is now completely out of control. Hiding spirits in the outbuildings – for God's sake, you haven't drunk spirits all the time I've known you. You are on a route to self-destruction, and I'm not going there with you, that's why I'm sleeping in a separate room. Number two, there never will be any development on the land we are retaining because your brain is too addled to plan it. If you had remained teetotal we wouldn't have had to sell anything and you could have planned it in one of your clever ways, but I am now having to make decisions affecting our lives on my own because you're always in bed sleeping off another drinking session. I can't find my way round multimillion pound development plans, it's completely beyond my abilities, and you have drunk yours away. And number three, you WILL sign the agreement I have made with Mr and Mrs Bird because you have no choice. Once we have sold the farmhouse we can hopefully convert the big barn into a house, then we will have that plus the cottage and the two smaller barns which I can manage on my own, regardless of what you want to do about your drinking.'

She disappeared on a modelling assignment and he went back to bed.

During the summer she kept the lawns mowed, the pool clean and the weeds at bay in all the gardens. She figured out how to repair guttering and generally ran herself ragged trying to keep on top of all that needed to be done. Modelling was done in her free time.

Dripping with perspiration she poured herself a glass of water and listened to Toby chatting to someone on the phone. His drinking had been much more moderated since her outburst. He seemed to have taken her tirade to heart.

'Who was that you were talking to?' she asked.

'The Court in Bromley,' he replied, sitting back in his chair with a smile. 'They said because I completed that driving course two years ago, all I have to do is send the certificate in and I can drive again straight away. Should get my licence back in a few days.' And he happily posted the certificate showing that he had indeed completed the course.

Sally was pleased by the Court's eventual response, Toby was not. He may indeed drive again for now, but was required to supply them with the results of an up to date blood test within 14 days to confirm his new alcohol free status.

He drove to the pub; in fact over the next few days he drove to the pub a lot. When the police stopped him as he started the car engine to drive home one afternoon he was livid. They had insisted he blow into their machine, and even with a deliberate half-hearted attempt it glowed red.

He stormed into the house, growling at Sally: 'Did you set the cops onto me?'

'Don't be ridiculous, of course I didn't. How would I know which of the pubs you had gone to?'

He was ordered to attend Court to answer a charge of drink driving.

She was away on the morning he was summoned. He drank a lot of Dutch courage, got into the car, reached the end of the driveway, then turned back and returned to bed. Nobody answered the door to the police with their arrest warrant at lunchtime, so they went away, but Sally heard about their visit from the elderly couple living in the cottage. They had been very concerned. Was everything all right?

She also heard from Toby that he had not attended Court because he had felt so unwell, and she made him ring the Court the following day to explain his absence to the Clerk. The matter would not go away, it would be re-listed.

By the time the farmhouse was finally sold in late summer she felt very fit from all the manual labour, and was very bronzed from so much time spent working outdoors. He had finally agreed to sign the sale papers, the elderly couple had moved out of the cottage, and Sally got as many strong arms as possible to help her move across to the cottage.

A week before the actual move she had a shock for Toby. She was not going to allow him to live in the cottage with her. Her patience had finally run out. Friends and family had all tried to help him, given advice, supported him at AA meetings, but all to no avail. The only option left now was to leave him to get on with it on his own. Perhaps if she had done that in the first place he might have come to his senses earlier.

'I've asked for details of rental properties in town for you,' she told him.

He didn't seem particularly bothered by his forthcoming homeless status. 'Bollocks! I'm not having everyone around here know my business, I'll live in the big barn, it's got a covering on the floor. I'll be quite happy there, and I'm sure you won't mind if your husband comes into the cottage for a shower and a meal, will you?' He poured himself another drink and buried his head in his newspaper.

OK, she could live with that for now, at least she could still keep half an eye on him. They had far too much furniture for the little cottage anyway, so she arranged half of their things into living accommodation for him in the barn, sofas, coffee tables, lamps, his bed and dressing table. There was an electrical supply and toilet facilities, and when she had finished it actually looked quite cosy.

But as she walked away and locked her front door against him on that first night, she couldn't help but reflect on some of the places he had called home.

Her world had been torn to shreds, now she had to start to rebuild it on her own. She knew she could never rely on him, or trust him, ever again.

Chapter 46

Things went from very bad to much worse. Toby spent his days sitting in the barn drinking from the 3-litre box of wine he ensured was always by his side, and in the evenings he sat in the cottage to have a meal and watch some television with his wife. He rose to refill his glass, took two shaky steps towards the kitchen and fell headlong, smashing the glass in his hand. 'My bloody back, it's gone again.'

'The reason your back has gone is because of your drinking. Your muscles are in such an exaggerated state of relax they are not supporting your spine – that's why your back is not as it should be.'

'Crap! I need to see the quack about it. I'm sure he can give me some tablets, or something. Soon sort me out.' He left the broken glass on the carpet for Sally to clear and staggered back to his makeshift bed in the barn.

They were granted consent to convert the big barn into a house, and Sally knew she had to begin the process by having the existing services disconnected. There was no way he could continue to live there with no power or water, so she broached the subject of rented accommodation again. The centre of town would be a good choice since the Court had thrown the book at him when he finally answered the latest charges of drink driving, in fact she didn't know how he had escaped a jail sentence. There was no possibility of him driving again for many years to come, perhaps ever.

'Bollocks.' he mumbled angrily. 'I've told you I'm not having anyone else know my business. I've decided I'm going to go and live in Greece, and you can send money out to me when I need it.'

'Greece? Why Greece?' she asked, he'd never been to Greece in his life.

'Why the fuck not? You don't want me here and at least it's warm over there, and no-one to nag me. Plus I can drive in Greece. Don't worry, I'll sort it out.'

'You can't drive in Greece, they will see the endorsements on your driving licence and know you are banned from driving.'

'That's only in the UK. Anyway, listen, you of all people ought to know you've got to get up early in the morning to catch Havers. My original licence may have endorsements on it but my duplicate hasn't. Remember getting it for me when I lost the original when we were in The Old Lodge? The Greeks won't know the address is wrong. Knew it would come in handy one day.'

She knew she had to leave him to his own devices, had to let him make his own mistakes now and not rely on her for support, he needed to sort out his problems himself. She also knew she had to drive him to the airport and let him go, but go where? Greek jail perhaps? Well, maybe that wouldn't be such a bad thing, maybe something like that was what was needed to bring him to his senses; she had to let him find out.

After dropping him at Gatwick it was all she could do to reach the petrol station 300 yards away before breaking down. She was torn within herself; on the one hand she loved him so much, and her natural instinct was to try to protect and help him. But isn't that just what she had spent the last few years doing? And what good had it done? Was it maybe her fault that he had as serious a problem as he had? Now she had to try the alternative route, let him get on with it on his own – learn the hard way.

Memories of all my girls
Will guide me through my day.
Memories of each of them
Who always had their say.

Don't think my life is over,
It's only just begun
I go 'midst fields of clover
As those before have done.

I'm going to fields and pastures new
To build a different life.
When you arrive you'll find it's true
My world is free of strife.

Another life's before me now,
I know not what's in store.
I hope it fills me full of joy
As life has done before.

I give my thanks to all I've known,
To family and friends;
But most of all my wife, mine own,
You loved me till the end.

The memories we shared as one,

The fun of life we had;
The myriad of things we've done
Together. I am glad.

And now the time has come for me
To turn the page, to read
Another chapter, one more scene,
And find out where 'twill lead.

Be glad for me. I'm sad to leave,
But I've tasks I must pursue;
And I will tackle them, don't grieve,
Whilst I shall wait for you.

The big gas-guzzling car had to go. He wouldn't be driving again and she had no need of status symbols, besides it was a very costly car to run. Instead she bought a small sporty car that was plenty big enough for her and much more economical to run.

Two weeks later his credit card statement arrived. According to the details itemised on the statement he had not gone to Greece, but to Ibiza.

A week later he called to tell her he had lost his glasses and was coming home to get a new pair. He didn't sound too good.

Her every fibre screamed at her to beg him to please, please come home and let her make it all better for him, but she knew she couldn't do that – no one could. She steeled herself and knew she had to tell him he didn't need to come home just for new glasses. 'If that's your only problem just go to an opticians in Ibiza and get a new pair.'

'How did you know I was in Ibiza?' he mumbled.

'Do you think it might have been details from your use of the credit card perhaps?'

'Please love, just pick me up from the airport tomorrow. I'll be landing at Gatwick at 7 o'clock in the evening.'

He was brought out to the car in a wheelchair and her heart broke for the hundredth time at the sight of him. He clearly hadn't shaved since he'd been away, and when he crawled shakily into the car it was also evident that he had neither eaten nor washed for some time. He was a gaunt, yellow, hollow eyed caricature of the man he used to be. How on earth had they even let him board a plane?

'We've got to find somewhere else for you to stay,' she told him on the way home. He didn't reply, he stayed silent during the journey, his head lolling from side to side. She sent up a silent prayer of thanks that he had come home when he had. Was this rock bottom for him? Would he now be able to turn the corner and begin the road to recovery?

Her new car smelt clean and fresh, and that was the way she meant to keep it, not like his car that stank of his constant smoking, so when he pulled a cigarette out of the packet and started to light it she asked him: 'Please don't smoke in the car, I don't want the smell of cigarette smoke lingering in the upholstery. We'll be home in 15 minutes and you can smoke to your heart's content when we get there'.

'Bollocks. If I want a cigarette I'll have a fucking cigarette!' And he lit up. That made her angry, how dare he be so discourteous. She grabbed the cigarette from his lips, and together with the half full packet and lighter, threw the whole lot out of the window.

'What the hell did you do that for? What a fucking waste of money throwing away perfectly good cigarettes – obviously money is no object to you. You're getting as stupid as Hilary, you are.'

Taking a shower had become impossible for him because he couldn't stand steadily for long enough, so she ran a bath for him instead, laid out some fresh clothes and watched him eat the hot meal she had prepared. The sight of his crumpled, shaking figure frightened her, and she made no protest when he asked her for a glass of wine – red or white, it didn't matter. But this was no time for weakness, and she knew she still had to send him out to the freezing barn to sleep and they would discuss his future accommodation the next day.

'I don't see why you won't let me stay here with you, paying out rent to someone else is just more expense. Besides, I'm your husband and my place is with you, unless you've got someone else lined up of course.'

'That's not fair,' she replied quietly. 'You know exactly why I won't live with you any more. I have spent the last five years or so helping you to fight your drinking problem, and I've finally had to accept defeat and move on to try and save my own sanity. You will have to sort it out on your own – maybe I should never have tried to help in the first place; perhaps you'd have hit rock bottom more quickly. All I know is you are drinking yourself to death, literally. I don't know how much time you have left in this world, certainly not long at this rate, and I can't stand by and watch you slowly killing yourself. You're on your own now.'

His son George had bought a small terraced town house in the next village; a quaint little 17th century place with an old oak door that opened directly onto the high street, the narrowness of its façade being compensated for by the four floors of rooms, but commuting to London every day was becoming tiresome, so he planned to find a tenant for it and rent something in London for himself.

'I'll rent George's place,' declared a much brighter Toby the next day. 'He's looking for a tenant, so it might as well be me. Everyone'll be happy then, including you – I know you want me out of your hair.' She couldn't believe the change in him. It was almost as though nothing was wrong with him. He was still shaking and looked very gaunt and yellow, but he appeared much more sprightly and alert than the night before, even after a night wrapped in a duvet against the freezing cold November night air in the unheated barn. After another bath and a proper shave, but with lots of nicked skin because he was shaking so badly, he was looking a little less like the tramp she had collected from the airport the day before.

George called round to see his father, and was happy to agree to him living in his house – he would stay with friends until he moved into his London pad. The only concern was the very steep, narrow staircases that curled and twisted upwards through the house. 'You will have to take great care on those stairs dad, because if you slip there will be no one to pick you up.'

'What a load of bollocks, I'm not an invalid. Nothing wrong with me that a swift pint can't put right. Bloody Spanish beer, how I hate it. I'm really looking forward to a good old-fashioned British pint in a proper jug with a proper handle.'

Sally packed up a suitcase for him, put his bedding into the boot of the car together with his coats and dressing gown, and drove over to the next village to George's house, where the reverse procedure was employed. The bed was made up, the little fridge stocked with food from the local shop, and she fussed over him till she could find no further excuse to stay.

'I'll come over tomorrow and make sure that you're all right, and please take care on those stairs.' He sat on the sofa, looking so small, crumpled and sad, his eyes pleading with her not to go, but he said not a word as she bent over and kissed him gently. It took her several minutes before she was composed enough to drive off, and deliberately went to the busy supermarket to get more groceries for him. She didn't want to be alone just at that moment.

She made him as comfortable as she could and visited him every day to collect his laundry and keep his fridge topped up, although the only thing he seemed to be cooking for himself was spaghetti. He had a local pub just across the road, and no doubt was making himself known there.

George came over to see him just before Christmas, and they had a drink together in the evening at the local pub. Toby was just topping up his alcohol level from his lunchtime session, and as they left the pub together his body crumbled into the gutter. He wasn't hurt, just confused, and he opened his eyes, squinting up at the young man in the dark overcoat bending over him and asked: 'Hello son, you the old bill?'

'No dad, it's me, George. Let me help you over the road. Come on, steady now, lean on me, that's right. I'll soon have you tucked up in bed.'

Sally came round the next morning and saw the mud on his sheepskin jacket. 'Look at this – what ever happened to you? I'll get it cleaned for you after Christmas.'

'I haven't the faintest idea – must have slipped on some ice or something. Fancy a drink, sweetheart?'

'No thank you. It's Christmas Eve and I promised Sarah I would get a turkey for her. Do you need me to get you anything?'

'A wife would be nice.'

Ouch, that hurt, her eyes stung. What had she done that was so wrong? Caring too much? Not enough? What more could she have done for him?

She turned away so he would not see the weakness and misery in her eyes. 'You know I'm spending tomorrow with Sarah and Tony and will stay over with them, but I'll pick you up on my way home on Boxing Day and we'll have our Christmas Day together then.' It was hard to bend over and kiss him without crying her heart out and begging him to stop drinking. But what good would that do?

After she had gone he sat quietly gazing through the window at the busy street; people hurrying by, some laughing with friends, others probably on their way to join friends or family. He picked up a pencil:

> *Dream of peace this Christmas,*
> *An end to war and fear.*
> *And as you feast on Christmas Day*
> *Spare thoughts – perhaps a tear*
> *For those who are not so happy,*
> *For those who are alone,*
> *For those who are poor and old,*
> *For those without a home.*
>
> *Dream of love this Christmas,*
> *A world that's always free.*
> *And as you love – just spread your love*
> *Like the angel on the tree.*

Let's live 'longside our fellow man,
Let's try for harmony.
Let's share our love with all around.
Dear God, just let it be.

Dream of peace this Christmas,
An end to war and fear.
Dream of love and happiness
And strive to end the fear.
For if black and white and differences
Can start another year
Loving one another –
That's the end of war and fear.

Early evening he put on his overcoat, it really was very cold out that night, and he crossed the road for his usual pint. The little bar was full to overflowing with noisy revellers, all looking forward to Christmas Day. He took himself off to a slightly quieter corner where he could drink undisturbed; he wasn't feeling terribly sociable, he'd only stay for one, he decided. Got some wine at home.

'Hey, Bob, you open tomorrow?' he called to the landlord.

'No mate. Christmas is for the family, the one day of the year we have to ourselves. That's where you should be.'

Might as well stay for a bit more then, he thought to himself since he couldn't have a beer tomorrow, only the wine he had in the fridge.

He really felt very unsteady on his feet as he left the pub for the short walk home, and found the opening in the lock with his key more by luck than judgement. It was cold in the little house, the heating had switched itself off hours ago, and so he stumbled awkwardly up the stairs with his warm, bulky coat still on. 'I'm so cold I could sleep in the fucking thing,' he muttered to himself.

As he rounded the bend in the steep staircase his left foot missed the narrow angled tread, and he felt himself floating through the air. 'Ooops!'

It was Christmas morning, and the phone rang four times in the kitchen of George's little house before the answer machine cut in. Sally's disembodied voice wafted softly around the empty room. 'Morning darling, it's 10 o'clock on Christmas morning. I'm at Sarah's – where are you? I'm just ringing to say hello, but you're obviously still in the bath, or something, so I'll call you again later. Bye for now.'

An hour later her mobile phone rang. The caller display showed it was George's house, and relieved that he had made it through another night unscathed, Sally answered the call.

'Sally? It's Simon.' Toby's youngest son's voice sounded a little shaky.

'Oh, hello Simon, Merry Christmas. Is everything all right?'

'Sally. Are you sitting down? I'm afraid I've got some bad news. I just called round to see dad and give him a present. It looks as though he fell down the stairs. He's dead.

NO, NO, NO – PLEASE DEAR GOD, NO!'

And when it's over – chapter ended,
You nor I must be offended,
For perhaps our book will hold
A thousand memories to unfold.

Other books by Carole Anne Goodman

She's Not Heavy . . .
A story of unfailing loyalty and friendship

The school bullies made eleven year old Jessie Harrison's life absolutely miserable. Ellie Davis had exactly the same problem, and as they each searched for solace in their individual misery, both looking down a long, dark, lonely tunnel of unhappiness, they bumped into each other as they both drew comfort from the vast bulk of a wise old oak tree, and they discovered that as they joined forces against their tormentors, they became strong.

A borrowed television set, beds taken from their respective family homes and cheap beanbags were all they could afford for the first flat they shared together, their jobs only just providing sufficient funds to make end meet each month, but it was their first foray into independence.

The warmth of Ellie's friendship carried Jessie through a brutal attack in a darkened park, and when Ellie's world exploded as a result of the abduction of her small son, Jessie was there with her constant, unwavering support. As Jessie suffered in her marriage, reviving all the mistrust she had felt at the hands of men, Ellie took control and helped to guide her friend back to sanity.

Then, a revelation by Ellie's mother threatened to cost Ellie the love of the man with whom she was planning a future. But Jessie's friendship was there, as ever, to hold her hand and help her through the ordeal.

Their shield of togetherness protected and supported them both as they came through the traumas that life threw at them.

Other Peoples' Lives
12 quirky tales with a twist – and a connection

1) Prison Gates:
1969, Northern Borders
The bleak, majestic hills of Cumbria had been Bertie Gibbons's view for 12 long years, but now his time was over. At last he was able to return to a life of freedom and leisure, determined never again to enter those prison gates – until the unexpected telephone call.

2) The Yellow Tie:
1969, Northern Borders
Two young people, by chance catching just the briefest glimpse of the other, both planning to meet. But fate was to conspire against them. Could they conquer fate?

3) All About Timing:
1982, Home Counties
Sherridan Smallbone's acting ability was far superior to others, he knew he was the best; it was the rest of them that were wrong. His loyal, long term partner put up with his high-handed ways and supported him – right to the end.

4) The Hotel Porter:
1982, London
Recently arrived in England from Montego Bay, Raynard was determined to make something of himself in his new country, and the hotel trade was what he knew best. After all, his family had owned a small one in Jamaica, so that was the trade where he felt most at home. But life for a black man in England held its challenges.

5) Cleaning Windows:
1990, Sussex
Early mornings did not rock 19-year old Jimmy Eaves's boat at all – until he discovered a way of making money that he quite enjoyed. He did his best for his customers, and his best friend, but everyone can make a mistake – can't they?

6) The School Reunion:
1990, Marbella

Property scams were run to make money, and a lot of people made a lot of money from such scams in Spain, never mind who got hurt in the process. Sarah Freeth had scores to settle, and the scam put her on just the right path to settle them.

7) Katie's Revenge:
1990, Brighton

Ed and Katie had been married for ten happy years. No children, but that was the hand they had been dealt, so they accepted it. At least that was what Ed had thought. Katie had obviously felt differently, a difference that was to shatter his life beyond redemption.

8) Gloria's Light:
1990, Midlands

As a young ballerina Gloria had been tipped for great things in her future, perhaps even Prima Ballerina, but when compelled to accept the fact that it was not going be, she found a new path as wife and mother. Now she danced to clear the trauma of her past in her head until eventually forced to confront it.

9) The Man:
2010, London

The man sat on the bench. Nadia felt threatened by his presence, though she didn't know why. Was it perhaps because of the way he stared at her eldest daughter with his dark, brooding eyes? Did he really keep appearing at the school and the house, or was it all in her fertile, depressed imagination? Who was he? What did he want with her child?

10) Social Climbing:
2010, Essex

Chloe wasn't interested in a relationship that required her to look after a man; in her world things should be the other way round. She had her life all mapped out, and someone was going to be targeted to provide the fruits.

11) Secrets of the Scissors:
2010, Northern Borders

There was something about the two ladies who had just moved into the Old Vicarage, and the elderly ladies at the hairdressers were dying to know.

Julie knew, but she could keep a secret.

12) The Circle of Life:
2010, The North

Well into his retirement years, Buzzer Bates recalls his life as a young bin man. Someone had to do the smelly job, and when the work provided him with an opportunity to enhance his modest wages and provide a few extra treats for his wife, he jumped at it. Pity he hadn't chosen a wiser route.